Devil's Fire

'Your dress . . . why is it crumpled?' asked the abbot.

Mrs Goodin had found me with Hyde Fortune, so there was little point lying. 'I was leaning against some flour sacks, sir.'

'And Hyde was humping you from behind, like a crazed dog.'

'I wouldn't describe it like –'

'Remove your dress,' interrupted the abbot. 'It defiles you.'

My jaw dropped; here was a man of God commanding me to disrobe. I was about to protest but the narrowing of his feral eyes warned me not to. I fumbled with the buttons.

'Just rip it off. You won't be wearing it again, anyway.'

I wrenched it open and stepped out of the green-and-ivory striped gown. This left me standing before my arrogant host wearing only my lace corset and bloomers.

'And why are your drawers sticking to your thighs?' he asked slowly. 'Did you wet yourself, girl?'

'Of course not!'

'Then whose sex do you reek of? And is that a hole in the seam of your bloomers?'

This cruel man was determined to humiliate me. He seemed extremely interested in the most intimate and degrading details.

Devil's Fire

MELISSA MACNEAL

BLACK
lace

Black Lace novels contain sexual fantasies.
In real life, make sure you practise safe sex.

First published in 2000 by
Black Lace
Thames Wharf Studios,
Rainville Road, London W6 9HA

Typeset by SetSystems Ltd, Saffron Walden, Essex
Printed and bound by Mackays of Chatham PLC

ISBN 0 352 33527 0

Contents

Chapter One
A Man of Dubious Repute

Colorado Springs. January, 1897

*T*he back door was bracketed by overgrown bushes that clittered in the wind, making me pause as I reached for the knocker. MOUNT CALVARY, said the weathered brass plaque. HYDE A. FORTUNE, MORTICIAN.

Although the words were prettily engraved, they had the finality of a tombstone inscription. I used to laugh about the name Hyde A. Fortune, considering he sold burial plots and coffins. But on this cold January morning I couldn't afford to mock him: should I entrust my future to this sandy-haired rogue with eyes the colour of cinnamon sticks? Would I regret discussing the employment he'd mentioned, now that I truly needed it?

Most people avoid undertakers, because their arcane trade is a necessary evil, associated with grief. My first dealings with Mr Fortune came seven years ago, when Mama died, and we met again last month when we buried my father. Our acquaintance was as pleasant as I could expect under such circumstances, yet oddly unsettling: as we stood among the mourners at Papa's graveside, praying, Hyde's hand slithered down my back to fondle my bottom. It sent a streak of white heat through

1

me, a delicious wickedness that settled between my legs and got rekindled every time I thought of him.

Rumour had it Hyde kept his mother locked away in a room of this rambling mansion, where he lived on the top two floors. But that couldn't be true: I'd read Madeleine Fortune's obituary years ago, and I walked past her headstone each time I visited my parents' graves.

And my father, the Reverend Jeremiah Michaels, had announced his dislike of Mr Fortune early on, saying Hyde couldn't be trusted with the deceased's valuables – that he replaced their gemstones with paste. Worse, however, Papa believed our local undertaker took unspeakable liberties with the dead of either sex.

So, my father made me promise his burial would be handled by the mortician in Manitou Springs. However, a series of events set in motion by his own greed had prevented me from carrying out his final request.

It was Hyde Fortune who brought Papa's body up from the chasm where he'd thrown himself. And he'd waived his fee when we learned my inheritance – a topic Papa discussed constantly as his mental condition declined – was a large donation he'd stashed beneath his mattress, instead of depositing it in the church's bank account. I returned this money when his misdeed was discovered, which left me nothing to live on.

So Mr Fortune's services were all I could afford. And as I stood at his private entrance, trembling with trepidation and the cold, I wondered if his reference to a possible position was merely a way to lure me into his clutches, now that I had nowhere else to go.

I despised being destitute. I despised being at any man's mercy.

Yet the handsome mortician and his dubious reputation fascinated me. His magnetic eyes and mesmerising voice made promises I didn't dare keep – but which I longed to explore, anyway. A woman past her twentieth birthday, without marital prospects or money, can't allow such opportunities to pass her by.

With my first nervous clatter of the brass knocker, his office door swung open. I felt like the heroine of a Gothic novel, my inner voice screaming that I entered this office at my own peril. But inside, a cheerful fire crackled and the ambiance of polished woodwork and leather drew me in. After spending a dismal night at the Home for the Friendless, I craved the warmth and sense of solidity this place offered. As I stepped in out of the wind, brushing the snow from my cloak, I saw a snifter half-filled with brandy beside the open ledger on his desk. Mr Fortune would soon return from whatever errand had called him away.

Raucous female laughter came from the next room, followed by shrieks of ecstasy. I blinked. Fortune displayed his coffins in that parlour, yet the frantic calling of his name suggested anything but a grieving – or deceased – client.

My first impulse was to leave, before I stumbled into a very embarrassing situation. Yet my curiosity nipped at me like a pup. I tiptoed to the parlour door, my nerves crackling with an audacity I didn't know I had.

Hyde Fortune was humping someone in a glossy walnut coffin. From this angle, I could only see her stockinged legs flailing on either side of his very active backside. His white shirt-tails fluttered wildly around his arse – and what a fine arse he had, sculpted with muscles that would make a Greek god envious! Up and down he pumped, as the woman beneath him howled like a coyote bitch in heat. I was so riveted by this spectacle that only her final triumphant cry sent me skittering away from the door. But not before I caught sight of Hyde's stiff, dripping cock as he pulled away from her.

My pulse raced as I clutched my crotch. I'd never seen such an act of abandon, nor felt such brazen desire. Just the fact that I'd thought of Fortune's exposed parts in

3

such vulgar terms shocked me, for I'd been taught to keep my thoughts tightly reined. Had this house and its occupant cast a spell? Or had walking in on such a provocative act sent me out of control?

I grabbed the snifter from Hyde's desk, calming myself with brandy so I could act as though I'd seen nothing. But I wasn't accustomed to alcohol. The first sip sent a sweet fire singing through my insides, and the sensations went straight to that already-aroused area between my legs. The second sip put a flush on my face, betraying my secret observations.

I was sipping again when Fortune walked in. His eyes nailed me – such a curious colour of topaz mixed with russet – and he stopped in the doorway. Then a sly grin overtook his face, the look of a fox entering his lair to find he'd cornered an unsuspecting morsel.

'You've come to discuss that position I mentioned?' he asked in a silky voice.

Fumbling with his goblet, I blurted, 'If it's the same position you had that other woman in, I'm not interested!' This was a lie, but my upbringing forced me to be modest.

Realisation dawned on his face just as embarrassment reddened mine. Raking his hand through hair the colour of wild honey, Hyde glanced peevishly towards the parlour door.

'Insidious bitch!' he whispered. 'Bought herself the most expensive coffin I carry. Then said if I didn't supply other services each time she came to pay an instalment, she would publicly announce that I'd stiffed her by burying her husband in a false-bottomed box.'

'There is such a thing?'

Hyde chuckled, again making sure the woman in question didn't lurk behind the door. 'There's a recession on, and some of our finest families wish to keep up appearances as they bury loved ones, but they can't afford it. So I devised an ornate model with a drop

4

bottom, which the sexton and I take from the grave once the mourners have left.'

My eyes widened at this revelation.

'And Delores Poppington requested this model, so she could put her money towards her own luxurious coffin and let poor Terrence rot in the ground. Disgusting woman! And I wanted to strangle her for throwing you out of the parsonage! Most un-Christian for a pillar of the church, and the wife of a departed deacon.'

Delores Poppington. Her name brought bile up my throat, because Terrence had discovered Papa's misplacement of that donated money. He resembled a plucked chicken with a nervous tic, and confronting my unbalanced father – then learning of his suicide a few days later – had put Mr Poppington in his grave, as well. Had Delores handled this matter privately, rather than announcing it during a Sunday service, we'd all have been better off.

'Seems the Widow Poppington is recovering nicely from her loss,' I muttered. 'And we can guess where she got the money for that fine casket, can't we?'

As though on cue, footsteps approached the office. Delores then poked her head in to say goodbye to her lover, who was young enough to be her son. She had straightened her clothing, but her broad-brimmed hat sat cockeyed, with a few curls of grey hair hanging askew above her ears. When I flashed her a defiant smile, her expression curdled. She left in a huff, the rapid tattoo of her heels echoing through the parlour.

At the slam of the front door, Hyde laughed uncontrollably. 'Fine show, Miss Michaels!' he crowed. 'I always knew you were a trouper! I hope you're proud of yourself!'

To celebrate, he reached towards his desk – and then discovered I'd sipped from his snifter, rather than pouring brandy into a fresh one. His mood changed like quicksilver. As he slowly approached me, his eyes fastened on mine, excitement surged through my entire body.

'So you've shared my cup, Mary Grace?' he murmured, slipping his fingers over mine. 'I consider that a highly personal act. Far more intimate than the coupling you watched.'

The memory of his bared backside, his muscles bunching as he pumped, and then his impressive erection, had me nipping my lip. Hyde smiled, lifting the snifter to his mouth, holding my hand hostage. I wanted to lick the film of liquor from his lips and feel the roughness of his shaved skin as I kissed my way down to that knot where he swallowed. His breath fell warmly on my face, scented with brandy and desire.

'I've dreamed of making love to you since we first met,' he whispered. He closed his eyes, easing his face towards mine.

I backed away. 'I was hardly more than a child! Had just turned –'

'Thirteen, as I recall,' he murmured. 'And I was the undertaker's apprentice – terribly embarrassed by it, but who else would hire me? I was the local whore's illegitimate son, lusting after the preacher's lovely red-haired daughter. Even then I wanted to be your friend, hoping your unsullied reputation – your angelic ways – would raise me to a level of acceptability. But mostly I wanted to yank down your drawers.'

When my mouth dropped open, he caught my head in his hand and kissed me deeply. This surprise, plus the effect of the brandy, made my head spin. What could I do but kiss him back? Never before had any man delivered such a compliment, nor had my sheltered ears been so eager to hear it, and my heart to believe. Hyde's tongue led mine in a dance I'd never had the chance to learn, and I got so dizzy I had to grab him to remain standing.

A chuckle rumbled low in his throat while he continued his assault, teasing at me with his teeth, nipping the silk of my inner lips. Setting the snifter aside, he held me so tightly my breasts pressed against his midsection while I felt a hard ridge riding my lower belly. My legs were shaking, and the warmth that had pooled between them broke free to trickle down one thigh.

I gasped for air. 'This is a sin! We mustn't –'

'No,' he insisted, making me wriggle with the delight of his wet tongue inside my ear. 'The sin was the way your father kept you home, forcing you to sacrifice your youth and your chances for a husband.'

'But I was caring for Mama! We came to the Springs for her consumptive lungs!'

'And everyone admired your devotion, Mary Grace. You were a loving daughter to the end,' he murmured, pulling the pins from my upswept hair. 'But it was pure selfishness on your father's part to keep you home, locked away.'

'I was only fourteen!'

'And you grew up before your time by becoming your mother's nurse,' Hyde said savagely. His hands found my aching breasts, kneading them until I thought my nipples would poke through my threadbare dress. 'Your father –'

'Needed me after Mama died.'

'– could have married any of the available ladies panting after him, Mary Grace. Lord knows he didn't observe the same celibacy he required of you!'

I gasped, shoving him away. 'How dare you insinuate that a man of God –'

'Jeremiah Michaels was just that – a man,' Fortune replied in an impassioned voice. 'And, as a creature of God, he had needs just like the rest of us. How shallow of him, to sneak around at every opportunity while denying his daughter the right to bloom – keeping her home, enslaved by duty, under the guise of righteousness. Even if he hadn't voiced his slanderous opinions of me, I would've considered him a hypocrite for the way he treated you, Mary Grace.'

7

While this outburst shocked me, Hyde Fortune had honed in on a resentment I'd kept hidden in the darkest recesses of my heart. I was only a girl when my mother took sick, and I tended her frail body out of the boundless love she had always shown me. I had learned religion from Papa's pulpit, but I found my faith in Mama. Her death had devastated me. I recovered by keeping busy around the house, seeing to the needs of my grieving father.

But yes, he'd called upon plenty of women as part of his pastoral duty; women who smiled eagerly as they presented him with cakes they made or socks they knitted. Most of them were married, so everyone assumed their sympathy and gifts were given with honourable intent. I was too naïve to see their ulterior motives, or to suspect my father's response. But Hyde had just told me what I'd been too sheltered to guess.

And his words rang sweetly in my lonely heart, telling me I was lovely and that he'd wanted me for years. And yes, I'd sacrificed the prime of my life out of a sense of duty rather than love. Jeremiah Michaels was a demanding man who set me upon an impossible pedestal, as an example of virtue and modesty. So by the time he took to liquor as an attempt at staying sane, I had no choice but to cover for him. I'd accepted this form of servitude as my fate, my life's purpose as his daughter.

I sagged against the desk, absently rubbing my wrists as though bound by invisible chains.

Hyde sighed. 'I'm sorry. I've heaped even more sorrow and guilt on you. How can I make it up to you, dear lady?'

Dear lady, he called me. Although Mr Fortune was only five or six years older than I, his profession had rendered him worldly and sophisticated. He might've been born to a whore out of wedlock, but he'd carved himself a niche: death was the great equaliser, and as its gatekeeper, Hyde had attained a lucrative – if unenviable

– position. No one really liked him, but everybody needed him in the end.

So when he called me a dear lady, he was, in effect, raising me to a higher level by association. And at that moment, I felt too wonderful for words, because I sensed he could help me find the life I'd been denied. I no longer had to be poor and beholden. I could be Mary Grace Michaels, a woman in my own right ... maybe with my own means.

'You did mention possible employment,' I reminded him.

Those eyes took on a devilish glow that held promises beyond my wildest dreams. 'Come relax by the fire,' he insisted, guiding me to the settee beside the hearth. He put on another log and poured us more brandy while I sank into the supple leather. 'Let me pleasure you while I talk about Heaven's Gate.'

The snick of both locks prevented anyone from intruding, and sent a jolt of desire through me. I knew exactly what he planned to do – which was the very thing I'd been taught not to want, or even think about. But as Hyde Fortune knelt before me to remove my shoes, a wanton waywardness set my captive soul free. I sensed it would be a long, long time before I got it back.

And I was too far gone to care.

Chapter Two

Lessons in Ecstasy

'Look at these exquisite legs and feet. Mary Grace, you're even lovelier than I imagined.'

He'd thought about how I looked without my clothes? Even more exciting than this novel notion was the way he massaged my foot. No one had ever touched me like this, thinking I might enjoy such treatment. I sipped the brandy, letting its sweet heat roll over my tongue, and then held the snifter to Hyde's lips.

He took a swig, grinning. 'You're becoming a sensualist, it seems.'

'Teach me everything you know,' I breathed, slipping forward on the couch. 'Which is what I've always been taught not to want. But then, how did I know what I was missing?'

It was the brandy talking, just as it had led my father down the primrose path. But I paid no attention to that warning, because as Hyde rubbed the muscles of my calves and continued upward I felt so delicious I couldn't possibly stop him. I'd spent my life striving towards Heaven, yet in a few effortless moments this man had taken me there.

Hyde had been raising my skirts with his massage, and when his lips went where his fingers had been, I

10

gasped. How could I shiver this way without sliding forward on to his face? He was kneeling between my knees, kissing the skin of my upper thighs until I thought I'd explode. My inner muscles tensed and then went even tighter, sending shock waves through my body.

I lifted my hips, and with one swift movement Hyde took down my drawers. It was wicked, to willingly expose my intimate parts to him. But the brandy was stirring me, making so much slick, liquid heat that the pressure of the seam against my slit was unbearable.

'Jesus, woman,' Hyde breathed, and suddenly he buried his face in the muslin crotch. He began inhaling deeply, eyes closed, as though my personal scent contained the only essence he needed to live.

'God, you excite me!' he whispered, gazing up at me with eyes like embers. 'And I'm going to send you just as far over the edge, Mary Grace. So far you won't want to come back – except to come again. And again.'

I wanted to thrust myself at him, to relieve the awful aching that inflamed my inner lips and the bud they enfolded. But Hyde refused to humour me. He kissed my thighs with bold abandon, grasping my arse, purposely avoiding the feverish skin that craved his attention. Then he burrowed along my belly, while his fingers found the placket of my blouse. Buttons popped in all directions as he parted the thin fabric.

'Hyde, I've nothing to wear back to –'

'So you'll stay here, with me.'

'– and this is my only shift –'

'So I'll buy you a dozen of them, my love. Lacy little things that I'll forever delight in tearing away, so I can kiss your marvellous skin.' And with the splitting of the threadbare muslin, he was doing just that. His mouth set my breasts on fire as he licked and sucked and teased my nipples, toying with his tongue until I cried out. The silk of his lips contrasted with the roughness of his cheek as he nestled against my chest, like an infant begging to be fed.

11

Then his thumb found that little nub he'd ignored before, making me gasp with spasms. Hyde continued to suckle, while kindling a wildfire between my legs with the circling of his fingers. His body held me prisoner on the leather settee as he stroked and sucked more intently. I began to writhe, my head tossing like I was possessed, and I gave up all pretence at control.

My hips wiggled and strained. The ache inside me threatened to explode, spiralling deeper. Just when I thought I could take no more, Hyde lightly bit my nipple and slipped a finger up my hole. In and out he dipped, brushing my clit with a rapidity that made my head spin.

'Harder,' I begged, thinking I'd slide off the couch in all my wetness.

With a devious chuckle, Hyde inserted a second finger and began squeezing, faster now. My body flared and my senses reeled. The wet suction encircling my breast and the hot hand pounding against my mound were driving me towards certain insanity.

Suddenly I soared, riding waves that bore me high and free. A wail escaped me, followed by a louder, more desperate one, and as Hyde drove a third finger inside me, I shattered. I was vaguely aware of arms that kept me from flying off the couch and breathing that had become as laboured as my own, but otherwise there was nothing except the starbursts behind my eyes. I lost all track of time and the world around me.

When I could focus again, he was gazing at me with a tenderness I couldn't fathom, an affection like I'd never known. And at that moment Hyde Fortune became much more than my lover: he became my love. With every beat of my sheltered heart – every pulse of my awakening womanhood – I felt the rightness of what had just happened. We'd been born to this purpose, destined to create this fine, shining madness between us.

There would never be another man for me.

I didn't tell him this, of course. It was too dangerous

to think about, much less announce to the knave kneeling between my knees. As though he had no idea what he'd just put me through, his fingers began to massage me again.

'What are you doing?' I murmured. 'Give me the words, Hyde, because my mother certainly didn't.'

'I'm stroking your pussy. Fondling your lovely cunt. Fingering your slit . . . your twat.'

'My what?' I rhymed with a low laugh. I spread even further for him, guiding his finger deeper. 'Which word do you prefer?'

'Whatever suits the moment. Actually, just the thought of this enticing little entry has brought Solomon more pleasure than you'll ever know, on many a lonely night,' he whispered.

I stopped wiggling. 'Solomon?'

'My cock. He has such an upstanding reputation, he deserves the name of a great king, don't you think?'

I giggled, and Hyde responded by rising higher on his knees. With one hand he raised my curl-covered mound, which made the button hiding beneath it jut out like a little tongue. He then circled this sensitive area with his finger, apparently fascinated by the dew he saw seeping out.

'That position I mentioned?' he asked, looking anything but businesslike.

'Yes?' My head felt fogged in, and rational thought was now beyond me.

'It's at Heaven's Gate, the monastery in the mountains where they make those irresistible chocolates and brandy cakes.'

'I couldn't eat a thing. In fact, at this moment, I could swear I'll never be hungry again.'

Hyde chuckled, still massaging my juices. 'It just occurred to me, sweet Mary, that this little keyhole we've discovered is its own celestial opening . . . for which I alone now hold the key. Heaven's Gate, indeed.'

His words stopped my heart. Was he thinking, as I

had, that we were destined to be together? Or had his tone taken on a possessiveness I was too naïve to hear?

It didn't matter. When his thumb found my erect little clit again, the intense sensation sent me up off the couch, clutching at him. 'Hyde, please! I can't bear any more!'

He hugged me to his warm, solid body. I felt the rumble of laughter in his chest as he tugged my blouse from my waistband. 'You're delightful,' he said, kissing the sensitive spot beneath my ear, 'but what makes you think I'm finished? By the time I cast my entire spell, you'll never be able to look at another man without getting aroused – wanting me, sweet lady.'

It was a prophecy I dared not deny, for what did I know about the intimacies between a man and his woman? And why would I ever care about other men, when the one who now looked at me so lovingly had made me feel so complete? Cherished, in ways I never dreamed of.

'You're wearing too many clothes,' Hyde teased, so we peeled away every layer of fabric that covered me. A few hours ago I would've been mortified to sit naked before a man; my conscience would've smouldered like coals from the Devil's own fire. Yet now, my lover's admiring gaze made me thrust out my chest, and I let out a laugh so brazen it could've drifted from a whore-house window.

'Seems you're the one who's overdressed now,' I said, my fingers flying to his buttons.

'That's the spirit!' Hyde's smile tightened, and he ripped at his clothing with the same abandon he'd used on mine.

When I saw his broad shoulders – the pattern of curls that curved around his chest, forming an arrow pointing to his arousal – I sat back to watch. The only man I'd seen in the altogether had been my ailing father when I bathed him, so this display amazed me. Hyde moved with a sure, masculine grace as he threw his shirt aside and then stood to unfasten his pants.

He looked feral, like a lone wolf on the prowl, as he stripped. His eyes never left me. Had I inspired that magnificent stiffening? Lord, his cock looked formidable! I doubted I had room for it all. Solomon swayed before me as though it had a life all its own, the head reddened and the firm, tall shaft standing proudly pink. A tiny bead of moisture formed at the hole, and then dripped off.

'My word,' I breathed, wanting to touch it, yet not knowing if I should. 'You realise that Mama never explained these things –'

'You were young when she died.'

'– while Papa was too set on my salvation to talk about anatomy. He told me sex was for procreation, not pleasure. Never even said the word.'

'But did he consider that we were created this way? That, if God didn't want us to enjoy our bodies, He could find other ways to keep our species alive?'

He wrapped his arms around me, and I revelled in the warmth of his bare skin against mine. Coaxing me higher on the couch, Hyde kissed me with even more intensity than before. He gnawed my lower lip and then slipped his tongue past my teeth, taking me by surprise: its rhythm suggested the movement of his cock inside that Poppington woman, which I would soon enjoy myself! And as I felt his insistent prodding, and heard Sol rustling among my coarse curls, I instinctively raised my hips to take him in.

Hyde cried out with a desperation matching my own, plunging deep. I paced my thrusting with his, finding an even more primitive heat than he'd kindled while staying outside me. I spread my legs to allow him fullest access, hearing impassioned little whimpers that could only be my own – and which were coming faster as those waves rose within me again.

'Hyde . . . Hyde, my Lord,' I breathed.

'Am I hurting you, love?'

'Not a chance! Just don't stop, oh please don't stop!'

With a wicked grin, he raised himself up so he could look into my eyes. 'Squeeze me,' he commanded. 'Squeeze my cock like you're going to milk it dry, Mary Grace.'

When I did, Hyde's ecstatic grimace sent a shimmer up my spine. Then he angled himself higher, putting more pressure on that aching place that so desperately wanted his attention. 'Grip it,' he rasped. 'Drive us both over the edge. My God, but you're perfect.'

Inspired by his praise, I concentrated on those inner muscles. I gripped and let go, gripped and let go, until I was bucking beneath him. The settee groaned with our commotion, its leather allowing me to slide in the wetness we created. Pumping faster, Hyde challenged me with those relentless eyes, until the clamping of his jaw sent me ahead of him. My climax was noisy, and my lover's cries drove me to dizzier heights as he shot his hot seed inside me.

Hyde collapsed against me. My head fell back on to the upholstery. I felt rubbery and jointless as I draped an arm over his damp, heaving back. For a moment, there was only the cheery crackling of the fire.

And again I knew it: I loved Hyde Fortune like I could never love another. Despite my earlier reservations about this man of dubious repute, I had accepted him into myself, body and soul. And there could be no turning back.

He let out a contented sigh. 'Are you all right, sweetheart?'

'Never better. You've made me feel like quite the woman.'

'That you are. I'd swear you were made expressly to satisfy me.' He raised his head, grinning. 'I'll tell Delores Poppington to pay off her damn coffin and be done with it. After loving you, Mary Grace, the thought of plowing her furrow again makes me sick.'

We laughed together, a low, sweet sound that wrapped around us like a cosy old shawl. Hyde rested against me for several minutes before rising. 'I'll send in my housekeeper, Yu Ling, with a basin of water. I'll find you some clothes while you wash up, and then we can discuss your choices of employment.'

He was kind enough to tuck my old clothing around me before he dressed and left the room. With a languid sigh, I settled back on the settee to consider how my situation had changed in the past hour. I'd arrived here destitute, and had discovered a whole new frenzy – and a future I might share with a handsome man.

Did I dare dream of marriage? Could I hope for the home and children I'd been denied by Papa's demands?

It was too soon. Naïve as I was, I knew my confused heart had jumped at the first possibility that came its way. I'd given myself to a man without considering the consequences. Such compulsiveness wasn't like me, for I'd been raised to meet the needs of others without thought for my own happiness.

Indeed, happiness had always seemed a fleeting notion, like a butterfly I might capture some day, but never right now. So as I sat back, breathing the mingled scents of our sex, I had to laugh. This feeling was so far beyond mere happiness, I couldn't comprehend it. And I didn't want to ruin it by thinking about it too much.

Outside, the wind howled and an eerie ticking, like a deathwatch beetle, made me grip my makeshift coverlet. The frozen bushes by the window were clattering against the glass, I reasoned, but then I swore I heard voices above me, followed by a high-pitched keening that made me go cold all over.

I was in the undertaker's office, after all, so there might be corpses lying in the secret regions of this mansion. For all my belief in an afterlife, dead bodies spooked me. Hearing that Banshee-like wail again, plus the uncanny tapping on the wall, made my neck prickle with gooseflesh. What was taking Hyde so long?

The parlour door opened silently, and I jumped. I was greeted by the smile of an almond-eyed Celestial about my own age, who carried a basin of steaming water and some towels. She leaned against the door to shut it, studying me with a rapt expression. Her raven hair was wound into a fat knot atop her head; her breasts barely protruded above the wide sash of her kimono. Its poppy-coloured silk was shot with gold, and as she floated towards me she exuded all the mystery of the Orient – and another aura I didn't recognise.

'Missy Mary,' she said with a slight bow. 'Yu Ling come for your bath.'

Hyde's housekeeper intended to bathe me? I didn't want assistance while I washed, and I certainly didn't want this stranger touching private parts that oozed with my juices, and Hyde's! I clutched at the clothing draped over me, aware of how exposed I was beneath the flimsy fabric.

'I – thank you, but I can bathe myself,' I murmured.

Her bow-shaped mouth curved as she bobbed again. 'Mister Hyde, he give me job of everybody's care. Yu Ling much rather tend Missy Mary, with her hair like fire and her pretty skin, than the stiffs downstairs.'

I laughed. That Mr Fortune's serving girl kept her sense of humour despite her ghastly job impressed me. I could only speculate about the sort of care she gave Hyde – but that wasn't my place, was it? Maybe he'd saved this exotic young woman from the streets, just as he was about to act on my behalf. So I concentrated on the matter at hand.

'You may set the basin down and go on about your other duties,' I insisted gently. 'I'd rather wash myself. Thank you.'

Was that disappointment in her eyes? Before she could press her point again, Hyde opened the door, carrying a large fabric bundle and some dresses on hangers. He quickly assessed the situation. 'Let's discuss tonight's dinner, Yu Ling. Then you can prepare a guest room for Miss Michaels. The lavender one in the west wing would be the warmest, don't you think?'

I flashed him a grateful smile as he and his house-keeper gave me some privacy. Kneeling to straddle the basin, I lathered myself with soap that smelled like lemon grass. The hot water felt heavenly against my sticky thighs, while rubbing myself with the washcloth rekindled the sensations Hyde had awakened between my legs.

The image of Yu Ling washing me there, intent on removing our juices from my auburn curls, aroused me by surprise. I could imagine her enigmatic smile as she parted my thighs, kneeling to inspect me ... separating my swollen lips with her slender fingers while cupping handfuls of water against my quivering slit.

As I imagined her teasing me there, then thrusting her fingers inside like Hyde had done, my thoughts raced out of control. My hand went between my legs. Some-how Fortune's image appeared, as well, urging Yu Ling to fondle me while he held me from behind, a captive in their conspiracy. Heat rushed through me, and these illicit images – my secret, solitary act – drove me to another blinding climax.

Where had all this passion come from? I felt so sticky I had to wash myself again. On wobbly legs, I crossed to where Hyde had left two dresses, plus lacy bloomers and a matching shift. I tried not to think about who they'd belonged to – he'd had any number of customers and lovers, after all – as I slipped into the underthings. I chose the gown of green and ivory stripes. It felt large, but was nicer than any dress I owned, made from a lightweight wool that draped richly around my figure.

I was pulling my hair into a presentable twist when a low whistle coaxed me to turn around. Hyde had slipped in behind me.

'I thought that dress would become you, Mary Grace,' he said as he paused beside the chair. 'Leave your hair down. That untamed fire falling around your shoulders excites me.'

19

'And what doesn't?' I shot back. Then I turned away, embarrassed.

Hyde chuckled kindly as he took me by the shoulders. 'You're right,' he whispered, 'and I make no apologies for my desires. You've led a sheltered life, so you don't realise how men gaze at you and wish they could love you the way I have. No need to be ashamed of your natural beauty, or your need for affection, Mary Grace. Our Creator made you this way.'

How did he always draw upon my religious beliefs to twist a point to his own advantage? I laughed as he peppered my neck with kisses designed to make me feel better about my outburst, and myself.

'I shouldn't make fun of you, Mr Fortune,' I replied. 'I believe we were about to discuss my possible employment at Heaven's Gate.'

Chapter Three
Twice Frightened

'*L*et me start by inviting you to stay here, with me,' he said. His baritone voice flowed like the fudge sauce the monks made, rich and sweet, while his eyes glowed with that beguiling cinnamon glint. 'Now that I've discovered such a wonderful lover, I hate to let her go.'

Could he hear my heart thundering? Or see the way his words made my pulse pound? 'You flatter me.'

'This is not flattery, love,' Hyde whispered. 'I've never met a woman like you. Despite what you've heard – and what you walked in on – I'm a man of few friends. I crave your companionship as much as your passion, Mary Grace. My intentions are honourable, I assure you.'

His loneliness touched me deeply, as his expression entreated me to stay. And what young woman didn't dream of a handsome man falling in love with her, as quickly as she herself had succumbed?

The temptation to accept Hyde's offer almost overrode logic. Mr Fortune was wealthy, if not well liked. Never again would I wear threadbare dresses or be subject to the sneers of my father's congregation. I could set my worries behind me and pursue my dreams of a comfortable home and a loving family.

Or could I? Once again the tapping on the wall made

me stiffen. What if Hyde didn't want children? Would I, too, become a pariah by associating with this mysterious mortician? I told myself that his was an honest, necessary occupation, but the thought of occupying a house where corpses spent their final hours still gave me the shivers.

And it was too soon. My first taste of loving had ushered me to new heights, but I was too giddy to make reliable decisions while Hyde held me with his beguiling gaze. When I realised what he'd left in the wingback chair, my mind returned to the matter at hand.

'This is one of my quilts!' I unrolled the bundle, grinning. Emerald velvet made a leafy jungle background, scattered with parrots of sequinned crimson and peacocks cut from sapphire and turquoise brocades. For flowers, I'd appliquéd paisley petals that shone like stained glass.

'It's one of my earliest pieces, designed while I was caring for Mama. I found these jewel-toned gowns at a second-hand shop, thinking the lush colours would cheer her,' I continued in a more subdued tone. 'I donated it to the Home for the Friendless shortly after she died.'

'And I bought it at their charity auction, for my own mother,' Hyde replied, his voice rising with excitement. 'Several society types were there, and once they recognised the quilt's originality – and the auctioneer noted the Art Nouveau influence, like Tiffany glass – the price soared. But it was worth every bit of the four hundred dollars I paid, because Mother dearly loved this piece.'

'Four hundred . . .?'

'The colours fascinated her, Mary Grace. She'd stroke each different type of fabric as though she knew its story. As though she'd worn such finery herself, in a long-forgotten life.

'She hadn't, of course,' he added bitterly. 'She was an unwed mother, marked by her so-called sin. It was all she could do to keep us fed, and to send me to school in presentable clothing.'

I admired Hyde for rising above the circumstances of his birth, and providing for his mother in her declining years. Our eyes met in a gaze that recalled the women we both missed so much, which formed another bond between us. It hadn't occurred to me that Mr Fortune would grieve like the rest of us: I had assumed if his occupation hadn't made him immune, Madeleine's tawdry trade would have hardened his heart.

But the forlorn shine in those eyes told me I was seriously mistaken. He had loved his mother, as I had mine. One was a prostitute and one a preacher's wife, but both losses had left unmendable holes in the fabric of our lives.

'I'm glad it brought her comfort,' I murmured. 'But four hundred dollars?'

'Never underestimate the value of your work,' he replied pointedly. 'Brother Christy has been wanting a different product – something that nets more than a jar of jelly or a pound cake – so your illustrated quilts would make you a welcome addition at Heaven's Gate. Most people don't realise those brandy cakes and sinfully delicious chocolates are made at the abbey pictured on their tins, by the monks and those they take in as assistants. It's not far from here, you know.'

'I had no idea. Why, Mama's favourite raspberry jam bore that label. It was an indulgence Papa allowed her because her appetite was so unpredictable.' I thought of the familiar cream-and-olive label, which pictured a fortress reminiscent of Old World religious retreats. 'The jam was so terribly expensive –'

'Father Luc and his monks depend on those profits for their support.'

'– that I was punished for sneaking a little on to my own toast,' I recalled with a rueful smile. 'And I was strictly forbidden to sample Papa's favourite, which was the bourbon-pecan pound cake. Why, I got tipsy just lifting the lid from the tin!'

As Hyde smiled, I realised that Papa had acquired his

taste for this liquor-laced cake about the time he came into that large donation. I glanced at the brandy bottle on Mr Fortune's desk, and sure enough, there was that same label.

'The monks raise the fruits they use, in their vineyards and orchards. They're practically self-sufficient, and they finance the Home, as well,' he added proudly. 'Although I've invited you to stay with me, you could do worse than working there for a few months. Since your quilts would sell for so much more than their other products – and since you alone would sew them – I could strike a deal with Father Luc. Seems only fair that a portion of the quilt income be deposited in your own account, to establish your finances for when you return.'

Images of Friar Tuck, or perhaps St Francis of Assisi, stomping grapes and stirring great vats of chocolate, made me look more closely at Hyde's brandy bottle. The stone bulwark on the label, with its towers and lozenge-shaped windows, came straight from a medieval fantasy. Germanic script made the name HEAVEN'S GATE equally appealing, as did the glowing product description and a paragraph about the monastery.

'These products have always been sold in Colorado?' I asked.

'That's right.'

'Then why don't I know anyone who's been to Heaven's Gate?' I challenged. 'Surely carriage tours – or a cog railroad like the one on Pike's Peak – to this fascinating place would bring in a big income.'

Hyde's laughter made his dimples flicker. 'It's a religious refuge, Mary Grace, not a tourist attraction! A rather reclusive order, where the residents devote themselves to prayer when they're not making pralines or bottling brandy. Many of the orchard and kitchen workers once stayed at the Home, or were labourers who lost their jobs in this recent recession. They live in cottages and receive their meals and clothing as their pay.

'And it's as though the laws of nature conform to the

abbey's needs,' he continued in awe. 'Snow like we're having now is unheard of at Heaven's Gate. The temperatures stay balmy enough that the vineyards thrive, and the inhabitants don't even need coats.'

A glance out the window startled me. While I'd been at Mount Calvary these three hours, the world outside had been blanketed with white. I shivered, trying to imagine a place like Hyde described.

It sounded appealing. Yet my visions of prayerful, hooded figures chanting down candlelit aisles felt foreign to me. 'I'm not Roman Catholic,' I pointed out, 'and despite my religious upbringing, I'm not really suited to the contemplative, celibate life – as we've both discovered.'

'I'm hardly a candidate myself,' he said with a chuckle. 'But I'm in charge of distributing Heaven's Gate's products, and I oversee the budget for the Home. Brother Christy appreciates my work, and he'll welcome you for your pleasant disposition, Mary Grace. Not to mention for the profits from your quilts.' Hyde's eyes glowed as he came up behind me, urging me back against his tall, sturdy frame.

'But I'll miss you,' I whispered. 'And – and these stone walls on the label look so intimidating. What if I can't live up to my agreement? What if I don't fit in?'

Turning me, Hyde smiled his reassurance. 'I'll gladly pay off whatever remains of the agreement we draw up, Mary Grace. I'm the last man who wants to see you unhappy. You could establish yourself as an artisan whose work is not only recognised but sought after. Work that could provide you with a tidy income.

'And although you think you'll miss my attentions while you're there,' he went on softly, 'I suspect you have ... reservations about taking up with a man who lives in a morgue. That's quite understandable, you know.'

My cheeks went hot. He'd sensed my fears, knowing the elegance of this house would never disguise its distasteful function. Hyde kissed me until I melted against him, returning his passion with gratitude and a rising desire.

He laughed, stroking my hair. 'If we decide to take up housekeeping, I'll buy us a cosy little love-nest, Mary Grace. A haven where you can sew, and a refuge from the morbidity I deal with each day. I want you to sleep on your decision, however. I travel to the abbey on Fridays, but this snowfall might keep us here until the road up the mountain becomes passable . . .'

His voice faded into a promise of lovemaking to come, which made me tingle with the warm breath that was tickling my ear. Spearing his fingers into my hair, Hyde captured my mouth with his tongue and pulled me so close I could feel his arousal through our clothing. Would either of us get any work done, if we lived together?

As I reached for his shirt buttons, he gently ended our embrace. 'Such a responsive woman,' he murmured. 'But I'm a negligent host, keeping you from the dinner Yu Ling's prepared. And it's unfair of me to influence your decision with kisses.'

'All's fair in love and war,' I quipped, and allowed him to usher me upstairs to his living quarters.

By not looking at the coffins displayed in the parlour, I could appreciate the mansion's architectural details – the grand staircase, polished to a proud shine, lit by a crystal chandelier that glistened like a million stars. The flocked wallpaper and the carpets were the rich reds and blues of Impressionist paintings, and as I ascended on Hyde's arm I pretended I was already the lady of such a fine house. A pleasant fantasy indeed, considering how he pulled me close on each landing, for a soul-searing kiss.

When we entered the second-floor hallway, Hyde escorted me towards a large room at the back of the house. 'When this mansion was converted into a mortuary, the kitchen remained on the main floor,' he explained, 'so Yu Ling sends up the meals on a dumb waiter for Sebastian to set out. I hope you don't mind if they join us. Seems ridiculous to dine alone, when my staff need to eat, too.'

We stepped into a room dominated by a massive walnut table, where stew and fresh bread were laid out. Twelve chairs waited like silent guests, but only four places at one end were set. Tapers flickered in the brass candelabra, lending a romantic air to this room full of ponderous sideboards and gilt-framed mirrors. I was about to compliment the china pattern – elegance like I'd never known at home – when hearty male laughter rang out in the room we'd just passed.

Hyde pulled out a chair to seat me, but when the laughter mixed with lusty moans, he grinned impishly. Holding a finger to his lips, he motioned for me to follow him to the wall. Then, silent as a thief, he slid a small section of panelling aside to reveal a rectangular hole just large enough for the two of us to peek through.

What I saw made me gasp, so as Hyde pulled me closer he covered my mouth with his hand. Yu Ling stood before a beefy, bearded man who sprawled in an armchair with his pants around his ankles. As she teased his large, red erection with an ostrich plume, he grasped himself as though he were aiming a fire hose at her. The Celestial squealed with delight, dodging his quivering feet while tormenting him with her feather.

'They love this game,' Hyde whispered. 'It's a contest to see who lasts longest when –'

'Oh, God, drink me,' the man rasped, his face contorting. 'Hurry it up, or Hyde'll think he wants to share you.'

My eyes widened. Yu Ling positioned herself between the man's knees with a coy grin. She then made her mouth into a tight 'O' and approached his bobbing cock, with a hunger that made my insides flutter.

The man beside me sucked in air, watching this scene with growing arousal. His nostrils flared, and then the

27

hand at my waist snaked down to grab my skirts. Within seconds, Hyde's fingers slipped into my bloomers and he'd braced himself against my backside.

When Yu Ling's lips met the man's bulbous red head, my lover gyrated against me. 'Oh, Mary Grace,' he breathed, 'if you could do that to me some time ... the touch of your tongue would make me insane. That lucky bastard Sebastian.'

The two people we watched seemed to act out Hyde's fondest fantasy. Sebastian's dark head rolled from side to side with his outbursts. Like a man possessed, he grasped the Celestial's neck and urged her on. Yu Ling seemed just as caught up in his pleasure, pumping her head repeatedly, bearing down, then sucking up the length of his impressive shaft.

The fingers inside my sex lips matched the pair's frenetic rhythm. My inner voice told me I should be appalled at what I now witnessed, yet I writhed against Hyde's hand, unable to take my eyes from the spectacle in the next room. When my legs parted of their own accord, he plunged his thumb up my pussy until I almost cried out from the unexpected pressure.

Sebastian's hips twitched so unpredictably, I wondered how the serving girl could keep up with his wild motions. She continued to suck him in and let him out, with the ease of a sword-swallower at a side show. He grimaced and bucked, throwing his shoulders back, and let out a hoarse cry that sent my own spasms spiralling. I ground myself on to Hyde's hand, while he in turn rutted against my backside. The wetness I shot out triggered a groan he muffled against my shoulder. His own urgent throbbing followed.

When rational thought returned, Hyde slid the panel back into place. He steadied me while I caught my breath, then licked his fingers.

'Quite a nice appetiser,' he said with a wink. 'More appealing than oysters. And much nicer than having to share a woman, too.'

His eyes plumbed mine, as though to ask if the favour his Celestial had done for Sebastian seemed feasible to me. Then he helped me smooth my skirts and guided me to the table. With utmost courtliness, he seated me at a corner and took his place at the head, beside me.

Seconds later we were joined by the couple we'd spied upon, who were acting as though nothing out of the ordinary had happened. Hyde stood, smiling at the man whose dark beard and hair made such a contrast to his own features. 'Mary Grace, this is Sebastian Hatch, my sextant and business assistant. Sebastian, you probably remember Miss Michaels from when we –'

'What man could forget such an angelic face, and such stunning auburn hair?' Hatch crooned. He bowed over my hand, kissing it slyly. 'We're pleased to have you, Mary Grace. Yu Ling seldom meets young ladies her own age, and she was terribly excited about readying your room for the night.'

His beard tickled my skin as he bussed my knuckles, his dark eyes fixed on mine. How could such common, polite words sound as though secret meanings peeked out from behind them? And how could this debonair man, dressed as fashionably as his employer, act like he could devour me while Hyde looked on – even though he, too, had just enjoyed a stunning appetiser?

These mysteries played with me as we ate our delicious stew. Men had never expressed such open admiration for my attributes, and being seated across from one and beside another set me on edge. I was also aware of Yu Ling's sloe-eyed gaze, as she sat beside Sebastian. Her obvious interest unsettled me, after watching her suck on the sextant.

Our conversation implied subtle double meanings while we all pretended we hadn't pleasured ourselves before dinner. This charade would've excited me more if I hadn't been the newcomer – unaware of household customs, and wondering if I were to be served up as dessert.

The Celestial brought us a raisin-studded bread pudding, however. I tasted brandy as well, and by the time I finished the dessert and my wine, my entire body tingled. Before today I'd rarely imbibed, so the laughter and attentions of my new friends went to my head. I found out how tipsy I'd become when I tried to stand up, and Hyde had to steady me.

'You've had a tiring day,' he said kindly, excusing us with a nod to his staff. 'Thank you both for a wonderful meal. I think Mary Grace is ready to retire.'

'Shall I run her a bath?' Yu Ling asked. She cocked her head at a coquettish angle, her eyes alight with Oriental mystique.

'That would be lovely,' Hyde replied.

Once again I had the feeling this young woman couldn't wait to get her hands on me, and that Hyde would indulge her. Yet now, after such good food and drink, the idea didn't seem as repugnant ... perhaps because of the shine in my benefactor's eyes. I sensed he wouldn't allow the play to go further than my relative innocence would tolerate. I'd simply have to trust him.

He showed me through the parlour where Sebastian and the serving girl had performed, and the adjoining library. Both rooms featured deep green walls and overstuffed furnishings of sage and tan, without the ostentatious air of the first floor. His own suite, dominated by a four-poster bed of mahogany, exuded a rich masculinity in its royal blue, red and gold decor.

Hyde smiled at my awestruck gaze until the sound of running water beckoned us. We then entered the largest bathing room I'd ever seen, and were enveloped in rose-scented steam rising from the clawfoot tub. Candles chased the evening shadows into the corners, inviting me to slip into the soothing water.

I turned to my host with a shy smile, which he kissed. Cradling my face in his hands, he opened my lips with his tongue to explore, to ignite my inner fires so effortlessly. As I wondered just how many times we could make love in a day, I realised the water had been shut off. The hands unfastening my dress belonged to a silent someone who'd come in behind me.

When I balked, Hyde's kiss became more insistent. I understood then that he was distracting me so Yu Ling could perform her duties, as well as to accustom my body to a woman's touch ... a potentially exciting exploration of my sensuality.

The Celestial made quick work of removing my clothes. Her breath teased my skin as my shift fell around my ankles. Her murmurings, a soft Chinese chatter, conveyed an excitement she couldn't contain as she slipped her fingers beneath my stockings to remove them.

Still kissing me fervently, Hyde kept his body apart from mine – thwarting my inclination to cling to him, while I submitted to his serving girl's ministrations. Their teamwork sent me into an unexpected frenzy: when his tongue began to duel with mine, Yu Ling ran her hands up the insides of my naked thighs.

I realised that she, too, wore nothing as she made a deliberate sweep of my backside with her lips and breasts. Those taut buds blazing trails up my hips were her nipples, and the thought made my own breasts bead up, sending a shiver through me.

Yu Ling responded by standing against me, spanning my abdomen with her hands and then drawing them lightly up the sensitive skin of my belly until they cupped my breasts. Her moan made my insides coil, right above the slit that was growing slick in spite of my reservations. I almost pulled away, but then Hyde began to suckle the breasts the Celestial offered him with her attentive hands.

I moaned in surprise and surrender. Sandwiched between the man who licked my nipples with his warm, wet tongue and the serving girl whose mound gyrated against my hips, I could only play the victim. A more willing victim than I dared to admit.

And when feminine fingers parted my folds to grant Hyde's hand access, the pressure of at least three male fingers made me gasp. Merciless, my captors continued to thrust and knead and press me between their undulating bodies until I thought I'd explode. My cries reverberated in the steamy room as I bucked between them, the waves of shimmering delight cresting on and on until my knees buckled.

With a knowing chuckle, Hyde swept me up and carried me to the tub. 'May I watch Yu Ling bathe you, sweetheart?' he whispered. 'What a fetching contrast – your auburn fairness and her blue-black hair and eyes.'

I felt too loose and jointless to refuse him. I lay like a helpless child in his arms, sighing languidly when the warm bath water lapped around my body. When I leaned against the gentle slope of the bathtub, the Oriental joined me rather than remaining alongside the tub, as I'd expected.

I had never seen another woman naked. Yu Ling, with her ebony hair knotted on her head, appeared so at ease as to be displaying herself for my benefit. Her golden grace was accentuated by the flickering candlelight, while her obsidian eyes riveted mine. As she knelt to rub her sponge against a bar of rose-scented soap, her breasts bobbed. They rode high and firm on her chest, with the velvety perfection of pansy petals begging for my caress.

Then she stood up, slight but proud, her gaze daring me to drink in her loveliness as rivulets of bath water trickled from her bush down her parted thighs. The scrape of the soap against her sponge played a suggestive song as she stepped between my legs. Her tongue darted between her lips as she knelt in the water. The steam rising between us intensified our silence.

I gripped the rim of the tub, waiting.

Yu Ling slowly extended the sponge. Still holding my gaze, she squeezed, dropping dollops of foam on to my chest. When a gasp escaped me, she smiled, crouching like an exotic predator, well aware of her power. With my legs and arms following the curves of the tub I was completely open to her advances. I'd never felt so vulnerable in my life.

Her lips parted, inches from mine. 'You so ready,' she panted. 'Yu Ling watch while Mister Hyde couple with Missy Mary, so she been hot and wet between legs all this time. Want you to touch her down there ... yes? Please?'

My fingers tingled as the Celestial guided my hand through the water. When my wrist grazed her thigh, her eyelids flickered. Her face, misted with steam and desire, took on a wanton expression as her jaw went slack. Moaning, Yu Ling eased my palm against her coarse curls and skin so slick it felt wetter than the bath water.

'Jesus, Mary, and Joseph,' Hyde muttered thickly.

This utterance – because of whom it named, and because it reminded me Hyde was watching – brought me back to reality. I suddenly realised that a woman had my hand trapped between her quivering legs, and that she was about to kiss me.

'No! I – please!' I jerked my hand back, twisting my head away from Yu Ling's glare to beg Hyde's understanding. 'I can't let her – not while you watch us –'

The Celestial threw her sponge in my face, cursing in Chinese. Waves spilled over the tub's edge and her stiff, angular walk across the room hinted at a wrath she might try to avenge.

Hyde sagged like a deflating balloon.

'I'm sorry,' I whimpered, 'but I just can't –'

'I understand, Mary Grace. We've pushed you beyond your limits. I can only hope that some of what you've experienced has been pleasurable?'

How could I deny that? And how could I not be grateful for the way he helped me up, and then dried me with a soft towel? Moments later he was carrying me into the next room, where a single candle lit the lavender dimness. On the bed's soft sheets he laid me, smiling as he shucked off his clothes.

'Shall we rest, and take up tomorrow where we've left off?' he asked with a roguish grin. Then, more seriously, he added, 'I'll never expect you to do things you dislike, or place my own pleasure ahead of yours, Mary Grace. Just speak up, like you did tonight.'

'Thank you,' I whispered.

He blew out the candle and slipped between the sheets. When he curled his warm body around me from behind, I had never felt so protected. So cherished. So free from the ghosts who'd haunted my dreams, and from the agony my life had become. Despite my excitement at sharing a man's bed for the first time, I drifted into a deeply contented sleep.

I awoke disoriented, my eyes flying open in the darkness. When Hyde shifted and mumbled in his sleep, I remembered where I was, but remnants of an unsettling dream hung like fog in my head. I recalled an ominous sound, like the pounding of a nail into a coffin.

And there it was again, metal striking metal. The racket came from a distance, somewhere below.

Hyde pushed up on to his elbows, scowling. 'Someone's at the door,' he muttered, 'and Sebastian sleeps like the dead. I'm sorry it woke you.'

He padded across the room, to be swallowed by the shadows. I lay there wishing for his warmth, or the comfort of the nightgown I'd left at home, for I felt more than the chill of a winter's night. Voices below reminded me that I slept above a mortuary. I wondered why a corpse couldn't wait until morning, yet realised that, in the absence of a doctor, an undertaker was often asked to find the signs of life or death. This wasn't the first time Hyde Fortune had been summoned in the night, and it wouldn't be his last.

I snuggled deeper into the mattress, trying to still my imagination. I was alone upstairs, in a house of the dead, in those darkest hours before dawn. That shuffling I heard might be Hyde returning ... or the tread of something undead that had escaped from the bowels of the house. Enough moonlight lit the room that I saw the curtains fluttering in the draught from the window. Or was it a departed soul making them move?

I squeezed my eyes shut so the shapes in the shadows would go away. It would be just like my father to haunt me, shaking his finger at my shameless fall from grace. My conscience prickled when I reviewed yesterday's events: I'd succumbed to Hyde Fortune with barely a protest. Something about this house and its inhabitants had transformed Mary Grace Michaels into a wayward woman I barely recognised – a wanton my dear mother wouldn't want me to associate with, let alone become.

A brittle cough sent gooseflesh up my spine.

I gripped the blankets, willing away this figment of my imagination. Yet the laboured breathing, and the clearing of a very old throat sounded too real to be a product of my overwrought mind. I remembered the heaviness of Mama's congestion, the way her consumption gurgled in her lungs, and wondered if it were she, rather than my father, who'd come back to chastise me.

I peeked through the slit of one eyelid and my breath caught. A stooped-over crone loomed between the bed and the doorway. Was it the moonlight? Or was her translucent white gown the gossamer of dreams gone awry? The wraith was studying me with a gaze so piercing I wanted to disappear into the weave of the sheets.

I was very naked, and very cold, and very scared. And this visitor knew it.

'Don't go,' she rasped, and the effort made her cough again. The voice wasn't Mama's, but this poor soul's condition sounded painfully familiar.

'Heaven's Gate,' the apparition continued, 'is not what they ... not as it ... appears. Those who go ... are lost ... forever, Mary Grace.'

One of those pale arms rose, and the thought of this zombie touching me made me scream. I burrowed beneath the blankets, into an airless haven that offered no real protection. Was I to become the victim of my own visions? Would I be frightened to death by this shimmering figure and her warning?

I stopped breathing to listen, until I thought my lungs would burst. I pressed my forehead to my knees and prayed to God like I'd never petitioned Him before. Minutes crept by like hours before I dared uncurl myself for a breath of air.

The woman – or whatever she was – had warned against going to Heaven's Gate, and my thundering heart believed her. Yet when the first glimmer of dawn brought back my safety, my sanity, I knew what I had to do.

Despite my benefactor's offer of a fresh start, something about Mount Calvary set my teeth on edge. Its shroudlike atmosphere might suck me under, never to emerge as the wife and mother I wished to be. Sebastian Hatch and his Chinese accomplice would hold me hostage with their little tricks, and not even Hyde Fortune's avowed love – and he had never used that word, I reminded myself – would save me from this humiliation. His cinnamon-eyed smile and promises couldn't raise me from disgrace or keep that weird, nether-worldly woman from haunting me again.

And what advantage would it be to live here, to become the fuel for new rumours? My father's crimes had made me enough of a conversation piece already.

So I would go to Heaven's Gate.

And as far as I was concerned, we couldn't leave soon enough.

Chapter Four
Our Perilous Journey

*A*gainst his better judgment, Hyde agreed to drive me to Heaven's Gate immediately after breakfast. The sky, a gun-metal grey edged with heavy clouds, promised more snow – not the best of conditions for driving up a narrow mountain road, but he sensed my eagerness to leave Mount Calvary. Sebastian Hatch helped him load large sacks of supplies into the carriage, and waved us off with a look of unmistakable concern.

'I'm sorry to be such a Nervous Nellie,' I whispered, clutching my cloak around the ivory and green striped gown he'd given me. 'And thank you for fetching my sewing supplies and clothing from the Home. I just couldn't show my face there again.'

Hyde shifted beside me on the padded seat, holding the reins that came through a slot centred before him. The rectangular black carriage was completely enclosed, with small windows on either side and a larger one that spanned the front. For several moments there were only the clip-cloppings of Beau's hooves and the hum of our wheels on the brick street.

When he looked at me, I glanced down at my lap. 'Are you having second thoughts, Mary Grace? About becoming my lover, or –'

'No!'

His expression showed a vulnerability, a loneliness I glimpsed yesterday. I slipped my hand under his elbow, hoping this contact comforted him as much as it did me.

'Then what's happened? Yesterday you had the world by the tail and this morning you act as though you've seen a ghost.'

If I told him about the old crone who appeared in my room, he'd think I was insane. Yet if I didn't explain my turnabout in attitude, Hyde would assume he'd done something for which I couldn't forgive him.

'I ... when you were summoned downstairs in the night, I had a frightening experience,' I began. 'Perhaps I imagined her, but I could swear a withered old woman came in, warning me not to go to Heaven's Gate. Her white nightgown shimmered in the moonlight, hanging so loosely she appeared not to have any substance. And her voice ... that cough like Mama's ...'

The man beside me paled – or maybe that was my imagination, too. My pulse was pounding in my temples as I recalled the panic the apparition had caused, and how I'd burrowed beneath the covers like a frightened child. Hyde scooted against me.

'I'm sorry I had to leave you, sweetheart,' he said quietly. 'I didn't realise how deeply Mount Calvary affected you. I've grown so accustomed to its creakings and shadows, I forget others assume the house is haunted by whoever might lie dead downstairs. I had no bodies last night, by the way.'

The twinkle in his cinnamon eyes made me smile in spite of my nerves. I felt so foolish. I could almost convince myself the visitor was indeed a figment of my overactive imagination, something dredged up from those Gothic novels I'd thought of when the office door opened of its own accord yesterday.

'Thank you for humouring me,' I murmured. 'I got skittish in the night and had scary dreams while Mama was so ill, and again when Papa lost his mind. He'd get up to roam around at all hours, and sometimes I'd awaken to find him gone in the morning. Just like . . . just like when he finally threw himself into that chasm.'

Hyde's arm slipped around my shoulders. 'You've been through some terrible times, Mary Grace. Enough to give anyone nightmares. I think it's best you're going to Heaven's Gate for a fresh start, among new friends who will encourage your work. I'll come to see you every week, of course.'

This thought, and the mischievous tilt of his grin, brought me out of my troubled mood. On impulse I kissed him, and Hyde continued the embrace with a vengeance. His mouth closed and opened over mine, becoming hungrier as our tongues explored. I was vaguely aware that he dropped the reins, and that the carriage began to tilt slightly as we started up the mountainside. As he held me close for another long, tempestuous kiss, I felt his hand slipping under my shift, slithering along my calves until his fingers found the bare skin above my stockings.

'Hyde! What if the horse –'

'Beau knows the way blindfolded,' he assured me as his hand stole under the hem of my new bloomers. 'This is our only chance to be alone for God knows how long, and I intend to make the most of it. I had to do some tall talking to keep Hatch at home. He thinks you'd be a tasty morsel, Mary Grace.'

'But I – sweet Jesus!'

I slid my hips forward, eager for the feel of him. His fingers found their mark and had me quivering against the back of the bench, shameless with desire. Hyde then crouched between the seat and the front wall of the wagon, lifting my leg over his shoulder as he tossed my skirts out of his way. He grasped my arse, planting feverish kisses along my stockings and into my soft, inner thighs until my lacy bloomers were all that came between his mouth and my sex. Undaunted, he licked and sucked and pressed his lips into me until the silken seam cut into my aching clit.

I was panting, my cries punctuating his urgent grunts. With his thumbs, he lifted the cushion of my mound and ground his mouth against me until I could feel his teeth riding up and down the seam in a quickening rhythm. I screamed, parting my thighs to thrust against him as the spasms overtook me. Wetness shot out of me, and Hyde pulled at the straining silk until it split open along the stitching, to lap at me with greedy satisfaction.

'Mary Grace ... Mary Grace,' he whispered when I fell back. 'Sol's so desperate to be inside you, I can't stand up without splitting my pants.'

I giggled, still half out of my head. 'And who am I to deny a king his every wish?'

'I thought you'd see it that way. Climb over the back of the seat.'

Slowly the world around me came into focus again: the rising, narrow road before us, the steady sway of Beau's sleek haunches, the creaking wheels that made an occasional pebble ping sideways at the mountain on our right. Hyde cupped his privates, which were creating quite a bulge in his trousers, and then stepped cautiously on to the upholstered bench. Once he was over the back of it, he extended his hands in an invitation to follow him.

But when I sat up, I could only stare. All I saw to the left of us was sky. Growing darker by the moment, those storm clouds rolled towards us like sacks of quarrelling cats. The edge of the road disappeared over a drop-off, and except for the rugged rise of terrain on our other side we appeared to be ascending on air.

My heart dropped into my stomach. I was certain the carriage would plunge over the cliff. 'Hyde, I – I can't breathe!'

'You'll be fine if you concentrate on something else, love,' he insisted gently. 'And I have just the diversion in mind, back here where you won't be so aware of the winding curves and rising elevation.'

I didn't believe him for a minute. I was certain Beau's next step would send us careening into a rocky grave. I stiffened, the bile rising in my throat.

'Close your eyes, sweetheart,' his baritone tickled my ear. 'I've made this drive countless times, and I've always returned, haven't I?'

I did as he instructed, squeezing my eyes shut.

'Now turn, slowly. I'm right here for you, Mary Grace. I'll never leave you.'

Such tender words from a man who could so effortlessly control me. I reached around for him. As soon as my foot found the padded seat, Hyde's hands spanned my waist and I felt myself floating over the back of the bench, into his embrace. He held me close for a moment, reassuring me with soft kisses along my hairline.

Such a kind, gentle man he was. How could I not trust him to get me safely to my destination? And how could I deny him the pleasure he'd given me? Hyde Fortune had allowed me to choose my future, putting my need for independence ahead of his own desire for affection. The least I could do was set aside my fears and return the favor he'd granted me. It was the best way I could imagine to ignore the disorienting sights outside the windows.

As if sensing my thoughts, he pulled the curtains across the glass. The back of the carriage dimmed cosily, and he turned me so I faced the rear wall, where he and Hatch had stacked my quilting materials as well as mammoth sacks of flour and pecans and coffee. Scents of cinnamon, cloves, and cocoa mingled with the perfume of my sex, coaxing me to breathe deeply.

I relaxed. With Hyde standing behind me, caressing my breasts while he kissed the sensitive skin beneath my ears, I forgot all about being afraid. I began to move in his rhythm, rubbing my backside against his blatant erection. He coaxed me forward, and I nestled against

41

the stack of sacks, which cushioned me like a soft pillow. Flour wheezed out and made me laugh as it landed on my nose.

'If you bend at the waist and lean into those bags, you'll discover a whole new range of sensations from this direction.'

I stiffened. 'You're not going up my arse, are you?'

'No, no,' he assured me, his breath sending streaks of lightning down my spine. 'Simply entering that same little gate from another way. You'll love it. I know you will.'

His words were becoming thick with desire, his movements more desperate. I leaned forward as he'd suggested. Seconds later, I felt a draught when my gown swished up over my back and my drawers fell to the floor. Hyde fumbled with his fly buttons while he placed his other hand between my legs.

'Spread for me. Lord, I'm so thick and heavy, I might –'

My gasp drowned him out, because he'd parted my folds and shoved two fingers inside me. I was dripping already, so the friction of our skin made a secretive, sucking sound – yet another sensation to add to the repertoire I'd begun yesterday. With a moan, Hyde slid his cock between my folds, rubbing the outside of me with quick, frantic strokes.

'Bend lower,' he rasped.

As I did, he entered me. Hugging the soft, pillowy sacks, I braced myself to withstand his thrusts. I felt myself rising quickly towards climax again. His guttural cries told of a need only I could satisfy, while the thumb he pressed against my aching nub reminded me that he still put my pleasure first. His cock pumped relentlessly; his privates made a slapping sound each time he buried that column deep within me. A now-familiar tightness devoured me and I cried out with my own release. It sent Hyde into a series of spasms that filled me with his hot, gushing seed.

When he collapsed against me, our weight caused an avalanche of supply sacks. I landed beneath him with a squeal, giggling helplessly as more of the flour and coffee fell around us. The carriage air grew hazy with white powder, which settled on our clothes and faces, but we were too busy kissing to care. Hyde rolled on top of me, his low chuckles vibrating against my chest.

'I might have to visit the monastery more than once a week,' he teased. His eyes glowed as he brushed flour off my cheeks. 'Leaving you there among the monks might not be such a good idea. I know damn well they'll want you as badly as I do, sweetheart.'

'Ah, but they have their vows of celibacy,' I reminded him. 'And what you said yesterday is true. You've cast your spell, Hyde. I couldn't possibly want another man.'

His smile sent little streaks of joy through me. After we caught our breath, he helped me up from the carriage floor and we straightened our clothing, sharing playful kisses. It felt so wonderful to engage in these things without being spied upon, and without the morbidity of Mount Calvary pressing upon me.

When we returned to the seat, however, reality set in. Beau's back was now laced with snow and the sky churned with whiteness. The horse instinctively kept close to the mountain, shaking his massive head to clear his vision. Hyde took the reins again. Although his face remained calm as he surveyed the landscape – or lack of it – I sensed he'd require his total concentration to guide us safely through this impending blizzard.

I sat silently beside him. My panic flared again, yet I knew better than to distract him with nervous chatter. I tried not to think about what disasters might lie ahead; tried not to see phantasms and eerie, shifting faces as the snow hissed and swirled against the windows. Pulling my cloak closer around my shoulders, I shut my eyes. Hyde had assured me the weather at Heaven's Gate remained balmy enough for the vineyards to thrive, so I told myself that once we passed through this atmos-

43

pheric layer, we'd ascend into sunshine again. After all, he had no reason to lie to me. Did he?

How many desperate young women had he escorted up this mountain? How many had been so flattered by his attention – easy prey for such a handsome man of means – that they gave themselves to him as eagerly as I had? For all I knew, I'd arrive at the abbey to find Hyde's previous conquests awaiting his return. Each believing herself Mr Fortune's favourite, these women would snub me and do their best to intimidate me.

I must have shuddered, because his arm slipped around me. 'You can open your eyes now, Mary Grace,' he said softly. 'We've passed through the worst of it, and we'll arrive within the hour.'

How much time had gone by since our lovemaking? I'd lost all track, so it was a great relief to hazard a glance through one eye and see only dull grey rain hitting the window. I relaxed against him. He pressed his lips to my temple, and I decided I was foolish to fret over his other women. My stay at Heaven's Gate would allow me time to consider my feelings for Hyde, and a chance at an income, as well. I would simply have to have faith in the future, and in my ability to make the most of it.

Poor Beau struggled along a stretch of the road where rocks and mud had washed down the mountain. The carriage lurched precariously, but we made it around the obstacles without sliding over the canyon's edge. Had I not been so preoccupied with whether solid ground remained under our wheels, the view would've been breathtaking. Higher we climbed, until we left the stately stands of lodgepole pine and spruce behind us. The sky remained heavy and dark, and the rain pelted us like a barrage of gunfire.

But then we rounded another bend, and there it was. Even from a distance, Heaven's Gate exuded the quaint charm drawn into the labels on its products. On a brighter day, I could imagine it resembled a fine cathedral, up here close to God, so I held that image in my mind while we plodded along. Beau's breath encircled his head and his muscles bunched with the exertion of hauling such a heavy load. The man beside me had relaxed, so I fantasised about the fine quilts I would soon design. No sense in dwelling on the ominous shadows behind those towers, or in the sense of foreboding that loomed around the abbey when the clouds covered the sun.

I must have dozed again. It was a dreamlike kiss that awakened me, to discover that the inner tinglings I felt came from the warm hand covering my breast. I allowed myself to remain in that state between wakefulness and sleep while Hyde unbuttoned my bodice to caress my bare skin. My nipple stood at rigid attention already, and his damp tongue drew circles that made me whisper his name.

'So responsive,' he murmured, 'so perfect. I'm going to miss you, sweet lady.'

I moaned, shifting lower on the seat. He must have stopped the carriage somewhere while I was asleep, because we weren't moving. Instead of the storm, I heard the rustling of wings, as though birds were settling in for the night.

'Open your eyes, Mary Grace. I want you to be looking at me when you come.'

My eyes did indeed fly open, because a decisive thrust of Hyde's fingers wakened my entire body. Somehow he'd found a sweet new spot inside me, a pleasure-pain so intense I clutched his shoulders. His face was a study in seduction, its manly contours shaded by a slight stubble and its square jaw clenched. Those russet eyes glowed from behind a thick wedge of his hair, which was mussed from being under my skirts. When his nostrils flared, I realised he was as caught up in my passion as I, and a final, deep lunge of his hand made me scream and squirt a torrent of juice.

I grimaced, mortified. 'My Lord, I've relieved myself all over you.'

'No, it's not what you're thinking,' he assured me with an awed smile. 'Some women can climax from deep within, when touched in the right place, and it seems you and I have accomplished that! Just another reason I want to keep loving you – to discover how much pleasure you're capable of enjoying.'

I was too muddled to understand what he meant, but I had faith Hyde Fortune would bring me to further glories over time. And he wanted to keep loving me!

He stroked my hair, his expression pensive. 'May I ask a favour, while we're still alone?'

'Anything,' I whispered.

His smile made my insides shimmer, for it was obvious he cared for me. 'Would you . . . do you recall what Yu Ling did for Sebastian, as we watched through the peep-hole?'

He sounded almost shy, as though afraid he were asking too much. I saw the Celestial quite vividly in my mind, taking the sextant's thick, red erection into her mouth. It gave me pause, knowing how long and strong Hyde's member felt when he thrust it inside me. Yet how could I refuse him? He'd mentioned this desire before. And he'd always seen to my pleasure first, as he promised.

I ran my thumbnail up the bulge in his trousers with more confidence than I felt. If that little serving girl could please him with either set of lips, I would have to aspire to even bolder heights to prove I was a better lover than she. So I reached for Hyde's front buttons, and was rewarded by an eager smile.

Solomon jutted out proudly as we freed him from the constraints of clothing. I grasped the solid, pink base and squeezed, letting Hyde guide my hand's rhythm and pressure. Once more I imagined the scene we'd spied upon, and extended my tongue towards the jewel of juice at his tip. With a moan, Hyde braced his foot against the edge of the seat. My licking made him pant in desperation while his hips quivered.

'Take me – God, take me in your mouth, sweetheart. Now.'

Making my lips into an O, I slid them down his shaft. He smelled of sex and sweat, and the secretive taste of him was nothing like I'd expected. Up and down I slid, letting my tongue slither wetly around him while I fondled his sac. His excited little gasps cheered me on; he speared his fingers through my hair to increase the speed of my strokes. I could feel him tightening, straining towards release. Solomon filled my mouth and prodded the back of my throat, until Hyde paused with the tip of him just inside my lips. He made a strangled sound, and then filled my mouth with warm spurts of cream that tasted like salty-sweet butter.

For a moment, I was at a loss. Now that he was spent, what did I do with this liquid? Hyde was catching his breath, his member deflating but still between my lips while I feared my mouth might overflow. Again calling upon recollection, I realised Yu Ling hadn't spat afterwards. So I swallowed in two big gulps. Hyde cradled my head against his flat lower belly, his pleasure evident in his sigh.

'What a woman,' he crooned. 'You've given me another fond memory to fill the hours until we can play this way again. Lord, but you're a natural at this, Mary –'

The sudden opening of the carriage door made us both jump. Cold air blew in around us, but it was a chilly female voice that sent gooseflesh all over me.

'Brother Christy is waiting,' the intruder insisted. 'We thought you'd been detained by the storm, until Ahmad came to report your carriage parked at the edge of the vineyard.'

I wanted to die. Through the slit of one eyelid I saw a woman who suited that disdainful voice perfectly: with her steely hair pulled back in a tight knot, wearing the severe black uniform of a maid, she was the picture of a shrewish spinster who delighted in making others feel unworthy. Behind her, several people clad in simple brown tunics peered curiously into the carriage. At the sound of a snicker from among them, Hyde snatched the door from her.

'We'll see Brother Christy momentarily. Meanwhile, I know my way to the abbey without a group escort. Thank you.'

He slammed the door. 'Should've known Mrs Goodin would sniff us out!' he said in a disgusted whisper. 'Once we entered the grounds, I pulled over, hoping the rain would stop before we unloaded the kitchen supplies. But I couldn't help wanting you one last time.'

I was frantically adjusting my dress, wishing for a mirror so I could straighten my hair. 'Nothing like making a grand entrance,' I hissed. 'Now all those people will think I'm some sort of hussy, come to –'

He stopped fumbling with his buttons to take my face between his hands. 'You're more a lady than any of them can ever hope to be – because I say so, and because you're mine,' he insisted. 'So stand tall and walk proud, Mary Grace Michaels. And stop blushing. It's far too becoming.'

As though his words weren't confirmation enough, Hyde suddenly plucked the remaining pins from my hair. 'We'll show them just what sort of woman you are, sweetheart. We'll make them wish they had half your inner strength and beauty. After all, you're going to lay them several golden eggs, so to speak.'

Ah, but the goose in that story lost her head, I mused.

As Hyde took up the reins and urged Beau back on to the vineyard path, however, I kept my concerns to myself. Perhaps he was right: perhaps my quilts would redeem my unseemly entrance into this mountaintop world. I knew better than to assume Mrs Goodin would ever have a better impression of me, but I trusted Hyde's judgment. I would only be a whore if I let them treat me like one.

Chapter Five
Stripped and Cleansed

A s the carriage approached the abbey, with its Gothic spires and leering gargoyles, I sensed we were being watched even though none of those previous onlookers loitered outside its massive double doors. Heaven's Gate loomed like an ancient sentinel, and in my imagination's eye the stone pattern above those tall, lozenge-shaped windows formed eyebrows raised in disdain. Those who came here were being warned to repent and prepare for the Kingdom.

I tried to brush the flour from my skirt. 'Hyde, I'm a sight! What will these monks think when they see us? They'll know damn well what we've been doing.'

He pulled Beau to a halt. 'They'll regret ever taking a vow of celibacy. And they'll envy me as the luckiest man alive. No doubt they'll have a lot of praying to do, to get beyond their lust and covetous thoughts.'

His gaze remained steadfast – not a hint of a grin – until I scolded him.

'Why, that's the most – you're incorrigible!' I swatted the hand he was easing up my thigh. 'I've come here to work, Mr Fortune. I care about making a bad impression already.'

His face relaxed into the boyish grin I'd come to love.

'They must accept you as you are, Mary Grace. Some of the vagrants who've come here from the Home for the Friendless are guilty of far more grievous sins than ours, yet I've never taken anyone back down the mountain. Lost souls seem to find a purpose here that makes them stay.'

When I looked beyond the forbidding facade of the monastery, his words rang true. Although it was January, the grass grew lush and clusters of white cottages gave the place a more homely air. Beyond these living quarters grew groves of trees laden with fruit, and a huge garden laid out like a patchwork quilt. Then row upon row of well-tended vines stretched towards the horizon, heavy with grapes that glistened in the late-afternoon sun. This little world atop the Rockies could've been a still life rendered by an idealistic artist, perfect in every detail of form and colour.

Hyde was right. Work well done was its own reward, and I was silly to let my state of disarray override my reason for coming here. This was my chance to start fresh as an artisan whose talent would justify her presence until she was on her feet again, emotionally and financially. Not many females got such an opportunity. I decided to stop whining and present myself as a resident worthy of respect, whose dignity would not be compromised by unseemly appearances.

I'd no sooner stepped out of the carriage into Hyde's arms than those heavy fortress doors opened. That shrew in the dark uniform stalked towards us, followed by a shorter, plumper monk with the most cherubic face I'd ever seen. I liked him immediately, but we first had to endure another scolding from the woman who'd thrown open the carriage door.

'High time you arrived,' she said in an accusing voice. 'Brother Christy and Father Luc have been forced to delay their afternoon prayers, thinking you'd be here sooner.'

Hyde bowed slightly, still holding my hand. 'Mrs

Goodin, I'd like you to meet Miss Mary Grace Michaels. As her father, the Reverend Jeremiah Michaels, has recently passed on, she's come to share her quilting abilities – and the profits from them – here at Heaven's Gate. I'm sure you'll make her welcome.'

The woman's expression soured and her fist found her hip. 'Your explanations for these foundlings grow more incredible with each one you leave us, Mr Fortune.'

'And where would we be without the people he brings, and his promotion of our products?' the monk behind her demanded. He stepped forward with his hand extended to Hyde, but his bright smile was all for me. 'We're delighted to have you, Miss Michaels. We hope your stay here will ease the grief of your father's passing and bring you the peace you seek.'

'Thank you,' I murmured. It was the first time anyone had expressed concern about my situation without blaming me for my father's suicide and the wrongdoing that drove him to it.

'Mary Grace, this is the Brother Christy you've heard me speak of,' Hyde said with a smile. 'I have no qualms whatsoever about entrusting you to his care between my visits.'

After being caught by those curiosity-seekers, I felt immediate relief when the chubby monk took my hands in his as Hyde looked on. Brother Christy's round face beamed like an angel's in a religious painting, although I saw no halo floating above the sun-streaked blond hair, which fitted his head like a bowl. Blue eyes twinkled behind rimless spectacles. Although he exuded a fatherly air as he gazed up into my face, I sensed he was young in outlook if not in years. He seemed ageless in an almost mystical way, and I couldn't help smiling at him. Just being near this diminutive man made me feel happier than I had in months.

He turned to Mrs Goodin. 'Our friends are tired and hungry after a longer trip than usual,' he remarked. 'Would you please have a meal and a basin of warm water brought into the guest quarters? I'm sure Hyde and Miss Michaels would like to freshen up before they meet with Father Luc.'

The woman turned on her heel, giving the impression she wasn't accustomed to taking orders. When she'd passed beyond earshot, the monk flashed me an apologetic smile. 'Mrs Goodin serves as the abbey's housekeeper, as well as tending the laundry for everyone here at Heaven's Gate,' he explained quietly. 'We all wonder if her exposure to lye soap and starch hasn't affected her disposition.'

I stifled a chuckle. 'Poor Mister Goodin. How does he stand it?'

Brother Christy's laugh resounded against the stone facade of the abbey, but he then sobered. 'None of us knows what happened to the man and we don't dare ask, for fear we meet the same fate. You'd be well advised to stay on her better side, Mary Grace. Mrs Goodin's temper is legendary, and she has an excellent memory of all our shortcomings.'

I nodded, realising that already.

'Well! Shall we fetch our lady's luggage and quilting materials from the back?' Hyde said as he walked to the rear of the carriage. 'The rest of the load is flour and cocoa and such, which Sybil ordered for the kitchen.'

'Fine. We'll have one of her helpers unload it while you two refresh yourselves. I'll tell Father Luc we'll meet him in an hour.' The beneficent monk then bowed slightly, smiling at me. 'Make yourself at home, Mary Grace. Everyone here will be so pleased to have you.'

Those last words, and the way Brother Christy's gaze lingered within mine, sent a warning tremor along my spine. I dismissed it, however, as a sign that I was tired from our treacherous journey up the mountainside. After all, Hyde trusted the little man completely, and he'd been gracious enough to provide food and warm water instead of making an issue of my disarray. He took the large box of sewing supplies Hyde handed him, and I then followed him through the abbey doors, hugging two of my illustrated quilts.

Our footsteps echoed in the vaulted entrance. The high stone walls glimmered in fragile pastels where light came through the stained-glass windows, and a hint of ancient incense inspired the hushed reverence of a grand cathedral. Although I knew better than to intrude upon monastic rituals, or to overstep my place as a guest, I couldn't wait to wander around this abbey and drink in its magnificence. I was wondering why being the caretaker of such hallowed halls hadn't softened Mrs Goodin's hard edges, when she shot like a bullet from a narrow hallway, aimed straight at me.

'Drop those at once! Father Luc insists upon meeting with you immediately!'

My arms tightened around my unwieldy bundles. 'But Brother Christy said –'

'The first thing you'll learn here, young lady, is that no one's instructions come before the abbot's,' she barked. 'And your next lessons will be in humility and decency. I'll see to it myself.'

With that, she gripped my arm to steer me down the passageway. Since Brother Christy had gone on ahead, and Hyde hadn't yet returned from the kitchen, neither man could come to my defence. I trotted along like an errant schoolgirl being hauled to the front of the classroom, struggling to keep hold of the quilt in each arm. The starched laundress propelled me through a doorway and slammed the door behind us.

'Here she is, Your Excellence. The latest of Mr Fortune's indigents.'

The small chamber rang with silence while I closed my eyes against my quilts. Then a low, sinuous voice said, 'This is the one you found kneeling before him in the carriage? Licking his jism from her lips?'

'Yes, Your Excellence.'

'Thank you, Mrs Goodin. You may go now, confident

53

that your watchfulness and concern for this young woman's soul will be rewarded.'

I felt the weight of her mocking smile as she walked away. My knees were knocking and my cheeks burned with rage. I'd hoped to impress Father Luc and Brother Christy with my quilting skills, and instead I'd been dumped like a slut to await the abbot's judgment. It was too much to hope that Hyde would find me. No doubt the housekeeper was now detaining him in some insidious way.

'You may lower your bundles and present yourself, Miss Michaels.'

Slowly, I let the ribbon-tied quilts slide to the floor. Summoning my earlier confidence, I reminded myself that no one could make me feel dirty or worthless unless I allowed it, but I was unprepared for this audience. My hair tumbled around my shoulders and my dress was smudged with flour, rumpled from lovemaking. The heat of this moment was reviving the scent of our sex, and in a room this small the abbot was sure to smell it.

'Has anyone ever told you your hair glows like hellfire?'

I looked up into the most arresting face I'd ever seen. Father Luc, his thronelike chair raised on a small dais, frowned like a disapproving patriarch of the Bible. His hair swept back like raven's wings from a deep widow's peak; a close-clipped beard accentuated his lean features and matched the brows now raised in a haughty sneer. It was a Valentine-shaped face, yet the narrow black moustache framing those sinister lips suggested a heart of darkness, completely the opposite of Brother Christy's. His eyes locked into mine. He cleared his throat, waiting.

'I – I beg your pardon, sir?'

His expression remained inscrutable, suggesting I should take some sort of cue from it. 'If you can't hear me, you must step closer,' he finally muttered.

It was the sort of manipulation my father had used. I bit my lip against a retort, deciding to shorten this ordeal by going along with him. 'No, sir. You're the first to tell me I resemble anything from hell.'

For a moment he seemed amused, but then he stiffened. 'There's no pride in that, you know. From here on, you'll wear your hair discreetly fastened back, rather than flaunting it like some hussy. And that dress – why is it crumpled?'

He knew, of course, how Mrs Goodin had found us, so there was little point in lying. 'I was leaning against stacked flour sacks, in the back of Mr Fortune's carriage.'

'And Hyde was humping you from behind, like a crazed dog?'

'I wouldn't describe it like –'

'Remove the dress. It defiles you.'

My jaw dropped. This was an abbot, a man of God, commanding me to disrobe. I was about to protest, but the narrowing of those feral eyes warned me not to. Reaching awkwardly behind me, I fumbled with the buttons down my back, aware of how this thrust my breasts forward for Father Luc's scrutiny. He allowed me to struggle this way for several minutes, until I'd undone all but the buttons between my shoulder blades.

'Just rip it off. You won't be wearing it again, anyway.'

Wondering desperately where Hyde and Brother Christy were, I wrenched open the dress. The colour rose up my neck and into my face as I stepped out of the green-and-ivory striped gown. This left me standing before my arrogant host wearing only my lace corset and bloomers, with cotton stockings and pumps.

'And why are your drawers sticking to your thighs? Did you wet yourself, girl?'

'Of course not!'

'Then whose sex do you reek of? Hyde's?'

'No! I –'

'Ah, yes, I remember now. Mrs Goodin and the others witnessed that little act first-hand, didn't they?' Father Luc leaned forward, his gaze burning over my body before honing in on my face. 'What exactly happened to Hyde's semen?'

At that moment it was roiling in my stomach, threatening to spew up my throat. A sheen of sweat sprang over my body and the room suddenly felt airless.

'Look at me when I'm speaking to you, Mary Grace.'

I raised my face, opening my clenched eyes. The abbot wore a mocking smile as he enjoyed every moment of my humiliation.

'Now what happened in that carriage? Where did Hyde climax?'

'In my mouth,' I murmured.

'And what did you do with his juice, Miss Michaels?'

My face burned a shade redder. 'Swallowed.'

Father Luc stroked his black moustache again and again, contemplating my punishment, no doubt. His piercing gaze roved over me and then fixed upon the fabric clinging to my thighs. 'Is that a hole in your seam?'

'Yes.'

'And how did that happen, Mary Grace? I refuse to believe your bloomers were so worn they split of their own accord.'

Damn him! I'd thought of trying that line, since I came to Heaven's Gate destitute, but this cruel man in the black cassock seemed to read my mind – and seemed extremely interested in the most intimate and degrading details. So I decided to humour him.

'No, sir, Hyde gave them to me new this morning – after I spent the night in his bed,' I added in a coiled voice. 'And on the trip up the mountain, he couldn't get enough of me. Threw up my skirts and began to lick and suck and gnaw at my cunt through the fabric. Ran his teeth along the seam until I was crying out his name, and then ripped open a hole so he could stick his tongue up me. I shot my juice all over him, and it hasn't had a chance to dry.'

Father Luc's eyes had caught fire and his olive complexion darkened. 'Show me the slit,' he breathed.

I did him one better, as I was tiring of this game. Curling my fingers on either side of the gaping seam, I tore my drawers so hard they split all the way up to the drawstring. No sense in them hanging there, tattered, so I let them drop to the floor. With the toe of my shoe, I swung the limp garment so it landed on the dais, in front of the abbot's chair. 'I suppose you'll be wanting to sniff that.'

His hand darted towards his lap but stopped in mid-air. Father Luc leaned forward then, glowering. 'Your depravity does not serve you well, Miss Michaels. Here at Heaven's Gate we allow no sexual activity – neither fornication nor speaking of it, nor the solitary, secretive pleasures to be found at one's own fingertips. You will apologise to me for your brazen behaviour, or you'll be leaving with Mr Fortune.'

The thought of going back sounded good, until I realised I'd have to explain my change of plans to Hyde – and I sensed Father Luc would be sure he heard every damning detail of how I'd ripped off my bloomers, by making me tell him about it myself. Surely the monastery's code of celibacy would protect me from further incidents of this nature. So if I caved in to this initial humiliation, I'd be giving up my chance for independence – the chance to decide if I truly loved my handsome benefactor.

Yet the abbot's expression spurred me on. 'Apologise for what, sir? I gave you precisely what you asked for.'

He stood up, towering above me with a scowl that spelled out my doom. 'You will fetch the basin and soap in this side room, and you'll return here to cleanse yourself,' he muttered. 'Then you'll don the tunic of Heaven's Gate residents, and we will discuss the tasks you're to perform to earn your keep. I will then absolve you of your wickedness, so you may start a clean and honourable life among us. Do you understand me, Miss Michaels?'

How was I to answer a man who was openly staring at my crotch? 'No, I don't understand how you can condemn my wickedness while indulging your own, at my expense! I'll wash myself and dress behind that door, thank you!'

It was the wrong thing to say. Father Luc stepped down and clamped a hand on my bare shoulder. 'Mrs Goodin,' he called out, 'we'll be needing your assistance now.'

The door to his chamber opened, and with unabashed glee the uniformed housekeeper entered. Clearly these two had scripted this little drama before I'd come in from the orchard, and she'd been waiting – ear pressed to the wall – for her cue to come onstage. When she returned from the little room with a basin of steaming water, a bar of soap, and a towel, I knew I'd fallen into their trap.

Was Hyde aware of their connivings? I surmised this pair had cleansed new residents before, and that my benefactor had supplied them with several. I didn't want to believe he'd played a part in humiliating me ... but there was no way to find out until I saw him again. If I ever did. Perhaps his whole story was a lie. Perhaps he wouldn't come back up the mountain until he had another unsuspecting victim in tow.

But I couldn't worry about that now. The housekeeper crouched before me and set the basin on the floor. 'Straddle this,' she commanded.

As though he thought I'd bolt, Father Luc kept his hold on me until I placed my feet on either side of the large basin. 'Turn around and face me,' he ordered, and when I hesitated he twisted my shoulders around until my legs were forced to follow along. I nearly tripped, and one foot landed in the water, ruining my shoe.

'You should do as you're told, Miss Michaels,' the housekeeper suggested. 'Now spread your legs. Further.'

I had never felt more awkward, standing in my corset, stockings and shoes with my ankles against the opposite rims of a basin. Mrs Goodin dipped the soap into the water and lathered it between her hands, her face alight with anticipation. Up the inside of one leg she rubbed, with strokes so vigorous I nearly tumbled forward. I grabbed her shoulder to keep my balance, and she retaliated by sliding the soap up into my pussy.

The sting of the lye against my intimate parts made tears spring to my eyes. I clenched my jaw, determined not to cry in front of this nefarious pair. Mrs Goodin seemed so intent on getting my privates clean, I wondered if she would use the entire cake of soap: white, frothy lather clung to my bush and then slithered down my thighs, or dripped into the water below me.

'Stand behind her, Mrs Goodin. I can't see if you're cleansing her thoroughly.'

With a smirk, the housekeeper dropped the soap so she could unfasten my corset. 'You're not helpless,' she hissed near my ear. 'You're to keep washing yourself until Father Luc declares you clean.'

With lightning speed, she removed my remaining undergarment and then grabbed my hands. 'Slow learner, are we?' she sneered, guiding my fingers to my soapy slit. 'Now rub yourself, Mary Grace. I'm going to wash the rest of you.'

For a fleeting moment I thought of Yu Ling, the Celestial who'd wanted to wash me as an act of gratification. Had I not been so squeamish, perhaps I wouldn't have fled to what I believed was a safer haven, only to learn that the world held far more perverse people than a serving girl who truly enjoyed her work.

Mrs Goodin skimmed the foam from my bush and worked it up my belly in rough spirals, until she was circling my breasts. She palmed my nipples until they beaded out, her breathing becoming shallower with her efforts. Then her rough hands cupped me from the sides, pushing out my bosom as though she were offering it to Father Luc as a gift.

His eyes were riveted to my fingers, and his hands had slipped into his cassock pockets. The glazing of his face gave the only indication of what was going on beneath his black robe, and gave me something to smile about: Father Luc couldn't take his own medicine. He'd forbidden me to engage in sexual behaviour, yet he appeared ready to explode with his own.

'Kneel with me. I feel a prayer coming on,' I said. And before the housekeeper could second-guess me, I went down on my knees, catching myself when I fell forward. I sloshed warm water where the soap was burning the lips of my sex, and then let my weight carry me backwards, so my arse landed in the basin with a splash. Mrs Goodin jumped away, her shoes saturated.

'You conniving little bitch!' she shrieked, and when I caught her ankle before she could kick me, the housekeeper let out a wail that would've done a witch proud. 'You've cooked your goose now, Miss Michaels! I will not be made a fool of in the presence –'

'Hush, they're coming!' Father Luc warned in a low voice.

I heard those footsteps in the hallway, too, so I sprang up and grabbed the towel. My heart pounded with gratitude as I sprinted into the little room at the side of the dais: Mrs Goodin's hysteria would divert whoever was coming in, allowing me to escape any further embarrassment she'd planned for the abbot's entertainment. A tunic the colour of walnut meats hung on the back of the door. After I dried myself I dropped it over my head, meanwhile listening to the conversation in the main room.

'Mrs Goodin, are you all right? We'd have been here sooner, but Sybil asked for our help unloading her kitchen supplies.'

I knew damn well the chore Brother Christy spoke of had been arranged by that howling bitch who baptised me with lye, but he – and Hyde, I assumed – had at least arrived in time to rescue me from a deteriorating situation. While the abbot insinuated my audience with him had sent Mrs Goodin into an outrage, I tied the belt at my waist. Since I had no hairpins, I removed my shoes and cotton stockings, and tied my hair back with the stocking that was driest. Better to appear barefoot and penitent than to arouse any more uproar.

When I opened the door, I saw Father Luc had somehow whisked my clothing out of sight. His dark glance warned me not to contradict his story, and apparently Mrs Goodin had gone just as Hyde and Brother Christy arrived. To the casual observer, the basin positioned before the abbot's chair signified a baptism, perhaps, or some other ritual observance. Hyde's weighty gaze said he suspected discrepancies between what he was hearing and what he saw, but he knew better than to ask questions.

I smiled demurely. Fortune appeared unaware of Father Luc's cleansing method or Mrs Goodin's part in it, so it was to my advantage not to let on. It was enough to know Hyde hadn't been involved with it and that later, when we were out of earshot, we might discuss it.

'Mary Grace has complied with my instructions concerning her entrance into our monastic life, and I believe she's ready to discuss those bundles she brought with her,' Father Luc was saying. His benign smile sickened me, for I knew he was secretly smirking. But I played along, because what chance did I stand, if he revealed how I'd already mocked him and got on Mrs Goodin's bad side? It was his word against mine.

Hyde was unrolling the coverlet closest to him. 'When Mary Grace expressed a need for employment, and I realised she created these magnificent illustrated quilts, I saw this as the new opportunity Brother Christy has been hoping for – a way for the abbey to raise a lot of money at no expense. Miss Michaels proposes to stay here through the spring, sewing her quilts for you, asking for only a percentage of the profits after I take them to auction.'

He was showing the abbot and Brother Christy a quilt depicting a brilliant Colorado sky and a mountainside ablaze with bright yellow aspen trees at their autumn peak. The leaves, cut and stitched individually, shimmered like their live counterparts when he shifted the quilt to show it to full advantage.

'Oh my,' Brother Christy breathed, running a reverent finger over the shining satins and taffetas. 'I've never seen anything like this! It reminds me of stained glass, the way the colours and textures are arranged to capture the light. You do beautiful work, Mary Grace.'

My smile was genuine, but I was watching the abbot's reaction. He sat forward in his chair, studying the detail while trying not to act excited. The attention he paid to his own appearance suggested a man attuned to line and balance and proportion, but while Brother Christy expressed his admiration for my artwork, the abbot saw cash.

I didn't need another cue. 'I can complete a quilt like this in about three weeks,' I said as I unfolded my second example. 'I'll be needing more scraps of exquisite fabric –'

'We can supply that,' Father Luc murmured.

'– but otherwise, all I ask is a place to work and, as Hyde suggested, a part of the profits.'

'What can we expect them to sell for?'

Hyde grinned at me as I held up the jungle scene with the bright, sequinned parrots. 'I bought this one six years ago for four hundred dollars, so they're surely worth more now.'

'And what percentage are you requesting, Miss Michaels?'

The glint in Father Luc's eyes made me bold. 'Half,' I replied, 'because no one else's work compares to it. If you allow me to create my quilts, without responsibility for other tasks – and without interference,' I added pointedly, 'I'll produce six by the end of May. That means you can expect twelve hundred dollars, at the very least.'

The abbot blinked, surprised that I could so quickly calculate the sum. 'I'd be a fool to refuse you,' he said in a low voice, 'but what assurance do I have that you'll carry through on your projections? You're obviously attracted to Mr Fortune. A lot can happen in the next four months.'

Hyde spoke on my behalf. 'I've assured Mary Grace I'd cover any part of this bargain she fell short on, because as you've noted,' he said, returning the abbot's unwavering gaze, 'she's a beautiful young woman, and I have my own hopes for her future.'

Father Luc raised a dark eyebrow. 'Then why don't you keep her in town? Why let her spend four months with us?'

With a smile that put his dimples out to play, Hyde took my hand. 'She's asked for time to recover from her father's suicide, and to adjust to becoming an undertaker's wife. It's best to give a woman what she wants, don't you agree?'

My heart leaped at his words, but I knew better than to show excitement the abbot could later use against me. In the moments before his response, I saw an almost diabolical purpose at work behind his eyes.

'Miss Michaels shall have a workroom down this hall, with access to the fabrics she needs, and she'll receive her food and lodging for four months,' he decreed as he stood up. 'Sybil will accommodate her as a room-mate. While I would enjoy continuing this conversation, I must prepare for the evening's vespers.'

With that he excused himself, as though no further explanation were needed. Hyde and Brother Christy let him pass in silence, but once Father Luc's measured tread couldn't be heard in the hallway, they exchanged puzzled looks.

'Sybil won't want to share her cottage,' Hyde said

quietly. He began to roll the blue and gold quilt into a tight bundle. 'She's the chief cook, as well as the creator of Heaven's Gate's most delectable confections, so she's always been privileged with a place of her own.'

Brother Christy's expression confirmed his doubts, as well. 'And she's not terribly inclined towards bowing to someone else's orders – even if the abbot himself made this decision. If we break the news to her now, she's liable to ruin the evening meal for us all, out of spite.'

Although this Sybil sounded as disagreeable as Mrs Goodin, I admired her attitude: I wasn't keen on accepting the abbot's commands, either. But instinct told me if anyone could influence Father Luc, the monastery's chef certainly had the best leverage.

'Shall we go to the kitchens and find out?' I suggested. 'And perhaps we can ask her for something to eat – before we announce me as her new room-mate. It's been a long day, and I'm famished.'

Chapter Six
Sybil

'*F*ather Luc thinks I need a room-mate, does he? Well, Father Luc can eat shit for dinner!' The vixen standing alongside the bubbling pots of stew ripped off her apron and headed for the back door. 'And he'd better watch out. I'm just pissy enough to poke him a new arsehole!'

The handful of helpers who were slicing bread smiled among themselves, and then looked to Brother Christy for his reaction. The monk let out his breath, relieved nothing more catastrophic had happened.

'Well, you've met our Sybil,' he remarked, running a spoon through the nearest kettle. 'Don't take it personally, Mary Grace, but I wouldn't be surprised to find your belongings thrown out the window when you return to the cottage.'

'I'd probably react the same way to having a new-comer foisted upon me.'

I hadn't said so, but when we took my valise to the bungalow nearest the Heaven's Gate kitchens, I had immediate doubts about the arrangement. While the large room was immaculate and cosily furnished, there was only one narrow bed. I considered bunking in my workroom instead, using the aspen quilt for a pallet, because sleeping so close to a stranger would be an adjustment: except for napping with Mama while she was so ill, and last night with Hyde, I'd slept alone all my life.

Yet something drew me to the woman who'd stormed out. With a little wave to suggest Hyde and Brother Christy stay behind, I meandered between the work tables and the hearth where black, bulbous pots hung over the fire. The evening meal smelled heavenly, redolent with beef and vegetables and brown gravy. What a shame if a surly cook spoiled it for everyone to spite Father Luc!

I stepped out into the cool evening air, cautiously looking for Sybil. Had she been a man, she would have impressed me as the type who might carry a knife in her boot. Standing in silhouette against the abbey wall, she appeared small but formidable: she was indeed wearing boots, with dark trousers and a man's black shirt tucked in at her slender, belted waist. And she was smoking a cigarette!

As I approached, she scrutinised me, her cigarette cocked in the corner of her mouth. Its tip glowed red and then she exhaled through her nostrils, like a dragon looking for a fight. 'What're you staring at?'

I stopped a few feet away. 'I'll answer that question when you do, Sybil. It's not like I asked to share your cottage, you know.'

Her laugh was short and cynical. 'All right. I'm staring at a naïve little girl who follows all the rules because she's too unimaginative to know better. She never shows her true feelings because she's too busy indulging the sensibilities of others, hoping men will adore her for it. Hyde loves that type. He fancies himself a protector of fallen women.'

'And did Mr Fortune bring you here?'

'Nope. I showed Father Luc my tits and told him my bourbon-pecan pound cake would make his cock throb. I've been the mainstay of this monastery ever since.'

66

Now I knew why Papa had loved that expensive confection, and why he'd been so unwilling to share it. And I felt somewhat relieved that Hyde wasn't counting this sultry little elf as one of his success stories: although she wore male attire, Sybil exuded the aura of a tigress in heat. She leaned against the back of the abbey with one leg bent so her boot sole rested several inches up the wall, which thrust out her bosom in provocative profile. No wonder Father Luc was impressed. No wonder she was accustomed to having things her way.

'So now – what are you staring at?' she challenged again.

I considered Sybil carefully, noting kohl-rimmed eyes and tinted lips I wouldn't associate with monastic life. Not to mention a mane of untamed henna waves flowing back from her fine-boned face, and gold hoops like gypsies wore. She was everything the abbot had instructed me not to be. He'd had a subversive motive in mind when he assigned me to share her cottage.

'I see a woman who plays devil's advocate to make herself feel superior, and to get herself noticed. A woman afraid to trust – or to love – anything she can't control. Perhaps because her heart's been stomped on once too often.'

Where that conjecture came from, I didn't know, but Sybil's eyes widened. Perhaps I was an unimaginative type, but I'd just risen a notch in her estimation, even if she would never admit it aloud.

'Is it true what Mrs Goodin told everyone? That you were sucking Fortune in the orchard, and you gulped him down?'

Would there be no end to this infamous tale? I sensed another effort at intimidation, so I feigned nonchalance. 'Why would she make up such a story? She impresses me as a seeker of the truth, so she can shape it into a whip and flog us repeatedly. In the interest of our immortal souls, of course.'

Sybil's laughter sounded like the tinkling of fairies'

bells – which didn't match her decadent demeanour. She took a last draw on her cigarette and flicked the butt away, never taking her eyes off me. This seemed an improvement in her attitude, until the gaze continued beyond the boundaries of proper conversation.

I shifted my weight, determined not to back down. 'Does this mean you like what you see? Or that you've changed your assessment of me?'

'I think not!' she jeered, pushing herself from the wall. The shadows were lengthening, and as Sybil stopped in front of me, some animosity remained in her dusky gaze. 'But I no longer feel like adding belladonna berries to the cobbler, just to wreak revenge on our fine, upstanding abbot. No sense in giving everyone a bellyache on your account.'

I let her enter her domain alone, taking a few moments to breathe the refreshing air. Heaven's Gate was not at all what I'd expected. Considering the way Mrs Goodin greeted us, and then humiliated me during my audience with the abbot, and the reception I was now receiving from my room-mate, going home with Hyde sounded like the rational decision. He kept corpses in the bowels of his house, but at least none of them would treat me with such scorn! From what I'd seen of the abbey so far, these residents had no concept of brotherly love or compassion. Each one I met seemed more arrogant and demeaning than the last, except for Brother Christy.

I was pleased to sit across from this cheerful friar at one of the long tables in the dining hall, where everyone assembled at the tolling of the large bell in the front tower. As we passed baskets of fresh bread and heaped our plates with steaming stew, the pudgy monk again complimented my colourful quilts. He suggested that Hyde buy more of the fine velvets, satins and brocades which made the scenes glimmer so richly, using some of the money he collected from merchants for the abbey's cakes and jams.

'Some day soon I'll show you the catacombs – which

we now use as storage,' he added when he saw my hesitant expression. 'No old bones there any more. But over the years we've accumulated clothing no longer in fashion, and you might as well put it to good use.'

I considered this as I chewed my stew. Heaven's Gate again presented me with an enigma, because Brother Christy spoke as though the catacombs dated back at least a century, an image confirmed by the abbey's ancient architectural details. Yet the territory that included Colorado was populated only by Indians and wild animals – and the white trappers making a profit from them – less than fifty years ago. And why were the grass and vineyards at their peak here, when at the base of the Rockies we fought the cold and snow of a typical winter?

'. . . It would seem our Mary has fallen asleep on us.'

I blinked, realising the round-faced monk was addressing me. 'No, simply drinking things in, Brother Christy. It's been an unusual day.'

He nodded wisely, reaching for another chunk of bread. 'Here at Heaven's Gate, one day feels pretty much like the next. We tend our vines and orchards, we garden, we produce jars of jelly or bake cakes. With Christmas behind us, we can relax a bit. It's a long stretch until the Vernal Equinox, when we take time out to celebrate the rites of spring.'

I nodded, smiling. I would be nearing the end of my stay by then, and perhaps would fit into the ebb and flow with Brother Christy and the others, rather than feeling like such a spectacle. Although the roomful of men wearing brown tunics, and the women scattered among them, seemed amiable enough, I still detected a glimmer of interest in my unorthodox arrival. Every few moments, I caught someone looking at me with a secretive smile.

'And how do you celebrate?' I asked, hoping our conversation would keep me alert. The long day was making itself felt in my tired back and muscles.

The monk's eyes lit up. 'Oh, it's quite a festival. A little different each year, yet always a madcap party by the time we sample our new wines and offer up a celebrant.'

Was he referring to a sacrificial offering, like ancient pagans made of virgins? Something about the way he gazed at me quelled any further questions – although being established as Hyde's latest lover would certainly disqualify me as pure and untouched.

I suddenly felt very tired. And though I wanted to spend the night with Hyde, who sat as close to me on the bench as we dared, the thought of getting to that bed first – of being asleep before Sybil finished her kitchen duties – appealed to me. No doubt Mrs Goodin would make sure the roguish Mr Fortune spent the night in the abbey's guest quarters, anyway. And, as much as I longed for the touch of the man I loved, I didn't feel like defying our all-knowing, all-seeing housekeeper right now.

'Time for bed,' I suggested, stifling a yawn.

Hyde's cinnamon eyes searched mine with a yearning I recognised. 'I'll walk you to your cottage and say my goodbyes,' he said softly. 'The carriage is already loaded for the trip home, and Mrs Goodin's a stickler for sending guests on their way at first light. Shall we go?'

The night sky formed a canopy of azure velvet studded with silver sequins. All was quiet, since everyone else still sat at table, so for these precious moments I could pretend the grounds beyond the monastery were my private estate and Hyde Fortune was the man I'd invited to share it with me. We walked past the cottage, meandering along a grassy path where a stream burbled in the moonlight.

'What are you wearing under your tunic, Mary Grace?'

'Nothing.'

The arm around me tightened. 'What happened to your underthings? Your dress?'

I hesitated, not wanting to spoil our last moments

70

together. 'Father Luc must have disposed of them while I changed. The bloomers were torn, after all, and that poor dress was smudged with flour and crumpled in some tell-tale places.'

'You don't like him, do you?'

Again I thought before I spoke. 'I get the feeling he and Mrs Goodin know my every move before I make it, and that they'll try to catch me engaging in sexual behaviour, or pleasuring myself – both of which are strictly forbidden, you know. They don't trust me. I'm too quick with improper, irreverent remarks.'

Hyde's laughter saddened me. Several days would pass before I heard it again, so I toyed with the idea of telling him how badly I'd been treated in his absence. He would offer to take me home with him, and I would jump at that chance.

But the opportunity got lost in our kiss. Without missing a beat, he pulled me close, pressing his lips into mine. My hunger for him flared like wildfire. I coaxed him into the cover of some trees, away from inquisitive eyes that might easily find us in the moonlight.

'Make love to me,' I whispered. 'Oh, Hyde, how will I survive a week without touching you, without losing myself in the luxury of your kiss?'

He moaned softly, running his warm mouth down the column of my neck. 'I'll miss you, too, Mary Grace. But I understand why you want to stay, and I know you'll do well here.'

How could I protest without sounding like an ungrateful coward? I set aside my doubts and longings, to glory in these last moments before he left me, by leading him deeper into the trees. We came upon a secluded spot where rock formations rose above the sandy creek bank, and a small waterfall marked the source of the brook we'd followed. A shared look had us shedding our clothes.

'If this water flows down from the mountains, it's too cold for swimming.'

'We're in luck,' Hyde said in a husky voice. He

grabbed my hand and led me to the silvery edge of the stream. 'This is where Mrs Goodin does the laundry, and where the drinking water is drawn. It's never been known to ice over. Not even a thin layer on the top.'

Yet another natural wonder about this mountaintop retreat intrigued me, but Hyde's smile invited me to forget everything except his wondrous loving. He walked me into the flowing water, until we stood waist-deep. Gathering me into a passionate kiss, he ran his hands all over my body, as though trying to wipe away the traces of our coupling in the carriage. Squeezing the halves of my arse, he pulled me against an erection that prodded my belly.

I revelled in his caress because I would miss it, and because it soothed the places chafed by Mrs Goodin's lye soap. Parting my legs, I moved against him as his hand sought the warm, slick skin there. The water felt so refreshing, rinsing away images of the cruel cleansing I'd endured in Father Luc's office.

'I love little pussy ... her coat is so warm,' Hyde whispered against my ear.

I giggled at his nursery rhyme, matching the thrust of my hips to that of his hand.

'And if I don't hurt her, she'll do me no harm,' he continued, slipping only his fingertips into my hole to tease its outer rim. 'So I'll not pull her tail, nor drive her away –'

He tugged at a tuft of my bush, sending shivers through my insides.

'– and pussy and I very gently ... will play.'

With that he drove his thumb inside me, bracing me from behind with his other arm. I arched back, mouthing silent screams as Hyde gave me a vigorous foretaste of what he intended to do with his erection. I panted and splashed, spiralling upward with inner heat and the desperate need for release.

'Are you ready for me, love?' He circled my nipples with a rough, wet tongue.

'Yes! Please – oh, please take me!'

'How much will you miss me?' He breathed against my damp skin, making the dark little buttons pucker and harden.

I reached around his neck, and then clambered up his legs to position myself for his tall, solid cock. 'I probably won't eat or sleep, for wanting you, Hyde. I wish you didn't have to go.'

'And will you save yourself only for me?'

Hyde suddenly raised me out of the water. Holding me by the hips, he watched the rivulets trickle down my thighs, and then brought his gaze slowly back to my dripping bush, and up my wet belly to where my breasts bobbed in front of his face. Then he gazed straight into my soul, his eyes dark with a potent magic he alone possessed.

'I was serious when I told the abbot I want you for my wife, Mary Grace. I hope your love will catch up to mine, and that you'll give yourself freely to me – only to me – when you leave here in the spring.'

'I already love you fiercely, Hyde! Maybe we should just go home and –'

'I want you to be sure,' he interrupted in a hoarse whisper, 'because once you've said yes, there's no going back, Mary Grace. I will not love you and then lose you to someone else – or to your doubts about my household, and my occupation.'

Images of Yu Ling and that wailing wraith vanished in the heat of our gaze. Hyde's eyes reflected the moon, glowing like golden coals as he silently demanded my answer. With a little sob, I reached for him. He loved me, and wanted me for his wife!

He lowered me into a savage kiss. My hips searched until I felt the tip of him insisting on entry. With a grunt and a deep thrust, I impaled myself on his jutting shaft. Hyde spread his legs, and then cradled my hips so he could lunge freely and with increasing speed. As my cries echoed around the little cove, I banged my itching

73

clit against the base of his cock. Maybe it was from that harsh soap, but my cunt and its little nub wanted him faster, and harder, and deeper, until all my muscles contracted at once. Hyde buried his face in my hair, stifling a guttural groan as he shuddered and shot.

For a few moments we clung to each other, breathing rapidly. 'God, I love you,' he confessed against my ear.

I wanted to laugh and cry at the same time. 'Maybe we should just slip back into the carriage, before anyone misses us.'

'Oh, but I would miss you!' a jaded voice called out.

Hyde clutched me, instinctively lowering us into the water. I turned towards shore to see the red ember of a cigarette, and then Sybil's shadowy form as she lounged atop a rock like a cat who'd trapped a fat canary.

'And aren't you a pretty pair?' she crooned. 'Too bad men demand such possessive promises of their women, who are too fickle to keep them.'

I wanted to lunge from the water and drag her in. Wanted to hold her head under until her cynical tongue was silenced. Hyde tightened his arms around me.

'Speak for yourself,' he replied tersely. 'Mary Grace embraces such virtues as faith and fidelity and trust. Things you'd know little about.'

'Does she now?' With a flick of her finger, Sybil sent her glowing cigarette into an arc that ended with a hiss beside our shoulders. 'We'll see whose virtues rub off on whom. I'm betting Miss Michaels will embrace all manner of things – begging for that deep, sweet release you just gave her, from whomever – or whatever – happens along.'

Sybil stood up with the grace of a dancer, then threw us a smug smile. 'By the way, you'll have quite an audience if you stay here any longer. Everyone saw you leave together, before our final prayer, so after Father Luc petitioned for both your souls he suggested a search party. Rather like hide and seek,' she added with a sultry chuckle. 'I guess I've won.'

Chapter Seven
A Fine, Forbidden Madness

S ybil stood naked beside the vanity table, with one leg on its padded bench, smoothing lotion into her skin. The glow from the oil lamp cast a spell over the cottage, and perhaps over me, because I could only stand motionless in the doorway, watching her. Her body glistened. Her muscles rippled, lithe and lean, as she lavished the lotion over her thigh.

When she changed legs, our eyes met. I licked my lips nervously, wanting to come inside before any of the others found me, yet not wanting to intrude – or to appear eager. She'd turned down the bed, and I longed to crawl into it, but she'd be only a few feet away, massaging herself. I felt oafish and unsophisticated, my hair still dripping and my tunic clinging wetly to my breasts and hips. I caught the scent of lemongrass, and my skin ached for some of that lotion where Mrs Goodin's soap had burned me.

Sybil smiled coyly. 'Cat got your tongue? Or shall I take up where Fortune left off?'

She laughed at my anxiety. Then she poured lotion between her palms and languorously fondled her breasts. For such a diminutive pixie she was well endowed, yet firm and pert. The dark skin around her nipples bounced at a saucy angle when she brought her hands up from her belly, and then she stood as though offering herself to me.

'You might as well come in,' she said. 'I've graciously decided to share my home with you, Mary Grace. Don't stand there gawking like the village idiot. It's highly offensive.'

Nodding, I stepped in far enough to shut the door. 'I suppose you'll tell Father Luc how you found Hyde and me. No doubt he has a prize for the winner of tonight's game.'

She chuckled, her hands still moving in that hypnotic motion, up to her shoulders now. Sybil arched her back to let her hair swing free, so she could apply the lotion to her neck. This canted her hips towards me in an even more blatant invitation, because I could see the petals of her sex peeking out from her russet-coloured nest. This was the second time I'd beheld a female naked, displaying herself, and I tightened inside. No one had ever told me women could want each other: it went against my grain to even consider such a coupling. Or perhaps my horrified fascination with this taboo excited me more than I realised.

'You want me to tattle?' she challenged. 'You don't impress me as the type who craves pain and punishment.'

'No! I – I just figured you would report us. Everyone here seems set on embarrassing me. Mostly because I'm too new to know the routine.'

I wondered now why Brother Christy hadn't informed me about staying for the closing prayer, just as I had assumed Hyde would know about it. But it was too late to fret about that. And as I watched my room-mate caress herself, I sensed Sybil had figured out my foibles and weaknesses, and was already planning to work them to her advantage.

She offered me the lotion bottle. 'There's a spot in the

76

middle of my back I can never reach, Mary Grace. If you'd be so kind . . .'

It was the nicest thing she'd said since we met, yet again I smelled an ulterior motive along with the light scent of lemon: this was the favour she wanted in exchange for her silence. Her dark-rimmed eyes pulled me forward. Her nostrils flared daintily.

'I won't bite,' she said lightly. 'And never forget what an advantage it can be, having the queen of Heaven's Gate as your friend. I can be very persuasive.'

I didn't doubt it. Against my instincts I stepped towards her, as though entranced by the light in her eyes and the fullness of her lower lip. I took the lotion, trying not to look at the two flawless breasts only inches from mine.

Thank goodness Sybil turned then, and with slow, sensual grace she lifted her honey-red hair from her shoulders. My first impulse was to quickly slather on the lotion and be done with it, yet when my fingertips met her skin, I lingered in that concave between her shoulder blades. She felt like velvet, her softness the ultimate contrast to her defiant nature. As I rubbed in wider circles, I told myself I was doing nothing more erotic than when I'd performed this same service for Mama, when she was ill.

But my mother hadn't undulated and swayed her hips.

'Use both your hands,' Sybil sighed. 'You have a wonderful touch. Tender, yet firm.'

I wouldn't have guessed the word 'tender' might fit Sybil's vocabulary, except perhaps to describe meat she'd roasted for dinner, or pastries she baked. Encouraged, I puddled lotion in one palm and set aside the bottle, spreading the creamy liquid over her shoulders in rhythmic double arcs that eventually dared their way down to her waist.

Still holding up her hair, she turned. 'Now let me do the same for you.'

With her elbows pointed at the ceiling and her hips

cocked to one side, Sybil could've seduced the most righteous man on earth. Yet she stood in front of me, those gypsy earrings swinging in the lamplight while her nipples bobbed on breasts that begged for my attention.

'Don't be shy,' she said, and then she raised one eyebrow knowingly. 'If we're to share this cottage, we might as well get accustomed to each other, don't you think? You certainly didn't back away when Hyde touched you.'

'Hyde's a man,' I stammered, feeling the heat creep into my cheeks.

'God, yes! And the sight of him holding you up, as though you were light as a child, and then ramming his rod into you until you both screamed – well, it was quite a sight,' she admitted. 'I envy you, Mary Grace. Fortune actually believes he loves you.'

While I wondered if this were another of Sybil's wiles, at that moment I felt sorry for her. She thought true love was merely a fantasy, found only in fairy tales. I had the advantage of knowing Hyde loved me as much as I loved him, so perhaps I was even more fortunate than I had assumed. And because I'd pledged myself to him – and Sybil had witnessed it – I decided not to feel threatened by her touch. My poor skin was crying out for the lotion's relief, and letting my room-mate rub it in would establish some trust between us. It was a long time until the end of May, so becoming Sybil's friend would be a wise move.

I turned towards the bed and nervously removed my tunic. 'Does anyone wear underthings beneath these?' I asked as I draped it over the ironing board to dry.

Sybil let out an unladylike snort. 'Really, Mary Grace! What makes you think I've checked?'

I was about to protest, when her two hands followed the outer curves of my behind. Slow and sweet her touch was, and in a fit of jitters I lifted my hair so she could lotion my back. The lemony cream felt cool and smooth as it soaked into my skin, yet prickles of heat shot like lightning through my insides. Sybil continued her gentle exploration by kneeling behind me to massage my right thigh, working her thorough hands down both sides of it. When she tickled the sensitive spot behind my knee, I giggled and fell forward, catching myself on the bed.

'Now there's a sight,' she murmured.

It was then I realised we were in front of the vanity mirror. My breath caught as I watched our reflection: I stood naked, braced against the bed with my legs apart and my hair falling about my shoulders. Sybil, however, wasn't looking at how our complexions and hair were such a near match in the lamplight. She was focused on my pussy. With rapt hands she slathered my calf, easing up it with slow, purposeful strokes that made me hold my breath.

When I tensed, she caught my eye in the mirror. 'What on God's earth did Hyde do to you? Your crotch looks raw, and all along your thighs. It must hurt like hell.'

I closed my eyes, mortified. 'That's Mrs Goodin's handiwork,' I breathed. 'She and Father Luc insisted I needed cleansing, after the way they caught Hyde and me in the carriage.'

Her jaw dropped. 'What'd she use, a scrub brush?'

'Lye soap.'

'Jesus Christ,' she muttered, and then she quickly yanked open a vanity drawer. 'Some day that woman's going to swallow her own medicine. Here, I'll apply some ointment we use in the kitchen, for burns. No wonder you wanted Hyde to take you home!'

Before I could anticipate her, Sybil had dipped into the jar and was fingering my slit. Those few moments of her sympathy had caught me off-guard, and I yelped when she worked the slick salve between the lips of my sex. She chuckled knowingly and continued her ministrations, rubbing my clit between the knuckles of her left hand while she reached for more ointment with the other.

'Yes ... relax and let your honey flow, Mary Grace,' she whispered, once again focused on my hole. 'It's the best medicine, your own natural juice ... so creamy-white, like liquid pearls.'

Shocked at my rapid reaction, I tried desperately to think of something else. I wanted to pull away, but Sybil instinctively slipped her arm around my hips.

'I know how to scratch your itch,' she continued in that feathery voice, 'so stop fighting me, pretty Mary. Let your arse wiggle and let the fire catch inside you. You don't think you should allow a woman to touch you this way, but you like it too much to stop me. Don't you?'

My breath escaped in a rush, and without any conscious command, my legs opened further. Was it the illicit thrill of Sybil's touch and voice that sent such a fine fire singing through my veins? Or was she speaking a truth I couldn't have known when Yu Ling approached me, wanting this same sort of contact?

'I've got salve on the middle finger of this other hand,' she went on in a voice I strained to hear, 'and now that my knuckles have kneaded your sweet little clit from behind, until it's sticking out, begging me for more, I want you to guess where my fingertip's going.'

My eyes widened and my pussy went tight. The waves of pleasure were rising like flood waters and I couldn't have stilled my hips if I'd tried. I was gripping the sheets, bearing my weight on my hands, as I glanced towards a most shocking reflection in the mirror: crouched behind me, Sybil moved in time with my body, her breasts bobbing and her spine curved down to her shapely arse, which swayed forward and back with the motion of her forked knuckles.

'Tell me where,' she said in a more determined whisper.

My eyes closed as my desire for release intensified. A trickle of my juice ran between her insistent fingers. 'You ... you're going to put it inside me.'

'I'm going to shove it up your hungry little cunt,' Sybil confirmed hoarsely. 'I'm going to start right here –'

I sucked air as her finger found the front side of my aching clit, and gasped again when she gripped that finger between her other knuckles. She stopped moving, stopped breathing, and just held me suspended from both sides. I rose to my toes with the tension, clenching my teeth against the need to feel her swirling the salve inside me.

'– and I'm going no further until you beg me to fill your squirming little pussy. You know you want it.'

I stood at attention, my body throbbing with a need I didn't want to admit. Sybil tightened her knuckles around her fingertip, which pressured my cramped clit until a low cry escaped me. 'Sybil – please –'

'Please what, Miss Mary?' With an impish giggle, she wiggled the fingertip and inched it closer to my hole.

My hips thrust forward and my juice surged again. 'Stick it up me – God, please!'

With a triumphant cry, she slid her middle finger inside me, maintaining the pressure of her knuckles to create a double pleasure-pain like nothing I'd ever felt. I moved against her hand until I was humping shamelessly, wild for release. In and out her finger slithered, each time igniting that sweet ache as though she knew exactly which spot would send me through the roof.

I was panting madly, on the verge of a crashing climax, when Sybil pulled away. 'That'll be all,' she said with a cool smirk. 'I've more than repaid you for rubbing my back.'

I turned like a crazed animal and hauled her up to face me. 'Just what do you think you're – you can't stop! I won't let you!'

Sybil only narrowed her eyes at me, the green feline eyes of a night cat mesmerising her prey. 'But I did stop,' she murmured, 'and there's not a pussy in the world that can make me –'

What possessed me, I don't know. I turned, propelling

her on to the bed so she landed on her back with me sprawling on top of her. Our lotioned fronts slid together and I thrust my hand between her legs, fighting fire with fire. Sybil struggled, but I had the advantage of size and pinned her down with my upper body. Her breasts thrust up into mine, and when my middle finger found its way through her coarse curls, her sleek wetness awaited me.

'Can you take what you dish out?' I grunted, shoving two fingers inside her.

She squealed and acted as though she were wriggling away, but I realised then that this was her crafty way of pushing me beyond my inhibitions. I stroked her with the intensity she'd used on me, leaning into that nub where all her nerve endings would set her afire. Moaning now, she locked her gaze into mine and answered the rhythm of my hand with her thrusting hips.

'Harder,' she gasped. 'Pound it into me. Like Hyde did with you.'

I thrust my fingers as far as they would go and held them there, pressing her clit beneath my thumb. In that amazing moment I felt her pulse thrumming with mine, felt her trembling towards orgasm as frantically as I had been.

'Finish what you started, damn it,' I muttered. 'Then maybe you'll get yours.'

That voice didn't come from the Mary Grace Michaels I knew, but from a brazen slut who had suddenly discovered her own power. I pushed a little harder with my thumb, circling surreptitiously to spread the wetness there, while raising my upper leg.

'Do it, Sybil. I can lie here pinching your clit all night, or we can both get what we want, and then get some sleep,' I said in a clenched voice.

She eyed me defiantly, as though she might spit in my face. 'Kiss me,' she hissed.

'Don't you dare!' I clamped harder on the slick flesh between my fingers. I saw no connection whatsoever between the intimate act she demanded and the way our hot, damp bodies moved against each other, making the sheets rustle seductively. Her juice was oozing into my palm and her breasts quivered against mine with her rapid, shallow breathing.

Like a striking snake, her hand found my pussy and the surprise of it allowed her to roll me on to my side. From there it was a contest to see who could inflict the most delicious pain. With feverish fingers we went at each other, raising our legs and jostling our way around the bed. Sybil challenged me with a sultry glare I didn't dare look away from; her practised fingers danced against my slick skin while I answered her thrust for thrust. When she saw her chance, she rolled me on my back to straddle me, like a cowgirl astride a contrary mare.

Lifting my mound, she drove several fingers inside me, mercilessly, until I was raising her up with the arching of my spine. The spasms were gathering, inspiring me to writhe and stare brazenly at the nymph whose manipulations kept me craving more, riding a fine edge of madness. Sybil's hair framed her body like a halo of flames; her earrings swayed crazily and her moans became low and frenzied. Her breasts loomed large from this angle, slapping softly against her body as she rode my fingers and kept pressing her own into my wet sex.

My head thrashed, and I cried out with the extreme pleasure cresting inside me. Cupping her with the heel of my hand, I wiggled my fingers against Sybil's clit until her head fell back and she clenched wetly. When she collapsed on top of me, I didn't have the strength to pull away, or to feel appalled by what we'd just done. She'd goaded me into it, and we had indeed got accustomed to each other.

'Well, at least I came out ahead in something today,' I murmured. 'You didn't expect me to win that one, did you, Sybil?'

My room-mate sat up, pushing her hair back so I

could see her arch expression. 'You call that winning?' she mocked. 'Seems to me you succumbed first, which signifies inexperience – or lack of control. So you lose, Mary Grace. Make your pallet on the floor. The bed's all mine until you've got me begging for it the way you were.'

Although she was fighting a smile, I didn't challenge her for bedding rights. It seemed no matter what I did here at Heaven's Gate, the rules got changed just when I thought I'd figured them out, and Sybil was the mistress of the game. I slipped my nightgown over my head, and curled up on the small sofa across the room. I felt her watching me, ready to challenge the place I'd chosen to sleep.

But then the lamp went out and the bed creaked softly. I was too exhausted to know or care about anything else.

Chapter Eight
Startling Rituals

I awoke with a horrible feeling I was off to a bad start because everyone else knew things I didn't: the bed was neatly made, and Sybil was long gone to oversee breakfast. After donning my tunic and winding my hair into a knot, I hurried towards the back door of the abbey.

The kitchen was empty, except for the sweet yeastiness of freshly baked bread. I walked past the large fireplace, rejoicing when I saw heads bowed silently in the dining room. I could slip into a spot without calling attention to myself, or interrupting the morning meditation.

The only vacant seat was beside Father Luc. His eyes opened the moment I entered, so he could watch me trying to slip in without anyone being the wiser. His mouth quirked, making his moustache look even more sinister. As I was sliding on to the end of the bench, he stood up, taking me with him.

'I'd like to introduce our newest resident,' he announced in a voice that filled the room. About a hundred eyes took in my disgrace and half as many mouths fought smiles.

'Mary Grace Michaels comes to us courtesy of Mr Fortune, and will be creating some extraordinary quilts,' the abbot continued. 'I trust you'll make her welcome and assist her as she becomes accustomed to our schedule and our . . . chaste ways.'

Someone behind me snickered. Was I never to be free of that ignominious moment when Mrs Goodin threw open the carriage door to catch me with Hyde's pants down? She was staring at me now, as though she'd also witnessed what Sybil and I did last night. The cottage had no curtains, so for all I knew, every person in this room considered us the grand finale of the hunt Father Luc sent them on.

'We trust you rested well, and we've been praying for your arrival,' my nemesis said with a slight bow. 'It's our custom to wait patiently, until all are present, before we break bread.'

Heat flared in my cheeks. Not only had I kept everyone else from eating, but the abbot had once again used my ignorance to humiliate me. 'I – please excuse me, I didn't know –'

With a lordly nod, Father Luc signalled for the serving to begin. The man at the end of each table stood, and began ladling oatmeal into bowls that were stacked in front of him. When a large pitcher of milk made its way around, a platter of plump raisin rolls followed it.

I took my seat, humbled. My room-mate had obviously risen hours ago to bake those glazed, cinnamon-scented treats. While I detested Sybil for not waking me before she left, or at least telling me about the meal-time customs, I realised I would have to take responsibility for myself now. I would have to ask a lot of questions, for no one volunteered any information.

A bowl of oatmeal clattered on to the table in front of me. 'Thank you,' I murmured.

The monk beside me, a wiry, balding fellow who wore rimless spectacles, placed the milk within my reach. When I mumbled my thanks again, his eyes widened ominously and he pressed his finger to his lips. Indeed, the hall was silent, except for the scraping of spoons. I'd committed a second sin, and I hadn't been there three minutes.

Frustration welled up in my throat until I could hardly swallow the thick cereal. I thought of Hyde, probably halfway back to Mount Calvary by now, and desperately wished I'd gone with him. What had I got myself into? Why hadn't he warned me about the monastery's rules and rituals? I distinctly remembered talking during last night's dinner, when I sat with him and Brother Christy. But the rules had apparently changed since then.

I was nibbling my raisin roll, thinking it might be the only thing I would enjoy all day, when the abbot stood up again. 'Let us begin our work,' he sang out. 'Let us rejoice in this life, and make good use of our time and talents.'

The monks rose in unison, filling the room with the scraping of benches and their quiet conversation. I was jerked away from the table when the others scooted my bench back – and squeezed my roll too hard, to keep from dropping it. As I noted how everyone else had eaten very quickly, I also felt Father Luc looking down his imperious nose at me.

'Shall we set up your work space, Miss Michaels? I know you're eager to be useful.' His gaze shifted to the misshapen morsel I held in a hand smeared with glaze, implying I was to leave my treat behind as punishment for being late and slow.

'Certainly,' I muttered, taking a bite despite his glare. The roll was as sweet and soft as I'd imagined, and I considered sitting on my bench until I'd savoured every delectable mouthful. The hall had emptied, however, and I thought better of being left alone with the abbot. 'Where will I be working? I have a quilt top in progress, so once I've unpacked my fabrics, I'll get busy. "Idle hands are the Devil's workshop", they say.'

The abbot seemed amused, but something in his expression set me on edge. Sensing that each moment of my defiance would cost me, I preceded him towards the door. I would not allow him to deprive me of my breakfast! When I stepped outside, Father Luc followed me so closely his cassock swayed against the back of my tunic. I took another bite of my roll, trying to ignore his hovering.

The sky bloomed like a morning glory above us, the grass seemed set with emeralds, and the sun warmed my face. Brown-clad figures were walking towards the orchard, and others worked the garden with rakes and hoes. A few knelt along the walkway, clipping grass, and it was one of these monks the abbot hailed.

'Brother Ben! I'd like you to meet Mary Grace,' he said in a jovial voice. 'She's eager to learn our ways, so perhaps you can demonstrate the virtue of sharing what we have with others.'

When he raised his face, I saw he was the man I'd just sat beside – the monk who'd looked none too eager to share a smile with a confused newcomer. Now, however, his eyes glittered behind his lenses. He grabbed my hand and guided it to his mouth, taking a huge bite of my roll.

'The pleasure's all mine, Mary Grace,' he said while chewing greedily.

'I'm sure it is!'

My stunned expression made him laugh, a reedy sound that curdled my breakfast. And damned if Brother Ben didn't go after more! He bit right to the ends of my fingers, swallowed, and then stuck my thumb between his lips. I released the last bite as though it were a burning coal, appalled at his audacity. He was licking the frosting from each of my fingers, making a lusty sucking sound as he moved from one to the next.

'Brother Ben is performing a thoughtful service,' observed Father Luc with a foxlike grin. 'We wouldn't want glaze getting on your quilt. He has also reminded you it's far better to give than to receive. Just look at the enjoyment he's found in your acquaintance.'

I stood speechless. The monk's face shone as bright as

his bald spot. His eyes were closed as he ran my middle finger in and out of his mouth with frightening reverence.

'I think you've had enough,' I said, withdrawing from his grasp. 'Gluttony is a sin, you know. I'd hate to lead you down that heathen path.'

Brother Ben smiled, his eyes meeting mine only for a moment. 'I thank you for your indulgence, Mary Grace. And I look forward to our meeting again.'

What sort of people inhabited Heaven's Gate? I had assumed the unfortunates Hyde brought here might be misfits, and that those called 'Brother' were men of a religious bent – and that I'd be able to tell the difference. As I continued towards the main entrance with Father Luc, however, I wasn't so sure. Brother Ben had looked downright aroused, and it wasn't the glaze making him sweet on me.

When the abbot opened the monastery door, the gargoyles seemed to leer down upon us and the air inside felt stagnant, like the coolness of a tomb. I shook these thoughts away: I was a preacher's daughter, accustomed to finding God even in the draftiest sanctuaries. When Father Luc ushered me towards the room where Mrs Goodin scrubbed me, however, a different chill crept down my spine.

'I offered you work space here in the abbey without realising all our nooks were occupied,' he said, opening that door to my humiliation again. 'So you'll have a corner here in my office. Perhaps over by the window.'

It was an outrageous lie, which Father Luc's diabolical smile made no effort to cover. Somewhere on the grounds, there had to be space where I could sew without his constant supervision . . . his unnerving presence. But since I'd only seen Sybil's cottage, the kitchen area and this little room, I had no idea where that might be.

What had I done to inspire this man's meanness? I thought quickly, grasping at the only straw I knew. 'I hate to intrude upon your privacy, sir, so perhaps I could work in the cottage. Sybil will surely –'

'Sybil has nothing to say about it. I've made my decision.'

'– be working in the . . .'

His stern expression warned me to accept my fate. The abbot gestured towards my new corner with a grandiose sweep of his arm: few residents warranted their own work space, so he probably expected me to bow and scrape for this favour he'd granted me. Rather than humour him, I assessed my cramped domain.

'I'll need a table – the size of two of those in the dining hall,' I asserted quietly. 'And some shelves for my fabric. And an armless upholstered chair, with an ottoman.'

'You'll be content with what I provide you. Trying to crowd me – or land yourself a different place – won't get you far, Mary Grace,' Father Luc replied. 'Your self-serving inconsideration appalls me. We'll have to work on that.'

With a sigh I walked over to where my trunks and two quilts awaited me. I could only hope that sewing every available hour – and earning a lot of money at auctions – would prove my worth to this unpleasant man, as well as convince him I didn't need his constant supervision or whatever penance he had in mind for my selfish requests. There was no negotiating with the abbot. I knew, because I'd been raised by a clergyman who was very much like him.

I took my current project from a trunk, thankful that most of its pieces were cut and ready to sew. Then I unrolled the aspen quilt and sat cross-legged upon it, threaded a needle with scarlet embroidery floss, and began to appliqué a satin tulip petal to the muslin sheet where I'd sketched my design. Good working light came through the little window, but it didn't compensate for the weight of Father Luc's stare upon my back. He sat shuffling papers at his desk, but I sensed his attention was often directed at me. What he found so fascinating, I didn't know. I didn't really want to know.

An hour passed, and then two, marked by the ominous chimes of a clock somewhere in the abbey. My back and legs became so stiff I decided sitting against the wall, where I had to face the abbot, was better than suffering in my Indian-style position any longer. He watched me as I shifted, but I refused to acknowledge him. I simply lost myself in the bouquet of bright colours that would become a spring garden where a black velvet cat watched a trio of brocade butterflies. I'd learned to escape this way when Mama was asleep yet restless with pain I couldn't alleviate, and the technique served me well.

I was so caught up, embellishing a butterfly's wings with orange and green embroidery, that I didn't hear anyone enter the room. It was the sucking-in of breath that made me look up into Brother Christy's admiring eyes. He squatted beside me so he could see the picture right-side up, fingering the crimson tulips I'd completed.

'Exquisite,' he murmured, studying the sketch lines. 'We're in a garden, with tulips and daffodils and lilacs, so lifelike I can almost smell their perfume.'

'Thank you,' I breathed.

'But sitting on the floor will ruin your spine, Mary Grace. Don't you prefer a chair?'

I glanced surreptitiously across the office. 'Perhaps the Lord will provide where the abbot hasn't.'

Brother Christy's forehead furrowed. 'We'll see to that after dinner. Meanwhile, I thought you might like a tour of Heaven's Gate, since you arrived too late yesterday to see anything.'

He didn't need to ask twice. Gripping the pudgy hand he offered, I rose to my feet as gracefully as my tunic and stiff legs would allow. My escort gave the abbot a little wave. 'I'll return her after we've walked the grounds and eaten dinner. You've got to allow our lady

91

some fresh air and exercise or she'll wither away, you know.'

Father Luc grunted and returned to his bookkeeping. If I hadn't felt his gaze on me so often, I would've thought he considered me an imposition. I wasn't sure I should discuss this with Brother Christy, however. My words and deeds had a way of reaching the wrong people, and then haunting me later.

The moment we stepped outside, I lifted my arms and face to the sun. Something about the monastery felt oppressive – perhaps because I was still unfamiliar with the routine and expectations of its inhabitants – so this moment of freedom was a blessing. I smiled over at the monk beside me, who observed my stretching with a curious grin.

'As much as I love quilting,' I began, 'I appreciate this chance to get out and move among the others, and drink in the beauty of these surroundings. Thank you for understanding that.'

His expression turned quizzical. 'Mary Grace, you're free to move about whenever you choose. You're not the abbot's prisoner.'

I smiled ruefully. Brother Christy sounded sincerely puzzled about a situation I knew better than to question.

'Matter of fact, he's never situated anyone in his office. He's taken a fancy to you.'

It was one of the least suggestive statements I'd heard since I arrived: Brother Christy impressed me as being too kind to think badly of anyone – not the abbot, nor his shrewish housekeeper, nor a young woman caught in a compromising position in a man's carriage.

'It's not like I asked for special treatment,' I insisted.

'If you did, you wouldn't receive it.'

'And I would rather work anywhere than in his office,' I went on, hoping this gentle monk would hear my plea without finding me ungrateful, as the abbot had.

Brother Christy's expression resumed its benign boyishness as we strolled towards the cottages. 'You're the only new resident who's come with her own vocation. Father Luc suspects Hyde's lofty claims about your talents – and their income potential – might be too good to be true, so he's keeping close watch on you.'

'But why would Hyde lie about me?'

'Because he loves you. In all the years he's been the liaison between our monastery and the markets in town, I've never seen him this way.' The monk adjusted his spectacles, as though to view me from a clearer perspective. 'But then, why wouldn't he want you for his wife? Perhaps Father Luc is curious about the woman who finally won Fortune over, so he's making sure you're more than just a pretty face.'

'You're too kind,' I murmured.

'I merely express my honest opinion.'

I wished everyone here would do the same. I wished I could believe the abbot was looking after Hyde's best interests, rather than some dark purpose of his own. As we walked along the path that ran between a double row of neat white cottages, however, I decided to lay aside my concerns and enjoy the company of the friar beside me.

'Everything here's so ... idyllic,' I commented. 'So picturesque. Look at this thick grass, and these white-washed houses set against a cloudless sky of cornflower blue – in January! Why, I feel like I'm living in an artist's rendering of a quaint little village where all goes well.'

'Hence the name Heaven's Gate.' Brother Christy stopped to admire the fine day, grasping his hands behind him. His blond hair shone in the sunlight, and his rounded brown shape brought to mind a kindly Friar Tuck. 'How Father Luc located this patch of perfection, we don't know. But we give thanks each day for the friendly weather and the bountiful crops we can raise, and the opportunity to carry out our purpose here.'

Was he implying that the abbot founded this mountaintop retreat? I wondered how that could possibly be, since the aged stone and style of the monastery suggested a structure dating back at least two hundred years. I was brought out of my ponderings, however, when the monk beside me resumed our leisurely stroll.

'How are you and Sybil getting along?' he asked, implying only the most respectable interest. 'I had my doubts about that arrangement, because Sybil, in her way, is every bit as bullheaded as the abbot. And on some days, her temper makes Mrs Goodin seem absolutely sweet.'

I had no desire to reveal how my room-mate and I came to terms last night, so I considered my reply carefully. 'We must dance to the tune the piper's playing, until invited to play along – or until we can outperform her.'

'Wisely put. Learning tolerance, as a preacher's daughter, will serve you well here.'

I wondered if I were too tolerant; too willing to accept whatever my father had dished up as my lot in life. But I wasn't of a mind to challenge Brother Christy's compliment. The discrepancies I was beginning to see, between this monk's interpretation of things and Father Luc's view, would take hours to fathom. And, as we approached the orchard, an interesting sight presented yet another ripple in the picture.

I stopped walking, to stare. Monks of every size and shape stood naked around a pear tree, relieving themselves. Their streams of pee glittered in the sunlight, and every few seconds they took a step backward. From this distance I couldn't distinguish their words, but I could tell they were enjoying themselves immensely.

'I know how odd this must appear to you,' said Brother Christy. 'Our morning ritual not only fertilises the soil around the trees, but it's an exercise in control, and a way to put such common elements as bodily fluids to a practical use.'

I fought a snicker. He was perfectly serious, yet this control he spoke of resembled a contest to see who could shoot the farthest and last the longest. And after the last monk peeing was cheered, the men tightened their circle again, each placing a hand on the arse of the man to his left while grabbing the shaft of the man on his right.

To say I was stunned was an understatement. I gawked, much like that village idiot Sybil had referred to, as the men leaned into their purpose and began to chant a single sound on a low, sustained note. They established a steady rhythm, and then I saw fingers flicking at puckery rectums and fists beginning to pump, slowly up and slowly down, with the entire ring moving a step to the right on every fourth beat.

'I suppose this is another sort of ritual,' I breathed, my eyes roving over the variety of body shapes. I'd seen only three men without clothing, and the sight of so many backs and arses, some hairy and some bare, fascinated me. There were twelve in this group, a few of them around my father's age, yet a surprising number nearer my own.

'A ceremonial cleansing, done each morning to rid the body of tension and inclination towards sexual indulgence – which, as you know, is expressly forbidden here,' Brother Christy added matter-of-factly. 'At Heaven's Gate we believe the naked body of itself holds no shame, and that releasing our pent-up desires each morning, as a corporate act of joy and contrition, frees us to become the spiritual, productive people we were created to be.'

I considered this, while the men stepped more quickly and their music rose in pitch. Many of them had inserted a finger into the arse at hand, and the handling of hardened cocks was quickened, yet still controlled by the rhythm of their monotone chant. Perhaps an evening with Sybil had made me more jaded, but I couldn't help thinking these monks had merely devised a method of jerking themselves off as a form of worship, perhaps because so few women lived here. Which brought to mind questions I didn't dare ask Brother Christy.

'If you look off in the distance, towards the vineyard,'

he said as he pointed, 'you'll notice a line of men performing a similar act along the grapevines. Our women, who assist Sybil in the kitchen or do the laundry with Mrs Goodin each day, have their own ceremonies. For obvious reasons, we keep the two groups separate.'

I could not in my wildest imaginings picture the chief housekeeper throwing aside her bleak black uniform to fondle the females in her charge. And yet . . . she'd had no qualms about running her hands and that damn lye soap all over me. The memory made me twitch with embarrassment. Or was it the rising tide of passion in the men's chant that made my clit tingle?

The voices sounded more urgent now, and the beat accelerated. The faces I could see tightened, the need for release becoming the lyric to their singular song. Would they each climax at will, or did the ritual demand utmost control – a unison shooting of their seed? I was beginning to fidget at the sight of so many cocks being pumped and so many arses wagging, so I tried to return to rational conversation.

'And what about Father Luc? Does he participate in these rituals?' I asked in a tight voice.

'No, Mary Grace, we believe men who have achieved the status of abbot possess enough control and wisdom that they've risen above the needs of ordinary brethren.'

I looked pointedly at the monk, partly because I didn't agree and partly because I wondered what his own answer would be. From what I'd seen, Brother Christy exemplified the Christian ideal – and the control and wisdom he'd just mentioned – in far greater measure than the man he answered to. But it wasn't my place to point that out.

'As for me,' he replied with a knowing smile, 'I felt I should escort you around at this hour, so you'd be aware of our daily practices. Coming from your background, I can imagine you find this rather foreign. Perhaps repugnant?'

Could he see how my upper thighs were squeezing in

time to the men's beat? How my nipples had hardened beneath the heavy weave of my tunic? Their chant had landed on a note that sent lightning streaking through my veins while making the moisture pool in my pussy. I suddenly wanted to stand in the centre of their circle and study each man closely . . . perhaps feel them releasing upon me. 'It – it is a little different,' I rasped, wishing I could relieve the pressure between my quaking legs.

'And of course, now that you know about our morning exercises, you shall participate in them.' Brother Christy flashed me a conspiratorial smile, lowering his voice beneath the wail of the men we'd been observing. 'I understand your inclinations tend toward a sexual direction, Mary Grace, so perhaps you should engage in our acts of open cleansing starting tomorrow, before you begin your sewing. You'll be a calmer, more spiritually attuned woman, if you do.'

I would also be free from the abbot's arrogant stares, at least for a short time each day. And these exercises, though far removed from any religious practices I held dear, would acquaint me with the other women working here at the abbey. This group groping was sounding better by the second to my agitated body, even though it would require my disrobing before total strangers.

A glance at the rather perverted version of Ring Around the Rosie made me forget my fears – and pretty much everything else. With a triumphant cry, all heads fell back and all bodies convulsed. Streams of cream shot from one cock and then another and another, until the trunk of that pear tree ran with their gooey fluid. Some of the men thrust and spurted for an incredible length of time. I couldn't take my eyes off them, and I was getting dizzy from the quivering I tried to hide from the man beside me, and from the musky scent adrift on the breeze.

'Mary Grace? Oh dear, this was too intense for your first day, wasn't it?'

Before I realised what was happening, Brother Christy

led me towards the men who'd just spent themselves. My slit was throbbing so hard I could barely walk and my juice flowed freely down my leg. I couldn't imagine what was coming next, but I certainly wanted to come myself.

'My brothers, Mary Grace was so deeply affected by your ceremony, she finds herself in need of similar release. I fear we're too late for the women's exercises. We should assist in her cleansing while the spirit moves her.'

Before I could protest, or simply ask for a few moments alone in the cottage, I had a naked man on either side of me. 'Don't be alarmed, dear Mary – we won't let you fall!' the younger one said. 'I'm Brother Jack and this is Brother Gregory. Lean into us, now. That's our girl.'

I fell back into a seat they made by clasping hands behind my shoulders and under my thighs. 'But I'll be fine – really! I don't want to interrupt your work, or –'

'The health and happiness of every member is our mission here,' Brother Gregory said. He smiled kindly, making creases around his green eyes. 'You're pale and trembling, sure to faint if left untended.'

'Let me help! There's no time to lose!' A third monk, very slim and sleek, with long brown hair, knelt before us to assess the situation. 'Hold her by the knees.'

The men supporting me shifted their arms so my weight suddenly hung suspended, and the third monk shoved my tunic up my legs. All of this happened so quickly, I had no chance to protest. 'Is this what's called having one's arse in a sling?' I asked, feeling utterly ridiculous yet intrigued by their quick efficiency.

'Brother Nolan's a doctor,' Brother Jack assured me. 'He'll have you at rights in no time.'

Indeed, a squeal of delight escaped me before I realised what this physician's methods would be. He was licking the slickness from my inner thigh, inciting a riot of sensations as his tongue eased upward and his palms spread my legs. The monks who held me complied by each taking a knee in the crook of an elbow and stepping sideways, which left me hanging with my bare arse and my wet sex exposed. When I saw the other men gathering around, I shut my eyes. What would Hyde think? What if the abbot came out here and discovered these brethren indulging in this illicit game?

My reservations flew skyward with the first thrust of Brother Nolan's tongue. In and out and around he drove it, thoroughly lapping the liquid hidden in my heated folds. Back and forth he moved me with the pressure of his mouth, until I was swinging like the pendulum of a clock ... a clock racing against time and the urge to explode.

'Is this what you're needing, Mary Grace?' Brother Gregory asked quietly.

'Oh, yes – dear God –'

'And will you promise to take good care of yourself while you're among us?' Brother Jack asked just as sincerely. 'You must attend to your libidinous needs, or they're sure to rage beyond your control.'

Control. With a nude man crooning in each ear while another one nibbled my clit, I hadn't any idea how to regain it. I simply bobbed back and forth at the whim of Brother Nolan's fine, flexing tongue, feeling those inner spirallings growing wilder with each expert stroke. The doctor knew how to cure what ailed me, all right, and I began to quake and quiver in earnest as he worked his lips into mine.

'No act of contrition and cleansing is complete without a few heartfelt words, Mary Grace. A confession, perhaps,' Brother Gregory hinted, and then he ran his tongue along the edge of my ear.

'Dear Lord,' I whispered.

'That's a good start,' Brother Jack murmured, nuzzling my neck, 'and perhaps the doctor's methods will be even more effective if you tell him where it hurts ... where you're needing his attention the most.'

'Right there!' The tongue inside me curved to fit around my clit, and then delved in and out with an intensity that threatened to drive me insane. My muscles clenched, ready to spring me upward and into sweet oblivion. My head fell back and my hips thrust forward, beyond the point of no return ... beyond the point where modesty or discretion meant anything. 'Sweet Jesus, take me! Take me home!' I called out.

As my spasms crested I was vaguely aware of men murmuring in approval, and perhaps in awe. Brother Nolan gripped my hips to bring me slowly back to grounded reality, and with a few final kisses and licks, he completed his treatment. Smiling almost reverently, he tugged my tunic over my legs again and assisted me to my feet.

It occurred to me then that I had willingly allowed three complete strangers – naked strangers – to bring me to climax while their friends and Brother Christy watched. I stood for a moment, dazed but, yes, feeling at peace. Nowhere did I see eyebrows arched in disapproval or hear men muttering that I was a slut who deserved punishment. In fact, they all introduced themselves to me with sincere smiles, and then agreed that it was time for the day's work. As they headed to the little shed where they'd left their tools and their tunics, I stood amazed at their relaxed attitudes while watching their backsides wink and wiggle as they walked.

Brother Christy gestured towards the vineyard, as though nothing out of the ordinary had just happened. I gazed at him, blinking, still slightly dazed.

'I ... I don't know what to say,' I murmured. Was he judging me? Finding me weak and wanton for falling prey to my newly discovered sensuality?

He smiled, adjusting his spectacles in that scholarly way he had. 'Sometimes words are inadequate, Mary Grace. The moment we lose control is often the time we reach a sublime understanding – an acceptance of things

100

that confused or eluded us before. May it be that way for you, sweet lamb.'

I nodded, feeling he'd given a sort of benediction.

'Shall we proceed to the vineyard? Ahmad is quite eager to meet you.'

Chapter Nine
Ahmad, The Prophet

When I saw him, I realised why Ahmad's name sounded familiar: he'd been the one to find Hyde's carriage parked in the orchard. He stood out because he was the only man of colour, and as Brother Christy and I approached him, other attributes set him apart, as well.

Besides a name that conjured up turbaned sages from far-away lands, Ahmad had a tangible presence – an aura of Eastern mysticism mixed with an earthy, rebellious demeanour. His height alone intimidated me, for he stood head and shoulders above everyone else. His smooth, coal-coloured skin contrasted sharply with his teeth and the whites of his eyes, and gave no hint of his age. His close-cropped curls fitted his head like a cap, yet didn't detract from his ethereal beauty. A ruby sparkled on one side of his nose.

When he took my hand during Brother Christy's introduction, a jolt of awareness shot up my arm: this man exuded a power every bit as potent as Father Luc's, but of a different essence. Ahmad impressed me as a deeply spiritual man, a seer attuned to the mysteries of the universe who made no effort to disguise his blatant sexuality. His erection protruded from the folds of his

Indian-style loincloth, like another hand awaiting my grasp.

'Ah, Mary Grace,' he pronounced in an accented whisper. 'You have doubts about leaving Hyde to live among us, but let me assure you, my precious primrose – I knew of your coming long ago, and your arrival is but a fulfilment of prophecy. You have a purpose here, a place among us, like a much-loved guest for whom we've set a plate at the table. Be at peace within yourself.'

I tried not to stare at the coffee-coloured eye of his cock, which seemed to be watching me closely. Had it hurt when that little gold ring pierced his tip? 'I – thank you,' I murmured. 'Although Heaven's Gate is nothing like I expected.'

Ahmad focused his chocolate eyes on mine until I wondered if he were mesmerising me. 'How so?' he mused aloud. 'How are we different from what Mr Fortune led you to believe?'

I sensed I should answer carefully while within Brother Christy's hearing, because the rotund little monk seemed genuinely concerned for my welfare. I couldn't tell them about the warning I received from that spectre at Mount Calvary, either, or both men would think me insane. 'Oh, Hyde spoke quite highly of the people here,' I assured them with a smile. 'I suppose I just didn't know much about monastic life. About your rituals, and such.'

'You didn't expect to find us fertilising the trees as a means of spiritual enlightenment?'

'That was a shock, yes.' I chuckled, recalling those naked men dancing in a circle.

Ahmad took my hand again, looking steadily into my face. 'I shall tell you then, Mary Grace, that Heaven's Gate will hold many surprises, some not as pleasant as others. But as your time with us passes, I hope you'll ponder not only the unexpected realities around you, but the ones you find inside yourself, as well.'

He paused, including Brother Christy in his mystical

gaze. 'You won't be the same woman when you leave here, my perceptive peach. You will have embarked upon an inner journey, where you encounter facets of your soul you never knew existed. It's a wise woman who accepts the changes within herself as new truths, rather than doubting herself – or doubting the new path she's chosen.'

Again I recalled that wraith hovering near my bed, warning me that I'd be lost if I came here. The old crone had spoken with such urgency I still couldn't write her off as a figment of my imagination, and she was right: things at this monastery were not as they appeared. Yet as Ahmad stroked my hand with his long, pliant fingers, imploring me to understand the meanings hidden beneath this life's surface – beneath my own inexperience – I felt reassured. I had the impression that neither man standing with me now would allow events or personalities at Heaven's Gate to overwhelm me.

As if to reconfirm this, Brother Christy grinned. 'You realise, I hope, that if I allowed anything vile to happen to you, Hyde would never forgive me? And where would we be if he refused to distribute our products? Of all the new residents we've received here, you, Mary Grace, embody the most responsibility. The most risk.'

Before I could grasp this, or ask why anyone here should be associated with risk, Ahmad rested his hand at the base of my neck to continue our tour. 'So you see, my pleasant periwinkle, Christy and I consider you a sacred vessel entrusted to our care. No harm shall befall you. You should prepare yourself to see things in a different light, however – much as we expect the life after this one to present us new challenges, and mysteries we couldn't comprehend while here on this earth.'

I would have to ponder these things later, when I was alone with my sewing. Flanked by my two self-proclaimed protectors, I strolled towards parallel rows of vines that lined the terrain like the spokes of a wheel. Even from this distance I saw bunches of plump red grapes glistening in the dew, and noted occasional brown-clad figures filling oblong baskets with the harvest.

'To our left, where the trees bearing our apples, pears and cherries give way to the grapevines, you'll see our apiary,' Ahmad remarked, gesturing elegantly towards rows of stacked white boxes. 'The bees, of course, play an important part in our production. Not only do they pollinate our fruit blossoms, but they provide honey for our cakes and table use, and wax for our candles.'

In the sunlight, tiny flying specks drifted to and from the hives. Insects with stingers weren't my favourite creatures, so I was hoping our stroll didn't take us much closer to them. Beside me, Ahmad chuckled.

'You stiffen,' he said in that foreign voice. 'And you're wise to behave cautiously in their presence, for they're easily aroused by those they perceive as intruders.'

'Most beekeepers wear mesh around their heads, and heavy gloves, while carrying a smoking rag to sedate the bees,' Brother Christy added. 'But Ahmad is so attuned to them, and they to him, that he gathers their combs of honey without wearing any protective gear at all.'

'Without wearing anything,' the darker man amended.

Despite their reassurances, the image of Ahmad working these hives naked made me shudder. I turned my attention to the vineyard again, hoping to direct us to a tamer, more pleasant subject; trying not to picture bees buzzing around the ringed erection that still stuck out of this man's thigh-length wrap-around pants, or around the nipples that glistened like pink beads on his brown chest.

It occurred to me that Ahmad and Brother Christy might expect something in return for keeping me, their sacred vessel, out of harm's way – just as Father Luc, Mrs Goodin and Sybil demanded their due. But I hesitated to raise this subject. I had seen and heard enough this morning to keep me pondering my discoveries for quite some time. Just as I was wondering about repayment, however, the shaman-like man beside me cocked his head, as though listening closely to my unspoken thoughts.

'You are thinking my guidance comes with a price,' he said in that faraway whisper. He continued to walk me around the shade-dappled grounds, back to a grove of apple trees encircled by an outcropping of rocks. It resembled some sort of ceremonial area, because the trees grew in a semicircle around a grassy clearing.

Ahmad plucked a huge red apple from the nearest tree, polished it against his hip, and handed it to me. 'You recall, of course, the story of Eve and the apple? The debt she incurred for eating of the Tree of Knowledge?'

'Oh, yes,' I murmured, almost afraid of what this apple might symbolise. It was the largest, most perfectly beautiful fruit I'd ever seen, and I had an undeniable urge to bite into it. 'Mankind has borne the burden of her sin ever since. She and Adam were suddenly aware they were naked, and that they had reason to hide and feel shame.'

He closed his eyes, his ruby twinkling as he bowed to my reply. 'Their knowledge required repayment, just as everyone's choices have consequences. Here at Heaven's Gate, things are no different. We acknowledge that we all fall short of our intended glory – but without our sins, we wouldn't require redemption, would we? Since grace is ours for the asking, we believe in sinning boldly, and we trust a fitting afterlife will be ours, as well.'

I could see my widened eyes reflected in the apple's shine. Ahmad's theology struck me as quite radical, compared to my father's, yet I could argue with nothing the enigmatic man said. I looked up at him, swallowing hard. 'What are you saying? What should this mean to me?'

He and Brother Christy smiled indulgently and ushered me towards the distant monastery. 'The sooner you accept our ways, Mary Grace, the sooner you will find your peace. From that self-acknowledgement will come your willingness to give back to our little community, to repay those who have helped you become the woman you were created to be.'

'It will feel quite natural to you, once you attain that spiritual state Ahmad speaks of,' Brother Christy continued. 'From what I've observed, you're a lover of beauty and a seeker of truth. Giving and compassionate by nature. We will all rejoice in your inner epiphany. We await it . . . quite eagerly.'

Something in the monk's voice belied a darker message I couldn't yet decipher. In my confusion, I clutched the apple. We were approaching the grounds around the abbey, which meant I would soon face Father Luc again. An unpleasant prospect, after the morning I'd spent enjoying the outdoors while witnessing so much that piqued my curiosity.

Again, Ahmad sensed my mood. Pulling me gently into an embrace, he murmured, 'We will meet again soon, Mary Grace, for it is my calling to instruct you. To enlighten you.'

How should I respond? This man's cock was prodding my midsection while his hand wandered down my backside to tease the crease between its cheeks. Brother Christy looked on benignly, and then glanced towards the abbey.

'I'll find you a chair,' he said, 'and I'll tell Father Luc to expect you back after the noon meal. This will allow you about half an hour with Ahmad, to further explore the morning's revelations.'

The monk dismissed himself with an amiable smile, leaving me to wonder what might happen next. On the one hand I feared Father Luc's reprisal for staying away from my work so long, and on the other I allowed that as a newcomer, I had every right to become acquainted with the grounds and the people I'd be living among for the next few months. Ahmad had taken my face between his hands and was compelling me to listen, to open myself to the mysteries behind those arresting umber eyes.

'Come, let us kneel together,' he whispered, guiding me towards what looked like an altar – a large, smooth rock surrounded by tall bushes that flowered in magenta and pink. 'It is good to humble ourselves, to separate from others as we ponder the opportunities afforded us in this abundant life.'

We entered the enclosure, and when he fell to his knees facing the boulder, I followed his example. Ahmad took the apple from me, placing it above us, on the stone. 'A thank offering,' he explained. 'A worthy return from the harvest, as we offer ourselves, as well.'

I couldn't dispute this offering, or my need for meditation. I sensed this exotic man would instruct me further, and followed his example of bending low over my legs so my palms pressed the grass and my forehead rested on my hands. The rustling of the flowers and an occasional bird call were the only sounds around us, while the breeze riffled my tunic. I hadn't felt this quiet, this peaceful, since I'd arrived at the monastery.

'Be still, and accept the knowledge that is mine to impart,' Ahmad's voice lulled me. 'This position of humility opens us to many wonderful possibilities.'

My tunic was eased up over my back, by hands that then followed the curve of my spine to fondle my bottom. As Ahmad's fingers grazed the crevice there and then slid forward to stroke my bush, I sucked in my breath.

'Let go of your doubts, my prized pupil,' the man behind me intoned. 'Let your body respond to my teaching, for to reject such a gift would be not only selfish but foolish, in light of all I have to offer you.'

I was being given the chance to thank Ahmad for his kindness, yet I balked. The erection I'd been trying not to stare at was now stroking me like a thick finger, inching down to rub against a hole I didn't intend to open for anyone. 'I – I've promised myself to Hyde!' I protested. 'I assured him of my love and faithfulness, yet everywhere I turn people mock my intentions.'

'All the better reason to learn from Ahmad, who will enhance your present understanding of pleasure while honouring your promise to a fine man.'

His fingers found the cleft of my sex, making me gasp with the intense sensation – and making me immediately wet. It was embarrassing how quickly I responded to the touch of this charismatic man, yet I'd been drawn in since the moment he took my hand in greeting.

'Ah, that's better,' he crooned. 'I shall prepare you for what I sense is a new experience, Mary Grace. Be still, and accept the sincere giving of my gift.'

He was leaving me no room to refuse without appearing ungrateful. I nipped my lip as his purposeful fingers circled my clit and then dipped again into the cream that pooled beneath it. As I expected, his fingers slipped back to anoint the puckery portal that tightened instinctively against his intrusion.

Ahmad chuckled and continued spreading my moisture until the entire crevice between my legs was dripping. He then gripped the halves of my bottom and kneaded them in a hypnotic rhythm, letting the head of his cock tease forward and then back in my moisture. Sensations reeled within me when his ring rubbed my privates, yet part of me knew – and rebelled against – the penetration he sought.

'Please, Ahmad,' I whimpered, 'please don't ram yourself up my backside! I can't even think about the pain!'

He responded by lifting my hips so quickly I couldn't anticipate the wet tip of his tongue, which briefly licked behind my pussy and then circled the rim of my tightest hole. He plunged it into me, wiggling its length against inner walls that spasmed in surprise. I cried out, but it only inspired him to insert his tongue further than I believed possible. The passageway felt full and curiously pressured, and when I realised he wasn't hurting me, I relaxed.

Ahmad responded with a sensual moan that reverberated up my spine. A furtive fingertip slipped into my slit and I began to follow its rhythm, driven almost helplessly towards a mounting tightness that promised climax. I hovered awkwardly, half-standing, balancing myself by placing my hands against the boulder in front of us, at the command of an amazingly adroit tongue and finger.

And then, as my need increased to a thick, churning demand, Ahmad slipped a finger in where his tongue had been. He began slowly, working a knuckle at a time with several moments of excruciating pleasure-pain between his moves.

'You do well, my perfect pearl,' he whispered, kissing my thighs to incite yet another riot of sensations. 'You will soon be ready to receive me. Where most men are thick and forceful, you will find me slim and resilient, ever mindful of your comfort. Attentive to your needs and deepest desires.'

I let out a long sigh, still moving tentatively to avoid pain. Ahmad, the sly fox, inserted a second finger into my slit, which sent me quivering into a near-panic state. I felt suspended above the ground – above all I had experienced before – yet wary of the man's next move. 'Please, may I turn around?' I pleaded. 'I want you – so badly – inside me!'

'There are times we must bend to another's wishes,' he replied quietly. 'Times when we must learn while others instruct. Have you arrived at this level of acceptance, Mary Grace?'

I could only pant and drive my aching clit against the fist he manipulated me with. I closed my eyes for fear of losing myself, my very soul, to the man squatting behind me.

'Very well,' he murmured. Still thrusting two fingers deep inside my slit, he placed his knees behind mine and raised himself until the head of his shaft pressed against my other entrance. 'Now let yourself fall back,

110

Mary Grace, and let me catch you . . . catch you up in a rapture of fulfilment like you've –'

I screamed as his cock gained entry, lunging forward to escape what still repelled me. Ahmad fell backwards into the grass while I landed hard against the large stone. It scared me more than it hurt, but I'd reached my limit: I curled against the warm rock and sobbed. I cried for the loss of familiar places and pleasures, and for the man who'd offered to share them with me. I bemoaned my decision to come here among jaded strangers so eager to lead me down a dark path.

Behind me, I heard a disgruntled sigh. Hoping Ahmad would simply leave me to my misery, I kept my face in the crook of my arm, sniffling pitifully. The breeze tickled me between the legs, where I was still wet but had lost all interest in my climax. Then I felt hands on either side of my bare hips.

'We will compromise,' Ahmad stated impatiently. 'For days I've awaited you, and I must have my release. Turn and face me, as you wanted to a moment ago.'

Something in his voice told me not to argue. When I glanced over my shoulder, I saw a belligerent edge to Ahmad's dark features, yet still those eyes and that voice held me in their thrall. 'I – I'm sorry I disappointed you.'

'Disappointment has its place. It provides room for improvement.' His gaze settled on my sex, and one hand wrapped around the erection that now protruded even further out of the folds of his pants. 'Lie back against the rock and spread yourself. By taking the pleasure I've saved up for you, I'll show you what you have denied yourself. I'll teach you to trust, to override your fears and open yourself to me.'

My impulse was to bolt. I'd explained that I wished to remain faithful to Hyde – a perfectly honourable request – and by allowing this man to enter me I was breaking my promises. Yet again he read my thoughts.

'I won't take you against your will,' he muttered, his hand actions becoming faster. 'And I won't ask you to indulge me the way we found you with Fortune – it will teach you nothing, and I take no pleasure from gagging my partners with my extended length. They invariably bite down.'

I remained quiet, slowly turning to face him. His ebony features tightened, yet he remained in utmost control.

'Lie back, offering yourself to me. Spread your legs wide.'

I felt like a sacrificial lamb, yet I sensed Ahmad intended no harm as he relieved himself in a way I had yet to understand. I took hold of that perfect apple so it wouldn't fall to the ground, and then hoisted myself on to the rock as he'd instructed.

'Wider,' he breathed, his gaze so penetrating my slit felt the same tinglings he'd inspired before with his fingers. Again I felt swept into his power, free to choose yet wanting to do as he willed. Wanting to make up for the way I'd rejected his original attempt.

'Touch yourself,' Ahmad instructed, bucking forward and back as though he rode a cantankerous horse. 'Slip your fingers between those rosy lips and show me your most secret, sacred place. Make me welcome, Mary Grace. Open yourself as you could not before, and let me come . . . let me come –'

With a guttural gasp, he aimed and kept pumping. The cream spurted out of him like streamers, thick and white and warm as it landed against my open hole. 'Yes . . . yes . . .' he moaned when I began to rub the slick substance against my skin. 'Anoint yourself with me. Let me pour myself into you, my paroxysm of passion. Let me fill you until you can hold no more.'

His low voice urged me on until I was writhing in time with him. I thrust myself at him, opening further to receive yet another burst of his seemingly endless seed. This was indeed an unanticipated experience, for had someone told me I would find such a dousing erotic, I wouldn't have believed it. When Ahmad at last sank to his knees, I flicked my fingers in and out and around, driving myself into the spirals that would bring release. My head lolled back and, knowing Ahmad watched with great interest, I thrust three fingers inside myself, still spreading his wetness over my engorged clit.

Just as I was arching upward, he grabbed my hands to pull me into a standing position. My eyes flew open, and so did my mouth. 'You bastard! You spiteful –'

Ahmad laughed, swatting the hem of my tunic back to my knees. 'Just as there is a lesson in unanswered prayer, we have much to learn from desires left unsatisfied,' he crooned in that exotic accent. 'When I see you again, we will resume our quest. Meanwhile, ponder what you've seen and heard and learned, my puckery persimmon.'

'I am not your –' I hurled the apple at him, aching all over from this latest lesson in frustration. At least Sybil had allowed me release, even if she turned it against me at bedtime.

But Ahmad nimbly snatched the apple from the air. His mystical aura had returned, marked by brown eyes that sparkled with mirth. Stepping towards me, he bit smugly into the apple, spraying my face with its juice.

'Knowledge is power,' he said in a snake-like voice. 'Pay its price, or be forever damned.'

Chapter Ten
Some Realities Revealed

I curled up on the couch that night, hoping to fall asleep before Sybil finished her kitchen duties. When she opened the cottage door, flicking her cigarette behind her, I was wide awake but didn't greet her. The afternoon in Father Luc's office had passed without any direct conflicts, although he seemed to consider my upholstered chair and worktable a challenge to his authority. I sat engrossed in my sewing, facing the window, so I could sort through the confusing events I'd seen during my tour. But I had reached no conclusions. That inner peace Ahmad kept referring to eluded me, chased away by images I didn't fully understand.

My room-mate walked silently as a cat, so I felt rather than heard her presence at the end of the sofa. 'Well, damn! I was hoping for another wrestling match tonight.'

'Better find yourself a different partner, then.' Through the slit of one eye I watched her cross her arms in the darkness, backlit by the moon.

'But it's you I want, Mary Grace. Someone as quick with a retort as I am. Someone who sees this place with fresh eyes.' Her gaze seemed to penetrate my blanket. 'Someone fresh, and soft, and so much lovelier than she realises.'

I sighed, curling inward. 'Sorry to disappoint you – and you're not the first I've done that to today. But take heart,' I added ruefully. 'There's a place for disappointment. It gives us room to improve.'

'Ah-hah! I have Ahmad to thank for your mood.'

Without preamble, Sybil lifted my feet and sat on the sofa beneath them. She took one foot between her hands and began to knead it with a surprisingly strong grasp. 'I wondered why you didn't speak to me at dinner, but I was hoping you were too busy flirting with Brothers Gregory and Jack. Not to mention that fine specimen, Brother Nolan. Now there's a tongue that knows its way around a cunt.'

I chuckled in spite of myself.

'So you've met him. Tell me about your day, dear. Sister Sybil sees all and knows all, but that doesn't mean she betrays a confidence.'

This was another facet of my brazen room-mate, a softer side I needed after such an extraordinary first day at Heaven's Gate. I turned on to my back, folding my arms beneath my head as she continued to ply my foot with firm, soothing strokes. 'This is the nicest thing that's happened to me all day. Thank you.'

Sybil's brow arched. When she turned to look at me in the dimness, I saw a shine in her eyes. 'Really? Nolan must be losing his touch.'

'No! It's just that –'

'So he did lick you! You're getting around faster than I'd have thought, Mary Grace!' She gripped my toes together in a tight bunch, her grin mischievous. 'I won't finish this foot until you tell me about it. Every delicious detail.'

I knew better than to deny her, if I wanted any sleep. And it felt good to have a sympathetic listener, someone who might understand my plight better than a man. 'Brother Christy rescued me from Father Luc's office for a tour of the grounds this morning, and –'

'You're not getting along with the abbot?'

I sighed. 'He's overbearing, at best. Peeved because Brother Christy fetched me a chair and a worktable, which he originally denied me.'

'He'll get over it. Is your quilt going well?'

'Oh, yes. The picture's nearly complete, and I'll put the layers together tomorrow.'

'Then he has no reason to glare down his bony nose at you ... unless he's so taken with you he can't get his own work done. Go on – you were touring.' Her hands took up my other foot, magically massaging away the knots of tension.

'I was just in time for the orchard ritual where they fertilise a tree.'

Sybil giggled. 'Impressive, isn't it? Just like a bunch of men to rationalise such ludicrous behaviour by calling it a ceremony, when they're really measuring each other up while having a pissing contest, followed by a come-off.'

I blinked, yet her assessment matched mine. 'Brother Christy said the women have similar morning exercises with you and Mrs Goodin, in the interest of keeping everyone spiritually attuned rather than –'

'Horny? Out of control?' Sybil let out an incredulous snort. 'Now honestly, Mary Grace! Can you picture Hortense Goodin directing a circle of women who're fondling themselves?'

'Well, no,' I admitted. 'Her name is Hortense?'

'Appropriate, eh? As in a whore who's tense?' Laughing at her own joke, Sybil ran her fingernails along the soles of my feet. 'Christy's a bit deluded if he thinks we kitchen workers hold organised shooting sprees. We take care of our needs as they arise, and then we're back to work. Much tidier and more efficient.'

'Oh.' I tried not to squirm as her touch sent streaks of fine lightning up my legs. 'I was hoping to use that as a reason for getting out of Father Luc's office each morning.'

'You'd rather play with the ladies than pay constant homage to –'

'It's not like that! I just want a chance to be around other –'

Sybil silenced me by pressing my feet together and then planting a loud kiss on one of them. 'Don't mind me. I'm just throwing you a line, because you're so willing to be reeled in, sweet Mary.' She cast me a pensive glance, her warm hands still stroking my ankles. 'Come visit us any time you like. You're probably quite competent in the kitchen.'

'I don't have the impression I'm free to come and go.'

'Rubbish! Are you chained to that chair?' she demanded, her eyes shining in the darkness. 'Just walk out! Hyde didn't bring you here to be the abbot's shadow.'

Once again Sybil was showing me a perspective I hadn't considered, probably because I was so accustomed to doing as I was told ... or as I'd been intimidated into believing. Perhaps Ahmad's talk about new realities and challenges had merit, after all. 'You may be right.'

'Of course I'm right! Now get on with your story. Cut right to the part about Brother Nolan,' she said coyly. 'Truly an inspiration, that man. Nothing I enjoy more than watching him wink and flash those big blue eyes at me while he's working his tongue under my muff.'

I cleared my throat self-consciously. 'He volunteered his medical expertise after I was overcome by the sight of that uh, ceremony. It's good we have a doctor here at the abbey.'

'Doctor?' Sybil laughed raucously. 'Nolan likes to play doctor, but as far as I know he was doing carpentry and chimney sweeping before he came here.'

Another discrepancy revealed. Or was my room-mate playing Devil's advocate – throwing me another of those lines because I was such a naïve little fish? Her hands were working up my calves now, relaxing me wonderfully, so I didn't challenge her. And it wasn't like I was about to reveal something about other residents she didn't already know.

'Well, Brother Nolan did indeed sweep my chimney,' I quipped, 'while Brother Jack and Brother Gregory suspended me between them, holding me open for him. Quite a sensation, being held by two naked men while their friend purged me of my distracting libidinous impulses. And Brother Christy looked on as though it happened every day.'

'That's all he ever does. I'm not sure if he pleasures himself, or if there's no equipment hanging under that cassock.' Sybil glanced at me, while her hands climbed higher. 'So then you met Ahmad?'

'Yes. And speaking of equipment,' I mused aloud, 'does that man's pecker always poke out of his pants?'

'Amazing, isn't he? I don't know if he goes around in a constant state of arousal, or if he's just that glad to be with me – and now you! See how quickly everyone's come to love you, Mary Grace?'

I wished I could believe that. I wished I felt as comfortable with my new friends as Hyde had promised I would. 'Did you have trouble adjusting when you first came here, Sybil? I – I feel like a very square peg in a world of round holes.'

My words came out sounding more pathetic than I intended, but the lithe elf at my feet responded with almost maternal compassion. She rose on to her knees, positioning herself between my legs as she faced me. After shoving the coverlet to the floor, she resumed her massage by placing a hand on each of my thighs, levering her weight into each stroke. I realised now where her ministrations might lead, yet I so badly wanted her counsel I didn't protest.

'Let me guess which round hole Ahmad tried to peg,' she ventured softly. 'And is that why you supposedly disappointed him?'

I nodded, watching her move above me in a steady

rhythm that had become the metre of my own breathing. She again wore black pants and shirt, and her panther-like movements made her seem a creature of the night; far more erotic, even fully dressed, than any of the men I'd encountered here. This thought surprised me, for I still had no designs upon Sybil, nor the desire to pursue her as anything other than a friend.

'Well, we all have our preferences,' she explained quietly, 'and dear old Ahmad just likes to enter through the back door. We have no one else of colour here, so who knows how he'd act if he could be with others from his part of the world.'

Her voice had lost the edge she'd cut me with last night. She was simply Sybil, talking woman to woman, and working a subtle spell with her touch. Her fingertips ran up the insides of my thighs, pushing my flimsy nightgown ahead of them. She held it there, studying me for a long moment before letting out a sigh.

'Look at you,' she breathed, folding back the fabric so it stayed out of her way. 'Firm, lovely legs crowned by a heart-shaped bush. Pouty little lips sticking out, begging me to –'

She almost touched me, but then clasped her hands against herself. 'I forget that not everyone shares my enthusiasm for this. If you want me to leave you be, just say so, Mary Grace. I was rude last night, testing you, but I can see you've had a perplexing day.'

'I asked you a question,' I replied just as softly.

She smiled, sitting back on her heels. Her expressive hands spanned her own thighs, sighing along the fabric of her pants. 'Did I have trouble adjusting? you ask. Did I ever feel like a very square peg among a lot of round holes?' She let her head fall back in thought, making a very provocative silhouette against the moonlit window.

'I think it was easier for me to come here because, first of all, I wrote my own ticket with Father Luc. I was slaving away in my maiden aunt's bakery. She raised

119

me, and considered every day's gruelling work my penance for possessing such a wayward state of mind.'

I chuckled, glad for this insight into Sybil's past. 'And you told him your bourbon pecan pound cake would make his cock throb?'

'Yes, ma'am! And he took me up on that, as well as on various other offers, so I arrived at the monastery with a talent that would make him money, among other things. But I suppose I had an easier time, once I established myself among the monks, because I've never been bothered by a conscience.'

She leaned forward again, bracing her hands on my thighs so she could look me directly in the eye. 'You're a preacher's daughter, so guilt and shame come as naturally to you as greed and seduction do to me. Is this making sense, Mary Grace?'

I blinked. 'It never occurred to me that a human could exist without a conscience. I've always been told it was what put us a step above the animals, and kept us on the upward way.'

'Some of us prefer the low road.'

Did this make Sybil an evil woman? A daughter of the Devil himself? She was now pressing so close against me I could smell cigarette smoke and feel the heat of her body. All I heard was the pounding of my pulse, which matched the throbbing down where my clitoris met the fabric of her pants. She had me trapped, awaiting my spoken reply and my body's response, yet this felt so different from being Father Luc's prisoner. I lay beneath her willingly; expectantly. My mouth went dry as I stared up into her slender, sloe-eyed face.

'I'm trying to understand,' I rasped. 'If Heaven's Gate is a religious retreat where I've been told sexual activity is strictly forbidden, why does everyone around me pursue release while calling it something else?'

She flashed me the grin of a vixen, slipping a finger into my wet cleft. 'Why do children do exactly as they're told not to? Why do men sneak into whorehouses while their wives take secret lovers?'

I couldn't answer that. Until I'd met Hyde Fortune and his staff, with their rampant appetites, I wasn't aware such yearnings existed. I was the daughter of the Reverend Jeremiah Michaels, and I simply hadn't been exposed to this side of life.

'Some day you'll figure it out, Mary Grace,' Sybil whispered, leaning so low her breath caressed my face. Her fingers stroked steadily between our bodies, further igniting that forbidden fire. 'And when you do, Lord love us all! I may have to step aside as the Queen of Cunts.'

'Hah! You'll never give up that throne!'

With a wicked giggle, she threw her head back and rocked against me in earnest, her gypsy hoops bobbing as her hand probed the depths of my sex. Three of her fingers plied my pussy into a quivering itch demanding to be scratched, while her thumb settled against the nub that now stuck out as blatantly as Ahmad's amazing member. I bucked against her, raising my legs to invite even deeper thrusts. The sofa creaked and shifted beneath us, until I feared it might collapse, but I was too caught up in those wild inner tightenings to care.

'Oh, Sybil . . . Jesus me!' I rasped, and for all I knew I flew up towards the ceiling with my release. When I came back into myself, I was aware of hands gently stroking my hips as the woman between my shaking legs slowed my breathing by regulating her own.

She sighed. 'You spent yourself so gloriously I have very wet pants.'

'Wet from the inside,' I quipped, and then giggled uncontrollably. 'And it's your own damn fault, you know. I was lying here minding my own business when you came in.'

'Feeling dejected and miserable. Admit it now! Aren't you just glowing with goodwill and a sense that all's right with the world?'

Sybil spoke the truth. And I had an inkling of what it might be like to choose the low road, without the inconvenience of a conscience. 'I feel guilty, indulging in this gratification when I've promised myself to Hyde.'

'Well forget your guilt! Think of how pleased he'll be that you've learned so much about your body's responses,' she insisted. 'And how grateful he'll be that instead of a simpering little thing too afraid – or ignorant – to ask for what she wants, he'll be taking up with a lover anyone would delight in. Think of it as a gift only you can give him.'

Sybil eased herself from between my legs. The scent of my sex teased me as she stood beside the sofa, smiling. 'You've had a remarkable day, dear Mary. Get your rest now. Tomorrow promises to be another adventure.'

Chapter Eleven
Caught in the Act – Again

I sat sewing, embroidering the final details of a gloriously golden butterfly, while the abbot and Mrs Goodin reviewed their accounts. With the sun beaming through my little window, I was content to spend the day on this quilt, because I loved working with the fabrics and colours – and because with both of my wardens close by, the opportunity for getting away seemed unlikely.

I had plenty to think about, anyway: three intimate encounters with people I'd known less than a day made me wonder if I'd left my conscience behind with Hyde, or even forfeited it when I gave myself to him. I wasn't so far from that low road Sybil had mentioned, and this change in my behaviour concerned me.

Startled by a pounding on the door, I pricked my finger. Before Father Luc could grant permission for our visitor to enter, Sybil carried in a cake topped with prettily arranged apple slices and cherries, so redolent with brandy we could've gotten tipsy on the aroma alone. She winked slyly at me.

'Father Luc! Mrs Goodin!' she exclaimed. 'We've concocted a recipe for upside-down cake, and want your opinion on whether it should become a new product.

And since our main project today will be dipping cherries, I'm hoping Mary Grace can assist us. Best to work quickly, with several hands, so the chocolate doesn't clot, you know.'

Something told me my room-mate had concocted more than cake: her story reeked of that adventure she'd spoken of last night, if her secretive grins were any clue. Mrs Goodin's raised eyebrow told me she smelled something behind Sybil's visit as well, but the man beside her accepted the gift as though his favourite kitchen wench were offering herself on a platter.

'What a thoughtful gesture. And if you devised this recipe, Sybil, I can count on its success without even tasting it.'

High praise, from a man who had only rules and criticism for me. But then, Sybil had known how to flatter and appeal to this man's desires from the start. I watched their exchange of glances, sucking the blood from my fingertip. Her catlike green eyes danced with his darker ones; her hips shifted as she talked, and her hair – swept back from her forehead into a ribbon, tumbling down her back in a cascade of smoky auburn waves – swung seductively as she suggested names for the new recipe.

When they'd finished flirting, Father Luc glanced my way. 'Well? Are you going to sit there with your finger in your mouth, or will you dip cherries with Sybil?'

'Sorry, sir. Fingered my prick – er, pricked my finger.'

Colour rose in the abbot's cheeks, and I saw the hint of a bulge in his cassock. Sybil, meanwhile, was braying with laughter, which Mrs Goodin found inappropriate.

'I think we all have work to do,' she said stiffly. 'And if these accounts are accurate, we've seen an increase in kitchen expenditures these past few months, which our sales don't justify. Look well to your budget, Sister Sybil. We support several people here, and if you waste our food, we'll have to cut back to two meals a day. That won't be a popular decision.'

'So don't make it,' the redhead retorted. 'Mr Fortune will bring our Christmas profits with him this Friday. Your ledger – among other things – will look more flush once he arrives.'

Damn her, for looking at me when she said that! I rose from my chair before Warden Hortense or the abbot could change their minds about my going.

'You're obnoxious!' I hissed as Sybil and I strode through the front doors of the abbey.

'Got you out of there, didn't I? And this is my thanks for making up that cake, and the story to go with it?' She snickered as we approached the back side of the building. 'Between the liquor in that cake and the hot talk, Father Luc will be steamed all morning.'

'What about Goodin? What if she comes to watch us dip our cherries?'

'She's probably fingering her own right now,' my companion said with a smirk. 'Old Hor-tense puts up a frigid front, but underneath that uniform she's got a twat just like the rest of us. Did you see her eyeing that bulge in the abbot's cassock? They couldn't wait for us to leave.'

I had trouble picturing the abbot allowing his house-keeper to pleasure him – especially since it was Sybil who got him aroused. But stranger things had happened at Heaven's Gate, and I was a poor predictor of what might transpire between any of those who lived here.

The kitchen smelled like a chocolate shop, with an undertone of brandy. Sybil smiled, pleased with the industriousness of her helpers while she'd been away. 'I've brought our newest resident, Mary Grace, to see how we make our sweets,' she announced. 'She's eager to help, so I bet she'll be as good at dipping her cherry as the rest of us, by the time we finish this morning!'

The three women and two men greeted me with warm smiles, and I was introduced around the room. They were dressed in cloister brown tunics, too, so I relaxed: no one here appeared driven to enlighten me, or to overwhelm me with pithy remarks. They acknowledged Sybil as their leader, and because she kept a hand on my shoulder they accepted me as someone who deserved to be here.

The first two women were arranging sheets of parchment on rectangular trays. 'Mary Grace, I'd like you to meet Violet and her sister Zerelda, whom we call Vee and Zee. They're preparing trays where the chocolate-covered cherries will dry.'

They bade me a cheery hello, each of them offering a hand. 'How nice of you to help us,' Vee said. She stood taller than her sibling, and a spattering of freckles made her appear girlish, although I suspected she was near thirty. 'I understand you sew the most beautiful quilts.'

'I can't wait to see them!' Zee chimed in. 'When Mr Fortune brought us here, we had no particular skills or talents, so I envy your ability to earn your keep from the start.'

'And if either of you ladies were working at something else, how would we ever make our tins full of temptation?' Sybil asked kindly. Then she smiled at me. 'These two lost the rest of their family in a tragic fire several years ago, and have made their home here.'

'Sybil was a saint for taking us under her wing,' Vee explained.

'And we'd have been stuck at the Home for the Friendless, had Hyde not taken pity on us,' her sister added with a wide-eyed grin. 'You're so lucky he found you, too, Mary Grace. There's no sweeter, dearer man to be found on the face of this earth.'

Had these sisters been in the crowd that caught me with him when that carriage door flew open? As Sybil guided me on, I smiled at them, wondering just how sweet and dear Hyde had been. We paused so that two robust men carrying a large cauldron between them could set their chocolate-filled burden on wooden slats in the centre of the floor.

'And these fine fellows are Brother Paul,' Sybil said,

nodding towards the muscular blond, 'and Brother Quentin – the only two men capable of pleasing me in the kitchen.'

'The only two who could put up with her day after day,' Quentin teased. Built like a lumberjack, tall and broad, with his sorrel hair pulled back at his nape, he was the last man I'd imagine as a kitchen assistant.

Brother Paul adjusted the steaming cauldron on the slats, and then focused his full attention on me. 'We're glad to have you,' he said with a playful grin. 'You'll find our cooking methods a bit unorthodox, but we make the best chocolate you'll ever put in your mouth –'

'Or anywhere else,' Brother Quentin added slyly.

'– and thanks to Sybil, the work here is more like play. Yet we produce the cakes and candies that support the entire monastery. The finest desserts to be found anywhere.'

'And we do it with such modesty, too.' Brother Quentin clapped his companion on the shoulder, letting his hand drift down to the other man's backside. 'If we make a tasty show of it, perhaps Mary Grace will join us often.'

Something about the two of them struck me as different from the other men I'd met there, yet I liked them immensely. And when I was presented to the last of Sybil's aides, I was even more aware that her crew consisted of individuals who probably wouldn't work with Ahmad or Mrs Goodin – or anyone else – because Sister Sybil alone gave them the same outspoken yet unconditional acceptance she'd shown me.

'And this is Elvira, a talented kitchen wench unlike anyone else you've ever met.' My room-mate spoke with pride, yet her word choice alerted me to qualities that didn't show on the surface. 'Elvira helps me devise new recipes, and also designs the distinctive tins that set Heaven's Gate products apart from others.'

Elvira sat on a stool, inspecting a shallow pan filled with plump cherries that swam in brandy, and when she

127

stood to greet me I was astounded at her height. Her blue-black hair was caught up in curls that would do a debutante proud, yet she was anything but delicate or simpering. Like Sybil, she edged her eyes in kohl and wore daring earrings; her bosom put everyone else's to shame. Elvira was thicker and broader than was fashionable, yet her proportions allowed for an undeniably feminine allure to shine through. Her smile radiated warmth, but I knew immediately not to put myself at odds with her.

'Hello, Elvira,' I said shyly, and for want of more intelligent conversation, I glanced at her pan of brandied cherries. 'You seem to have the most intoxicating job of all.'

She offered her hand, perusing my every move with great interest. 'Not every cherry we start with will be worthy of the Heaven's Gate label,' she replied in a husky voice. 'Only the plumpest and ripest and sweetest will go into tins today, Miss Mary. Those not succulent enough to be chosen shall meet a different end.'

Her tone made me feel sorry for those little fruits that didn't measure up to her exacting standards. I eased my hand from her larger one, aware of mixed sensations: Elvira was the most stunning woman I'd ever met, yet something in her demeanour whispered of dark, provocative secrets. I sensed my innocent eyes would be opened some day, and I hoped I could take in this new reality without making a fool of myself, or inspiring Elvira's wrath.

'Shall we begin?' Sybil called out. 'Our chocolate won't wait forever. And of course, the sooner we finish the morning's work, the sooner we can play.'

Like cogs in a well-designed clock, the assistants assumed their places. Elvira kept sorting, while Vee held a pan of acceptable cherries for Zee and Brother Paul to dip into the chocolate, which Brother Quentin kept stirring. Sybil handed me one of the trays lined with parchment. 'If you'll position this so the dippers can place

128

their cherries on the paper, and then set the full trays over on the tables, it would help us immensely.'

I grinned, glad to be useful while I could observe their precision operation. Sybil acted as go-between, fetching more cherries for Elvira and more parchment-lined trays for me, as well as standing in my place until I returned from the table.

Zee and Brother Paul stood facing each other across the pan of brandied cherries, plucking two in each hand, shaking them once, and then dipping them in the chocolate coating, which magically adhered to the fruit. With practised motions, they rotated the stems so the rich brown liquid stopped dripping and sealed itself, with uniform shape and thickness, before placing the finished sweets on my tray. I was so fascinated I had to remind myself to rotate the tray for them and then carry it off when it was full.

The kitchen hummed with the silent concentration of friends who worked well together, anticipating each other's moves. When an occasional cherry fell off its stem into the chocolate, Brother Quentin deftly picked it out with his spoon and dropped it into a pan beside him. 'That one just couldn't stand the strain of becoming such an exceptional treat!' he explained with a wink. 'But she'll find her place, sooner or later. We only dip cherries a few times a year, so we save some of the fallen fruit for our seasons' ceremonials.'

'Or for when we'd like something sweet and juicy to play with,' Brother Paul added coyly. 'We have to be careful, though. If those assigned to the vineyards or gardens found out how much we enjoy ourselves, they'd all want to work here, too.'

'And that would spoil everything,' Vee said with a grin. Then she turned towards Elvira. 'How many left, oh Amazon Queen?'

'Just the one pan,' came the throaty reply. 'I'm guessing we've done a record number this morning – perhaps fifty dozen – with damn few rejected ones.'

'We'll have to use those wisely, then,' Zee remarked. Her smile looked unusually sultry for a young woman with such an unassuming face.

'And we've very few saved back for this spring's ritual,' Sybil informed them, 'so we should set some aside before we get carried away.'

Their laughter spoke of a secret too delicious to share with those outside this close-knit circle, so I felt honoured to be standing among them. When Elvira rose from her stool, exclaiming, 'Done!' the excitement mounted. Brother Paul and Zee moved faster, in a contest to see who would coat the last cherry. Brother Quentin stirred carefully, as the chocolate at the bottom of the pot had thickened. I gripped my tray, trying to guess how the race would end.

'Mine!' Paul cried as he snatched the last two stems from the pan.

Quentin wagged his eyebrows at me. 'This means Brother Paul will decide the fate of our remaining cherries, and who gets them, and in what order.'

'Sort of a master of ceremonies,' I ventured.

'Precisely. And he always makes a fine one. There!' the bullish man beside me crowed. 'You may now carry these safely into the dining room, dear Mary, while we prepare for the festivities. Sybil's chosen one of our favourite days for you to join us, and we hope you'll come again. And again.'

Something in his words called up an image I couldn't pinpoint, yet its association sent a tingle through my insides. Even a novice like myself couldn't miss the insinuation that bawdy, provocative games were about to be played, by people who loved to outdo each other. I sensed these activities would be much more palatable than watching a dozen men pee on a tree.

'Let us practise wild abandon!' Brother Paul proclaimed, lifting a ceremonious hand. 'Our first event will be dipping dildoes, and creating a bust of Miss Sybil. Vee and Zee, if you ladies will do the anointing and assist us with the chocolate, I'll ask Elvira to hold our Kitchen Queen in position while her likeness is being cast.'

He paused, challenging the raven-haired woman with a look I didn't comprehend. 'You're welcome to compete with Quentin and myself, Elvira dear. If you're up to it.'

Elvira rolled her eyes. 'I always win, you know.'

'That's why I'm having you balance Sybil on your lap. It gives the rest of us half a chance.'

As this playful banter was exchanged, the others were slipping out of their tunics. I watched warily as Brother Paul, Brother Quentin and the two blonde sisters bared themselves and hung their clothing on pegs along the wall. 'Mustn't get our clothes dirty,' Sybil explained as she sidled up to me, 'or everyone's favourite laundress will wonder what goes on here.'

'And investigate, so she can tattle to the abbot,' Zee chimed in. She smiled warmly, and then assisted as Sybil peeled off her dark shirt and trousers. She and her sister had beautifully smooth skin, and breasts that peaked in nipples resembling raspberries, and identical blonde bushes. They seemed completely at ease as they fetched a jar of golden liquid and slathered it all over Sybil's globular breasts.

'That's good . . . quite nice,' my room-mate murmured as their caress continued. 'Anoint Paul and Quentin now, ladies. We'd better be dipping before our chocolate thickens any more. Are you ready for our instructions, Elvira?'

The statuesque woman was moving more deliberately than the others – and, like me, she still wore her tunic. Her smile betrayed a shyness I wouldn't have imagined in one so physically outstanding. Elvira seemed to notice my hesitation, and stepped closer.

'You see, Mary Grace, how Brother Paul and Brother Quentin are preparing for our first event? The object of this game is to make the most shells of this chocolate coating before climaxing, which requires great control.

131

We then fill the hollow, cock-shaped containers with nougat or other candy filling – or use the last of the thickened chocolate inside, which creates a most delicious dildo.'

I blinked with sudden understanding. Brother Quentin, the beefier of the two, now sported an impressive erection as Zerelda oiled it lovingly. Her sister worked on Paul, who eyed his opponent's pecker as though using it for inspiration.

'So you cover these, uh, body parts with the chocolate, until it hardens?'

'That's right. Takes a good double dipping to produce a shell that will hold up to filling – and then, of course, there's the challenge of deflating carefully, so as not to break one's shell, before rising to the challenge of making as many more as each contestant can manage.'

My face must've registered my surprise, because Elvira laughed until her bosom shook. 'I'm going to hold Sybil suspended on my lap at whatever angle Brother Paul dictates, which will create a casting we'll probably fill with wine, for a sipping contest some time in the future.'

This image, too, made my eyes widen – and they grew bigger still when the giant of a woman beside me ran a finger along my face. 'This must feel foreign to you, as a newcomer,' she continued in that throaty voice. 'So if you simply want to watch, that's your privilege, Mary Grace. If you care to join in, however, you're invited to lend a hand ... or a tongue, or whatever you care to contribute. And you do find this rather enticing, don't you?'

My glance had wandered to where Brothers Quentin and Paul sat across from each other, ready to compete. Sybil came up beside us, her expression teasing. 'Don't let Little Miss Innocent here fool you, Elvira. She's a wildcat once she gets warmed up. If she appeals to you, you ought to give our other boys a run for their money.

No doubt in my mind you can do that while you're holding me.'

Elvira shifted, looking as affected by the aroused bodies as I was. 'Does she know?'

Sybil shook her head. 'I always let people disclose their own secrets, my dear. Once Mary Grace grasps yours – in whatever way she will – she'll be fine with it. She's a quick study.'

The two of them exchanged a purposeful look. Then Brother Paul glanced our way, resuming his role as director of the activities. 'Elvira! Sybil! Get into your positions. Quentin and I are ready!'

Sybil went to fetch the stool, leaving me quite curious about the tall, onyx-eyed woman towering above me. Holding my gaze, Elvira slipped out of her tunic, to reveal the most prodigious cock I had ever seen! She then unfastened the short, artfully stuffed camisole that provided her with such remarkable cleavage, and handed her clothing to me. 'Will you please hang these on a peg?' she asked.

I now realised why her voice sounded gravelly; I couldn't stop staring at a smooth, hairless body of magnificent proportion – but a male body with the face and hairstyle of an alluring woman. 'Does . . . does the abbot know?' I squeaked.

'Absolutely not. But Sybil's bringing you here tells me you can be trusted, Mary Grace.'

I nodded rapidly. What would I say, after all? I wasn't sure Mrs Goodin or Father Luc would believe me if I told them Elvira's secret, anyway.

'If you don't mind, we'll save my explanations for later,' Elvira said. 'Right now, I'm going to show Brother Paul and Brother Quentin that two men can't outdo a woman, once she puts her mind to something.'

My thoughts skittered when Elvira took my hand. 'Anoint me, Mary Grace. You can assist with Sybil's dipping, and then with mine. I have a feeling we'll be an unbeatable trio before it's all over. And feel free to make yourself more comfortable, whenever you wish.'

Without further ado, Elvira perched on the tall stool, her legs spread slightly. A couple of playful pats invited Sybil to balance atop those muscled thighs, facing out in a kneeling position as two strong arms held her suspended. 'Let's do Sybil's first dip,' the raven-haired contestant suggested, 'and then I'll give you gents a challenge like you haven't seen in weeks. Miss Mary has agreed to be my inspiration.'

Vee came over with a deep pan of the chocolate, offering one end to me. We stepped around Elvira's extended legs and then raised the pan between us so Sybil could lower her firm, rounded breasts into the coating.

'Mmmm . . . nice and warm,' she breathed, and then she raised herself up to let the excess drip off. 'All right, Paul. Put me where you want me – but quickly.'

Vee took the chocolate away, and all eyes were on Sybil. She leaned out over Elvira's sturdy arm to display her fudge-covered front, looking like an erotic statue on a ship's bow.

'A bit lower,' Brother Paul crooned. 'Perfect! Balanced, with the nipples at the most advantageous angle. Are you ready, Elvira? Quentin and I can't wait forever, you know!'

I found myself intrigued. With oiled hands, I grasped the cock jutting up towards Sybil's stomach, and produced an immediate low moan and two inches of additional length. There was still so much I didn't understand about Elvira, yet no one seemed to consider this man in woman's clothing freakish or abnormal. So I laid aside my doubts. The long, pink shaft quivered in my fingers, until its owner whispered, 'Stop, dear heart – the object is for me to outlast Paul and Quentin! You're doing a lovely job, by the way.'

I glanced up into kohl-lined eyes that held praise and admiration. Elvira was trusting me, so I took one of the smaller pots of chocolate Zee had poured for our contestants and knelt beneath Sybil.

'On your marks – get set –' the sisters chanted, pausing for an unbearable moment, 'go!'

The three dippers thrust into their individual chocolate pots. I could see where I'd have to assist Elvira, who bore the added burden of balancing Sybil – who must be kept still as her casting dried, so it wouldn't crack. I scooted closer, shoving the narrow pot up over the stiff, pink erection facing me, then lowering it to catch the drips.

'Splendid,' Elvira breathed. 'Both you, and this warm, luxurious chocolate, Mary Grace.'

'It's not too hot?'

'Feels absolutely divine.'

'What . . . what keeps it rigid, once it's cooled? I asked.

'We stir in beeswax as we melt it, which adds flavour and hardens quickly – as you saw with the cherries.'

I nodded, unable to stop staring at Elvira's chocolate rod. Sybil was looking down at me, giggling as much as her cast would allow. 'Dip me again, Mary, and then tend to Elvira. Mind you, don't do anything suggestive while she's shrinking herself. Licking me wouldn't be a good idea until she's ready for a second casting.'

Indeed, Sybil's neatly-trimmed slit was positioned right in front of my face. I dodged her hint by doing as I was told, holding the pan of liquid chocolate so she could re-coat her breasts. I was setting the pan aside when I heard Elvira letting out her breath with a victorious little gasp.

'There's number one! Oil me again, Mary.'

The casting Elvira handed me was a perfect replica of a splendid pecker, right down to the little hole in the top, and the ridged edge of the head, and the veins that corded the underside. I had no time to study this piece, however, because Paul and Quentin sounded ready for second dippings as well. I quickly oiled the shaft before me, marvelling at how it blossomed in my hand.

'May I ask how you shrivelled so quickly?' I whispered.

'Let's just say I think cold thoughts of cold people,' Elvira replied with a nasty chortle. 'Right now, however, your touch is reviving me quite nicely. Are you sure you can resist that lovely cunt in front of you? Watching you lick Sybil would be . . . such an inspiration.'

The moment of truth had arrived: while I'd learned to enjoy Sybil's attentions, I had yet to taste a woman's nectar. Hers was flowing, too – gathering around the rim of her pink hole like milky honey, ready to spill over. Closing my eyes, I advanced towards her with my tongue extended, eliciting a pair of delighted sighs when I made contact with Sybil's musky cunt.

'Dip me now, darling. And then get right back to what you're doing.'

I obeyed eagerly, aware that our competitors were catching up, making the most of the attention Vee and Zee were giving them. When Elvira's cock was coated, I leaned up again, letting my curiosity lead my tongue. Sybil moaned and shifted, spreading her thighs to urge me on.

'Go deeper,' she rasped. 'Jesus, Mary, I've wanted this for so long. Get me out of this damn cast so I can enjoy you!'

Licking the dew from my lips – and catching the yearning expression on the face behind Sybil's thighs – I stood to assist her. It seemed feasible to cup the lifelike chocolate casting so that, with Elvira's help, Sybil raised herself out of it. She breathed her relief, her nostrils flaring at me like a dainty colt's, but her intentions got cut short.

'We need another bust of Sybil!' Brother Paul cried out. His erection stood up, proud and brown, yet he had the presence of mind to heckle us. 'Have to keep that Head Wench occupied so she can't distract the rest of us. We know whose team she's pulling for, after all!'

And so it went. I dipped Elvira a second time and

then smeared sweet-smelling oil over Sybil's lovely breasts, more enthralled by the feel of them than I thought I'd be. With no time to lose, however, I assisted her dip and by that time Elvira was easing out of a second casting.

'Oil me again, sweetheart,' she breathed. 'Don't be afraid to knead and squeeze me. It gets trickier each time I go up, after shrivelling it.'

I complied, and on impulse I also renewed my attentions to Sybil. Her moans proved quite inspiring to Elvira, who watched so eagerly as I drove my tongue in and out of that creamy slit that she felt compelled to join in. When Sybil let out a louder wail, like a she-cat calling to its tom, I realised Elvira was tonguing the hole behind mine – and loving it, by the way that cock sprang to life in my hand again. My face was so close to those chiselled lips, I stopped breathing for a moment.

'Dip me,' Elvira whispered, and then kissed my lips.

'Dip me!' Sybil squealed. 'Don't you two even think about ignoring me down there!'

I moved as fast as I could, realising Brother Paul and Brother Quentin might soon gain the advantage because they each had an assistant – and no wiggling woman on their laps demanding her due. I reviewed Elvira's explanation of this game, and considered a counter-strategy I hoped would work. Our opponents appeared as randy and close to climax as Elvira would soon be, if I weren't careful – although I had the feeling that Paul's excitement came from ogling the man facing him.

Not that it mattered. Our game was everything at the moment, and as rapidly as Elvira was panting into Sybil's arse, I sensed it would end soon.

'Go cold!' I whispered, taking hold of the chocolate shell that had hardened sufficiently.

Elvira stopped wiggling, and as soon as that member shrivelled just enough, I slipped the casing off it. Once again I oiled it, this time slipping my mouth over its pulsing hardness as I inserted two fingers into Sybil.

Again the shaft shot up, and after its initial dip, I offered my wet fingers to the lush lips I curiously wanted to kiss.

'Warm in here,' I rasped, my pulse racing as Elvira sucked up to my knuckles. 'You tend Sybil while I derail our competition. I won't be long.'

With a covert chuckle I stepped from between those long, smooth legs so I could catch Brother Quentin's eye. As I anticipated, he was rocking on his seat, straining to contain himself while Zee reached for the pot to give him a second coating. I stepped in front of him. Then I lifted my tunic quickly over my head, exposing myself more lewdly than I'd ever dared before.

Brother Quentin's eyes bulged and his face reddened with the strain. And when I cupped my breasts from the sides, creating an offering of my cleavage, he let out a cry. The chocolate on his cock shattered, sending a stream of semen on to Paul's stomach. The blond fired back, only his coating shot like a long brown bullet and smashed against Quentin's chest.

'Bravo! That's my Mary!' Sybil crowed. 'Now get me out of this thing!'

With utmost care Elvira lowered the redhead from his lap to the floor and relieved her of the hardened chocolate encasing her chest. Sybil in turn eased the chocolate from Elvira's cock. She turned to congratulate me, her eyes warning me that I was being ambushed from behind – but my arms were already being playfully pinned to my sides.

'And what punishment shall we deliver to this wicked little vixen?' Brother Quentin said from behind me. His breath teased my ear, and I felt his laughter rumbling in his chest. 'Seems to me she deserves a licking, from everyone present.'

'And what better way to use the brandy left in the pans?' Sybil suggested. 'Just this morning, Mrs Goodin warned us not to waste our supplies. So we'd only be complying with her command, wouldn't we?'

I was laughing too hard to be afraid, only faintly anxious as Vee and Zee fetched the pans while my captor planted me in the pot of chocolate. Like warm mud, the fudge oozed up between my toes, and then the blonde sisters were giggling on either side of me, pouring the warm, sticky brandy so it ran in rivulets down my breasts and back. It went down the crack of my arse, and saturated my bush, and then slithered into my slit.

'I think she's ready,' Brother Paul announced in a feral voice. 'Let's see how long it takes to make her cry for mercy!'

They converged on me like a pack of hungry dogs. Lips and tongues teased every part of my body while sly fingers entered me from front and rear. Brother Quentin centred himself in front of me to kiss me hotly on the mouth, so I didn't know whose mouth massaged my bottom or who was suckling each breast. Female panting and laughter mixed with male, and my body threatened to overload from all the sensations of their probing tongues and exploring hands.

'I bet she has the most delicious feet,' Zee suggested, and I was suddenly uprooted from my pot of chocolate. Elvira cradled me against her smoothly muscled chest, while Brother Paul sucked on one foot and Zee latched on to the other. I writhed, amazed at such exquisite torture. Was it Sybil kneeling beneath me, separating the halves of my arse? I felt Vee kissing my neck, and closed my eyes for the more thorough kiss I saw in Elvira's shining gaze.

The lips were a man's, hard and demanding, and I opened eagerly to them. I squirmed against the arms that tightened passionately around me, certain I was incapable of accepting any more pleasure. Then I heard a devious chuckle – Quentin's – and after he lifted my bush to wetly tongue my clitoris, he shoved something inside me.

My eyes flew open. 'What – ? Whose – ?'

Quentin's laughter came from between my legs. 'Now

139

you know why we delight in making these chocolate cocks, sweet Mary. I filled one of Elvira's with some of that fudge, so even after you've climaxed, there will be luscious pleasure left for the rest of us. How much more can you handle? It's only halfway in.'

I curled upward with the next thrust, barely containing a scream of utter ecstasy. Elvira smiled, a mere inch above my face. 'That's how you'll feel when I get my turn, lovely Mary.'

Again and again the velvety dildo was pushed and pulled, coating my inside passage with its lush warmth until I could hold back no longer. I cried out with loud, lusty wails that ricocheted from the copper pots hung by the hearth. I convulsed as though possessed by the Devil himself, and then fell limp in Elvira's arms.

'Welcome to the Kitchen Club,' Vee said with a giggle.

'We're so glad you could come,' Brother Quentin quipped, and he gently placed the dripping dildo on my chest. It had shrunk considerably, and it reeked of heated chocolate and brandy and my own copious juice. 'Since you so gamely entered into our fun, Mary Grace, you get to choose who'll tongue you out. Can't let all those choice ingredients go dribbling down your legs, wasted.'

'Wouldn't want to defy Mrs Goodin,' Sybil chimed in, making them all laugh. 'And Lord knows old Hortense would be green with envy if she knew how we've all enjoyed making Mary's acquaintance.'

'Or just making Mary,' Brother Paul added with a chortle.

'Better to be green with envy than red and scorched from the fires of Hell.'

The group sucked in its collective breath and drew instinctively closer together. But that didn't keep the dour woman in the doorway from seeing our unclad bodies, all caught in the acts of pleasure from moments before. I clenched my eyes shut, doom roiling in my stomach as the seconds of Mrs Goodin's silence ticked by. Elvira gave my shoulder a sympathetic squeeze, but it did nothing to relieve my mounting fears.

'Father Luc will see you now, Miss Michaels,' the housekeeper announced, her voice ugly with glee. 'He wants to discuss your next quilts. I'll tell him you're on your way.'

Chapter Twelve
Yet Another Cleansing

*A*s I hurried along the path to the abbey's imposing entrance, where the gargoyles leered with more menace than before, my tunic was sticking to all the wrong spots on my body and my hair was a ghastly sight. I could only wonder what sort of punishment awaited me when I reached Father Luc's office. Mrs Goodin had only had five minutes to tell her tales – but I suspected she'd set a nasty trap before coming to the kitchen. My thighs chafed with the memory of her lye soap as my footsteps echoed down the stone corridors. I entered that solitary hallway, nipping my lip.

Father Luc awaited me alone. He was seated on his thronelike chair, his hands tented beneath his nose, following the sinister lines of his black moustache. 'What day is this, Miss Michaels?' he demanded.

As I calculated back to when I left Mount Calvary, it seemed I'd crammed weeks into only a few days. 'It's Sunday, sir,' I murmured, already sensing where this path would lead.

'And have you attended Sabbath services?'

'No,' I replied, the heat rising into my cheeks. 'Have you?'

'I conducted mass at sunrise, before breakfast. I noted

your absence, Mary Grace, and was appalled that you've so quickly departed from the way in which your parents raised you.'

'Let's leave my parents out of this!' I retorted. While I was ashamed for forgetting what day it was, no one else had mentioned any worship services – nor had they behaved as though today was different from any other. 'And why are you mentioning this now? I'm getting pretty damn tired of everyone else knowing the routine here, and leaving me out!'

His coiled laugh warned me that I was playing into his trap. 'Sybil didn't inform you? She hasn't missed a Sunday service since she's been here,' he continued smugly. 'And Elvira – whom you undoubtedly met during your kitchen visit – is the finest organist Heaven's Gate has ever enjoyed. If I were you, I'd be wondering why my so-called friends didn't tell me about these things ... why they allowed me to blunder, and then pay the consequences. Perhaps you're associating with the wrong people.'

My mouth dropped open. 'You're the one who assigned me to Sybil's cottage!'

'Because she had room for you. Because we have so few women's quarters.'

'And you have nothing but praise for her cooking!'

The abbot chuckled as though he were dealing with a dense, witless woman. 'What Sybil and her crew produce in the kitchen is our business, Mary Grace. Our livelihood. Let's not confuse our earthly work with seeking our souls' places in the hereafter.'

When Father Luc leaned towards me, I noticed how his eyes burned with something familiar, yet something so cruel and vindictive it frightened me. I braced against his scrutiny, because it would be a sign of defeat to shrink away from his gaze.

'What's that I smell?'

'I don't know, sir. Your cassock looks fresh,' I ventured. 'Perhaps it's the soap and sunshine from Mrs Goodin's laundering.'

His mouth quirked. 'You reek of brandy, Mary Grace. Sybil invited you to assist with the chocolate-covered cherries, but you didn't have to return here smelling like one. Did you bathe in that liquor?'

I would have to reply carefully to this line of questioning, or I'd betray my new friends. 'I must've sloshed some on my tunic. It has a delightful pungency, doesn't it?'

The hint of a twinkle in those piercing eyes was all the humour the abbot allowed for. I suspected Mrs Goodin was waiting in the wings to join him in this interrogation, so I had to speak carefully. He had probably heard her account of our kitchen activities, and would mete out my punishment according to how bad a lie he caught me in.

'Remove your tunic. I can't possibly work in this small room with you smelling like fermented cherries.'

'I assume you have another one for me?'

'No. You'll have to wait for this one to be washed.' The planes of his face creased with a nasty mirth. 'Each resident is issued one tunic upon arrival, in keeping with our vow of poverty. Perhaps after this you'll take better care of your clothing, Miss Michaels.'

Did this mean everyone went around naked while his tunic was being washed? I had a hard time believing the monastery coffers were so low, or the residents so tidy, that the monks made do without any additional clothing! And yet ... I'd seen those men circling that pear tree, and Sybil's assistants had no qualms about hanging up their tunics when their games began. Perhaps I'd have to set aside my modesty, even though I didn't plan to remain here past May.

'Where's the dress I wore here?' I demanded, stepping forward to challenge him. 'If you think I'm going to do my quilting naked –'

'You'll do as I tell you.'

'– then Hyde's going to hear about your perverted –'

'He won't believe you.' Father Luc raked his fingers back through his raven hair, smiling arrogantly. 'If you tell him I forced you to strip, he'll chalk it up to your own wantonness – which he knows about, first-hand. And I'll attest to your need for penance, if you're to continue to live here. You've been nothing but trouble since you arrived, Mary Grace, and I have more important matters to attend than your behaviour. The sooner you obey me, the sooner you'll have your tunic back.'

No laundry would be done today. I glanced at my little corner beside that window – where anyone passing by could look in and see my naked state – and wanted to put up more of a fight. Yet my punishment for defying him would only increase with each passing moment.

And he was right: no one else would defend me to Hyde, because they all seemed quite comfortable shucking their clothes. I closed my eyes and tugged the bottom of my tunic towards my waist, hoping this would satisfy Father Luc's penchant for humiliating me. Hoping he wouldn't notice other substances I'd tried to wipe off before coming here.

When I stood clutching my sticky tunic against my front, the abbot cleared his throat. 'Look at me when I'm speaking to you, Mary Grace.'

I opened my eyes, knowing he'd found another path to pursue.

'Drop your tunic beside you.'

I did so, wishing my nipples didn't react to my lack of clothing. It repelled me to think that Father Luc's lecherous gaze might inspire the hardening of these buds, or the clenching of muscles in my nether regions, where my honey began to flow in spite of my growing resentment towards this man's manipulations.

'At the risk of embarrassing you with an indelicate matter, Miss Michaels – what's trickling down the inside of your leg? I hope you haven't become so upset while talking with me that you've soiled yourself.'

My face went fiery-hot. I was tempted to say yes, it was excrement and it expressed exactly what I thought of him. But Mrs Goodin would be all too pleased to wash my mouth with her lye soap, if I got too cheeky.

'Perhaps, Father Luc, I smell so horrible you'll want me to work in the cottage. If you find my personal hygiene lacking, I'll gather my things and go.'

He laughed abruptly. 'You smell like chocolate. Chocolate and your own musk.'

I remained silent. He hadn't asked a question, so it was better not to respond.

'Melted chocolate is one of this world's greatest delights,' he went on in a voice that raised the hair at my nape. 'It coats the mouth with velvety sweetness, and makes the palette – one's very soul – sing for joy, and for more chocolate. Don't you agree, Mary Grace?'

I had visions of him spreading my legs to indulge in the treat he described so poetically, and my body's reaction to this fantasy made me wish I could disappear between the marble tiles I stood on. 'Yes.'

'Yes, what?' he demanded, scooting forward on his chair.

'Yes, Father Luc. Chocolate is delicious.'

'Then we shouldn't waste a single drop of it.' His expression tightened and he folded his hands below his waist, where I suspected he had a large bulge. 'Cleanse yourself, Mary Grace. Catch the drippings on your legs, and then lick your fingers. Reach higher, until no trace remains on your private parts, or your pubic hair, or inside you. Then I shall deem you fit to continue your work here.'

My shock made him chuckle darkly. 'And if you find this too revolting, I'm sure Mrs Goodin will oblige me. She craves chocolate even more than I do.'

Heart pounding, I reached down to scrape the warm liquid from the inside of one thigh. Quentin's chocolate phallus had thoroughly coated my inside passage, and now gravity was running its course in a sticky stream. I licked my fingers quickly, eager to be done with this repugnant display.

'You should savour that, Mary Grace. Sybil and her assistants stir up the finest chocolate in the world, so suck those fingers slowly,' the abbot murmured. 'And tell me – what do you taste? Besides cocoa and sugar, that is.'

My cheeks prickled again. 'Myself, sir.'

'And what flavour might that be?'

My belly went tight with his question, causing more liquid to seep out. 'Salty . . . buttery.'

'Mmmmmm . . . keep cleansing yourself, Mary Grace. You seem to create more sweet, salty honey-butter by the moment.'

I couldn't look at him. Pretending my closed eyes were a part of that savouring he demanded, I scraped my fingers along the other leg and inserted them into my mouth, pulling them out slowly so I could indeed enjoy the consequences of our contest in the kitchen. I thought again of Paul and Quentin, firing their chocolate shells, and of mysterious Elvira kissing me deeply, and I could forget about my lewd spectator, who was probably pleasuring himself beneath his cassock. Visions of Sybil came to mind, proudly poised on Elvira's lap with her breasts encased in hardening chocolate, parting her legs in invitation as I anointed the curious man who held her.

I began to use both hands, dipping and licking one before quickly following suit with the other. The sensitive skin of my thighs quivered and I caught myself writhing, more aroused than I would ever want to admit once this shameless exercise ended.

'Spread further, Mary Grace. Scoop that dark, sweet liquor from your outer folds. Dip your fingers deep . . . deep inside you.'

I complied, wiping at my bush and my outer lips, and then sucking off the chocolate. My breathing was becoming shallower and more rapid with each stroke. Although I had to run out of that buttery-brown nectar

147

soon, my pussy was pulsing it out continuously and growing more excited by the second. I reached up inside, using three fingers as a scoop, and heard a low moan.

'Lie down,' the abbot rasped. 'Keep reaching into yourself, with your thighs wide, until I declare you completely clean.'

He demanded the most intimate of views, the most explicit means of exposing myself. As I sank to the floor, bunching my tunic beneath my head, Father Luc walked quickly into the little room where I'd dressed after my earlier episode with Mrs Goodin. He returned with a basin of water and a towel, which he folded, lengthwise, and then draped across my eyes.

'You're not nearly finished,' he chided in a breathy voice. 'Now keep those fingers moving, Mary Grace. You know what's required of you. You know that to fully purge yourself of that chocolate – however it got up there – you'll need to convulse like a female giving birth.'

He spoke in a different metaphor than others I'd met here, but his meaning was clear. The towel created a dimness I could hide behind, even though my sex was still blatantly exposed to him. Relieved that his house-keeper wasn't being called in, and aroused enough that my initial hesitation had disappeared, I thrust my fingers up my cunt again. I was rocking on the floor, my movements becoming more frantic between tastes of the syrup I brought out with wet, furtive noises. I felt the inner spasms beginning, like low and distant thunder before a storm.

A hand clamped around my feet, pressing the balls of them together while pushing down slightly to keep my legs open wide. 'It's running clear now,' the abbot whispered. 'Time for the final act of contrition, Mary Grace.'

The position he held me in intensified every sensation as I strove towards the climax that would settle this matter. I was somewhat constricted, unable to see, yet between the confines of my thighs, my slit and clitoris pulsed so powerfully Father Luc could probably view their movements. He would be looking directly down at them, as I felt his feet flanking my hips and his cassock fluttering around my bent knees. My fingers slid quickly along my wet slit while my thumb rubbed the aching nub adjoining it, until the warmth and the wetness and the illicit nature of this penance had me writhing up towards release.

Father Luc raised my feet, which elevated the sensations until I grimaced with an exquisite tightness that refused to be denied. As I cried out, I heard an answering moan. A torrent of hot seed splattered against my breasts.

I fell limp, and the abbot released me. 'Use the towel and water to wipe yourself, and then continue with your work, Mary Grace. You'll be sequestered in this room until Mr Fortune visits on Friday, to prevent any further temptations and the need for purging them. Your solitude will provide the time to contemplate your purpose here among us, and to plan your future work.'

'Yes, sir.'

'I'll inform Sybil of this situation, and instruct the others that you are to be left completely alone, for your own benefit. Do I make myself clear?'

I sighed beneath the towel, imagining a week in this claustrophobic room, naked, with only the abbot and Mrs Goodin for company. 'Yes. Quite clear.'

'Fine. Make yourself respectable, and be thankful for my lenience today. Your penance will be much harsher and more humiliating next time.'

Chapter Thirteen
My Guardian Angel

I was so overjoyed to see Beau trotting ahead of that familiar black carriage, I nearly cried. My five days of confinement in Father Luc's office had been less of a punishment than I anticipated, but only because Brother Christy appointed himself my ambassador. Although the abbot forbade him – or anyone else – to speak to me, the kindly friar brought my clean tunic on Tuesday, and carried in all my meals. And when I spotted Hyde through my little window, it was this blond, bespectacled friend who came to escort me outside.

Not that I would've awaited permission to leave: throughout those days alone, thoughts of my handsome benefactor had kept me from caving in to the loneliness Father Luc imposed upon me. My heart knew Hyde would be happy to see me, too, so by Friday I was determined to rush into his arms, abbot be damned. I nearly knocked Brother Christy against the wall in my haste to greet the man I loved.

'Mary Grace!' he sang out. And then we were embracing, kissing like impassioned animals. 'My God, how I've missed you, sweetheart. I've lost count of the times I almost told Sebastian to hitch up the carriage.'

'I wish you had,' I whispered against his neck. 'Oh, I wish you'd been here.'

Hyde gazed at me with those distinctive cinnamon eyes, which burned with his affection. Had ever two strong arms felt so comforting? In the week since I'd seen him, I'd been caressed in ways and places I couldn't have imagined before, but this simple hug in the sunshine felt better than all those other touches combined. It made me feel loved. And I had sorely missed that emotion since coming to Heaven's Gate.

Ignoring Brother Christy and the abbot, Hyde searched my face. 'Have things gone well, Mary Grace?' he asked with quiet concern. 'I'll pay off our arrangement and take you home, if you have the slightest doubt about staying here.'

From beneath that wedge of brown hair that hung rakishly over one eye, Hyde Fortune appeared as eager for me to leave the abbey as I was to go with him. My first impulse was to shout, 'Yes! Take me with you! Please take me home!'

And yet, with the abbot looking smugly on, flanked by the monk who'd befriended me, I couldn't concede defeat. If I went down that mountain, I'd have to tell Hyde of the degradation I'd suffered here, without confessing the more arousing aspects of my stay. I'd be admitting I couldn't keep my part of a bargain, which would mean – at least to me – I couldn't support myself with my sewing. I loved Hyde dearly, but I wasn't ready to depend upon him like a parasite. Especially if it meant living above his mortuary.

But mostly I envisioned Father Luc's laughter as he counted Hyde's money, his sneer as he bade me goodbye. And it would be just like him to recount my sins and shortcomings when Hyde visited in the future. He would delight in telling how easily I became aroused, and with how many lovers in how many different ways, to shatter Hyde's trust in me.

No, I couldn't leave here a loser.

151

So I put on a brave face. 'I've finished a quilt and started another! I've made several new friends. And Sybil even invited me to make chocolate-covered cherries.'

'You and your room-mate are getting on all right, then?'

I smiled, hoping he didn't read between my lines. 'Oh, she puts up a tough front, but inside, Sybil's a cream puff – if she likes you. And thank goodness, she's decided I'm worthy of sleeping on her couch.'

A dimple played in his cheek, perhaps betraying a recollection of his own experiences with her. 'If you're sure this is working out, I suppose I can endure the next few months without you. The house feels empty. Even Sebastian and Yu Ling miss you, Mary Grace.'

I was tempted to admit the truth, to leave this place before I got myself into deeper erotic waters than I could tread. But Father Luc's purposeful cough brought me out of my pondering. Why should I give him the satisfaction of seeing me leave with my tail between my legs?

'I miss you, too, Hyde. Dreadfully,' I whispered. 'But I'm a woman of my word. I'll stay and earn out my part of this bargain.'

He nodded, and with a quick kiss he ended our private conversation. 'Father Luc will be wanting the balance of his Christmas profits,' he said more loudly, 'and I've brought supplies Sybil needs in the kitchen. For you, my love, I have a trunkful of ball gowns, donated by the Ladies Aide Society. Many of them want one of your illustrated quilts, and seeing pieces of their own finery worked into the designs will send the bidding higher yet.'

'Thank you!' I squealed. 'I can't wait to see them.'

'And so you won't.' He gestured towards Brother Christy and the abbot, steering me to the back of his carriage. 'If these gentlemen will carry the trunk into your work area, I'll fetch the cash, and we'll settle up.

Then,' he whispered, 'you and I will settle a few things. Alone.'

Opening that trunk felt like Christmas. I pulled out shiny taffetas and tulles, rich velvets, silks and *crêpe de Chine*, along with patterned brocades in bright jewel tones that lifted my spirits like nothing else could. I felt someone behind me and looked up to see Brother Christy.

'You have quite a rainbow here,' he remarked, testing some of the fabrics between his fingers. 'Perhaps one of your quilts could illustrate the Noah's Ark story. This tweed could be the gopher wood for the boat – and look! Wouldn't this gold velvet make a fine giraffe!'

'You have a wonderful eye,' I replied. I could already see the bow of the boat in the quilt's foreground, with a shimmering rainbow behind it. Some animals would stand on the deck, and a serene white dove would bear an olive branch across the sky.

Hyde had joined us, and he was smiling slyly. 'I could even persuade a certain someone to buy that quilt for the church, Mary Grace. Delores Poppington was asking about you this week, and I told her some of your creations would soon be up for auction.'

'Lord knows she has the money for it,' I muttered, recalling the false-bottomed casket she'd bought her husband – and her ecstatic shrieks when Hyde was humping her in her own. 'Perhaps her conscience will drive the price on this fine piece as high as Mount Ararat.'

Brother Christy laughed. 'My offer still stands, to show you other cast-offs you could use for your quilts. Remind me some day, and I'll take you to where we keep them.' He nodded to Hyde then, and went on his way.

The money Father Luc had just collected drew Mrs Goodin like a magnet, so we left the two of them poring over the ledgers. I felt supremely happy as I linked my arm through Hyde's, and then let him help me into the enclosed carriage, where he pulled me into a deep, yearning kiss.

'Be thinking about where we can go,' he whispered, clapping the reins across Beau's backside. 'My buttons are ready to pop from wanting you.'

Arousal highlighted his virile face, and his words sent the wanting right between my thighs. I'd gained a great deal of experience among these randy abbey residents, but none of them had the voice or the way with words Mr Fortune wooed me with. I sensed our budding romance was a vital part of our lovemaking to him, as it was to me, and this set his affection apart from the games and rituals my new friends engaged in.

We entered a sweet-smelling kitchen that buzzed like a hive. 'You're just in time for a taste of the morning's work,' Vee sang out, and her sister added, 'Come look at these pretties.'

Hyde and I followed them through the kitchen towards the dining tables, where delicate fruit and pastry creations cooled. I took a long, appreciative sniff. 'Tarts, eh?'

Elvira glanced around, wearing a furtive smile. 'No one here by that description, surely. How are you, Hyde? Good to see you again.'

I watched with veiled interest as the man wearing fashionable male attire took the hand offered by one who dressed as a woman. Did Hyde know Elvira's secret? Their greeting was brief, because Sybil sashayed in with a tray of tarts still steaming from the oven.

'Just the man I was hoping to see!' she crooned with a seductive wink. 'I hope you've brought me something, instead of saving it all for Miss Michaels. I could use a long piece of hard salami about now!'

Hyde smiled, his eyes sidling to mine. 'You'll have to get your rise out of the yeast I brought you, Sybil. The rest of my goods go to Mary Grace.'

'Fine way to treat the woman who never lets you down,' she teased. Then she playfully pressed a cooled tart to his lips. 'See if this cherry's to your liking. And ask your lady friend about covering hers with chocolate a few days ago. She had a memorable morning.'

Hyde bit down, then shared his pastry with me. 'Every morning with you is memorable, Sybil,' he quipped, 'but today I'm interested in a cosy nook where Mrs Goodin won't yank open the door, and spies won't taunt us in the water. The hide without the seek, in other words.'

Sybil's smile lit up her dark-rimmed eyes and made the bangles in her ears quiver. 'I know a little cottage where the mistress won't be in until after dinner's served,' she hinted. 'And everyone else will be here in the dining hall. Just leave me a little something on the sheets to remember you by.'

Within minutes, Hyde, Brother Paul and Brother Quentin had unloaded the supplies, and we were strolling towards the bungalow with as much nonchalance as our desire would allow. My escort placed a hand on my back, hurrying me along, but he also waved to Brother Gregory and Brother Jack, who were returning from the pecan grove with loaded baskets.

'Would you look at the nuts on those guys?' Hyde teased in a low voice.

'I like yours better. How's Solomon these days?'

'Hard pressed, and in search of female company,' he growled, running his fingernails up my spine. 'He's especially fond of redheads who don't wear underthings. Know of any?'

'Two, actually. But if he's as wise as the story goes, he'll choose me.' I paused at the cottage door, glancing around the grounds. 'I have the distinct impression the other one is arranging a visitation of some sort, despite how deserted things appear. These people thrive on . . . exposing each other.'

'Surely not! Father Luc wouldn't allow it.' As we entered the cottage and he leaned against the door to shut it, Hyde's eyes glowed. I couldn't tell if he knew of the highly-sexed undercurrent at Heaven's Gate, or if he was truly unaware of how life here didn't reflect the typical monastery. 'All I know, sweet Mary, is that the past week without you has been hell, and that we have a lot of catching up to do before I leave this afternoon.'

My face fell. 'Must you go so soon?'

'Big funeral tomorrow. Rumour had it Mayor Bateman fathered a child out of wedlock, and his wife shot him. By the time the smoke cleared, the new mother decided someone else had sired her child, so then poor Mrs Bateman ate the pistol herself.'

'How tragic!' I whispered, before Hyde's searing kiss silenced me.

'Not nearly so sad as this pistol of mine,' he breathed. He guided my hand between his legs, where a bulge threatened to split the seam of his pants. 'Unfired for a week now, growing despondent and cold in your absence. What do you intend to do about that, sweet lady?'

At least he wasn't asking if I, too, had gone unfulfilled. I returned his kiss with a vengeance, wanting him more than Sybil or Ahmad or anyone else who'd been my teacher this week. I unfastened his fly, grasping his erection to lead him to the bed. 'I'm going to straddle your face and feel your tongue thrusting up my cunt,' I murmured. 'And when I can't stand any more of that, I'm going to mount you like a wild mustang and hang on for dear life!'

'Oh, God,' he murmured, tugging my tunic up over my head. 'Suck me, and buck me ... and then you'll have to fuck me!'

Hyde's words sent heat rushing through my body, now exposed to his view. He cupped my breasts, his hands urgent as they reacquainted themselves with the size and the weight and the roundness of them. My nipples popped out, and as I yanked his shirt from his pants I couldn't contain a lustful yelp. I bared his chest, splaying my hands across the muscled planes and then tickling his rigid nipples with my tongue.

He grunted and shoved me back on to the mattress. 'I hope fast and loose will suit you this time, sweetheart. Sol gets a little unruly when he's been deprived.'

'He'll be needing some discipline, then!'

His trousers hit the floor. Hyde climbed on top of me, kissing and prodding, but I rolled him on to his back before he could claim what he was after. Clambering over his chest, I spread my slickened lips with two fingers. 'Got your eyes on the prize?'

'Only long enough to see what I'm eating. And I'm a starving man, Mary Grace.'

I squealed as he gripped my hips. Shoving his tongue between my fingers, he probed deep and hard, rubbing my inner ridges with broad strokes as I worked my hand up and down to mimic his rhythm. My head fell back, taking my body into a more advantageous angle. He responded by sucking hard, creating a vacuum that squelched with my wetness. Inside me, the spirals tightened. I didn't want to come too soon, so I flipped over and faced his fine cock.

'Yes, suck me,' he begged. 'Dear God, Mary Grace, don't hold anything back!'

His raw command made me obey. I slid my lips down his shaft and dragged them up again, over the rigid veins and tight pink skin. Sol was in his glory, thrusting against my tongue while Hyde made little groans in his throat. Then it was I who cried out, when his mouth found my pulsing sex again and began to work it mercilessly.

We see-sawed, our heads and bodies rocking towards the release we both craved. I tasted the salt of his first droplets and ran my tongue around the hard ridge of his head. Cradling his sac, I rubbed my thumb around the root of of him, inhaling his heavy male musk while continuing to suck up and down.

As we moved into a position where we could observe each other's ecstasy, a prickling at the back of my neck told me we were being watched. 'Have you noticed the cottage has no curtains?' I whispered, again guiding him on to his back.

'I'd much rather gaze at you than count the heads at the windows,' he answered with a low laugh. 'It's your call, Mary Grace. We can give them the show they're hoping for, or we can pull the coverlet up and fuck for dear life underneath it.'

I couldn't tell him how many times, in how many ways, people here had watched me climax, when just a week ago I'd considered lovemaking a private thing. Despite the way my modesty had vanished, my time with Hyde was too precious to be flaunted before the eyes at the window. I would beat Sybil at her own impish game.

'Cover my bare arse and let's get to it!' I breathed. 'There's something to be said for keeping the audience in the dark.'

Chuckling, Hyde hauled up the counterpane until we were immersed in a dim, airless heat that only increased our hunger. I straddled him, staying low as I slid down to his tip. He entered me with a muffled grunt, and I wriggled against him, squeezing his cock with muscles that had sorely missed Solomon's girth. Hyde planted his hands on my backside to guide the slow, steady motion that gave our onlookers little to go on, yet increased the internal heat our bodies had been stoking like a boiler ever since we'd caught sight of each other.

The air beneath the blankets grew heavy with our scents. We rocked together, keeping our movement to an absolute minimum. It had an astounding effect: stifling my senses of sight and sound, and limiting my ability to thrust, forced me to focus upon those inner subtleties, creating a delicious friction between us.

Our climax took us by storm. No sooner had I begun to buck than Hyde hugged me close and lunged upward, sucking air through his teeth. For long, lovely moments we shuddered with spasms that made the bed creak like a field of mating cicadas, until we fell limp. Solomon oozed out of me with a little river of cream, and I chuckled at the tickling sensation.

'I guess this juice dribbling down your thigh will be the memento Sybil requested,' I whispered. 'But right now I don't care who's at the window. I've got to have air!'

The quilted counterpane flew off us before I could reach it. I squinted at the sudden rush of daylight, to see my room mate's foxlike grin. She stood beside the bed naked, inhaling deeply on her cigarette as she gazed at our entwined bodies.

'So you finally got to use the bed, eh?' she teased in a smoky voice. 'Seems only fair I should collect a little something for that – not to mention for asking my kitchen assistants to keep everyone else occupied at the dining hall. What's my silence worth to you, Mary Grace?'

I wavered, wondering what Hyde must be thinking about this jaded woman.

'After all, I let you have Mr Fortune all to yourself, uninterrupted.'

'But you eavesdropped the whole time, didn't you? Dammit, Sybil, is nothing sacred?'

She rolled her kohled eyes and laughed, which made her breasts jiggle pertly. 'Sacred? You have a lot to learn, my naïve little friend. Would you rather I keep your secrets – and keep your sweet little pussy safe from all the men who want to invade it? Or would you prefer another stint of solitary confinement with Father Luc?'

My chest constricted. Sybil was saying far more than I wanted Hyde to hear, and she apparently intended to blackmail me with the abbot, as well. 'You wouldn't tell him what Hyde and I have been doing!'

She arched an eyebrow. 'In case you haven't noticed, the abbot and I have a rather unique relationship. I'm only asking for something I suspect you really want to give me, Mary Grace,' she whispered. 'And I know Hyde would like to watch. But he must promise not to question you about our ways here at Heaven's Gate. He must entrust you to my care for the duration of your stay. And you must give yourself over to me, too, pretty Mary.'

Hyde had followed our exchange as he lay beneath me. He raised up on to his elbow, frowning. 'Are you saying Mary Grace is in danger?'

'Of a life-and-death nature? Of course not.'

'Then why am I not to ask any questions?'

Sybil grinned slyly, thrusting her breasts forward as she stepped closer to the bed. 'Because I said so!' she teased. 'Because if you interrogate her too much, she'll revert to that shy, unsophisticated state in which she came, missing the chance to develop her full potential as a woman – as a much more enjoyable wife for you, dear man.'

'But I came here to sew. To establish myself as an artisan,' I protested.

'And you're doing a beautiful job of it,' my room-mate crooned. Then she smiled, cocking one knee up on the edge of the bed. 'But think of all the other things you've learned this week, and how they might improve your enjoyment of marriage when you leave us. Hyde will never be satisfied with a submissive wife who lies flat on her back. He also loves to watch women who are hungry for each other.'

Sybil caressed my dishevelled hair, her gaze intense. 'If I live to be a hundred, I'll never forget the way you threw me down on this bed that first night, and rammed your hand up me,' she murmured. 'And you'll always recall the way I made you squirm and scream on the couch. Won't you?'

I swallowed hard, my eyes fixed on her slender face. She stood close enough that I caught the scent of her musk, and when her fingers trailed lightly down my neck I shivered with delight. Sybil wasn't demanding anything more than she'd already given me; the same sort of shared pleasures Hyde had encouraged with Yu

Ling. I thought back to being in the tub with the Celestial – to his guttural response when his serving girl guided my hand between her legs. I'd come a long way since then, on an inner journey that amazed me.

So when Sybil gently steered my fingers beneath her russet bush, I didn't jerk away. I explored her folds with a knuckle, watching her smile flicker as her honey wet my hand.

'So – we've reached an agreement? Hyde won't ask, and I won't tell? You'll become my protégée, and I your guardian angel?' Her tight voice betrayed her arousal, yet she controlled her reactions until her terms were met.

Fortune's face, so alluring with that masculine shadow along his jaw, reflected his interest in what was about to transpire. 'I can live with that, yes,' he murmured. 'And I'm getting out of your way, ladies, so I'll have a better view.' He shifted from under me and scooted an upholstered chair alongside us, as though the bed were a stage.

Sybil sprang on to the mattress, her eyes alight with triumph. 'You won't regret this,' she breathed. 'I've wanted you since you first came here, and I'm happiest when I get what I want! I can't wait to feel your tongue driving into my cunt, Mary Grace.'

She arranged the pillows against the wooden head board, and then sat back with her legs bent. After taking a last draw on her cigarette, she stubbed it into the ashtray on the vanity. Sybil made an engaging sight, with her honey-red waves falling over her bare shoulders and her breasts framed between her knees, but what I saw in the mirror stopped my heart.

Brother Christy stood in the doorway.

I'd been too surprised by Sybil's ambush to notice his presence, and I doubted Hyde had seen him, either. Something in the monk's expression told me he'd witnessed our entire conversation. His lenses caught the light in a way that obscured his eyes, but his stance

161

suggested an avid interest in the protective partnership my room-mate and I had just agreed upon.

Had Sybil asked him here? Or had he arrived in time to watch what he thought Hyde and I would be doing? I wasn't sure I wanted to know.

And since Sybil was simmering like a pot of chocolate, warm and sweet and fragrant, I didn't want to stop what she'd started. Her gaze was riveted on my body while she toyed with the coarse hair curling around her cunt. 'Isn't she lovely, Fortune?' she whispered, spreading her juice with a fingertip. 'You're a lucky man, and I'm grateful you're willing to share.'

Hyde smiled, dimpling his face. 'I wouldn't do that for just anyone, Sybil. You've made quite an impression on our Mary, while remaining aware of her sheltered upbringing. By the time she comes home to me, I'll be greatly indebted to you. And I'll appreciate knowing she hasn't been ravished by every randy monk at the monastery.'

Sybil glowed with his compliment. She focused on my face, her fingertip still working the moisture into her open folds. 'You've never studied a woman up close, have you?' she whispered. 'What do you see, Mary Grace? Did you expect the intricate textures and scent? The delicate palette of pinks and crimsons? I'm so damned excited I could come, but I'm holding back . . . waiting for you to move much, much closer and touch me. Waiting for you to taste me.'

My own slit quivered. I watched, fascinated, as cream the colour of pearls appeared around her open hole, pooling in the scarlet recesses. Sybil began to gyrate, sinking deeper into her pillow so she could display herself even more. Her sex was petalled like a poppy, with the deepest shades of red at its core, blending into the rosier hues of its outermost folds. With forked fingers she drew back her mound. Her clitoris stood proudly at attention, beckoning me.

I leaned forward to stroke it with a curious fingertip.

Sybil's sigh filled the room and elicited a deeper one from Hyde, so I became bolder. Flattening on to my stomach, I eased towards her mesmerising sex and the slender finger she probed it with. Sybil slipped lower, until she was offering herself up, only inches away.

'Lick me,' she whispered. 'Keep it light – just the tip of your tongue exploring the rim. I want to save that thundering little bud for last, all right?'

I nodded, knowing how sensitive she would be there. On impulse, I blew a stream of air across it, and her desperate laugh urged me on. She smelled of a secret heat destined to scorch me like the fires of hell, yet I dipped my tongue where her fingers had been. My first taste was but a delicate sipping, which I paused to consider as I ran my tongue over my lips. When I looked up, above the curls so like my own and the rounded peaks beaded out with desire, Sybil's intense gaze sent a tremor through me.

'Take me,' came her breathy command.

I plunged my tongue inside her, rolling it into a point to stroke her upper wall. Sybil moaned and thrust against my mouth, opening further to receive every inch of attention I could lavish upon her. I pushed her cushiony mound higher, to reveal the folds and creases around an opening that pulsed with more cream. With firm, lapping strokes I pleasured her, alternating inner exploration with teasing circles around the crinkly red rim.

She panted, spearing her fingers into my hair. 'I'm so close . . . so close . . . oh God, Mary Grace, you're driving me insane!'

I pressed my lips against hers and sucked, flattening my tongue inside her, driving it in and out. Her cries rang around us and she writhed wildly, gripping my head between her flapping legs. When I sensed she was nearing her peak, I flicked her distended little clit. Just three light flutterings and Sybil screamed, undulating with a dewy delight that crested and ebbed, and then crested again for several moments.

She finally fell back, panting. I kissed her thigh, amazed at the sleek muscles and the softness of her skin. When she relaxed her hold on my head, I glanced in the mirror. Brother Christy was gone. Hyde was fondling a cock that looked raring to go again, and when our eyes met he rose from his chair.

'Point that arse in the air, woman. I want you from behind.'

As he clambered on to the mattress, I was aware of my own sex throbbing for attention again, as well. He slipped into my cunt, until his blunt tip struck the sweet spot far up inside me. I rose on to my knees then, loving the wrap of his sturdy arms beneath my breasts. The spasms were gathering, coiled to spring, and I let my head fall back on his shoulder.

I felt the lips of my sex being licked, and when I opened my eyes, the reflection in the mirror riveted me. Hyde held me from behind, his expression tense with imminent climax, while Sybil's head bobbed between my legs. I felt her fingering Hyde's sac as she lapped at me, felt his shaft pumping like a piston. Never had I been so deliciously helpless, nor had I experienced such a mix of sensations. I abandoned myself to them, letting them carry me upward on a rapture that suddenly flashed like white lightning inside me.

My cries reached fever pitch and I felt Hyde convulse. Warm, creamy wetness filled me and I relaxed against him, panting. Sybil knelt before us, running her hands lightly over my thighs and belly, following her fingertip trails with airy kisses. She cupped my breasts, worshipping each one with a fervent mouth while I watched, fascinated. And when Hyde eased out of my slit, she smiled slyly.

'Hold her there, Fortune. Let's see how many more times she's good for.'

I was too surprised to protest – not that Sybil would've

listened. Like a thirsty dog, she lapped the juices running from my cunt. The room was redolent with all our scents, an intoxicating blend that drove her on. With fingers and lips and tongue she plied me, spreading my thighs further with the help of her accomplice. I scarcely regained my breath before I began to pant again, rising like a phoenix from the remains of my first release. Hyde was kissing my neck, whispering encouragements, as I reached a shattering peak. I rode on waves that rushed ashore and eased back, to rise higher and then linger in enticing little ripples before crashing yet again.

When I fell slack, Hyde caught me. His chuckle rumbled against my back as he held me close against him. 'Oh Mary, sweet Mary Grace,' he murmured. 'You've only begun to discover what loving can do. And I was lucky enough to be here for it. But I really must head down the mountain now.'

'Come again,' Sybil quipped. She fell back on to the bed, landing in the pillows with an exhausted plop. 'I think we've convinced her that, while others can walk her down a path of promises, Hyde and Sybil will deliver her . . . into ecstasy, and out of mischief that can't possibly measure up.'

Fortune smiled at me as he dressed. 'I'll be back next Friday, with money from your finished quilt. What shall we call it? "Pussy in the Garden"? Or, "Pussy on the Prowl"?'

I laughed weakly and let him kiss me, already aching with goodbye.

'I'll see myself out, ladies. Do try to behave in my absence.'

The door closed and silence filled the room. Sybil sat up, raking her unruly waves back from her face. I lay there watching her subtle, supple movements, the golden skin flowing over well-toned muscles. And while I admired her beautiful breasts and the flat of her belly and the flare of her hips, I rested content in the knowledge that Hyde excited me more.

She patted my calf as though she'd read my thoughts. 'You don't mind that I've appointed myself your guardian angel, I hope?'

'I may need one some day,' I replied, wondering about my answer if Father Luc asked how I'd spent my afternoon. 'You realise Brother Christy witnessed our pact?'

'It's just as well, since I can't be your constant shadow. If you wish to remain chaste for Hyde, Christy can be trusted above the others.' She smiled quizzically. 'The kitchen crew sometimes speculates as to whether he's been unmanned, or was born without all his parts. He doesn't have the same ... urges as the rest of us.'

I nodded, wondering if I had enough energy to dress. It was only mid-afternoon, so I had to account for my time with the abbot. 'He's shown an interest in my quilts, though,' I remarked. 'Gave me a good idea for my next one, and has offered to take me where they store the discarded clothing. With four more to sew, I'll be needing a variety of fabrics and ideas.'

'The catacombs, eh?' Sybil glanced away, her expression furtive. 'Be careful down there, Mary Grace. You never know what might spring out from those old crypts and crannies.'

Chapter Fourteen
A Snake in the Garden

*A*lthough I still thought of Sybil more as a fallen angel than a guardian, my life at Heaven's Gate settled into a cosy routine over the next several weeks. Whatever she'd said – whether in the form of warnings, threats, or ultimatums – I was no longer the target of every monk's lust, nor were my times with Hyde considered opportunity for group entertainment. I sat with my room-mate and her kitchen crew during Sunday services. I completed my second quilt, as well as the splendid Noah's Ark design Brother Christy had suggested. I was no longer an outsider, nor a woman to be tricked and ridiculed.

Best of all, because Hyde auctioned my garden quilt for five hundred dollars, and sold the second for almost as much, Father Luc allowed me to work unhindered, and to assist in the kitchen whenever I desired other company. It was the scene Hyde had sketched before bringing me here – or at least a closer match than I'd known my first week. And when Mr Fortune presented us with a cheque for three hundred and fifty dollars – half of what he'd convinced Delores Poppington to pay, to donate the Noah's Ark quilt to Papa's church – no one was more delighted than I! Mary Grace Michaels was becoming a recognised name about town; a respected talent whose work commanded a pretty price, and a woman who now had her own growing bank account.

When Hyde returned to town after that early-March visit, I gleefully shared my success with Brother Christy. 'Look at this,' I said, showing him the proceeds from my latest sale. 'That velvet giraffe and the rainbow of brocades was an inspired idea. What should I design next?'

The monk looked at the cheque, and then wiped off his spectacles to study it again. 'My stars,' he breathed. 'With what you've earned us so far, Heaven's Gate could function a year or more without producing another pound cake.'

He glanced up, his expression speculative. 'How many more quilts did you agree to make, Mary Grace?'

'Three, by the end of May. I could use my mountain aspen quilt as one of those, but right now I'm looking for another unique idea. Something bold and colourful.'

We stood in the sunshine, near the gardens where roses and azaleas bloomed in perpetual splendour. Brother Christy's hair shone like a halo, while his chubby cheeks took on that glow of saintly conviction I often saw there. 'Walk with me,' he suggested, taking my hand. 'Nature is often our best inspiration. Heaven and Earth provide a lush palette, if we observe with open minds and eyes attuned to a higher purpose.'

I had strolled these grounds between long stints of quilting, so the gardens and the cottage yards were now quite familiar. As we continued towards the orchards, I sensed the monk beside me had an ulterior purpose; something besides ideas for illustrations.

'Ahmad has been asking about you,' he remarked quietly. 'He wonders if you've been avoiding him, or shunning what he would teach you.'

I'd seen this mystical creature at meals, and had waved at him during my walks, but Brother Christy's comment summed up my attitude perfectly. How did I politely tell this friar I didn't want Ahmad's long, ring-pierced cock rammed up my backside?

'Often, when I need uplifting or inspiration, I come to the orchards to talk with him,' the man beside me went on. 'He has an innate sense of my needs. Because he's attained a high level of spiritual understanding, we often communicate without needing to speak.'

This brought to mind a ribald picture of Ahmad humping the chubby monk. Not good material for a quilt illustration, but food for thought nonetheless. 'Yes,' I replied, 'Ahmad has a definite presence. A way of transcending ordinary expectations to impart his wisdom in memorable ways.'

Brother Christy flashed me a wry smile. 'You don't like him, do you?'

I laughed. We'd suddenly come from the cosmic to rock-solid honesty. 'Actually, he fascinates me. But some of his ... teachings involve more intrusion than inspiration.'

'Perhaps today you'll be more receptive. Ahmad's a persistent sort, but once he's achieved his aim, he moves on without belabouring his point.'

I wasn't surprised Brother Christy knew how I'd refused the black man's advances, and as we approached the neat rows of apple, cherry and pear trees, his motive became clear. The two men who'd declared themselves my protectors had a plan: my afternoon would be spent pursuing that epiphany they'd mentioned. While I could choose not to accept such instruction, it would only prolong these secretive sessions designed for my enlightenment.

'Ah – there he is, among his beloved bees.'

I followed the monk's extended finger, looking beyond the trees to the stacked white hives. While I considered bees a necessary evil – and they were certainly a mainstay at Heaven's Gate – I could never trust creatures with stingers. They seemed far too interested in me, even when I did my best to avoid them.

Yet as we drew near enough to observe Ahmad working the hives, I stood in awe. The tall black man, naked, was nothing short of astounding: his muscles rippled with his measured movements and, yes, that eternal erection led the way as he lifted slats fat with honeycomb.

Brother Christy grasped my hand, a signal to walk no closer. 'He works without a smoker, so we must be careful not to disturb them,' the monk whispered.

Ahmad replaced the flat lid of the hive, and then turned towards us with utmost grace, smiling like a benign Nubian god. He was covered with bees. The shine surrounding his onyx body was actually the sunlight reflected from thousands of tiny wings. The insects had settled in his hair and on his face, and as he raised his arms to assume the shape of a cross, I saw bees crawling on his legs and upon that rod he pointed in my direction.

'Ah, Mary Grace, my petulant petunia,' he crooned. The movement of his facial muscles made the bees shift around his piercing black eyes. 'You've come to yourself, so you've come to me. You now witness the state of inner tranquillity to which you should aspire. Because I listen to the wisdom the bees impart, giving them my total devotion, they allow me to move among them unharmed, and to take the gift of their nectar. Are you ready for the next level of my instruction?'

I bit back an outburst about how I detested insects with stingers. 'What would you have me do?' I breathed.

The magnificent bee-covered Ahmad bowed slightly. 'I applaud the willingness in your voice, reflected in the openness of your soul. However, I cannot expect you to tolerate the bees' intimate attention just yet, so Brother Christy will escort you to our sacred grove. Immerse yourself in prayer as you await me, my precious pupil. Light the incense to create a holy smoke, and I will come to you, to anoint you with the wisdom of my words and the fire of my loins.'

170

I gladly followed Brother Christy out of the orchard, yet my insides tightened. There could be no mistaking what Ahmad intended, and my other protector would be his accomplice. To reassure myself, I whispered, 'Have you ever let the bees cover your body that way?'

'Oh, no!' he exclaimed. 'Ahmad is in charge of the apiary, and all of us rejoice in that!'

I breathed easier. At least hundreds of buzzing little bodies wouldn't accompany my instruction. As we came to the ring of trees laden with bright, shining apples, however, it became obvious this session had been planned.

'Now there's a picture for a quilt!' the monk said, gesturing towards the semicircle of green trees bearing their red fruit. 'Reminiscent of the Garden of Eden, don't you think?'

Or the Fall of Man, I mused, searching the grassy ground for a snake. 'I'll keep it in mind. I was hoping for a scene with a wider range of colours and texture.'

'And by the time you leave here – if you comply – you will have experienced a veritable kaleidoscope, Mary Grace.'

'And if I don't?' I blurted. I disliked the sharp, thin line his mouth had become.

'We'll try again. And again. Ahmad senses your potential, so considers it his mission to develop you to the highest level of comprehension. Anything less would be a waste of both your talents.' With that, Brother Christy slipped a bandanna from his pocket and wrapped it around my eyes. 'I am to prepare you for this journey. While I set the incense afire, you should remove your tunic.'

This monk had certainly seen me naked, yet I balked. 'I don't understand why –'

'Yes, you do,' he intoned from close behind me. His hands met at the juncture of my thighs, creating an awareness in my sex. 'And when Ahmad has finished, I'll reward you with colours and textures like you've

171

only dreamed of, sweet Mary. Fabrics fit for a queen will be yours, if you keep our commandments.'

I swallowed, wishing I could watch Ahmad's arrival. I reminded myself that these two men could allow no real harm to befall me, because I'd established myself as a source of income. Yet inside I quivered. And as I slowly peeled my tunic up over my hips, I realised my fear was feeding an excitement that now wet my sex. The memory of Ahmad's hands massaging my arse and my inner folds made those parts of me tingle as I bared them. I stood then, awaiting further instruction. I could feel Brother Christy's gaze upon me as I caught the first scent of smoke.

'Assume a position of humility, Mary Grace. Prepare yourself for the man who comes to us even as I speak. He'll expect your complete submission.'

I let my tunic drop and knelt in the cool, thick grass. Was I facing the correct direction? Would I be able to carry through with this intrusion of my most private part? As I flattened my hands on the ground to rest my forehead upon them, I had no more time to worry about it: I could feel Ahmad's approach. His charisma preceded him, causing a thrill of gooseflesh to cover my exposed parts, even as I heard a faint buzzing and felt an occasional flicker against my skin.

I clenched my teeth. Damn that man, to arrive with the beasts I most feared!

'I see you are preparing yourself, my precious peony,' came the familiar voice. 'And you flinch, shrinking from the bees who couldn't bear to leave my company. Be still, Mary Grace, and know that I am in control – unless your rash behaviour inspires their wrath. They only sting when provoked, you know. They will respect my presence and be lulled by the incense, as long as you accept my instruction . . . the affection I long to share with you, my pretty princess.'

With my head pressed to my hands and my arse in the air, I hardly felt like royalty. At the first contact of

Ahmad's hand, however, I let out the breath I'd been holding. His slender fingers slipped inside me, loosing my juices. He was kneeling behind me, his body large and warm against mine as he plied my inner passage with sure, steady strokes.

'Tell me how much you like this,' he murmured.

'Ohhhhhhhh . . .' The ring in his cock swept along my crevice, but made no effort to enter.

'We'll review our last lessons, and continue from there. My friend, if you'll bring that censer closer,' he instructed the monk, 'Mary Grace may inhale deeply and let the smoke work its magic while I beguile her.'

I was then enveloped by a heavy aroma that hung in my lungs. Curiously sweet it was, to the point of being cloying, yet Ahmad's insistent fingers coaxed me into breathing it in, several times in succession, until I experienced a heady weightlessness.

'Yes, precious Mary, relax,' the mysterious man behind me instructed. 'Let me have my way. Trust me to lead you along a path of new knowledge.'

My next cry was mixed with shrill laughter, because a damp, pointed tongue had found its way between the halves of my arse. I aimed my posterior higher, moaning as Ahmad dipped into that puckery portal I'd previously refused him. A light, flickering finger circled my clit, then spread my wetness around my folds and the hole that was aching for want of attention. Next thing I knew, he was spreading something thicker, and stickier.

'You must obey and submit,' he instructed, 'because the bees will be attracted to their honey – and your own. Raise yourself up, Mary Grace. Accept Brother Christy's assistance.'

'Or mine,' another voice cut into the spell he was weaving. 'Sybil sent me for apples, warning me to watch for serpents in the garden. And I see a long, black snake trying to bedevil you, Mary Grace.'

That low, hoarse voice could only belong to one woman – or man, as it were. 'Elvira?'

173

'At your service,' came the reply, and then she squatted beside me. 'If this isn't the sort of attention you want from Ahmad, I'll escort you back. Are you aware he and Christy are plying you with opium?'

I shook my head, awash in a pleasing sense of altered reality.

'She's come here of her own volition,' my teacher challenged. 'I'm relaxing her to make her more receptive, more accepting of the wisdom we've already prepared her for.'

'We're not expecting anything of Mary Grace she hasn't given to others,' the monk added. 'She's asked for colourful inspiration for her next quilt, and I'm granting her request.'

Elvira let out a sarcastic snort. Then she stroked the loose hair from my forehead. 'It's your choice,' she said softly. 'Sybil sent me to watch out for you, so your wish is my command, sweet Mary.'

I wavered for a moment, blindly reaching out – glad when a large, warm hand engulfed mine. 'Stay with me,' I whispered. 'Once this initiation is complete, I can move on to my next quilt. I just want to prove – to Ahmad and myself – that I'm open to new experiences.'

I must have made myself clear, despite my muddled state, because my newest protector shifted around in front of me.

'We will now resume,' Ahmad said testily. 'If you'll bring her to a state of arousal, in a form she enjoys, you'll divert her temporary discomfort as I raise her level of comprehension from a different direction.'

'And by doing so,' Brother Christy chimed in, 'we will allow Miss Michaels to chastely honour Mr Fortune's intentions towards matrimony.'

I smiled at the mention of Hyde's name as Elvira's fingers slipped into my slit. Her stroke was less confident, yet the unrhythmic attention gave me something to concentrate on as my arse was being honeyed like a bun. Up inside me Elvira ventured, with two probing

174

digits, squatting so close her breath fell upon my half-covered face. I imagined her upswept curls, and the male features disguised by kohl and rouge; it was a secret to savour, knowing a thick, randy shaft jutted beneath her tunic. In my curious mental state, it seemed only right to share my rising excitement: reaching discreetly beneath her clothing, I grasped Elvira's erection. The answering gasp spurred us both on, as though no one else were present.

Ahmad slid his finger in to the knuckle, and then to the next joint. I sucked air, and incense filled my nostrils.

'What do you see?' Brother Christy inquired.

Behind my blindfolded eyelids floated a panorama of images – some I recognised, and some which made no sense at all. 'A swirling of blue and yellow . . . throbbing purple dots with lots of little lightning strikes.'

Ahmad eased the rest of his finger up and then pulled it out slowly, repeating his little trick a few times. The sensation almost overwhelmed me, having the hand of one man rubbing against the hand of another, with only a thin wall of my inner muscles between them. I rose higher on my knees and began to pump, craving more of the intensity building from both sides.

'Ah, my little piece of paradise,' the man behind me encouraged. 'Ride with the current we're creating. Let yourself go, and let me go with you.'

At the prodding of his metal ring, I hesitated – but then received another noseful of that smoke. I felt strangely detached from myself, ready to float away, except the man on either side of me prevented it. Ahmad's chest expanded as he drew breath, and then he thrust through the honey and the muscles that had previously rebuked him, letting out a triumphant groan.

My cry echoed in the grove, the pressure inside me was so great. I was on the verge of exploding but didn't know which opening to let go of first.

'Take it slowly. The bees must savour this with us,' he whispered, so I clamped my mouth shut. Indeed, I still felt the occasional flickering touch and heard their buzzing, but the fact that I couldn't see made me extremely aware of my throbbing passageways. In and out the two men thrust, until I reached a height so bright with jewel-toned light I could scarcely bear it.

'Oh, God . . . the stars are pulsing behind my eyes, and my pussy is ready to – ready to –'

I screamed with a climax so shattering I didn't know if Ahmad or Elvira reached one. I felt myself slipping into a void of unconsciousness. I was vaguely aware of writhing, as though having an erotic dream while I slept, and then there was another voice calling me back to reality.

I shook myself, tugging at the blindfold. Mrs Goodin stood just inside the clearing, a basket of laundry perched on her hip. Her expression looked as starched as her uniform collar.

'I thought Father Luc's admonitions had finally taken hold, but I see I was wrong,' she said archly. 'What am I to think, finding you here naked with three men? What am I to tell the abbot?'

With that, she scurried between Elvira and Brother Christy to snatch my tunic from the ground. I called out in protest, but was too spent to chase her.

'Foul woman,' Ahmad muttered, glaring after the retreating housekeeper.

Elvira scowled and rose from the grass. 'I'll get your clothing back. For now, you can return to the kitchen with me –'

'Ah, but Mary Grace started her stroll with me, and we've not yet reached our destination,' Brother Christy interrupted. He offered me a thick hand, smiling as though nothing unseemly had taken place. 'I will not only replace her tunic, but will let her choose from a wide array of fine garments – for her own wearing, and for her quilts. And when we return to her work area, I'll be sure Father Luc understands the . . . spiritual nature of our gathering in the garden. Shall we proceed, my dear? We have much to see.'

I had reservations, but little choice: the monk helping me up from the cool grass had done me no harm, although he'd swung the censer of opium. When my head cleared, I realised I'd allowed an encounter I previously found repelling. Yet I felt at peace because I'd opened myself to it – and because Ahmad no longer had anything to prove. I couldn't cower behind Elvira, nor could I expect Sybil to watch over my every move during my remaining weeks at Heaven's Gate. So I stood up, only slightly embarrassed by my naked state.

After all, if I were to complete my last three quilts, I had to trust in the monk's providence. I had to believe he would keep me safe because he feared Hyde's reprisal more than Mrs Goodin's threats, or the penance the abbot demanded.

With a smile, I thanked Elvira. Her nod assured me her help would be mine at any time. Then I looked at Brother Christy, whose hair shone golden in the afternoon sun.

'I hope we can walk where I won't be totally exposed?' I teased. 'For once, I'd like someone else to appear more vulnerable than I.'

The little man's jaw clenched, but he then resumed his usual beneficent expression. 'Be careful what you wish for, Mary Grace,' he remarked as we left the circular grove, 'for sometimes wishes come true.'

Chapter Fifteen

Secrets of the Catacombs

'Just as Ahmad is the keeper of the bees here at Heaven's Gate, I am the keeper of the dead.'

Brother Christy announced this as though he were a gardener or an architect, and I suppose falling for Hyde Fortune should've accustomed me to the discomfort such a statement inspired. Indeed, as the monk ushered me down the central aisle of the empty sanctuary, with its vaulted ceilings and dark, carved panelling, he moved with more intensity than I'd ever seen him display. I held an arm over my breasts to keep them from bobbing, which seemed disrespectful in a place of worship, while goosebumps covered me like the flesh of a cold, plucked chicken.

I was wishing Elvira had come along. Brother Christy seemed oblivious to my anxiety as he marched me past the pews and the altar of Italian marble. During our brief Sunday services, I'd marvelled at this cavernous chapel's decor yet had come away feeling like I'd visited the home of a wealthy patron rather than a house of God. I became alarmed as my escort hurried me past the chairs with seats of black brocade, towards the crimson curtain behind the chancel.

'This is an honour I'm bestowing upon you,' Brother

Christy whispered. As his lenses caught the flickering light of the votives, his eyes were hidden by reflected flames. 'Show proper respect, Mary Grace. Those who have gone before us deserve a peaceful, undisturbed rest.'

I tried to swallow the lump in my throat. Did this cherub-like man think I'd dance with the dead? Or was he telling me the monastery's deceased had endured great pain before meeting their ends? As he opened a small door hidden behind the curtain, I wondered if I would ever emerge from this place he was taking me, or if anyone realised where I'd gone. I had always trusted Brother Christy, yet his manner – and the cold, dank air drifting through the door – made my skin crawl.

'I'd feel better about this if I were dressed,' I said, balking when he took my hand.

The monk blinked. 'You may choose more clothing when we reach the vaults. No reason to limit yourself to fabrics for your quilts, you know.'

I frowned. I'd assumed the nut-coloured robes were standard attire.

'Although most of us have chosen the tunics Father Luc issues, we're free to wear whatever we please,' he explained. 'Sybil, for instance, prefers trousers because her tunic caught fire one day.'

I could imagine the elfin redhead stirring pots at the open hearth, and swaying too close to the flames. 'And I suppose those India-style pants suit Ahmad's ... condition better than a hanging garment.'

Brother Christy grinned. 'His attributes can't be confined by clothing, it's true. Most of us choose tunics because we prefer their ease and freedom. It has nothing to do with a vow of poverty.'

'Easy on, easy off,' I mused.

I hugged myself as the chill from the passageway slithered around us. Wearing a dress with appropriate underthings appealed to me – made me less vulnerable to advances and thereby less likely to receive punishment from Father Luc. Yet, standing on the threshold of the catacombs, I knew who the garments Christy offered me had probably belonged to.

But where else would I find any clothing? My pitiful wardrobe from before Papa's death was best left behind, and I didn't want to become beholden to Hyde for new gowns. Sewing my illustrated quilts left me little time to be my own seamstress, so Brother Christy's offer seemed the most practical for my remaining three months at Heaven's Gate. He'd alluded to rich fabrics in brilliant hues, which sounded heavenly to a soul crying out for colour and stylish line.

So I took a deep breath and stooped through the doorway. We stood for a moment, letting our eyes adjust to the dimness. This small foyer's sconces matched the ones along the sanctuary walls, yet now that I stood close enough to discern their design, my eyes widened: one resembled male genitalia, with the flame flickering from the hole at its tip, while the other sconce was female. Brother Christy walked ahead of me, to descend a stone staircase, so I couldn't study that fire-breathing vagina. It was enough to make a preacher's daughter pale. What else in this monastery had I failed to notice in my naïveté?

My escort disappeared around a curve. I rushed to catch up, not wanting to be left alone in this nether region of the monastery where my assumptions were being so blatantly disproven. We were underground, judging from the stone walls rimmed with mineral deposits, entering a cave-like area lit by more of those suggestive sconces. Brother Christy's humming echoed eerily, punctuated by the slow drip of water from quartz and crystal stalactites that hung like huge, pointed breasts. He stopped in front of doors carved into the granite walls.

'I trust you've seen bodies of the deceased, prepared for their final rites?'

It was a logical question, considering my association

with Hyde. I clung to the hope, however, that hesitation might rescue me from this monk's mysterious plans. 'Only my grandmother, years ago,' I replied anxiously. 'Mama was emaciated by her consumption, and Papa so mangled after his fall, that their caskets remained closed.'

'And Fortune showed you nothing of his handiwork?'

'No one was brought to Mount Calvary the night I stayed there.'

Brother Christy's blue eyes sparkled. 'I'm indebted to Hyde for sharing his trade secrets,' he explained eagerly. 'He supplies me with the necessary chemicals, and has taught me much about the preservation of human flesh. I'll warn you, however, that our departed friends haven't been laid away in the usual manner. I consider it my final tribute – an art form, actually – to render them as beautiful in death as they were in life.'

Unbidden images flashed in my mind. I recalled Papa's accusations, about Hyde taking liberties with the dead, and my stomach knotted. Surely this man of angelic appearance didn't cavort with the cadavers he'd preserved ... yet Sybil had said Brother Christy didn't engage in the erotic games other residents enjoyed. And he had to be occupying himself somehow during all those hours I didn't see him.

When he took my hand, I didn't grip it.

'You're afraid,' he murmured. 'Or does your pulse race for the same reasons as mine?'

I yanked my hand from his grasp. 'I don't know what you're talking about! I have no desire to see – why don't you just bury your dead? Their souls have flown, so there's no earthly reason to preserve them!'

Brother Christy smiled patiently. 'You've surely noticed that here at Heaven's Gate, we live on limited land. It would be poor stewardship to turn our fertile fields into cemetery plots, when we depend upon the fruits and vegetables we raise.'

After digesting this, I nodded.

181

'And it's also monastic tradition, passed down through the ages, to inter the departed in catacombs or other areas within the abbey. As it happened, this large cavern occurred naturally, and we've improved upon it to meet our needs.'

The monk studied me, his eyes narrowing. 'There's nothing unnatural about preserving the dead, Mary Grace. Consider the way the Egyptians mummified their pharaohs, for instance. Your squeamishness will work against you – we must pass through the crypts to reach the vaults, where our fabulous old clothing is stored.

'So what will it be? May I show you what only a privileged few have beheld, or will you return to Father Luc's office naked and empty-handed?'

Something inside me railed against this choice. Since my arrival in January, Brother Christy had remained the one man I could trust – until today. He'd obviously conspired with Ahmad, to allow him his desired release, so coming to this emotional crossroads outside the crypt felt like another betrayal. I had believed this monk when he declared himself my protector, yet I wondered if his earlier behaviour had been a ruse leading me to where I now stood, cold and naked, at his mercy.

I shuddered, hugging myself against the dank chill of the cave. My imagination still ran amok as I envisioned what awaited me. It seemed prudent to follow through, however, hoping Brother Christy truly had my welfare in mind. 'All right,' I rasped. 'Let's go in.'

He turned, grasping both handles. The two carved doors groaned like souls in agony as a coppery film of fear coated my mouth. My gooseflesh returned, and I wanted to bolt back up the stairs, through the sanctuary and into the daylight. But with Brother Christy gripping my wrist, I was beyond escaping his dark diversions.

A dry warmth wafted from the room, scented with exotic herbs – a welcome change from the cave's wetness. We were greeted by life-sized statues that served as censers: an over-endowed male resembling Michaelangelo's David looked ready to ravish the woman beside him. Their hollowed mid-sections emitted the incense, while their other features were so vividly sculpted that only the dark veins in the marble prevented them from looking real and alive.

'Thank you for the admiration in your eyes, dear Mary,' Brother Christy murmured. 'When I'm not marketing our Heaven's Gate confections, I work with chisel and mallet.'

'You're a sculptor.' My gaze returned to the statues and I couldn't help caressing the male's chest. Firm and smoothly rounded it was, beaded with tiny nipples; the smouldering incense gave the marble a fleshlike warmth that soothed me, yet made me wary of other figures in the room ... images caught in the corner of my eye, which I didn't want to look at. 'You do beautiful work, Brother Christy. You have every right to be proud.'

His fragile smile told of a seldom-felt joy. 'I hope you'll feel that way when we leave. Come along, Mary Grace. Let me introduce you to my friends, so you can return to your work before the abbot and Mrs Goodin concoct your punishment.'

When I dared to look around, I felt like I'd arrived at a party where all the guests awaited me. Several sets of eyes drank me in, gazing from faces that no longer bloomed with life yet were by no means disfigured in death. These people were arranged as though for conversation – some sat in chairs, with two or three others standing nearby, while others depicted scenes from their lives. All were beautifully coiffed and clothed. Had the room not rung with their suspended silence, an unwitting visitor might've tried talking to them.

'Oh, my,' I finally breathed. 'How long have they been ...?'

Brother Christy smiled, guiding me towards the clutch at our far left. 'Ralph here – the gentleman in the frock coat, on the settee – was my first successful attempt at preservation. He was an avid supporter of the abbey,

183

until his financial empire crumbled and he had nowhere else to go. He's with Brother Daniel and Brother Will, and that's Katrina, a cook he admired.'

'How did he die?' I queried, my gaze fixed upon the quartet of lifelike figures.

'Collapsed on her, while taking her from behind.'

I blushed, even though I should have anticipated this answer. Although the friar hadn't answered my first question, I sensed I shouldn't press him for a reply that might frighten me. Assuming these figures wore clothing fashionable during their lifetimes, Ralph might've met his Maker near the end of the Civil War, more than thirty years ago. I puzzled over this, because Brother Christy didn't appear old enough to have produced such stunning work back then – nor could Hyde have assisted him.

Apparently my escort sensed my calculations, because he steered me towards the next grouping before I could ask any questions. I felt like a museum visitor, being guided through exhibits so I wouldn't fall behind my group or impede the progress of the next one.

'And this trio of angels were dear to me indeed,' he continued in a nostalgic tone. 'Etta, Emily and Eloise were orphaned in their teens. Had marvellous voices, all of them, and they went out singing.'

'Are the eyes real?' The girls seemed to look into my soul, and to follow us as we moved along.

'Glass, I'm afraid. Eyeballs contain a lot of liquid, so they deteriorate quickly. Which would detract from my desired effect.'

I nodded, still looking behind me with an odd twinge in my stomach. 'Are those their wedding gowns? Please don't tell me they died at the altar!'

Brother Christy cleared his throat. 'I think I've mentioned that here at Heaven's Gate, we celebrate the arrival of the seasons. For example, in two weeks we'll fête the coming of spring with the rites of the vernal equinox. The Rosen girls were our celebrants that year.'

That twinge in my stomach rose into my throat; I couldn't breathe, for thinking about how those three pretty young women might have died. I'd be better off if I didn't second-guess what my guide was saying between his carefully worded lines. 'And – and why is it so much warmer in here than out in the stairway? I'd think the heat would hasten the decomposition of ... of –'

'It's the moisture level that affects the tissues adversely,' he explained. 'By keeping the air dry, and circulating the essence of rare herbs, I can preserve my friends in their present state for years to come.'

I allowed him to introduce me to the others without further comment, because while the monk said nothing to suggest he enjoyed sex with the dead, he implied things that frightened me to the core. The sooner we finished here, the sooner we'd fetch my fabrics, so I completed the social circle at his quickening pace, to prevent myself from exploding with unthinkable thoughts.

As we reached the end of this rogues gallery, I noticed a door so cleverly concealed by the plaster pattern of the wall that it would be invisible to the casual observer ... or perhaps to those Brother Christy didn't want snooping beyond this funereal room. His fragrant chamber reeked of secrecy, which made me wonder what else he might reveal as we proceeded to the vaults. I didn't want to see any more, but I'd come too far to walk away empty-handed.

As though hearing my thoughts, Brother Christy smiled. 'You're doing well, Mary Grace. This last young man – Martin Crowley's his name – literally died of fright down here. The fool tried to slip away from our winter solstice ceremony last December, and couldn't find the pressure point for opening the doors, which have no handles on this side. We all know the dead don't walk, yet I suspect he imagined all manner of grotesque possibilities when he found himself trapped among these lifelike corpses.'

The agitation on Martin's face matched my own. I recalled how my fear had run rampant when that moon-lit crone came to my room at Mount Calvary; I didn't dare ask why young Crowley felt compelled to leave the celebration, or how long long he'd languished before expiring. 'Handsome fellow,' I remarked, not knowing what else to say.

'Yes, he was. All of us loved him.' Brother Christy's eyes met mine, telling me I should take a lesson from Martin's fate. 'But I'm wasting our time, and there's still much to see. And while precious few have viewed this room, only my closest, chosen companions even know about the next chamber. This should tell you how very special you are to me, Mary Grace.'

I couldn't miss the implication: the favour of his friendship came with a price. Although the room was cosy, I again shivered, wishing I weren't so exposed to the monk's attentive eyes – eyes that captured line and form so accurately and transferred them into his macabre art. I sorely wished Fortune had warned me about Brother Christy's peculiar pastimes – but then, he wouldn't have entrusted me into his keeping, had he known about them. With the fleeting thought that I might never again kiss the one I loved, I stood aside so my guide could open the disguised door.

What I saw in the next room made the blood rush from my head.

Noting my pallor, Christy draped an arm around my bare shoulders and began to speak in a low, controlled voice. 'At first glance, the eye fools us into believing that what we see is a continuation of what came before. But if you apply your rational mind, dear Mary, you'll realise the fallacy of this illusion.'

Concentrating on Brother Christy's voice – because I had to cling to something, or I'd faint – I focused intently on the figures in this room. It was a replica of the sanctuary, but with only three rows of pews between us and the chancel area. The dark panelling, marble altar and anatomical sconces were the same, but even in the dim lighting I could not mistake the faces and figures of Father Luc, Mrs Goodin, Elvira, Ahmad and Sybil.

Having seen the previous corpses, it took only a tiny leap of imagination to believe these people were dead, as well. 'I don't understand,' I murmured. 'And I don't think I want to.'

Brother Christy chuckled. 'This is my wax museum, Mary Grace. Because the human form fascinates me – and because we have an ample supply of beeswax – I've indulged myself in another medium that gives me even greater pleasure than preserving the dead. Perhaps you'll better appreciate my efforts after you sit down for a moment.'

Trancelike, I allowed him to usher me to the front pew. I was afraid to take my eyes off the wax models, fearing they might change positions to trick me – or reveal themselves as their live counterparts, playing a ghastly joke. Father Luc, dressed in a black cassock, sat on the majestic chair nearest the pulpit, while Hortense Goodin stood beside him with a fist in her hip, looking ready to scold the others.

And it was no wonder: my dear friend Sybil, stark naked, in a partial squat atop the altar with her russet waves and gypsy earrings, wagged her shapely arse at Ahmad. The inscrutable beekeeper, as mystical in wax as in reality, stood ready to skewer her from behind with that legendary pecker, while Elvira, clad in her tunic, leaned towards Sybil's crotch with her tongue extended.

That this brazen act was posed upon the altar was beside the point. Everything about the scene and this room, right down to the low lighting and the elusive scents of sweat and sex, suggested activities I didn't allow myself to imagine. After all, Brother Christy had made no mannequin of himself.

187

'Do you want to study them more closely? Touch them, perhaps?'

'No!' I blurted. My outcry echoed in the vaulted ceiling, mocking my deepest fears. Covered again in gooseflesh, I squirmed on the pew, my bare skin protesting against the polished walnut. My pulse was pounding, and I felt so ready to run from this room my shins twitched. And yet, when I saw that Sybil's eyes were fixed on mine – that she gazed at me over Elvira's ebony curls, with a longing I knew so well – the heat flared inside me.

'She's a wondrous creature, is she not?' the friar whispered. 'Forged in the Devil's own fire, it would seem, expressly to lead us into temptations beyond our wildest fantasies. I was so taken with her, she inspired my first work in wax the day after she arrived.'

Recalling the way this man watched from the cottage doorway as Sybil and I pleasured each other, his revelation didn't surprise me. 'Does she know about this . . . doll?'

'Of course not. And I think you realise why no one else does, either.'

I could only nod, mutely agreeing not to reveal Brother Christy's secret. Since she didn't feel the same level of affection for him, Sybil would be curious – and defiant – enough to sneak down here, to suffer Martin Crowley's horrible fate. Having her demise on my conscience would be more than I could bear, so I kept gazing at her lush breasts and the flush of arousal on her flawless face – admiring the perfection of the art so I wouldn't think about the twisted whims of the artist. As the wetness trickled between my legs, I swore Sybil winked at me.

'Sit here, if you wish, or you may look around. I've something else to show you.'

Brother Christy passed between the inert figures to the crimson curtain, which – like the one upstairs – concealed a door. He stepped through it, leaving me alone in this airless room inhabited by three-dimensional optical illusions. Wondering if I'd again been influenced by opium, I dared myself to stand up and touch Elvira's tan tunic.

It was as real as the one Mrs Goodin had snatched from the grass earlier.

Bolder now, I slowly circled the altar to study the monk's handiwork. Careful to remain at a distance, lest Sybil or Ahmad playfully grab for my breasts, I admired their skin tones, the skilfully arranged wigs, the facial features that captured them exactly as I knew them. I swore I could smell Sybil's wet sex. Ahmad's erection seemed to quiver, with a bubble of translucent fluid oozing from its tip. His cock ring glimmered in the dusky light, and the ruby in his nose caught the glow from the sconces as his piercing obsidian eyes tried to mesmerise me.

I turned quickly, thinking Elvira had shifted, but it was the rustling of the crimson curtain as Brother Christy returned. 'Now that you've had a chance to pass judgment on my earlier works, what do you think of this fine specimen?'

My hand flew to my mouth. He was rolling in a replica of Hyde Fortune.

At that moment I wanted Hyde's company so badly, a sob escaped me. This warned me of my distraught state, and of how vulnerable I was to whatever else the apple-cheeked monk had in mind, so I forced myself to study this life-sized image. Not only had Brother Christy captured the shadow of Hyde's jaw and the dimple near his chin, but he'd mussed the thick, sandy hair just enough to correlate with the handsome mortician's expression when he was ready to climax.

'I could swear he has a suit like that,' I managed, fighting to stay afloat in these emotion-charged waters.

The monk smiled slyly. 'They say clothes make the man, but I contend that our natural endowments are what make us memorable.'

189

With that, he unfastened the pants to reveal an erection so realistic I would've recognised it in the dark. The monk's chuckle came from all corners of the mock sanctuary as he let the trousers drop, watching my reaction. 'Feel free to indulge yourself, Mary Grace. I know how you miss him between his visits.'

Again I clapped my hand to my mouth, more frightened than I'd ever felt in my life, yet vibrantly aroused. Hyde might as well have been standing before me, imploring me to spread my legs or suck him. My sex ached with the need to know whether that cock of wax would fill me like the real one, but the way Christy caressed it – and himself – warned me not to step any closer.

'My sculpture's having the desired effect,' he murmured, slipping a hand through a vent in his tunic seam. 'It's one thing to react to my own art, but much more gratifying to see a beautiful woman respond so copiously, despite her knowledge that he's only a waxwork.'

Brother Christy's gaze remained at the apex of my legs. 'Would you please catch that honey dribbling down your leg, Mary Grace? You'll be doing us both a favour. The sooner we satisfy ourselves, the sooner we move on to the vaults.'

His manipulation stung, after I'd trusted him so long, but I didn't think he'd come after that honey himself: he'd had plenty of chances, yet allowed others to do the honours. As my fingers inched down to catch the slickness escaping from my slit, however, I knew the culmination I craved wouldn't come by my own hand.

My companion – as always – seemed to know what I was thinking. Brother Christy tipped the mannequin of Hyde backwards, just enough to level it horizontally, and then laid it carefully on the floor. Had I walked in at that moment, I would've assumed my lover was lying in wait, randy and ready for me. The cock rising proudly in the air seemed to quiver as I stared at it. It was my own excitement causing this illusion, no doubt, but I was too agitated to care.

'Straddle him, Mary Grace. Close your eyes and fuck him as though the two of you were alone.'

That was his price: Brother Christy wanted to watch me come, but this time he demanded a private showing. If I was to have the fabrics he'd baited me with, I would play his game and keep his secrets – hopefully before Father Luc and Mrs Goodin could plan another humiliating penance.

I lowered myself over the image of Hyde Fortune, reaching between my thighs for the shaft of wax. Undulating above it until its tip teased at my swollen folds, I circled my hole before testing it on my clit. Perhaps because the wax absorbed my own heat, it felt like the chocolate dildo Sybil's kitchen crew had slipped inside me – ridged, veined, and satisfyingly solid. With a sigh, I impaled myself and began to pump. Closing my eyes would allow me to pretend it was Hyde beneath me, lying very still at my command, yet I fed my fascination by gazing into that familiar face.

Brother Christy watched intently, following my movements up and down the cock he'd created. When he again slipped behind the crimson curtain, I assumed he wanted his own private release – so I humped faster, to please myself rather than putting on a show. Sitting higher, I threw my head back and thrust out my breasts as I angled myself to better advantage. My inner tensions had risen near the breaking point since I'd entered the monk's secret chambers, and I was eager for release. My body tightened until that familiar frenzy rose within me, breaking like waves before a cataclysmic storm.

Brother Christy returned as I was on the verge of screaming, and when I saw what he brought with him, my cries rang louder. He smiled, looking so very childlike and proud of another waxwork he'd made – of me.

His woman of wax wore the ivory-and-cream striped dress Hyde gave me, and her auburn waves had worked

191

loose from the knot at her crown. She was kneeling, with her eyes closed and her lips forming an O. Christy raised the front of his tunic. He was facing away from me, towards the seated figure of Father Luc, but I knew exactly what he was going to do.

Once again I was forced to recall when Mrs Goodin threw open the carriage door to catch me in that very position, but I was beyond humiliation: I squirmed against the false cock until release racked my body. Unable to stop, my hips kept driving against the shaft, finding that sweet, heated spot that sent ripples up from deep inside me for delicious minutes on end. Relieved, yet somewhat aghast at what I'd just done, I began to dismount the man so much like Hyde – until a rustling of the crimson curtain froze me in place.

Mrs Goodin stepped into the chancel, her eyes on Brother Christy. The monk was now thrusting madly into the mouth of my counterpart, perhaps pretending Father Luc watched while he slid between my lips. He was apparently so caught up in his pleasure he didn't realise who had joined us, while I hoped to avoid detection by lying flat upon the mannequin of Hyde, on the opposite side of the altar. Through the loose weave of the altar cloth I could see Mrs Goodin, however, and I knew the friar she approached in silence would soon feel her wrath.

But the dour housekeeper unfastened her skirt and let it drop to the floor. Then she stepped away from the puddle of stiff fabric, wearing only dark stockings held up by a black garter belt, which framed a bush of bristling jet hair. Without interrupting the humping monk, she threw aside the folds of Father Luc's cassock to reveal a wax erection beyond all possible human proportions. She was fingering her slit, feverishly spreading her wetness as she watched Brother Christy.

Backing towards the abbot's seated figure, Hortense straddled his lap to thrust herself upon his mammoth shaft. With a feral growl, she moved up and back, up and back, with the same speed and force of the monk a few feet in front of her. Now that I knew Father Luc's housekeeper was no stranger to this room, and was too engrossed in her own satisfaction to notice me, I slipped two fingers between my quivering folds. A delicious sense of irony spurred me on: while the two paragons of the monastery brought themselves to climax, I had caught them in the act – together!

The laundress was about to lose all her starch, judging from the dark sparkle in her eyes. As she gazed at Brother Christy, her nostrils flaring, she fumbled with the buttons of her blouse. 'Don't you dare pump your juice into that redheaded hussy, Christopher Goodin!' she snarled. 'Get over here where you belong. Prove yourself more a man than the abbot here.'

Brother Christy acknowledged her command with a desperate groan. As he yanked himself from the throat of the Mary Grace mannequin, Hortense removed her uniform blouse. She sucked in her breath to unhook her corset in one practised motion, freeing a pair of full, pendulous breasts. The man she'd summoned caught them in his hands, suckling them eagerly, as though he'd been deprived of human contact for days.

I could only stare: if I'd understood correctly, Brother Christy was the Mr Goodin we'd all wondered about and felt so sorry for. There was more to this story than I dared speculate over, but the housekeeper's enraptured face – and the hungry way the monk serviced her – told me these secret encounters occurred more often than anyone could guess. As I imagined telling Sybil about this, I doubted she'd believe me.

My fingers ventured farther up my cunt. I gazed blatantly through the altar cloth, goaded on by fear of discovery as well as this revelation of a most unusual couple. Hortense still writhed against the abbot's prick, appearing very near the point of no return, while Brother Christy's hips flexed uncontrollably beneath his tunic. The squelching of her wetness and their desperate moans echoed in the miniature chapel, driving me towards another climax as I spied upon them. Frustrated with the limitations of my fingers, I cautiously eased back on to the mannequin.

Hortense cried out, emitting a string of epithets no proper lady would utter in a church. Just the thought of her rutting against Father Luc sent my hips into a frenzy against Hyde's wax erection, and it was all I could do not to thrash about so loudly she'd hear me from the other side of the altar.

Her gratification waned quickly, however. 'Well, if you're going to take so damn long,' she muttered, 'you'll have to finish with Elvira. A peculiar bird like her is all you deserve, if –'

'No, please,' Brother Christy pleaded. 'I'm so close, so very –'

'Tell your troubles to Jesus. Now get your sorry self over here.'

Mrs Goodin strode to the wax model of Elvira and whipped the brown tunic up over its backside. This brought her so close I could've touched her sturdy black shoes, but instead I held my breath, trying not to writhe. Hortense stood like a teacher chastising a tardy student, holding the robe up with one hand while beckoning to Brother Christy with the other.

'Finish what you've started,' she ordered. 'Gawk at Sybil like the dribbling nitwit you are – like you do every time you see her – and blast away at Elvira here. It's the best you're going to get, Mr Goodin. You know my rules.'

Brother Christy looked desperate for release, and when he turned to obey her, I caught sight of his privates. He was hung like a proverbial horse, sporting a thick, blunt pecker that jutted ahead of him by several inches. With a groan, he shoved himself up the mannequin's hole, pumping so hard the altar rocked noisily. From where I lay atop Hyde's waxwork, I marvelled at the way the friar's ponderous balls slapped against

194

Elvira's backside as he put forth a Herculean effort to release himself.

It occurred to me then that the sculptor had erred: where his other work was uncannily accurate, he had fashioned Elvira with a pussy, complete with a neatly trimmed bush that formed a triangle. But I didn't have time to gloat over my superior knowledge of the kitchen assistant's anatomy: Mrs Goodin, never content to let well enough alone, was giving more orders.

'Ram it into her,' the housekeeper muttered. 'Feast your eyes on those tits Sybil thrusts at everyone, like the slut she is, and dream your way into her tight, wet pussy. You think you're in love with Mary Grace – and the two of them make a pretty pair – but it's Sybil you've always wanted to fuck, isn't it?'

The monk moaned, writhing frantically against Elvira's waxen buttocks.

'Answer me so I can understand you, Christopher.'

'Yes! Yes, I want her!'

'Then why don't you take her? She puts out for everyone else.'

Brother Christy stiffened, reaching a new plateau of stimulation. 'Because I belong to you, dear Hortense,' he rasped.

'That's right,' she replied, and to emphasise her point she slapped his quivering arse. 'And why else don't you fuck her, little man? You've lusted after her for years.'

'Because . . . because . . .'

The monk appeared on the verge of a cataclysmic orgasm, and it took all my strength not to thrash noisily against the shaft rammed inside me. I had a clear view of his thrusting into Elvira's cunt, and the bulging veins of his cock, and the reddened testicles that appeared ready to explode, which fed my own excitement. My juice was puddling in the hollow of Hyde's abdomen, and I felt ready to scream with my climax.

'Don't you dare come before you answer me! You know the consequences.'

His eyes clenched shut and he rocked back with the effort of withholding release. 'I don't ... fuck her because ... she'll see your name tattooed on my cock ... and laugh at me!'

His last agonised phrase echoed in the vaulted chamber as the spasms broke over him. Humping like a man possessed, Brother Christy squirted streams of thick, pungent cream into the mannequin's slit. It ran down the white thighs and splattered against the altar, some of it landing on my face. My pussy clenched around the warm cock, and I gave in to the shudders as quietly as I could, hoping the monk's outcries covered my own.

For what seemed an eternity, the man beside me convulsed like a tortured soul. It was probably best that he hadn't approached Sybil – or anyone else – because once his climax finally broke loose, it seemed more torrential than a normal partner could withstand. I didn't know the circumstances of his tattoo, but Hortense had certainly left her mark in ways that guaranteed her husband's fidelity.

As his climax subsided, Mrs Goodin dressed. All signs of her own passion had vanished, and putting on her corset brought back her inflexible disposition. 'You can thank me for this later,' she muttered as she stepped into her black skirt. 'Now mop up this mess! If I catch so much as a whiff of sex on these people or their clothing, you know exactly where I'll be using my scrub brush!'

'Yes, darling,' Brother Christy sighed, still catching his breath.

'I expect you to carry on as always,' she continued, 'so that no one suspects I'm even remotely connected to such a useless booby of a husband.'

'Quite right,' he rasped, brushing his hair from his sweaty brow. 'Why would any woman tolerate a man who prefers buggering his own waxworks? It's a waste of your lovely cunt and my equipment, as well, Hortense. I'm a lucky man that you'll even cast eyes upon me.'

'That you are. But you're also a fool, Mr Goodin.'

The monk's body jerked as though she'd swatted his butt again. 'What have I done now? If you ever want me inside you, you only have to –'

'I want nothing of the sort!'

My mouth went dry as I watched her through the woven parament. Mrs Goodin was gloating as she fastened the button at her starched collar, gazing steadily at Brother Christy's feet ... and beyond them. 'You should've known better than to bring Miss Michaels among your cherished friends. Your misplaced affection has now compromised you both! I'll be taking her upstairs for correction, so the two of you can contemplate the error of your ways.'

Brother Christy sucked air with the same terror that struck my heart. 'But I had offered her fabrics from –'

'Idiot! Do you really think she can keep these secrets to herself?' the housekeeper hissed. 'Did you think I wouldn't come down here looking for you, after what I witnessed in the grove?'

The staccato of her heels on the hard floor sounded like the driving of nails into my own coffin. I glared up at her as defiantly as I could, but she had the advantage and she knew it.

'Get up, you shameless whore!' she barked. 'Apparently my first cleansing didn't go deep enough! Father Luc has long suspected your subversive behaviour, and I can now confirm it – and bring about your just reward!'

Faster than I knew what was happening, the housekeeper hooked her hands under my armpits. I yelped, scrambling to get my feet beneath me, tripping over the life-sized form with its perennial erection. 'Please! I won't breathe a word about –'

'No, you won't,' the waspish woman assured me, 'because where I'm going to hide you, you'll have no contact with anyone until time for the rites.'

With a strength I never knew she had, Hortense Goodin yanked me into a walk. Again I stumbled, gasping when I kicked the mannequin's head, which went rolling across the floor . . . a nasty omen about my future with Hyde, it seemed. 'I – I don't understand,' I protested, looking over my shoulder for help from Brother Christy.

But the monk was already wiping the altar clean of his semen.

Mrs Goodin's smile sliced like a knife. 'I suppose he told you about the Rosen girls and Martin Crowley? How they were selected as honoured guests at our seasonal celebrations?'

My eyes widened. Brother Christy's allusions had left several things to my imagination, none of them good. 'He said they were much-loved.'

'And their popularity earned them the part of celebrant in our pageants. A role none of them lived to tell about, incidentally.'

She pivoted abruptly, her lurid gaze following the lines of my bare body as we approached the crimson curtain. 'Father Luc thought you perfect for the part the moment he laid eyes on you, Mary Grace. Your angelic face and religious upbringing – even your name, which suggests such purity! – are the ideal foils for the depraved soul that lurks within you! Oh, yes, the abbot will dearly love planning your debut – your coming out, in two weeks – at the rites of the vernal equinox.'

Chapter Sixteen
Alone With My Fears

Mrs Goodin shut me into a dungeon room, with only a slit for a window and space enough beneath the door to slide a daily tray of food. Spending the next two weeks here, awaiting my fate as celebrant, frightened me out of my mind. I passed my time wrapped in a scratchy blanket, sitting on a palette that smelled of mildew and unwashed bodies – or pacing, when the meagre sunlight allowed.

My confinement gave me time to ponder the mysteries confronting me since my arrival at Heaven's Gate, and my hurried walk past the vaults had added one more: some of the clothing Brother Christy had promised me dated back to before the discovery of America. As Hortense escorted me past costume collections any theatre troupe would've envied, I'd seen French silks and fine Irish lace; doublets reminiscent of the Renaissance; ermine capes that appeared Russian; ball gowns of brilliant textures and hues that dazzled me, just as the monk said they would.

Had these ensembles belonged to former residents? Or were they costumes for the abbey's pageants? Although I'd had no chance to study them, the mustiness and faded appearance of the more common clothing led me to believe the first assumption. After all, Brother Christy had already put my striped dress to use. It would follow that the other garments had been preserved down here in the crypts, just as their owners were.

But how could this be?

'I really must return to my work,' I protested as Mrs Goodin rushed me past these clothes. 'It's a part of my bargain, to sew three more quilts before –'

'Silly bitch!' she muttered. 'Father Luc doesn't need your money! If he never collected another cent, the monastery would go on as though you never existed. It was your idea to sew, and Hyde's idea to bring you here. You should've returned with him when you had the chance!'

Her malicious laughter filled the little cell she thrust me into, followed by the thudding of the door and the jangle of keys at the lock. Once again I felt like a Gothic heroine at the whim of her captors, whose only hope was the hero's realising something was amiss. Hyde would expect me to greet him as usual next Friday, and he would demand explanations from the abbot until he found me. Then he'd take me home.

This plan gave me strength as the days crept by. I spent the hours lost in fantasies of how it would be when I returned; I vowed to never again despise the morbidity of Mount Calvary, if only Hyde would keep me and love me. Days blended into nights, yet as I sensed the end of my first week of captivity, my spirits flitted like a butter-fly. It had to be Friday soon, and Mr Fortune wouldn't tolerate the mistreatment these people had heaped upon me!

When my next tray come under the door, I said, 'Wait! What day is it, please?'

I'd spoken to my food-bearer every afternoon, without response, but this time a familiar voice replied, 'It's Wednesday. Are you all right, Mary Grace?'

'If you cared, you'd let me out of here – I've talked to you before, but –'

'This is the first time Hortense has allowed me to come, and she has the only key,' Brother Christy replied dolefully. 'I'm sorry about all this. I had no idea she was watching us when I brought you down here from the grove. If I could –'

'Why hasn't Sybil done something? Surely she's asked about my disappearance!'

He cleared his throat nervously. 'She – along with everyone else – has learned you're to be the celebrant at the upcoming rites. And she realises that pleading on your behalf, or protesting your captivity, will inspire the abbot's vengeance. She doesn't know where you're hidden, anyway. I've been sworn to absolute secrecy, and I think you understand why I'm not crossing my wife!'

'She's right. You *are* a booby,' I muttered, wrapping my blanket more tightly around me. 'If this is the first time she's allowed you down here, she's got a reason for it.'

The friar sighed from behind the door. 'I'm supposed to tell you I'm going down the mountain this afternoon, so Hyde won't visit, and therefore won't know of your predicament.'

'And you think he won't suspect something? What sort of idiot do you take him for?'

The silence made me wish I could see Christy's face, to determine whether he was lying, or merely testing my reaction so he could report it to his wife.

'Seems Mrs Goodin has already considered that, and is sending a note – one you allegedly wrote – to convince him you no longer love him, nor do you wish to leave Heaven's Gate.' He cleared his throat again. 'I really must go, before she comes down here. I'll return every chance I get, to keep you apprised of the situation.'

'You do that,' I spat, and then I burst into tears. The fantasies that had kept me sane this week had been ripped to shreds by the feline woman who toyed with me as though I were her mouse. Yet before I lost contact with the tormentor she'd sent me, I had another question.

'Brother Christy!' I shouted through the door. 'Are you really a monk? A man who's promised himself to God?'

I'm not sure what my agitated mind intended to do with his reply, but I was relieved to hear his footsteps approach my cell again.

'Why do you ask, dear Mary?'

'What else do I have to do, but to puzzle out what's happened to me here?' I replied pitifully. 'At this point, your answer won't change my fate, so what will it matter?'

He chuckled. 'So you've seen through the discrepancies? I knew it wouldn't be long, bright as you are, so –'

'Just answer me, dammit! Do you want Bitch Goodin catching us?'

There was silence, when I think he was listening for her. 'No, I'm not a monk,' he admitted, so softly I had to press my ear to the door. 'We maintain the image of a monastery because it sells our products. We also support the Home for the Friendless, so Hyde believes we are doing the Lord's work.'

'So that means Father Luc isn't –'

His fading footsteps marked the end of the conversation, and presented more questions for me to ponder in my solitary state. I refused to believe Hyde would fall for Mrs Goodin's note, because he knew me too well . . . and because I couldn't face the future if Brother Christy convinced him it was true. So I wrapped my hopes around that subject as though it were a gift I could give myself later, when other mysteries were resolved.

It was slim satisfaction that over the past two months, I'd come to realise neither Father Luc nor Brother Christy ever quoted Scripture, or spoke about God the way any true clergyman would. While Ahmad and Christopher Goodin often alluded to spiritual matters, they didn't discuss the principles of Christianity. And who observed the commandment concerning adultery? Sexual gaming was the primary focus of the people here, when they weren't tending the orchards, cooking, or otherwise maintaining the idyllic lifestyle of this mountaintop retreat.

As I huddled beneath my blanket, I also pondered the mysteries of the perpetual spring weather. I'd been imprisoned without my tunic, and had taken it off several times for outdoor encounters, so I was grateful the wintry conditions in Colorado Springs didn't exist here. I wondered if Heaven's Gate had always posed as a monastery, or if the clothing I'd seen in the vaults indicated other types of communal situations over the years.

And what of Father Luc? If Brother Christy and the others weren't monks, did this mean their abbot was only pretending, as well? As his narrow face came to mind, framed within that close-cropped beard and sinister black moustache, I shuddered to think who he really might be. I told myself Sybil didn't know him any better, so couldn't warn me that the abbot's cover might differ from the book inside. I didn't want to believe that she too, had betrayed me, used me for her own wayward pleasure.

Then my thoughts wandered back to what Brother Christy had said about visiting Hyde. Did my lover know me well enough to suspect the story and note were fabrications? Would he drive up the mountain anyway? He trusted the angelic-looking monk – just as I had – so perhaps he'd believe the lies Mrs Goodin had written. My best chance was that, while settling details of my parents' funerals, he'd seen more of my handwriting than Hortense had, so he might recognise hers as a forgery.

Or was I fooling myself? Was Hyde just playing along like the others – supplying new members occasionally, for the enjoyment of those who lived here? I'd been all too willing to share my quilting profits, when Heaven's

Gate was apparently self-sufficient. And I'd certainly gone along with their erotic suggestions, swallowing explanations about pent-up energy and fertilising trees that now sounded hollow to my wiser heart. I didn't know what to believe any more, or who to believe in.

When I took a slice of bread from my tray, however, a fluttering piece of paper made me grin. It was a note, signed by Sybil, who must've scribbled it when she saw Brother Christy was to deliver my meal today.

'My dearest Mary Grace', the precise script began. 'Keep up your strength and your spirits! I have a plan for seeing you safely through the rites – Hortense and the abbot be damned! We all miss you! Your Sybil.

P.S. Here's something to entertain you. Dream of me as you enjoy it.'

Oh, how I wanted to believe her – to believe my roommate, rather than the warped woman who imprisoned me, had actually written these words. The tray was arranged like any other day, with two large slices of bread lying on top of some ham, and an apple alongside. When I picked up the second slice of bread, however, I laughed out loud. She'd sent me a chocolate cock!

Clear syrup oozed from its hole, so I put the candy to my lips. The sweet smoothness of the chocolate was spiked with a peppermint liqueur that tingled on my tongue. Its warmth blazed all the way down my throat as I sucked, closing my eyes dreamily. The dingy cell faded away. I imagined Sybil's sly smile as she'd tucked this under my bread – imagined what she would do with this chocolate novelty, if she were here. And if the syrup was making my mouth feel so warm and alive . . . what might it do to my privates?

I leaned against the wall and spread my thighs. The first contact with the candy had me exhaling blissfully, calling to mind the wax erection I'd straddled on Brother Christy's copy of Hyde. The peppermint sang delightfully wherever it touched my sensitive skin. My mouth went slack. I rubbed the tip of the cock around my inner lips, circling my clit until it throbbed to life.

It seemed a shame no one was there to lap at the chocolate as it melted around my pussy, but Sybil wouldn't want this to stand in the way of my enjoyment. I envisioned her kneeling between my legs, guiding the dildo around my hole, which ached at the thought of her gazing there, teasing me with just the right pressure. As the chocolate softened, mingling with my juice, I imagined my room-mate licking the sweetness from me with whimpers of desire – which, I then realised, came from my own throat.

I shoved the cock inside me, thrusting to meet Sybil's tongue and insistent lips. I squeezed the cylinder with my inner muscles, relishing its minty heat as my quivering began in earnest. In and out, quickening as my need rose, harder and faster I pumped, dreaming of the red-haired siren who'd enticed me so many times. She would be grasping my arse-flesh as she flicked her wicked tongue around my clit, still driving that shaft inside my eager cunt. My honey mixed with the melting candy, dribbling between my thighs as I worked myself to the point of climax.

With a series of soft cries, I succumbed. As the spasms began, it was Hyde I imagined, plunging deep into my pussy as he thumbed my clit. His cinnamon eyes burned into mine as the peppermint pleasure enveloped him. With a clenched grin, he drove his cock into me until we both convulsed in a wet ecstasy that smelled like he'd used a huge candy cane. I climaxed with a shriek that sounded very loud in the little cell. The only noise I'd ever heard from above was the rumbling of the pipe organ, so I felt confident no one could hear me.

As I fell back against the wall, however, the hinges creaked. My eyes flew open as my hand instinctively covered my dripping slit.

Father Luc stood in the doorway. His nostrils flared as he inhaled, while his gaze took on an unsettling glimmer.

In the fading light of afternoon, those eyes glowed like coals as he ogled every exposed angle of my body with obvious intent. The door shut behind him with an ominous thud. He then dropped the key ring to the floor, to kick it back through the slit.

Someone on the other side picked it up. Was Mrs Goodin, the keeper of those keys, his accomplice? Or had Brother Christy escorted the abbot down here, betraying me yet again? Father Luc's expression told me he'd heard every moan and shriek while I'd pleasured myself, and that he felt compelled to follow that same sweet path to his own satisfaction.

'Move your hand.' His gaze remained between my legs as he stepped closer.

I shuddered with the chill that suddenly filled my cell.

'I said move your hand!' the abbot barked, his eyes flaring with the volume of his voice. 'Your modesty fools no one, Miss Michaels, so we might as well stop playing games. I've come to make you an offer, but I must be obeyed!'

My heart thudded as I drew my hand up my abdomen. The candy cock remained in my slit, with chocolate syrup and my own juices dribbling out around it. Father Luc knelt, and then deftly removed the dwindling dildo with his thumb and forefinger.

'I can give you so much more than this,' he murmured, rubbing the melting pecker around my hole. 'In fact, I've come to invite you to be my protégée, Mary Grace. Along with this privilege comes a reprieve from the rites of the vernal equinox, where you'd be pawed and mauled beyond your worst nightmares ... perhaps beyond your endurance. Although I sense you're nearly as insatiable as Sybil and the rest of us.'

I shifted, trying to disguise my arousal. 'You're saying that if I accept your offer – to become yours, and yours alone – I won't have to serve as celebrant?'

'That's correct. And since your fear of that role is so strong I can smell it, you should seriously consider accepting.' The abbot continued to circle my slit with the chocolate cock, his face tightening with need. 'It's a generous offer – and I wouldn't hold you to making the rest of those quilts. You could live here without obligation, except to satisfy my desires. But I'm not leaving this locked room until I have your answer.'

I let out a ragged sigh as he lifted the padded canopy of my bush to expose my clitoris. 'And what of my promise to Hyde?' I breathed, trying not to writhe as he worked an uncanny magic on my most sensitive parts. 'He's promised me a good life, whenever I'm ready for it.'

Father Luc laughed humourlessly. 'Mr Fortune is never more than a funeral service away from meeting some poor, needy female who'd throw herself at his mercy, for the favour of one handsome smile. Is he, dear Mary?'

I moaned as he inserted two probing fingers. The abbot was illustrating my own desperate state after Papa died – and how could I forget the sight of Hyde humping Delores Poppington in her casket? My legs flailed, as that despicable woman's had, when Father Luc circled my clit more insistently with the chocolate while stroking up into my pussy with his fingers. Damn him for that imperious grin as he rekindled the need I'd sated only moments ago!

His features contracted with desire. 'Since you're no longer the little innocent Fortune brought to this mountain, you'll appreciate the advantages of staying here over returning to that tomb of a household, where your new appetites will go unsatisfied,' he continued. 'Before you answer, allow me to demonstrate my own superior skills.'

There was no allowing about it. Father Luc spread my thighs to attack my aching pussy with a mouth so hot I cried out in surprise. His tongue plunged inside me while his lips massaged the tingling, minted folds still dripping with chocolate. The suction he then created made me thrust myself at his face. The ridge of that clipped moustache sent me into paroxysms of pleasure, setting me on an edge I might jump from at any moment.

He slipped the remains of the chocolate shaft into his mouth, and then shoved it up my cunt with his tongue. I shrieked, spearing my fingers into his ebony hair. As I slid down the wall, Father Luc adjusted the palette beneath me to angle my bottom higher, all the while torturing me with his tongue. My legs splayed as far as they could go, and when my head fell back with my uncontrollable shrieks, I climbed to a wild climax like I'd never known. On and on it went, with the abbot coaxing one spasm after another, until I collapsed, senseless, on the floor of the cell.

He raised himself up, licking his lips. 'You do have a way with chocolate, my dear,' he crooned. And with a sly grin, he popped the last of the candy cock into his mouth. 'My compliments to Sybil for filling it with peppermint. Quite refreshing, don't you agree?'

My slit was still tingling from the mint, still pulsing madly after the abbot's attack. Father Luc dipped down to lap lightly around the edge where my bush met the slick skin of my pussy. His kisses then followed his caress up my abdomen, worshipping my sensitive skin until he met the tips of my breasts. After a playful peck at each aching nipple, he raised himself to gaze at my face, awaiting my answer. His erection prodded my pussy from beneath his cassock, an erection that felt as mammoth as the one Brother Christy had fashioned on the wax abbot. I could feel the tip of him pulsing through the black fabric, waiting to plunder me.

'How can you possibly refuse my offer?' he whispered, his eyes flaring above mine. 'I'll give you this ecstasy any time you like, Mary Grace. And I'll allow your attraction to Sybil full reign, as well. Instead of being at the mercy of every man – and woman – at Heaven's Gate during the rites of the vernal equinox, you could be writhing with unparalleled pleasure as I shove my cock into you again and again. I want to claim you with it now, sweet Mary. All you have to say is yes.'

My body almost betrayed me by curling up to encourage him. Yet something rang false about his offer. 'Why are you doing this?' I rasped. 'You could have Sybil, or anyone else who suits you.'

'But it's you I want, Mary Grace,' he whispered sinuously, prodding me with his cock. 'You're far too beautiful and erotic for Fortune. He's a mortician, after all – he's made death his livelihood! And they say his mother went insane in that house.'

I studied the face suspended above mine. The swarthy skin and fierce eyes gave nothing away about his age; his coal black hair accentuated his virile omnipotence. But I wasn't the least bit interested in becoming this man's lover, except to spare myself the pain Brother Christy's lifelike corpses had suffered as celebrants . . . and to give myself a chance to return to Hyde later, after Father Luc tired of me.

'You're stalling,' he prompted. 'The Mary Grace Michaels I've come to admire decides in favour of the right. She knows better than to believe a handsome man's pretty promises when a far more powerful lover is offering her the world. A world of eternal springtime, where her youth and beauty will never fade.'

It sounded perfect. Too perfect. And when his eyes bored into mine with a heat reminiscent of hellfire, I shivered. 'Mary Grace Michaels is also a woman of her word,' I replied. 'I love Hyde, and I'm honouring my promise to him.'

'Is that your final answer?' His erection prodded at my pussy until I thought it might tear through his cassock to get inside.

'Yes,' I hissed. 'Now get off me!'

With a feral snarl, Father Luc shoved himself up from the floor. He stood straddling my naked body, pointing a finger as though it were a pistol loaded with my doom. 'You'll live to regret those words, Mary Grace. And unless you change your mind, you'll also regret that you live!'

I reached for the tattered blanket to cover myself, but he kicked it away.

'You realise I can't possibly let you leave with Hyde,' he continued in a coiled voice. 'Brother Christy has revealed too much about our life here at Heaven's Gate, so I can't allow you to go anywhere, Miss Michaels.'

The abbot strode to the door and pounded on it, still glaring at me with those glowing eyes ... eyes that haunted me with a familiarity I couldn't place. 'You have a few days before the ceremony to reconsider. It's only a matter of time before I claim you, anyway. A matter of whether you come to me willingly, or for your own survival.'

I returned his stare with a defiance born of desperation. I had to believe Hyde would see through Brother Christy's trumped-up story. I told myself Sybil would ensure my safety, as she'd promised, no matter how blatant Father Luc's threats became.

My heart pounded as we heard the rasp of a key in the lock. The abbot stooped to snatch a piece of paper from the floor – the note Sybil tucked into my lunch. He scanned it with a smirk.

'If you believe for one minute Sybil will come to your rescue, then consider this,' he said, raising his brows for fiendish emphasis. 'She, too, had the chance to return to her previous home but saw the wisdom of remaining here with me, when I made her a similar offer years ago. If you think she'll place your wishes ahead of mine, you're a fool, Mary Grace. What a disappointment that would be. And I don't handle disappointment well.'

He swung open the door, slipped through it, and slammed it behind him.

'I told you she'd refuse,' came his accomplice's voice. 'Mary Grace still believes good will prevail over evil, even here at Heaven's Gate.'

Pain pierced my heart. It was Sybil who spoke, and

who'd just stated her betrayal. I clapped my hand over my mouth so they wouldn't hear my sobs.

What was I to believe? Whom could I trust?

Brother Christy had said that Hortense kept the keys to this prison, and that she'd sent him to mislead Hyde with a forged note. Yet it was Sybil, the one friend I thought remained, listening through the door as the abbot made me the same proposition he'd posed to her long ago. Everything I'd heard lately contradicted what I once believed. My trip to the catacombs had made me the unwitting witness to too many secrets.

One thing I knew for certain: Father Luc would prevail. It was merely a matter of whether I became his willing victim, or became another of Christy's macabre works of art in the crypt. I curled up on my palette beneath the old blanket, feeling totally lost and alone.

Chapter Seventeen
Rites of the Vernal Equinox

'*G*et off the floor! Act like the queen you're going to be – unless you're accepting the abbot's offer instead.'

The evil glee in Mrs Goodin's voice was a rude awakening. Not more than a day had passed since Father Luc's visit, so it couldn't be time for the rites. Except for the flickering flame of her candle, my cell was as dark as a moonless midnight, so it hardly seemed the hour for celebrating spring. The force of her foot against my backside convinced me to get up, however.

'Well?' she demanded, thrusting her candle in my face.

I backed away for fear my hair would catch fire. The housekeeper's expression looked downright wicked as she peered at me. 'I don't understand. What's happening?'

'Imbecile!' she snapped. 'You're being given a final chance at salvation. Are you staying with Father Luc, or going through the rites?'

'I'll take my chances on the ceremony.'

'You and Fortune will make a fine pair, then. I thought he had more sense than to come charging up here,' Hortense said with a snort. 'Damn shame such a handsome man will meet his fate along with you, but he wouldn't listen. Now get moving!'

She shoved me out the door ahead of her, into the dark, dank passageway. Instead of taking me back through the vaults and crypts, however, Mrs Goodin steered me around the side of the cell, to a stairway I hadn't seen before. I knew better than to dawdle – my warden would singe me with her candle if I didn't move fast enough to suit her. Past a cellar we climbed, where I made out racks of wine bottles and caught the scent of musty fruit. Then I noted large rooms where food was stored, so it was no surprise when Hortense threw the door open ahead of us, and we stepped into the back pantry of the kitchen.

'Get her ready,' she ordered. 'Don't keep the abbot waiting.'

As the housekeeper hurried on through the main kitchen, eager to prepare for my doom, Sybil stepped from behind the shelves. 'Ready for some fun, Mary Grace?' she asked when Mrs Goodin was out of earshot. 'This is where we show them what you're made of. Sugar and spice, and everything nice – until they discover the real you!'

Her conspiratorial grin wrenched my heart. 'Why should I even speak to you, after the way you brought Father Luc down to torment me?' I wheeled around, preferring the cheerfully lit kitchen to this dimness where a traitor lurked.

But Sybil grabbed my arm. 'It's not that way, Mary Grace,' she whispered. 'I had to play along. If you'll trust me, you'll be going home to forget any of this ever happened.'

'Is that what you told poor Martin Crowley? And those triplets in the white gowns?'

She frowned. 'The Rosen sisters? They left here a long time ago. And Martin was too pretty to labour in the vineyards and gardens, so he didn't last more than a week.'

'They're down in the crypts and you know it!'

'Shhhhh!' Sybil clapped a hand over my mouth, looking extremely confused. Then she glanced towards the kitchen, where Elvira and Brother Paul were dragging a bathtub to the hearth. 'Fill that tub, and I'll be out with Mary Grace in just a moment,' she called to them.

When she focused on me again, standing so close her dark trousers brushed my bare thighs, Sybil spoke in a whisper. 'I don't know what Brother Christy told you about those –'

'He said they were celebrants. He implied they died during the ceremony, and that he preserved them by –'

Again her hand covered my mouth. 'This is too bizarre to go into right now. We haven't time,' she insisted. 'But yes, the rites get raucous. If these men get excited beyond their control, you can't handle them alone. Since you rejected Father Luc's proposition –'

'Why didn't you warn me about that? He said you chose to be his lover long ago!'

Sybil nipped her lush lower lip. 'Yes, but I had nothing to go back for – no future with a kind, passionate man like you have with Hyde! I knew from the start you didn't belong here, Mary Grace. You've angered Father Luc beyond belief, so now I'm –'

'But he's got you! Why does he want me?'

'Because you're fresh and young and uncorrupted. But mostly because he doesn't want Hyde to have you. Now listen to me.'

Her hand framed my jaw, as though she were going to kiss me. Her feline green eyes plumbed mine, imploring me to believe what she was about to say. 'I can't tell you what my plan is, for fear the others will catch on. But once I get into that sanctuary, you follow my lead, understand me? Play it like your life depended on it, because the abbot's so jealous it just might come to that.'

The idea that I'd be surrounded by everyone else at Heaven's Gate, at the mercy of a vengeful abbot, made my heart stop. 'But I don't know what to do! How will I ever –'

'You hush that whining!' she snapped. 'Get it into that pretty, dense head that you are in control, because you hold them in your power until they get what they want. Men are like that, Mary Grace. So you lead them on with suggestive stories, or brazen demonstrations, or whatever works, and then you play along with me as though we'd planned our little performance all along. They'll love it, I promise you. And it's your best chance to grab Fortune and get the hell out of here.'

So Mrs Goodin wasn't lying: Hyde saw through the note, and came up here to investigate. And because he didn't wait until a Friday, Father Luc moved the rites forward ... probably to humiliate me into staying. I had no doubt the abbot intended to keep me here, if not to preserve the image of Heaven's Gate confections, then to satisfy his own insidious whims.

But Sybil planned to spring me from this prison, and what better hope did I have? I still had plenty of questions about what I'd seen and heard this past week, but they would wait. Right now my only choice was to trust the woman who stood before me.

'All right. Let's do it.'

'Good girl!' she breathed, hugging me close. 'It won't be easy to face all those excited cocks and outsmart the abbot, but I know you can do it! Now get that bath – and get rid of this filthy rag you've been cowering under.'

When Sybil yanked away the blanket, which smelled even nastier than I did, I managed a smile. In the kitchen, Elvira, Vee and Zee awaited me beside a curved tub from which the steam rose invitingly. I stepped into it, adjusting to their overt gazes by telling myself these friends were the least of my concerns.

'Like what you see?' My voice shook, yet conveyed a confidence I hoped to work up to.

'You'd better believe we like it,' Elvira crooned. 'We've been hoping you'd be chosen as our celebrant, because we wanted the honour of preparing you.'

I heard not a hint of bloodlust, nor did I note any eagerness to watch me suffer. These three were still my friends, and as they rubbed me with rose-scented soap and soft sponges I let my head loll back on the lip of the tub. Had I misconstrued Brother Christy's meaning down in the crypts, surrounded by those corpses and wax mannequins? Or had he been trying to frighten me, so that my imagination led me astray?

I let go of those grotesque images, allowing the steamy water to soothe my sorry state of mind. The blonde sisters were massaging lather around my thighs, inching higher as they spread my legs. I didn't resist their luxurious touch, nor did I protest when Elvira washed my neck and breasts. Six hands were circling my most sensitive areas, kindling an inner heat that rivalled the water's.

Just as the ebony-haired vixen leaned down to suck a nipple into her mouth, one of the sisters found my slit with her fingertips. With a moan I gave in to them, thinking this far more beautiful treatment than I received from Father Luc. In and out the fingers slid. I watched through a lazy haze as Vee plied my inner folds, her intent written all over her steam-flushed face. Inside me, that secret lust I'd come to love rose quickly, and I squirmed with the need for release.

'That's enough for now,' Zee teased, swatting her sister's hand away. 'It's our job to prepare you for the rites, not to satisfy you, Mary Grace. Now Brother Quentin will shave you. Here – sit on this stool, spreadeagle.'

My confusion made the large man approaching the tub chuckle. 'Trust me, dear Mary, when you see how we're going to anoint you, you'll be glad none of that mixture gets matted into your bush,' Quentin said, unfolding a blade that caught the fire's light. 'It's a shame to shave such a splendid patch of thatch, but it'll grow back – unless you and Hyde find your new nakedness more appealing.'

216

The blonde sisters were positioning me on a stool at the bathtub's back edge. I was dripping wet, pink from the steaming water, and so stunned I could only comply when Vee and Zee each took a leg again and leaned me back into Elvira's waiting arms. 'But I don't understand why –'

'Hold still, sweetheart.' Brother Quentin focused on the hair between my splayed legs. After rubbing a shaving brush around the rose soap, he lathered my mons and the plump folds of skin flanking my cherry-coloured pussy. 'Most women balk at this the first time, yet they find the result more exciting than they'd imagined. There now . . . steady . . . you're doing well . . .'

What choice did I have? As white lather laced with my auburn curls rose with each stroke of Quentin's razor, I knew better than to struggle. And once he had cleared away the visible hair to proceed lower, I found myself strangely enthralled by the scrape of his blade. He stood so near me his warm breath fell on my clitoris, as the cutting edge came achingly close to the folds around my hole.

Quentin, too, seemed fascinated by my emerging bareness. He stopped to inhale the scent of my private parts, which were seeping with a fragrance more pungent than the soap's. I quivered with a tingling sort of fear as he stroked close to my folds with his blade. Then he scooped hot water up from the tub to rinse me – a bold sensation, now that I had no coarse, curling hair to protect my protruding clitoris.

'Did you enjoy the chocolate toy I sent you, my Mary?' he whispered. 'I lay awake that night, imagining what you did with it, hoping you recognised it as mine.'

'I – I put it to good use, yes.' I sucked in my breath as he cupped more hot water against my newly exposed skin. His middle finger slipped into the naked pink cleft he'd created, making me rise up with need.

'Oh my, I can't let this chance pass,' he murmured, and immediately planted his mouth where his blade had

217

been. His tongue covered the bared skin with quick, wet confidence before probing deep into my cunt.

I moaned and spread further, my eyes fastened on the pink, innocent-looking flesh Quentin now devoured. The sisters and Elvira encouraged my enjoyment as I speared my fingers into the monk's soft, tied-back hair. With a grunt he swivelled me around so he could suck more freely, his bulky body moving between my legs until I bent them over his broad shoulders. The heat kindled during my bath flared again, only this time there was no holding it back. Spasms rippled out from my abdomen, making me thrash against his avid mouth. Had my friends not been holding me, I would have toppled off the stool as my climax reached its scintillating peak. My cries echoed around the hanging copper pots until I collapsed with a whimper.

Quentin rocked back, grinning as he wiped my wetness from his face. 'You'll be the most splendid celebrant we've had in years, Mary Grace. Just wait until the others see what glorious adornment we've planned for you!'

My fears faded with his teasing, and as I was dried with a warm towel I considered what Sybil had told me: I did indeed seem to hold these people in my power, because they all wanted a taste of me – or wanted to test their skill at pleasing me. Vee and Zee led me into the centre of the kitchen, where Brother Paul waited with a pot of honey and a paintbrush. His eyes sparkled as he coated me with the thick stickiness, careful not to miss a single inch of my skin as I stood with my arms raised and my legs spread. Meanwhile, Elvira was binding my hair into a Psyche knot which allowed the final length of my waves to swing alluringly, just above my shoulders.

'Close your eyes and hold your breath,' Zee instructed. 'This cocoa powder will make you sneeze.'

The flaxen-haired sisters were rubbing huge powder puffs into bowls of brown cocoa, and then playfully slapping them against me to cover the honey. A cloud of sweet-scented dust enveloped us as they worked, sneezing and laughing their way around my entire body. I squeezed my eyes shut as they powdered my face, and then I was finally allowed to breathe again.

'You're ready for a licking now,' Elvira crowed, circling me with admiring eyes. 'If we weren't pressed for time, I'd eat you up before the others had their chance!'

'Me, too!' the others chimed in.

I looked like a smaller, lighter version of Ahmad, with skin that resembled umber velvet. No doubt Sybil had concocted this outrageous costume to appeal to the abbot's love of chocolate, yet my cabin-mate disappeared from the doorway when my eyes met hers. Was she betraying me, despite her insistence to the contrary? Or was there more to her escape plan than I could imagine? When Paul came out of that same little room, carefully bearing a chocolate likeness of Sybil's bust, I chose to believe she was giving each of her assistants only a piece or two of the final puzzle so they couldn't ruin her scheme for my escape.

'I remember the day we made this,' I said with a chuckle. 'But I can tell you already I won't fill it out like the original model.'

'So we'll enhance you with some nougat, which will also hold the form to your body,' the slender man replied. 'Quentin seems to have all the luck today, as he drew the short straw.'

Behind him, the taller monk grinned and held up a bowl of thick, cocoa-coloured candy filling. 'I did, and I intend to take full advantage of the situation! Now Mary, you'll need to lean forward, so your breasts swing free of your body.'

As she'd done to Sybil the day we made the chocolate cocks, Elvira held my arms to steady me. Quentin scooped a handful of the nougat and smeared the undersides of my breasts with it, glancing occasionally at the chocolate mould I was to fill. He gently spread the sweet-smelling mortar around my nipples, chuckling when they poked through it in their excitement. Layer upon layer he applied, until he was satisfied that my enlarged breasts would fill the two chocolate forms and keep them from cracking, while holding the entire mould on my body. Then he and Paul eased me into the casting, pressing it until nougat oozed around the edges.

'You can help with this part,' Quentin told his assistant, and then they licked the excess nougat from around the chocolate mould. I giggled and squirmed, still held in Elvira's gentle grip, until Zee shooed the two men away from me. When she applied a final dusting of cocoa powder, my false front matched the rest of my body so perfectly, the unknowing observer would think I'd been born with Sybil's ample endowments. For further support, Vee criss-crossed a boa of woven grapes and cherries around between my protruding breasts, and then fastened it at the back. Another length of these artfully strung fruits slithered around each thigh and was tugged up into my chocolate-powdered pussy, and wrapped at my waist.

'The queen needs a crown and a sceptre!' Paul announced theatrically, and Quentin produced them from beneath the counter nearby. I stood very still as a cluster of pale green grapes, fitted on to a tiara sparkling with hard candy, was anchored into my upswept hair.

'Your jewels, madam,' Elvira breathed as she arranged my headpiece. Grinning, she then handed me a sceptre of imposing length. 'And if any man at Heaven's Gate tells you he moulded this around himself, I hope you'll introduce me to him!'

We all laughed as I surveyed the chocolate rod, which resembled an erect cock and stood at least thirty inches high. Jewels of hard candy were embedded in a ring beneath its ridge, and a stream of crystallised white nougat rose out of the hole to flow along one side. Indeed, my bizarre costume and the jovial faces of my friends had me believing the rites of the vernal equinox might be a party awash in chocolate gaiety, until Sybil stepped in front of me. With utmost solemnity, she fastened a gold hoop on to each of my ears, and then stood back to study me.

The kitchen grew quiet. My cabin-mate circled me slowly, adjusting the cherry boas and testing the weight of my oversized chocolate bosom. Without a word, she reached up to arrange the grapes in my tiara. I kept waiting for her impish smile to appear, so I could believe Mrs Goodin and Father Luc had been threatening me only for effect – that they, too, would be laughing and carousing in a candy-coated orgy when I appeared before them.

But when she stopped in front of me, Sybil remained as serious as I'd ever seen her. 'Remember what I told you,' she said softly. 'Tease them, and lead them astray, and make them wait. They've been anticipating you for weeks now, and you mustn't let them down. You mustn't disappoint them, Mary Grace.'

The abbot's final words about not handling disappointment well echoed in my ears, and I suddenly wanted a place to hide. I gazed into Sybil's wide green eyes, but she was giving nothing more away in the presence of her friends ... friends she would continue to live with after I'd gone, if her plan worked the way she wanted it to.

I was searching for words – anything to express my gratitude and stall my arrival in that sanctuary – when the back door flew open. In stepped an angelic vision arrayed in white, wearing a voluminous gown of layer upon gossamer layer of iridescent silk, complete with wings that shimmered in the light from the fire. We gazed at her in awe, trying to guess who hid behind the white satin mask.

'Father Luc – and Hyde! – have been waiting too long!' the visitor proclaimed, 'and all the others clamour for your presence, Mary Grace. It's time to meet your fate.'

221

There was no mistaking Hortense Goodin's voice, or her vengeful grin.

I looked longingly towards Sybil, but she'd disappeared. With a pounding heart, I followed my warden towards the sanctuary.

Chapter Eighteen
Sybil's Scheme Revealed

'What a disgusting spectacle!' Mrs Goodin muttered as she ushered me through the main doors. 'You'll pay for your defiance, young lady, because the abbot requested that you wear white, as befits a celebrant. I'm tempted to scrub you down and present you dripping wet and naked, but you've kept them waiting too long as it is.'

I smiled to myself: I could recall when such a diatribe would've had me pleading for mercy. Sybil had taken my fate into her own hands, however, and I trusted her judgment. If only for a moment, the element of surprise would be in my favour; I felt a smug delight knowing I'd broken Father Luc's rules. Mrs Goodin, in her spotless white attire, was trying not to touch my chocolate-coated skin, so perhaps she wouldn't participate in the ceremony.

When she swung open the door to the sanctuary, however, my previous fears returned. Incense stung my nose, and I wondered if the vapour from Brother Christy's censers contained opium. This would explain the higher pitch of his Latin chant as he strolled along the aisles with the ornate, smoking vessels. All the other residents sat awaiting my arrival, anticipation etched on their faces. Even the kitchen crew had slipped in, eagerly looking on from the front row at my left – except for Elvira, who gazed at some point above my shoulders, and Sybil, who focused on the floor. Her presence puzzled me, for I'd expected her to arrive after my ordeal began. Only the thought that she worked her secret mischief on my behalf kept me from a state of utter panic.

The pews were shifted to either side of the sanctuary, so everyone faced a large, open area with a table in its centre. Father Luc overlooked this arena from his majestic chair, in the elevated chancel. His face reddened as he stood for a closer look at me, but his wrath wasn't what made the bottom drop out of my stomach: Hyde Fortune sat in the high-backed chair alongside the abbot's, looking serenely detached, as though he couldn't care less about my welfare.

Had he betrayed me, too? The thought stabbed my heart like an ice-pick, and I nearly lost my nerve. Just as the abbot opened his mouth, however – probably to lecture me about my appearance – the congregation jumped to its feet, clapping wildly. Mrs Goodin gripped me gingerly by the wrist and led me to the stage, clucking as the catcalls became raucous. The mayhem reached such a deafening level, Father Luc tried several times to restore order.

I maintained a solemn expression, but I was secretly thrilled. Sybil was right: these people all wanted a piece of me. So rather than entering as though for my execution, I should hold court. The choice was a matter of attitude, but it was mine, even if I couldn't predict its outcome. I tried not to feel uneasy about the way Sybil, Elvira and Hyde sat – as though oblivious to the chaos around them, unconcerned about my predicament.

Finally, after several minutes of uproar, my audience sat down. Still they murmured among themselves, pointing at my exaggerated breasts and the garlands of grapes and cherries wound around my privates, until Father Luc thundered above them.

'Silence!' he proclaimed, raising his hands. 'Your encouragement of Mary Grace's misbehaviour appalls me! The rites of the vernal equinox remain a sacred tradition at Heaven's Gate, and I won't tolerate such sacrilege. We'll observe a moment of silent prayer, during which you will properly prepare yourselves for the ceremony.'

The faces around me looked anything but penitent as heads bowed. Ahmad wore his habitual other-worldly expression while gazing at his erection. Brother Christy held his forehead, as though regretting what had come to pass. The rest of them wiggled like chastised children determined to make mischief again as soon as the abbot turned his back.

When quiet organ music encouraged meditation, my eyes flew open. Elvira always played for our services, so how could she possibly be seated beside Sybil?

I stole a glance behind me, up into the organ loft. Sure enough, my friend of blended gender winked into her organ mirror ... which meant the ebony-haired wench on the pew was made of wax. As was the Sybil seated beside her. And if these two mannequins from Brother Christy's gallery had been planted prominently to mislead me, this explained the lack of emotion on Hyde's face, as well.

Hope welled within me, but it was short-lived. If the man beside the abbot was fashioned from wax, where was the real Hyde Fortune? Had Hortense tricked me by saying he'd come up the mountain? Or had Father Luc locked him away?

The abbot's Latin incantation brought the prayer to a close. Those around me inhaled, as though fortifying themselves with the smoke hovering around our heads. Father Luc focused on me as he descended the chancel steps. 'You may be seated, Mrs Goodin.'

My warden walked to a pew at my right, her voluminous skirts rustling.

Father Luc approached me, his expression taut. I returned his gaze, considering him a wizard who might resort to sorcery, to frighten me into denying Hyde and remaining at Heaven's Gate. Indeed, his crimson stole bore mystical symbols I'd never seen, and when he stopped in front of me, his piercing eyes reflected its blood-red colour.

'Why have you defied my order to wear a ceremonial robe of white?' His voice carried like a ventriloquist's, coming from several directions at once.

'I wasn't informed of your orders. I went with Mrs Goodin, and did as I was told.'

'Don't mock me, Mary Grace!'

I stood taller, knowing I shouldn't mention Sybil's part in this. 'You've told me of your love for chocolate, sir! So why would I question being coated with it – and then strung with cherries? You're fond of those, too, I understand.'

Laughter erupted around us, until the abbot's scowl restored order. 'Cheeky little whore! You've disobeyed me since the moment you arrived. You will now confess the sins of your wayward nature, so you'll be cleansed for the ceremony.'

Was it time to stall, as Sybil had instructed? If Father Luc had imprisoned Hyde, he might have had my wily cabin-mate locked away, too. Until enough time had passed to be certain, I needed to play this charade carefully. I glanced behind the abbot. 'You mean confess publicly, so everyone – even Hyde – will know I'm unworthy of the celebrant's role?'

He grinned maliciously. And as he circled me, I detected a protrusion beneath the front of his cassock. 'Loud and clear, Mary Grace. Mr Fortune should know exactly how you've behaved in his absence.'

'But Father Luc, I –'

'None of your wheedling! Or are you afraid your

benefactor will no longer love you, and will leave you here for eternal punishment?'

I refused to let this nasty abbot play upon my doubts. 'I'm not afraid, sir!' I blurted. 'My honey's dripping down my thighs, and I'm ready for the licking I so richly deserve!'

Once again the sanctuary rang with laughter and applause. As Father Luc's face reddened, I saw my chance to distract my audience until Sybil appeared – or didn't. When the crowd grew quiet, I extended an arm towards my tormentor, swaying so my chocolate breasts shimmied. 'I suppose, since you're the abbot, you'll want the first taste of me.'

Father Luc scowled as the hoots and hollers rang around us. 'Don't toy with me, Mary Grace,' he warned. 'I'll take what I want – at your expense.'

He spun around and stalked back to his chair. Trusting Sybil's view about this ceremony being an amusement, I stood at the base of the chancel steps, where all could see my face while I recited my sins.

'How many of you witnessed my arrival, when Mrs Goodin flung open Fortune's carriage door?' I spoke out. 'How many caught me after the act, licking the come from his cock?'

Grins flickered, and several hands were raised.

'And how many of you wished yourselves in Hyde's position?'

Additional hands arose, as did the volume of their chatter.

I glanced towards Hortense in her white finery, and then twisted to look at Father Luc, whose eyes were fastened on my bottom – until he saw the way my chocolate breasts teased him from this angle. 'Yet the abbot insists my sins are the exception rather than the rule here! So let's review my misbehaviour one incident at a time, and you can be the judge of my guilt.'

I turned to face Father Luc, addressing the waxwork beside him. 'Shall we re-enact that notorious scene that

227

sullied my reputation, Hyde? Drop your pants, dear man. Let me suck your lovely cock.'

The room rang with expectant silence. As I suspected, most of the onlookers were so excited about the rites being celebrated early, they hadn't noticed the lifelike figures seated among them.

'I've instructed Mr Fortune not to speak,' the abbot said imperiously. 'He has a great deal at stake here, so he's wisely complied.'

I didn't push my point. The congregation had been alerted to Father Luc's illusions, so I continued along a path I prayed wouldn't lead to disaster before Sybil showed up.

'Perhaps you would like to enact my next sin with me, then,' I suggested boldly. 'You ordered me to remove my dress when Mrs Goodin brought me into your office. You saw the hole in my bloomers, and made me admit they were soaked with my come. And then you wanted to sniff them!'

'That's enough, Mary Grace!' the abbot warned, leaning towards me with a menacing glare. 'These are your shortcomings we're confessing here.'

But my audience was warming to my methods. 'Did Father Luc yank your clothes off?' somebody called out.

'Did he fuck you right there on his floor?' another one asked.

Slipping my hand into my crotch, I backed towards the centre of the sanctuary. 'No,' I replied, 'but he told me I was unclean, and made me strip. Then he called Mrs Goodin, and watched while she scrubbed me all over . . . especially here, between my legs. The hot water brought out the scent of Hyde's jism and my own juice, until our illustrious housekeeper was sniffing around my cunt like a depraved dog – and Father Luc was fondling himself!'

'You'll go straight to hell for such lies!' Hortense cried, bouncing up from her seat. 'I was cleansing you in the interest of your immortal soul –'

228

'Oh, shut up!' somebody cried. 'You and the abbot go at it like rabbits, and we don't care! I for one want to help Mary Grace re-enact the scenes of her sins. I'm ready to stand in for Hyde, right now!'

I turned to see Brother Ben – the balding, bespectacled man who'd licked the frosting from my fingers – parting the folds of his tunic to reveal an impressive erection. The men around him clapped him on the back, noisily egging him on. Mrs Goodin protested loudly, while the abbot again called his followers to order, but the pandemonium only increased. I didn't really want to carry through Brother Ben's challenge, but I had to answer to my actions. When I brazenly raised my arms and shimmied my chocolate bosom at him, however, the crowd suddenly turned their attention towards the door.

'I see Sybil is whipping you into a nice hot lather,' our new arrival teased, 'but since these are my sins we're confessing, I should help her, don't you think?'

My mouth fell open, but then I grinned as though I'd been expecting such a grand entrance. I should've known she'd concoct such a creative foil for me.

The woman strutting down the aisle was my identical twin: her russet hair swung from a Psyche knot, in rhythm with her dangling gypsy hoops, and each step made her candy tiara twinkle in the light from the wall sconces. Her skin was cocoa velvet. Her moulded breasts protruded with lewd chocolate allure as she walked, naked except for the boas of woven cherries and grapes, which wound between her breasts and filled the cleft of her shaven pussy. She was grinning at me, approaching with open arms.

'You're perfect!' I murmured gleefully

She arched an eyebrow as only Sybil could. 'You're just now figuring that out?'

The crowd roared its approval when we met in a full body hug. As Sybil pretended to nibble my ear, she whispered, 'Let's keep their attention on us, rather than on Luc and Hortense. Less chance of retaliation that way.'

'You're right,' I replied, careful not to crack our breasts as we undulated. 'The man beside the abbot is made of wax, and Brother Christy has also placed likenesses of you and Elvira on the front pew.'

Sybil arched backwards for a better view of this situation, so I imitated her, pressing my pussy into hers. The applause became deafening, covering our further conversation as she leaned into me again.

'I could've sworn Fortune came in here with Father Luc. But don't worry,' she whispered urgently, 'his carriage is hitched up outside, ready to go. And there's Brother Christy, slinking off with my counterpart. Let's call his bluff. Those statues might be our best friends before this is over.'

Grabbing my hands, she spun me in several tight, fast circles – a ploy to mix our identities more completely – and let go with a giddy laugh. 'Brother Christy! Brother Christy! Has someone become ill?' she called to the retreating monk.

His crumpled expression belied a plan gone awry but, with everyone watching, he had to stop in the aisle.

'Why, Sybil – it's you!' Sybil cried to her likeness.

'By God, you're right!' I replied in a matching voice, following her across the floor. 'But how can that be? I feel fine – and I'm certainly better dressed than my look-alike! What do we have here, Brother Christy?'

As the people in the pews craned their necks, the friar blushed furiously. We'd caught him in a difficult position that might lead to trouble, so I quickly continued. 'If you fashioned this figure yourself, you've done a fine job! I never knew you created waxworks, dear man.'

'They say imitation's the highest form of flattery, and if I were Sybil, I'd be greatly flattered!' Sybil chimed in. 'Of course, the true test of the sculptor's skill would be to remove the clothing.'

'Oh, Mary Grace, you're always ripping off my clothes!' I crowed. 'We might as well strip her, in case these fellows can't wait for their turn with us, don't you think?'

As we spoke in matching stage voices, Sybil was relieving Brother Christy of the female form he carried. She started towards the table, cradling the mannequin in its sitting position, while I paused beside the front pew. 'What about Elvira here? She's looking left out. And rather stiff-necked about it.'

As the congregation laughed, Sybil turned towards me. 'I've never seen Elvira naked,' she replied, her cocoa-coated face flashing me a warning. 'Perhaps public exhibition isn't her style.'

Since I'd peered under the mannequin's tunic during my tour of the crypts, I decided we might be doing the real Elvira a favour – and creating another illusion to keep our audience off-balance. I looked up towards the organ loft, grinning boldly.

'What do you think, Elvira? Ever since I reached under your robe, that day we covered cherries, I've wanted a better show. I know you're every inch a lady – and Brother Christy has rendered your womanly charms in startling detail.'

Something in my tone earned her trust, because while the others clamoured for the baring of the waxwork, Elvira replied with a brassy organ fanfare. I carried the tall, black-haired waxwork to the table and joined Sybil.

'I think we've distracted Father Luc,' she whispered as she pulled the black shirt from her counterpart. 'Let's play this as long as we can, to buy some time for Hyde.'

'Fine idea,' I replied. 'Might be good to stage our own little show, too. It'll keep Father Luc guessing as to which of us is whom. And, well . . . since this will be our last time together, I'd like to go out with a bang. If you know what I mean.'

'Listen to you,' she teased with a wicked grin. 'I'd love nothing better. But if these people swarm down to join us – and this happens at the rites – promise me you'll

231

slip away at the first chance. I've gone to all this trouble for that very reason, you know.'

I nodded, sadly aware of how much I'd miss the vixen beside me. Meanwhile, we'd stripped away black trousers and the matching shirt, as well as Elvira's brown tunic. The audience sat enthralled as we revealed the lifelike features created by Brother Christy – who stood to one side, gauging reactions to his work. Enthusiastic applause filled the sanctuary when Sybil and I gestured theatrically towards the figures we'd bared. My cohort carried her likeness to the chancel steps, positioning it so it bowed to the abbot – which left its enticing arse sticking up in invitation, from the audience's viewpoint.

More laughter and wild applause covered our conversation as I placed Elvira's waxen twin on the opposite side of the stairs.

'My God, Christy even copied the two little moles on the edge of my sex,' Sybil muttered. Her amazement proved she knew nothing about his gallery in the crypts, which confirmed her fidelity. The rites were going in my favour so far, but it was good to know I had one true friend – an ally with influence over Father Luc.

'He's obviously never seen Elvira in the altogether,' I replied with a wink. 'It's nice we can preserve some essence of mystery around here, even if it's not our own.'

My friend nodded, a gleam coming into her eye as she raised her arm for silence. 'We digress from your confession, Miss Michaels,' she announced in a challenging voice. 'We can't forget your first night at my cottage. As I recall, you and Hyde had been splashing in the stream, naked. You were kissing passionately, and he lifted you on to his huge, hard cock –'

'And you had the nerve to spy on us!' I interjected, giving her rump a resounding smack.

Sybil pivoted, poised only inches away. 'And who came to my bedside, rubbed raw – in all the wrong places – from Mrs Goodin's cleansing? And what thanks did I get for smoothing on that ointment?'

'You stuck your finger up my cunt!'

'Like this?' Sybil backed me against the centre table. To our audience, it appeared she rammed her finger inside me, yet she was careful not to sever the garland of cherries and grapes nestled between my pussy lips.

'You don't fool me, Mary Grace Goody-Goody!' she taunted. 'Poor little preacher's girl, with nowhere else to go. But you came after me in a flash, didn't you?'

'You were naked. Shaking your tits in my face.'

'And you loved it! Get yourself on this table and spread those legs, celebrant!' she cried, boosting me backwards. 'Show these people how your soul is soiled as dark as your skin!'

My moan was only partly exaggerated, for Sybil was deftly stroking my hole while her thumb pressed a cherry into my clitoris. The crowd sat forward on their pews as my tormentor stepped between my splayed legs.

'You're the one who ruined me!' I protested. 'Teaching me all your dirty little tricks –'

'Like this?' Sybil attacked my mid-section with her mouth, seeking out the sensitive spots to make me howl beneath her. Playing to our audience, she worked her way down to my clean-shaven mound. Then, sticking her tongue out hard, she drove it into my aching slit while holding my thighs apart.

My excitement rose with the low moans around us. I saw tunics inching up, and hands pumping in laps. Had I thought consciously about giving such a brazen exhibition – in a sanctuary, before a large crowd – all passion would've vanished. Indeed, the Mary Grace Michaels who first came to Heaven's Gate could not have conceived of such a performance.

But Ahmad, the mystical prophet, had been correct: I had learned the ways of Heaven's Gate, and would be forever changed by them. So as Sybil lavished her attention on me, I allowed my body to respond to every nuance, every flicker of her practised tongue. A surge of raw heat made pretence unnecessary: right there in front of Father Luc, Hortense and the others, I let the waves of my impending climax climb until I was ready to scream.

Sybil pulled away, snickering.

My eyes flew open and I sat up. 'Damn you, bitch! That's what you did to me the first time! I ought to just –'

The come-on in her feline eyes told me to play it out. So I rolled forward to grab her shoulders. The audience went wild when we hit the floor, rolling with outbursts of lust and hatred. The unknowing observer would've thought us the worst of enemies, yet Sybil's cocoa-coated face told me she was every bit as aroused by this horseplay as I. I threw my weight against her, and then rammed three fingers inside her. Everyone heard the wet, squelching sound as I drove my hand in and out of her slit.

'I'm going to leave you hanging, too!' I vowed loudly. 'That night, you called me a loser because I came first – and shot it all over you. This time will be different!'

Sybil's body curled towards mine, to preserve the chocolate shell encasing her breasts, but out of sheer pleasure, as well. 'God, you're good!' she murmured. 'Give it to me, Mary Grace. Pop the cherries strung across my cunt. But be careful of your face, love. Once the chocolate comes off, Father Luc will know who's who.'

The audience cheered when I swung my leg over her. As I faced her firm, flexing thighs, I saw her juice mingling with the honey and chocolate that coated her pink pussy lips. The sight of her shaven mound gave me an unexpected thrill, so I licked it. Sybil responded in kind: she'd pulled the boa tight against my clitoris and was sucking my inflamed slit. Our guttural moans incited a riot of passion. A few others joined us on the floor.

I concentrated on Sybil, however. She returned thrust

234

for thrust, knowing just how and where to apply that exquisite tongue pressure. My cries were muffled by her honey-slicked skin, and when I felt her quivering towards release, I bared my teeth against her. Carefully I bit into the string of cherries and grapes, close to her clit. She screamed between my legs, rocking against the floorboards as she reached a monumental peak. Then she went after my cherry in return, pushing me beyond my limits with her teeth and relentless tongue.

Hot honey rushed from my hole and I cried out in climax. We didn't have the luxury of lying entwined, however: Sybil nudged my leg, signalling that we should see what was happening around us. Sure enough, Brother Paul's blond head bobbed above Quentin's lap, while others had stripped Vee and Zee of their tunics. A delicate hand drew my attention back to the nymph beside me.

'You're smudged,' she whispered. Placing light kisses all over my face for the benefit of an onlooking abbot, she also stroked my chocolate coating over bare spots. I did the same for her, knowing our facades would be my salvation.

'Thank you,' I replied softly. 'Thank you for everything you've –'

'Too early to declare victory, Mary Grace. Here comes Ahmad, and you know damn well what he wants. I'll handle this one, if you like.'

My sphincter tightened painfully as I watched the tall figure float towards us with an ethereal smile – and the anticipation of a tight, hot spot for that perennial pecker. A quick jerk sent his wrapped pants fluttering to the floor. His obsidian eyes focused upon Sybil and then on me. The ruby in his nose winked as he folded himself down to our level.

'Ahmad, most persuasive participant in my perdition,' I crooned low in my throat.

If he detected a difference from Sybil's smoky speech, he didn't let on. 'Imitation is indeed the highest form of flattery, oh peerless parrot of my speech pattern. I have come to provide our Mary Grace with her final lesson in the higher spiritual aspirations. Perhaps this shall replace the rest of her confession, before others attack her out of need for her sweetness.'

'She is a sweet little piece, isn't she?' I quipped. 'Your wisdom has ushered her up the path to higher under-standing and inner truth. And her arsehole quivers at the first sight of you.'

Ahmad was squatting alongside us, his hands entwined prayerfully atop his bended knees. At the mention of his favourite orifice, his erection came to life, producing an awesome bubble of fluid in its hole. Like a yellow-eyed cobra it swayed between his calves, hyp-notic in its movement as it appeared to study Sybil and then me.

'Oh, Ahmad,' Sybil pleaded in an admirable parody of my voice. 'Could you? Would you? When you enter me, caressing my most secret place – probing the depths of my being – just the thought of these other heathens having me renders the experience pale, by comparison.'

His white teeth flashed and that cobra swayed faster. 'Let us anoint you, my precious pearl,' he intoned, delving two dark fingers into her cleft. 'Your nectar flows, pungent and plentiful, and Ahmad understands your need for a pleasure only he can provide. Kneel, my child. Allow the abbot full view as we explore a bliss he – and these other poor fools – can't attain.'

With an obedient smile, Sybil turned. Father Luc was watching closely as my friend prostrated herself before him, giving him full view of her chocolate cleavage as the monastery's beekeeper positioned himself behind her. When her forehead met the backs of her hands, Ahmad massaged her lovely nates as a mother would caress a favoured child's face.

Ahmad slipped his finger up her slit and then mois-tened her puckery back entry. They rocked in a seductive rhythm, with her backside pointed at his lap and his long cock sliding in her liquid silk. The sanctuary grew hushed. None of the other revellers stopped their love-making: they moved in the same cadence Ahmad estab-lished, until the entire room pulsed and throbbed as one under the mystical man's control.

The beekeeper teased Sybil's anus with a honeyed finger, which he inserted to the second knuckle. She sighed, still moving in time with him. He smiled sweetly, positioned his erection, and then entered her with an ecstatic grimace. The whole congregation moaned along with them.

Sybil raised her head, thrusting out her magnificent breasts while her chocolate body – just a shade lighter than her lover's – undulated with his, accepting every deep thrust with guttural grunts of desire. Her broken boa of grapes and cherries dragged on the floor in front of her, which attracted Father Luc's attention like a magnet. He began rubbing the front of his cassock.

Brother Christy stood in awe of this spectacle. He gaped at Sybil, who writhed like a wild mustang, her auburn hair swinging with those gold earrings. Ahmad quickened their pace. Her eyes clenched shut and she bared her teeth in a feral grimace, while Ahmad behind her began to shudder. They climaxed so violently, the tiara flew from Sybil's head, shattering on the floor. Her headpiece of green grapes followed, and when she peaked, the strain on her upper boa made cherries and grapes pop away from her chocolate bust.

Our onlookers descended like a flock of ravenous sparrows, scrambling for the loose fruit. I stood still, hoping they wouldn't attack my adornments next – or lick the nougat that was seeping from beneath Sybil's chocolate bust shell, after her exertion.

Brother Christy's face flushed with desire, and he couldn't stand still. 'I want my turn now – with Sybil,' he told the abbot. 'And by the time she's spent, I'll be warmed up enough to give Mary Grace a ride.'

He adjusted his spectacles to focus on me. While I was

pleased our charade still held, the idea of this chubby monk pumping me gave me pause. I couldn't expect my lookalike to satisfy the entire monastery's lust, however. Glancing back at Sybil and Ahmad, who were separating, I racked my brain for a way to avoid Christy's affections.

Father Luc's laugh caught everyone's attention. 'People in Hell beg for ice water, too, Brother Christy. You'll content yourself with your imitation of Sybil – since that's why you make these models, anyway.'

'But I've never asked a favour, until now!'

'Perhaps that's why you've never got any,' the abbot quipped. He stroked his short, black beard, sneering. 'Might as well get on with it, as long as it takes you to work up your wad.'

The little blond bristled, looking anything but cherubic. 'I've wanted Sybil for years, and I'm going to have her, dammit!'

'Then you should've asked her! God knows she never refuses anyone!'

'You can't expect me to –'

'Someone has to make the decisions here, and it's going to be me!'

Father Luc stood up, lording over the pitiful man before him. 'Hike up your tunic and get humping, Christy. And the rest of you –' he commanded with a sweep of his hand, 'the rest of you vultures return to your seats! Things have gone too far awry, and by God I'll tell you when it's your turn!'

While I felt relieved Brother Christy wouldn't be heaving his bulk at me, the abbot's anger didn't bode well. An anxious hush fell over the crowd. Father Luc surveyed the scene with a stern silence that was interrupted only by the rhythmic bumping of his assistant against the waxwork. I recognised the proprietary smile on his thin lips, and I didn't like it.

'Mrs Goodin, you look absolutely divine today,' he

crooned. 'Would you grace me with your presence, please?'

From behind her white satin mask, Hortense beamed. She stepped lightly across the floor, her layers of silk floating around her like airy clouds.

'I've not had the pleasure of seeing you in that gown before,' Father Luc went on, clasping his hands to camouflage his erection. 'Did you make it for today's occasion?'

'Oh, yes. It took me hours to sew all these petals, with their beaded trim,' she gushed. She glanced at Brother Christy, who laboured over his waxen woman's backside, and stood taller in triumph. 'I knew you'd appreciate my efforts, because these rites are even more auspicious than usual, aren't they?'

Father Luc smiled, yet I doubted Hortense saw the look of a fox who's coaxed a chicken into a corner. She appeared ten years younger, giddy with her own expectations, after seeing her husband humiliated. 'What an astute observation, Hortense. And why do we find the ceremony especially tantalising this spring?'

'When have we ever had a celebrant like Mary Grace?' she twittered. 'Why, Father Luc, I haven't seen you so aroused since – well, since Sybil came to Heaven's Gate! And if you're excited, then I'm excited for you! Such a fresh young face is hard to come by.'

I felt ill. I stood absolutely still, hoping not to attract attention; not daring to look at my friend, who sat beside Ahmad on the floor. The only sound in the sanctuary came from the monk seeking his satisfaction on the stairs.

'A fresh face . . . yes,' the abbot mused. He rocked on his heels, as though he couldn't contain his mirth. 'And on the subject of faces, Mrs Goodin, would you bless me with the sunshine of yours? Your mask would make me a lovely souvenir.'

The housekeeper swept off the satin mask and extended it towards Father Luc, who held her fingertips a moment too long. This wasn't the Hortense Goodin I knew, and I sensed the other shoe was about to drop. Those around me shifted in suspense, wondering if the abbot would romance his housekeeper while we watched.

'I want your gown, too, Mrs Goodin,' he continued without batting an eye. 'Mary Grace and Sybil will assist you.'

Hortense gasped. 'But Father Luc –'

'Why do you argue with me?' he asked blandly. 'Is it because you desire humiliation similar to Brother Christy's? Or because you're not wearing underthings?'

She squawked like an enraged swan. 'But I prepared myself especially for –'

'For me?' he said with an arrogant laugh. 'I take my delight where I find it, Hortense. And I dearly love watching my subordinates endure the same punishments they dish out. Girls!'

The abbot snapped his fingers at Sybil and me, grinning gleefully. As Mrs Goodin pivoted to challenge us with a self-righteous glare, I whispered, 'This one's mine, Sybil. Assist me as you will, but I want my revenge.'

When we stood on either side of the housekeeper, Father Luc smiled down on us. 'Mrs Goodin has foolishly hoped to capture my attention today, knowing it's Mary Grace I favour. You chocolate-covered nymphs should put her in her place, just as she's humiliated you in the past. No holds barred – and believe me, she craves chocolate even more than I.'

While the abbot spoke words I'd yearned to hear, he was also aiming at me: once the forms came off our busts, and once our faces came clean, I would be his prey again – unless I found a way out before my unmasking. Yet I relished this opportunity.

'Wouldn't it be a shame, Mary Grace, if our laundress's beautiful white gown got soiled before we could give it to Father Luc?' I proposed in a throaty voice.

'And think of her horror, dear Sybil, if she had to cleanse us without her lye soap.'

I snickered. 'Surely you're mistaken, Sybil. I'm Mary Grace.'

'Oh, that can't be. My name is Mary Grace!'

'I think we should stop quibbling and make a Goodin sandwich.'

We moved in one fluid motion to catch Hortense between our chocolate bodies, Sybil undulating against her front while I wrapped my arms around her from behind. Mrs Goodin cursed, struggling between us – which smeared her gown even more. With the abbot's laughter goading us on, my assistant unfastened the pearl buttons down her front while I held her tightly.

'This is the most indecent waste of – Father Luc won't want this gown once it's ruined!' she screeched.

'Do you really think it's the dress he's after?' I mocked. 'He doesn't impress me as the type to wear them.'

'Oh yes, the abbot's all man!' Sybil chimed in. 'What he really wants is to see you stripped and cleansed of your sins. Naked before your Master.'

'Begging forgiveness for your adulterous ways.' I tugged on the gown's unbuttoned bodice to bare the housekeeper's upper body. The seamstress in me refused to tear such a magnificent fabric, so I said, 'Co-operate, Hortense. If you thrash about and rip this silk, the abbot will be sorely disappointed.'

'And we all know he doesn't handle disappointment well,' my friend mimicked.

Mrs Goodin stopped struggling. After Sybil handed the stained gown to Father Luc, we turned the housekeeper to face the congregation. For a woman her age, her body was remarkably firm, but as she stood there, wearing only her white stockings and opera pumps, Hortense shook until her pendulous breasts jiggled.

'Why do I sense this woman isn't quaking from shame?' I asked loudly. 'Could it be she secretly longs for the same degradation she hands out?'

Our spectators chuckled, and a few of them clapped.

'Like when she forced my legs apart, to watch Hyde's juice ooze down my thigh?' Sybil asked theatrically. 'She clucked like a biddy hen, but I had the impression she wanted to lick that jism! And she wanted Father Luc to watch!'

'And who are we to deprive her of her secret longings – eating hot twat, and gorging herself on chocolate!'

Sybil flashed me a wicked grin, and we headed for the table. Hortense kicked and flailed between us, while the applause rose in volume, but her expression told of her rising excitement.

'This is an outrage!' she cried as we boosted her on to the table. 'And you! You just mind your own business, Christopher!'

I glanced over my shoulder. Brother Christy had shifted the wax object of his affections so he could watch his wife's undoing. His cheeks shone with joy and he attacked his mannequin with renewed vigour when she landed on her back, with Sybil straddling her face.

'Lick me clean,' the russet-haired hellcat commanded. 'Love me with that vicious tongue, until you've lapped up every drop of Ahmad's spunk. If you pleasure me well, maybe I'll let you kiss my arse for that chocolate you're wanting. Get busy, bitch!'

Mrs Goodin's protest was muffled when Sybil pressed her pussy to the woman's mouth, which brought another round of cheers. As I held the housekeeper's tensing legs, I realised our hostage was glorying in this situation. I watched my friend's delectable chocolate buttocks flexing, forcing Hortense to either struggle for air, or to strain towards the juicy, pink passion fruit Sybil tormented her with. Mrs Goodin's sex glistened beneath her coiled, grey bush – and the sight of the sceptre I'd left on the floor inspired me further.

'Here comes a chocolate cock!' I crowed, cracking the long pole against the table's edge to make it a manage-

242

able length. 'Pretend it belongs to Father Luc. Live your dreams, Hortense.'

I shoved the shaft between her legs, up a cunt that gripped it fiercely. Mrs Goodin groaned as I plied the chocolate rod up and around, torturing her clitoris with the hard candy jewels embedded at its rim. Just then, Sybil raised herself high enough that her victim had to reach desperately, tongue extended, to regain contact with the slick skin she was lapping at.

My insides tightened: the sight of her pussy shaven clean, as I saw Sybil's engorged folds fluttering like a butterfly above a bud, sent a surge of hot longing through me. I thrust the dildo into Goodin's quivering cunt, redolent with melting chocolate and sex, until juice trickled down my own leg.

I sprang on to the table to straddle the housekeeper, grasping Sybil's waist to keep my balance. The watchers went wild when I found the chocolate cock, and then impaled myself upon it. I slid until I bumped Goodin's bush, using it to cushion my thrusts. Seven heavenly inches of candy filled my passageway, so the woman I sat upon was that full, too. Recalling why I wanted to humiliate her, I shoved against her relentlessly.

The sanctuary rang with a lusty roar while Sybil and I rode Hortense Goodin in tandem. Our two bodies pumped in time, forcing our captive to keep our beat at both ends. When our pace grew more frenzied, we tormentors became tormented, as well. The legs under mine curled around my backside, driving me at Goodin's own delirious speed, so I gave myself over to hot chocolate decadence until we squirmed in release. Sybil, too, succumbed with a startling series of squeals, until she and I collapsed against each other.

Our audience let out a collective sigh. Then all we heard were furtive gropings, and the rustle of clothing being shoved aside – and Brother Christy's near-hysterical grunts. When Hortense shook beneath us, however, I realised she was laughing.

'She enjoyed us too much,' I muttered. 'I have just the punishment in mind.'

'Have your way with her, then. Any woman this incorrigible deserves whatever revenge you can wreak upon her.'

Like a lithe chocolate frog, Sybil hopped over Mrs Goodin's head and on to the floor. I dismounted, too, delighting in the brown, gooey mess we'd made of the monastery's fastidious mistress.

'What're you doing?' she asked warily.

We helped her to a sitting position. 'I guess you'll find out, won't you?' Sybil quipped.

'But you can't leave me with this – this slop all over my face,' Hortense cried, whimpering when we caught her hands to keep her from wiping it off. 'It's going to gush down my legs when I stand up, if you don't –'

'Tell your troubles to Jesus!' I sang out. 'Meanwhile, I think poor Elvira could use a hug. And by the sound of it, Mister Christopher's about ready to shoot to the moon. High time you allowed him his husbandly rights, don't you think?'

We had hardly escorted the horrified Hortense over to the kneeling mannequin, before Brother Christy grabbed her from behind. She had no choice but to brace herself against his wax creation and bend with him. With a torrent of ecstatic murmurings, the monk positioned his prodigious red erection and claimed his prize. The applause was deafening, mixed with calls of encouragement as the friar pumped her so hard his spectacles flew off.

I glanced at Sybil, wondering what we could do next to distract the abbot. She squinted – and then so did I, half-blinded by a glare of light coming from above us. It was Elvira signalling us with the organ mirror. And beside her stood Hyde Fortune.

Never in my life had I been so overjoyed. I didn't care if he'd witnessed my debauchery against Mrs Goodin. Or that he saw me naked, except for my lewd breast casing and fruited boas, performing for all these people. I was finally going home with the man I loved!

I yelped and ran across the sanctuary.

'And now it's time for the rest of us to have our fun!' the abbot proclaimed behind me. 'Off with their chocolate!''

Chapter Nineteen
The Abbot Has His Way

'No! Let me go! Let me out of here!'

They fell upon me like a swarm of locusts. I could hear Sybil telling her kitchen assistants to get me out of the sanctuary, but she, too, had been caught up by the crowd. Our admirers, driven to their limits by the opium incense and our titillating behaviour, were too eager for a taste of us to allow our escape.

When I managed a glance at the organ loft, Hyde had disappeared. Had he left me, disgusted? Or would he fight his way through this delirious mob to save what was left of my virtue? I'd remained faithful to him – if only by a dubious stretch of definition – and to see that shattered now, at the abbot's whim, tore my heart out.

The boa around my waist popped when two monks hoisted me from the floor. Brother Nolan, the orchard worker with the wondrous tongue, had ducked between my legs during the mayhem and was kissing his way up my honeyed thighs with a look of absolute bliss. I couldn't see the mouths massaging my backside or the hands unfastening the cherries and grapes strung around my bust, but this frenetic energy frightened me. Rather than feeling pleasantly ravished or deliciously decadent, I was worried about being eaten alive. My entire body oozed honey and cocoa in the heat generated by all these people, and nougat was seeping from the bottom of my candy bust. When the chocolate shell cracked between my breasts, a wild cry arose from those who held me. My nightmare of becoming a living sacrifice had come true.

'You've had your fun now. Carry her to the table.'

It was Father Luc, demanding his due. The men who held me got in a few more licks, but then they bore me to the symbolic altar for my final rites. I was too frightened to cry. I had only myself to blame, for running towards Hyde in my happiness to see him. Desires had suddenly burgeoned beyond our control, and I couldn't expect Sybil to intercede for me now.

My aroused captors laid me on the table-top and then backed away like whipped puppies. As I watched the abbot approach, I understood why: stripped of his black cassock, he appeared several inches taller: a mighty, omnipotent god who commanded absolute obedience. His olive skin flexed as he walked, giving the appearance of a much younger man intent on having his way – a dark, disreputable master who could seduce the most reluctant woman with only a look.

Black hair hugged his chest, descending in a vee towards the most provocative cock I'd ever seen. Not only did it jut proudly skyward, but it looked three inches thick. Its plum-shaped head shone such a lustrous pink I wondered if I could see my reflection in it – not that I'd try. The entire shaft bobbed ponderously as he walked, and when he stopped in front of me I stared at it with a mixture of curiosity and dread . . . and desire.

'Patience, dear Mary. You'll have every inch of that, in good time.'

His arrogance brought me out of my trance. While some of the others took their pleasure with Sybil across the room, Father Luc appeared oblivious to the din in his scrutiny of me, the lamb finally brought to slaughter. His ebony beard glistened as his jaw clenched, pulling his moustache into a more malicious position. He crossed his arms upon his chest – to keep from grabbing me outright, I sensed – and continued to ravish me with his gaze.

'Mine at last,' he whispered, his nostrils flaring. 'We'll wait for Hyde, to make the consummation even more meaningful.'

I was ready to spit at him, but a jolt of realisation stopped me. Those devilish eyes held mine with a mesmerising heat I'd often found familiar, but now I knew why: his irises glowed like hellfire. It was the same smouldering cinnamon of Hyde's eyes, except far more potent. Hypnotic. Totally in control.

'Luc, please. I'll stand in for Mary Grace. I'll do anything you wish, if you let her go.'

The abbot's head snapped towards Sybil's voice. Her admirers had licked her clean and consumed the chocolate shell around her bosom, leaving her naked on the stage. 'Don't be ridiculous,' he said. 'I already have what I want from you.'

'But she doesn't belong here. She's not like us.'

'Nonsense. Mary Grace has taken to our ways like a swan to water. And everyone enjoys her immensely.' He rested his erection against the edge of the table, a thoughtful sneer angling across his dark face. 'You love her most of all, Sybil, so why are you eager to see her go? Planning to join her, perhaps?'

'Of course not! It's just –'

The crack in her voice matched the one in my heart as Sybil poured out her soul.

'– well, I think it's wonderful that Mary Grace has found someone who truly loves her. I'm the soul of depravity, but I can't keep her from a man like Hyde,' she continued plaintively. 'How different my life might be, had I found someone like Fortune before I came here.'

Laughter began as a low rumble in Father Luc's chest and then burst forth to fill the room. 'How absolutely touching!' he jeered. 'But this fit of conscience is too little, too late, my dear. And here comes our would-have-been bridegroom to plead for his beloved, as well!'

The sight of a bristling Hyde Fortune should've rallied my spirits, yet as the abbot placed a hand on my mid-section to lay me flat, I closed my eyes in resignation. All the others had slunk towards the pews, fully aware of the power this man embodied.

'I don't know what the hell's been going on here,' Hyde bellowed, his footsteps a loud tattoo on the wooden floor, 'but you're going to release Mary Grace –'

'Stand back!' the abbot warned, pointing at him with a diabolical sneer. 'You encouraged Miss Michaels to live among us, and you will now bear witness to a level of ecstasy few can attain, and only I can inspire. Watch her and weep, Fortune!'

A collective gasp made my eyes fly open. Although the two men had not touched, Hyde now stood stunned, as though rendered helpless by some unseen bolt of lightning shot from Father Luc's outstretched hand. He blinked, but had no further inclination to challenge the abbot. An eerie silence enveloped the sanctuary. Sybil sat down, and a rustling behind me indicated that Hortense and Brother Christy had taken themselves out of harm's way, as well.

My nemesis then turned his attention to me again. And as he gazed into my face, my body relaxed. I basked in the warmth from those eyes that glowed like coals – coals from the Devil's own fire. Yet I no longer felt the need to resist.

'Yes, dear Mary, entrust yourself to me,' he murmured. 'I loved you long before you came here, and have anticipated this moment with a joy you cannot comprehend. Be still, and let me show you what mere mortals miss.'

In the last rational fragment of my mind, I knew I should fight this demon posing as a priest, but I hadn't the strength. I felt serenely submerged in a womblike warmth that insulated me from all strife and shame, and I sensed this aura emanated from the abbot's gaze as well as the hand that still rested on my abdomen. His smile reassured me, and I returned it.

Father Luc then ran his fingers lightly along my sides. 'Lie back and enjoy this, my sweet. This is my gift to you, that you may never regret surrendering yourself.'

He began at the sole of one foot, taking it tenderly between his hands so he could kiss every inch of my skin. Where the others had devoured me like famished animals, the abbot lingered over each curve, lavishing his affection, taking only what remained of my cocoa coating for his own enjoyment. His tongue, warm and slightly rough, left a trail of tingling desire as he worked his way up my leg, until I simmered like a seductive love potion in a cosy pot.

'Yes, close your eyes,' he murmured when my lids got heavy. 'Wonders beyond imagination will unfold, if you accept my magic.'

What else could I do? I let out a blissful sigh, lost in the sense that time stood still and nothing mattered, save the sating of a desire that bubbled within me like fudge, sweet and rich and thick. Father Luc laved the length of my other leg and then gave my clitoris a teasing flick. 'We'll save the best for last,' he whispered.

With his fingertips he drew delightful lines, defining planes of erotic need along my sides and stomach. I squirmed with delight, seeing swirls of innocent pink behind my eyelids, feeling highly alive yet still so willfully submissive. The abbot's smile was so warm I could feel it, like a sun at the centre of my personal universe. My limbs hung limp. My pulse accelerated with the passion he inspired, yet I instinctively knew to lie still and accept his gift. I stretched with the utter luxury of a cat, thrumming with sexual energy. So very, very content.

He lifted away the chocolate casing around my breasts. 'We'll save this to enjoy later,' he said, setting the two hardened halves aside. Then he wiped the nougat from my chest with a soft cloth, filling the air around us with the sweetness of the melted candy while spreading an even sweeter heat through my insides. My slit trickled and the folds around it twitched with need.

'You have the most beautiful breasts I've ever seen,' Father Luc breathed, and when he cupped them and cradled their weight, I let out a languid sigh. His thumbs rubbed my nipples, which swelled into sharp, aching buds. So effortlessly he aroused me, caressing my chest and then enfolding my breasts in a seductive squeeze that made me see swirls of fuchsia and blue.

When he pressed his lips to my skin, my legs instinctively hugged his hips.

'Ah, so eager,' he teased, bracing his weight on his elbows. 'But you'll have to wait, my Mary. Lovemaking requires patience and finesse, and a fine sense of timing.'

Father Luc kissed my breasts more insistently then. The scrape of his beard and the slickness of his heated lips filled me with with a desperate desire. I dug my fingers into his hair, marvelling at its silkiness. Whimpering, I urged him to suck each of my breasts into his mouth while I writhed with the ecstasy this ignited.

'Kiss me ... kiss me,' I breathed. The colours in my mind's eye twirled more tightly now, the hot pink throbbing resembling a pussy, with a deep azure hole begging to be filled.

The abbot pressed himself into a fiery kiss, his body lying fully upon mine. Our mouths moved fiercely, seeking release. Every tendon in my body, every level of my being, pulsed to the beat set by this maniacal piper and I danced as I'd never done before. The tip of his huge cock rested against my cunt, spreading his wetness to blend with mine, yet holding back – withdrawing to torment me when I thrust up to engulf it.

'Ah, my Mary, I knew it would be this way,' he whispered near my ear. 'So passionate you are, so perfectly fashioned to satisfy me. I've brought you to the brink and I won't disappoint you. Let me take you higher, to a place you've never been.'

His hand slipped between our bodies so he could circle my clitoris. I yelped with my need, curling against the finger that inflamed me. It was scarlet I saw now, leaping and dancing flames, searing my soul beyond redemption as I felt the spasms begin. I slipped into a state akin to unconsciousness, yet I'd never flown so high nor felt so vibrantly alive as I arched and shuddered against him.

'Fuck me! Fuck me now!' I thrashed against him, searching for the shaft that would fill me with its power.

But Father Luc held us at the edge. 'Open your eyes, my love. I want you to be looking at me when we come together.'

I obeyed, and then cried out: he had positioned my head so it was Hyde I saw. The pain on Fortune's face sent me into a fit of sobbing, yet I couldn't stop thrusting against the man who held me captive on the table.

My greed for release consumed me, intensified by a blinding rage. 'Take me, you bastard.' I rasped. 'You know I can't stand this any longer. You know how I hate you, yet I have to have you.'

Father Luc's eyes glowed amber as he positioned his cock against my open, hungry hole. 'Congratulations, Mary Grace,' he said in a sibilant whisper. 'You've played our game with honour and commendable virtue. But it's time for me to win. I always win, you see.'

'Your game?' I demanded. 'You can't tell me –'

His chuckle paralysed me. 'It's true, sweet Mary. I saw you enslaved to your despotic father, and knew even then I had to have you. It was easy to send him over that edge – a victim to his own greed and our brandied cakes – and easier yet to make Hyde co-operate. He already believed in the higher purpose of Heaven's Gate; he's dedicated himself to noble causes all along. So you see, this moment is the culmination of all our hopes and highest aspirations. The reason for our being.'

Father Luc lunged, filling me with his fearsome cock. The force and size of it threw me back against the table, yet even in my dazed state I squeezed its throbbing girth to suck it deeper inside me. The colours in my head were spinning so fast I had the sensation of being levitated, weightless – or was it further evidence of the abbot's unearthly spell over me? A magic so black it swallowed me whole while catapulting me beyond all comprehension.

Like a sawdust doll I flailed as the abbot pumped me, yet I begged him like one possessed to fuck me harder. My head thumped the table, punctuating his grunts until he shot into me with such volcanic force I fell senseless. A final crack of my skull made stars explode behind my eyes, and a mind-shattering climax sent me into black oblivion.

Chapter Twenty
Fate, or Fortune?

'*T*he Lord is my shepherd, I shall not want. He maketh me to lie down in green pastures . . . He leadeth me beside the still waters . . . He restoreth my soul.'

I drifted into awareness, vaguely wondering if I were a spirit attending my own funeral. My body felt cushioned in warmth, and I would've been content to float in that semi-conscious state forever if my head hadn't been racked by a sharp pain. I moaned and my eyes flew open.

The soothing voice stopped. The candlelight dimmed as figures stepped in around me.

'Mary Grace? Welcome back, sweetheart. How are you feeling?'

My eyes took their time about focusing upon a man who seemed familiar, and then upon two other faces. One was distinctly female, her pale ochre skin set off by an elaborate topknot of ebony hair. The other, ruddy and defined by a close-cropped black beard, made my heart skitter. I shrank away, wishing I could escape into that deep, numbing sleep again.

'Easy now, love. Surely you remember Sebastian?' came the voice I'd heard earlier. 'You're not fully awake, Mary Grace. It'll all come back to you eventually.'

That's what frightened me most: that it would all come back, and the nightmarish images in my head would mean I hadn't escaped Heaven's Gate after all. My mind had vibrated, even in sleep, with the raucous calls of a crowd while I paraded naked, allowing dozens of men to fondle and lick my body. I smelled incense and my skin felt sticky. Most ominous, however, were visions of a dark demon wielding his power while I succumbed, without resistance, to unthinkable acts of humiliation and shame.

'Can you hear me, Mary Grace? Do you know who I am?'

The timbre of that low voice convinced me to concentrate on the face that was lowering towards mine. A wedge of sandy hair fell over his brow, accentuating eyes that shone with compassion. He radiated a love I longed for, and I wondered if it were the Saviour Himself bending over me. I whimpered, feeling inadequate, unworthy of his concern.

When he frowned, it all came back with horrible clarity: the same pain I'd seen on the face I loved most, as the abbot entered me.

'Hyde,' I murmured, turning my face from him.

'Yes. Oh, thank God!' he said, caressing my cheek. 'She's going to be fine. It was just a nasty whack on the head.'

This would explain the continuous throbbing that filled my skull. I hovered on the edge of sleep, to escape this pain as well as my betrayal of the man I recognised as Mr Fortune. If I could drift off again, I wouldn't have to face my degradation or the sense of failure filling my heart.

'I fetch missy some tea,' the woman said. 'You come, too, Sebastian. Mister Hyde need time alone with her. She been to hell and back, by the sound of things.'

As they walked away, the exotically accented words rang true. I had indeed been to hell. I'd survived the trip, and now had to own up to my actions.

The mattress dipped with Hyde's weight. 'You're home now, Mary Grace. Here among those who love you,' he murmured. 'I'd give twenty years of my life to turn back the calendar, to before I took you to Heaven's Gate. My God, if I'd had any idea – !'

He rose to pace beside the bed, his anguish resounding even more deeply than mine. I watched him, so magnificently handsome and consumed by a remorse I didn't understand.

'Can you ever forgive me, Mary Grace? Please say you will.'

I frowned, which intensified the aching in my head. 'As I recall, it was I who willingly went into that ceremony, wearing only honey and cocoa and . . . and strings of grapes and cherries. It's a wonder you brought me back, after the way I . . . let Father Luc . . .'

Hyde sat beside me again, scowling. 'He befuddled us both, sweetheart! I could tell by your eyes that he'd cast a spell – and then he nailed me in place! I've never felt so utterly useless. When I should've been snatching you away from him, I watched that bastard mock your honour before shoving his cock into you!'

My slit twitched. And although my mind recoiled at what I'd allowed to take place – begging Father Luc to fuck me, like some shameless hussy – my body came vibrantly awake. 'I'm sorry you drove all that way, only to watch my decadent display. It must've been awful.'

Hyde cleared his throat. 'Actually,' he began, 'you were a glorious sight, Mary Grace. While I detested the abbot for making us pawns in some insidious game, I found myself wishing it were I who made you scream with ecstasy on that table. I hope you'll give me the chance again some day.'

I wanted to smile and say yes, everything would be fine, as though I'd never gone to the monastery. But when I untangled the hair at my ear, and my fingers found a hoop – jewellery like Mary Grace Michaels had never owned – I snapped out of my wishful thinking.

It was all true. There really was a Sybil, and she'd disguised us as cocoa-covered twins to keep me safe from the abbot, and to return me to Hyde. Her earrings would forever remind me of the orgy gone awry in a sanctuary which was more like a brothel than a house of God.

Yet I cherished her friendship. She'd taught me some surprising things about myself.

It was Hyde's story I needed to concentrate on, however. Perhaps, now that I was fully awake, he could answer some nagging questions. With his assistance, I sat against the pillows he propped behind my back.

'Tell me about this game,' I murmured. 'While Brother Christy confessed he wasn't really a monk – and you wouldn't believe what he showed me, in the catacombs – I couldn't grasp what Father Luc was saying. Something about driving Papa over the cliff, and bringing you into the picture, all so he could get me to Heaven's Gate.'

Hyde again caressed my cheek. 'I couldn't believe what I was hearing, either. But I understand it a little better now that I've talked with my ... there's someone you need to meet, Mary Grace. I hope you'll understand why I've kept her hidden away.'

He looked towards the corner, where candlelight didn't penetrate the darkness; this was the bedroom Hyde and I slept in, before I fled Mount Calvary for the freedom I perceived at Heaven's Gate. The rustling of fabric made me peer around Hyde's body, and when a wizened figure stepped into the light, I sucked in my breath.

She wore the same translucent gown, and floated towards me with the same wispy hair and slightly wild eyes. Only Hyde's presence kept me from diving beneath the covers, as I'd done the first time I watched this wraith appear.

'Mother, I'd like to introduce Mary Grace Michaels,' he said gently.

My mind protested: I'd walked past Madeleine Fortune's headstone every time I visited Mama's grave. Yet Hyde talked as though his mother was part of his everyday life.

'Didn't I promise you she'd recover? Your idea about a Scripture vigil brought her around, just as we hoped,' he continued, as though reassuring a frightened child. 'Tell Mary Grace what you explained to me, about Father Luc and –'

'Don't go,' the woman wheezed. 'Those who enter Heaven's Gate are lost forever!'

Her body crumpled in a fit of coughing, and my fear was replaced by pity. Hyde towered above her stooping shoulders, tenderly guiding her towards the bed. His expression begged my indulgence.

'I didn't know, until last night, that Mother spent some time at the monastery as a young woman. Her story answers a lot of questions, if she's strong enough to repeat it for you.'

I reached for her withered hand, which felt like a little bundle of twigs in tissue paper. Madeleine Fortune looked fragile and dry, an autumn leaf that a breeze might carry away, yet the existence of a robust son meant she'd once been bursting with life. 'I'm so pleased to meet you,' I said. 'I hope you'll excuse my intrusion in your home – and my childish reaction when I saw you here several weeks ago.'

The hand inside mine squeezed back. 'I'm so glad you're here, Mary Grace. My son needs a responsible woman in his life, so that when I expire –'

'Now, Mother, you're fine,' Hyde insisted.

'– I know he'll be cared for,' she finished. Saying this seemed to bolster her courage. Her blue eyes sparkled in a face as pale as a daisy.

I sensed she'd wander unless we kept her on the subject, so I held her hand between both of mine. 'Hyde tells me you've met Father Luc.'

Her nostrils pinched in as she inhaled, but she regained her composure. 'His full name is Lucifer, you know. He didn't tell me that outright, but I'm sure a bright girl like yourself has figured it out.'

I tried not to let my head spin with her implication. For now, I wanted to listen rather than think, so I pressed on. 'And you went to Heaven's Gate? And it was an ancient monastery, where monks raised grapes and sold brandied sweets?'

'They were just beginning to make those cakes, as I recall,' she said in a faraway voice. She squinted then, studying my face. 'If I weren't getting a bit feeble, I'd swear you look exactly like the young woman who baked them.'

'Sybil,' I whispered.

'A lovely girl, but so brazen. Of course, everyone looked for an excuse to lose their clothes, so it's little wonder she behaved the same way.'

Madeleine fretted with the folds of her nightgown as though picking at loose threads, but after a few moments she focused on me again.

'I've never told anyone about these things, until Hyde brought you home last night, unconscious. I suspected trouble when I saw that pudgy blond monk through my window,' she continued in a hesitant voice. 'You see, I went to Heaven's Gate when I was about your age, after my parents died in a horrible fire. I thought it was the answer to my prayers, but as time went by, I realised something unthinkable was amiss. When I announced my intention to return to town, to become a school marm, I was made the celebrant for the celebration of the winter solstice. It was an orgy the likes of which I've never seen – and – and –'

'And Father Luc had his way with her,' Hyde went on, his lips in a bitter line. 'He got what he wanted, and he grew bored. Left her to wander down the mountain-side, in the dead of winter.'

The waif beside us nodded sadly. 'I was with child. I imagined the abbot laughing at my predicament, knowing I'd think of him every time I looked into my son's

259

eyes. I tried to give Hyde a normal childhood, and schooling –'

'I've told you how she sacrificed herself for me,' he said softly, calling to mind his mother's lot as a prostitute.

'– but I feared Luc would come after me and take his revenge for the way I defied him, and raised a good boy in spite of him.'

She shook with her horrible memories, so Hyde pulled her close, signalling the end of the conversation. I bade her a soft good night, and he carried her like a child, to some unknown region in the massive house.

I sat alone on the bed, sorting out this startling new information. My tired mind wasn't ready to dwell upon who Father Luc really might be, yet it explained the timeless, ongoing nature of Heaven's Gate, and its perfect climate, and so many other details about the life and the people there.

Hyde returned shortly, hesitating at my bedside. 'Do you understand why she lives as a recluse, eternally cloistered in this house?' he asked. 'As the years went by, her experience with Father Luc ate away at her sanity, until she became obsessed with the notion that he might come after her. The only way I could relieve her fears was to perform a closed-casket funeral, and erect a headstone, and promise her I'd see to all her needs.'

What a lonely, confining life – all because of Father Luc's intimidation. I had indeed been a game piece, as had Hyde. We'd provided diversions for the black-souled master of that monastic retreat, which resembled Paradise to the unwitting visitor.

'How horrible for you, to learn that Luc is your father, after what he made you watch.'

His smile flickered sadly. 'It was just another way of exerting his power and control. For all we know, he's left dozens of offspring in far worse circumstances than mine. I'm just grateful to Sybil – she helped me carry your things to the carriage, once the abbot was occupied with the ceremonies – and glad I arrived in time to reclaim you.'

I let out a resentful snort. 'Father Luc would've begun the ceremony whenever you showed up. It was his mission to humiliate you while he did the same to me.'

'It gave me quite a start, to see myself seated in that chair in the chancel, and to observe the frenzy the others had reached. If I'd had any idea about –'

'They only show you what they want you to see,' I offered.

'But we're sometimes blinded by our own arrogance. I should've realised things weren't as they seemed,' he said with a rueful smile. 'But I liked to think Sybil's propositions were a way to bend the rules, because she couldn't resist me.'

I smiled in spite of a tightness in my stomach.

'And I delighted in the changes I saw in you, Mary Grace, as you discovered new levels of excitement. New ways to attain pleasure. I hope we'll pursue some of those same . . . extremely erotic adventures, my love. My wish to marry you has never wavered, you know.'

Had I accepted his proposal last January, I could've opened my arms and enjoyed the affections of a handsome, compassionate man. Such comfort and love were the perfect antidotes to my poisonous thoughts, now that I realised the truth about Heaven's Gate. But I couldn't change the decision I'd made back then.

'You don't know half of what went on there,' I murmured. 'When I think back, I wonder if I weren't caught in some sort of unholy enchantment from the moment I met the abbot.'

'That's exactly how Mother put it. So you shouldn't hold yourself responsible for things beyond your control, dear Mary.'

'But I feel – unclean. Defiled.'

His dimple winked mischievously. 'Yu Ling was running a bath when I returned from tucking Mother in. Perhaps a hot soak is exactly what you need, considering the honey and chocolate you were wearing. And after a night's rest, I hope you'll feel up to a walk. I have a surprise for you, dear lady.'

What woman wouldn't flush with pleasure, knowing her man thought of her while she was away? Yet a sense of dread filled me. I didn't want to disappoint Hyde Fortune, after all his kindness. I didn't deserve him, and wanted him to be free of yet another parasite; another pariah he surely wouldn't want to be responsible for.

But my skin was sticky, so I agreed to the bath. As he escorted me into that steamy room, again scented with rose soap, his Celestial servant bowed with a catlike smile. 'Missy Mary want Yu Ling's assistance?'

'I'll be taking care of her, thank you,' Hyde replied quietly.

I recalled the last time I'd bathed here, when that exotic woman had climbed into the tub with me. I'd been such an innocent, I'd nearly jumped out of my skin when she put a sponge between my legs! For this bath, however, I was grateful for privacy. Hyde helped me from my nightgown and steadied my arm as I stepped into the water.

'Heavenly,' I murmured as the wet heat seeped into my skin. I closed my eyes, letting my head rest against the back of the clawfoot tub.

'Yes, you are,' came the soft reply.

As Hyde washed my neck and shoulders, the tension left my body. He was so gentle, massaging me with the soapy washcloth as though I were an invalid in need of tender care. My nipples sprang to life at his touch, and I languidly allowed him to caress my breasts and stomach before dipping between my open thighs.

'Feel good?' he whispered, kissing my damp temple.

'Wonderful ... absolutely divine,' I breathed, lifting my hips so he could wash those, too.

'I hope I haven't acted presumptuously, selecting your surprise without getting your opinion,' he said. His breath fell upon my wet neck, giving me gooseflesh despite my exhaustion. 'But I wanted you to see me as a man of my word, Mary Grace. I'd be ecstatic if I could call you my wife. But I don't expect you to marry me out of gratitude, or because you feel beholden. I want it to be because you love me, and can't conceive of spending your life with anyone else.'

I opened my eyes, to behold a smouldering russet gaze. Hyde, however, looked nothing like the diabolical man who'd offered to care for me under more lascivious circumstances. His eyes shone with warmth and hope and love, deep emotions I longed to return, yet simply couldn't. I smiled weakly, knowing he deserved far more.

When he'd washed my body as well as my hair, Hyde dried me with a thick towel and carried me to bed. Could any woman feel more pampered or beloved? And when he curled himself around me from behind, bending my knees with his, slipping his arm beneath my bare breasts, I'd never felt more protected or content.

'Good night, my sweet Mary,' he murmured against my ear.

Before I could thank him, I fell into a deep, dreamless sleep.

Hyde's excitement was contagious the next morning as we stepped outside. I felt like a new woman, well-fed and rested, with the song of the birds echoing in my heart. Spring was trying her best to come to the Rockies, and all around Mount Calvary the greening trees and columbine sky spoke of new life, fresh beginnings.

I was wearing a gown Mr Fortune had commissioned from a local seamstress, in shades of gold and rust-coloured wool, trimmed in lace. Yu Ling had made a special effort with my hair, pulling it back with a bow at the crown and letting my waves cascade over my shoulders, at Hyde's request.

'You look too lovely for words,' he told me, nearly stumbling because he couldn't seem to watch where we were going. 'And again, I hope you'll pardon any presumption on my part, for I know you like to make your own decisions. I love that about you, Mary Grace.'

I smiled at that statement, so different from the way most men spoke to their women.

'But when I found this place, I could see you waving at me from the verandah, and hear you humming in the kitchen . . . and the bed began creaking until I went crazy from wanting you! It was like you already lived here.'

My eyes widened when we stopped in front of a charming two-storey Queen Anne house, with a tidy white fence around the yard.

'I put your quilting materials in this bedroom, thinking you'd have the perfect light and work space,' he went on, pointing to the Palladian window on the second floor. His grin burst forth like the morning sun. 'Come in, won't you?'

He swung open the gate, placing his hand at the base of my spine. I eagerly took in the stone-lined flower beds and the neatly kept lawn, for I'd never lived in a place that exuded such cosiness. The verandah gave a welcoming creak as we stepped to the door, where Hyde paused with his hand on the knob.

'Welcome home, love,' he whispered.

He lowered his lips to mine in a sweet, confident kiss that had my arms twining around his neck. I pressed into him, seeking the affection I'd missed those long weeks at Heaven's Gate – the love that could've saved me from myself, had I allowed it to.

Hyde straightened, a sly light in his eyes. 'It doesn't bother me to take my pleasure while others watch, but I'd much rather make love to you without the neighbours looking on. Just you and me, Mary Grace. Naked. So brazen and hot we break the bed.'

My insides shimmered as he opened the door. We stepped into a vestibule with a glossy walnut floor and coral walls. Clean, white moulding framed each of four doorways opening off this little hall, which ended in a spindled staircase. I peeked into the front parlour, grinning. 'A bay window! And such a pretty shade of periwinkle. It's perfect!'

'So are you,' he growled, grabbing me in a playful embrace.

'I smell paint, don't I? And varnish. And lemon wax.'

'And I smell your rose-scented skin, and your warm hair ... and a place between your legs I'm longing to fill,' he replied, following me across the foyer.

This sitting room featured a fireplace tiled with Delft blue designs, and a large Persian rug in greens – which complemented the walls of seafoam. I could imagine the fun we'd have choosing furniture to make these rooms uniquely ours.

I pretended I didn't see the desire in his eyes, or the bulge below his belt. 'You had this house redecorated just for me, didn't you? It's nothing at all like Mount Calvary.'

'What else did I have to do while you were away?' he asked wistfully. 'I chose the brightest colours from your quilts, because they reminded me of your laughter and your indomitable spirit. Except for the bedroom, which is the exact shade of your pussy ... down deep, where Solomon has seen it gloriously inflamed.'

With a rakish grin, Hyde strode from the room. His steps echoed in the hall, and then each footfall on the carpeted stairs beckoned me to follow. I did – after a quick look into a striped dining room, a kitchen of buttercup and a solarium where the windows faced the distant mountains. I felt like a child with a wonderful new playhouse, for I'd lived in manses most of my life, where the rooms were furnished as the church saw fit.

My heart pattered rapidly as I mounted the stairs, overwhelmed by Hyde's gift. It would be the ideal place to live and work on my quilts, just a block from Mount Calvary yet a world apart. As I propelled myself gleefully around the polished curve of the bannister, I imagined the laughter of a son discovering how fast he could slide down it in corduroy pants.

But it was no boy who awaited me. Hyde stood framed in a bedroom doorway, backlit by the morning sun, glowing like some heavenly messenger come to issue my deliverance. His hair was tousled from removing his clothes, while his face formed a tight mask of desire as he watched me approach. His fingertips danced in anticipation, which drew my eye to his magnificent erection. It bobbed in greeting, sturdy and virile, ranging from a deep mulberry where his engorged sac hugged its base, to a pulsing pink at the tip.

'Perhaps I'm being presumptuous again, thinking you want what you're gawking at.' He lightly ran a hand down its length, parting his legs enough to fondle it.

'Judging from this house, you know me better than I thought,' I murmured.

'Excellent. I plan to make a life out of pleasing you, Mary Grace,' he said in a seductive voice. 'Which means I can never stop exploring, learning where your body longs to be caressed and where a tickle works best. Memorising the delectable scents of your navel, and your ears, and your slit when it quivers with juice. Am I wrong, or have your breasts swelled enough that your nipples now rasp against the inside of your corset?'

My jaw dropped, and as his gaze drew me closer, I felt like a girl about to have a man for her first time. It was an absurd notion, after all I'd experienced these past weeks. Yet none of those encounters were what I had previously considered normal, of a man penetrating a woman – unless I counted my final fiasco with the abbot. I closed my eyes, trying to put that ordeal from my mind.

Hyde touched me only with his lips, teasing little pecks to make me stretch up for the contact I craved. 'Yes, my sweet, close your eyes until your curiosity gets the best of you. It heightens the other senses.'

With incredible dexterity he unfastened my dress, slid

my shift over my shoulders, and then popped open my stiff new corset. 'Why you need this is beyond me, but the seamstress insisted young ladies of breeding depend upon them for a fashionable profile. So – gentleman that I am – I'll breed you, to ensure you fit the social mould. So to speak.'

My laughter got caught in his kiss, an open-mouthed duel between two hungry tongues. Hyde backed me against the door frame, rubbing his cock against my belly, inciting my pulse with featherlight landings of his fingertips along my sides. I dug my hands into his arse-flesh.

'Give it to me,' I rasped. 'All this talk about the future doesn't do a thing for a hungry little puss who needs filling right now.'

'Ah, there's the Mary Grace I've come to love,' he crooned, and he suddenly lifted me from the floor. Propping me against the wall, he wrapped my legs around his hips. 'If it's filling you want, I've got plenty of buttercream for you. But one of these days we'll try chocolate – and I'll marinate your cherry, too.'

I squealed when he placed the knob of his cock just inside my rim. And then he stood absolutely still. And he stopped kissing me.

I held my breath, waiting for him to plunge inside and end the unbearable tension. When that moment didn't come, I opened my eyes to find him studying my face. Words can't describe the wonder I saw, mingled with a sadness that nearly made me cry. 'What's wrong?' I whispered.

He shook his head. 'Just memorising your freckles, and the way these tendrils of hair follow your face ... and its colour, like the crackling fire in my office, the first time we made love.'

I looked away. 'Father Luc said it glowed like hellfire.'

Hyde's lip curled, and we were suddenly moving towards the four-poster bed. 'Father Luc be damned,' he muttered, sliding me on to the rumpled sheets. 'I should never have trusted him. I've wished a hundred times I hadn't listened to you that first visit, when I so badly wanted to haul you back with me.'

'I wish you had. I was being brave – a woman of my word – but my foolishness cost me.' I wriggled beneath his warm weight, trying to catch his cock again. 'Damn you, Hyde! What's a woman have to do to get laid around here?'

'All in good time, sweet Mary,' he teased. 'Solomon has advised me to take a closer look at where he's going. Somebody's changed the landscaping, and he can't find the bush marking the entrance to his cave.'

Hyde kissed my breasts, leaving a damp trail of arousal from one puckery nipple to the other, and down to my very ticklish navel, and then lower, until he held my legs apart. I propped my head on my arms to watch, fascinated by the fingernail he eased around my sex.

'What do you think?' I ventured after a few moments of this delectable torment.

'God, but you excite me,' he breathed. 'Your bud and its petals now bloom in full view, like a sultry rose. But I liked the sense of mystery in your curls, too. Maybe I should test for a change in taste – just in case Sol wants to know.'

Hyde dipped his tongue between my folds until, with a desperate moan, I took hold of his head. 'Inside me – please! It's been too long.'

'And getting longer,' he murmured against my feverish inner lips. With his thumbs he gently raised my mound, and then lapped at my clitoris with firm, steady strokes. I let my body ride the waves of heat he created, setting a faster pace by wiggling my hips. Wetness slithered all over my folds, and the spasms began deep inside me.

'Take me ... oh, please, please fuck me, Hyde,' I muttered in rhythm with my thrusts.

Raising a wry brow, he glanced down the valley of my abdomen and between my breasts. 'Such language, woman! I can recall when Miss Michaels didn't know that word, and wouldn't have dared say it! See how far you've come?'

'Come? Yes, I want to come. Now!'

'Patience, dear Mary. Lie back and enjoy this, because we're saving the best for last.'

With that, he inserted two fingers where his tongue had been. In and out he rubbed, pressing that spongy pad just inside my opening while manipulating my clit with his thumb. I spread my legs further, writhing with need. Something about his lovemaking rang familiar with what I'd heard at Heaven's Gate, but the rising sensations felt so much sweeter, I put that thought from my mind. The inner spasms suddenly erupted into a climax like fireworks, and I couldn't stop undulating and calling out Hyde's name.

When I could focus again, Fortune was lying half on top of me. 'Ready for another round? We must reward Sol for his patience, for letting you take your pleasure first.'

I giggled, still floating in delirium. 'How do you do this to me? How do you know exactly where to touch and how to kiss?

'Magic,' he whispered, 'and if you want a little more of it, turn on to your stomach, love. Face the mirror, and get an eyeful of ecstasy.'

Again I heard echoes. But as Hyde repositioned me, placing his cock at my slit, I realised this room was fully furnished, with a cheval mirror strategically angled nearby. 'Whose bed is this? Does someone still live here?'

'It's ours, Mary Grace,' he replied, coaxing me to lie flat. 'I couldn't resist spending a night here last week, dreaming of when you'd join me. Now point that pretty arse at Solomon, so he can slide –'

'No! I don't like it up my backside.'

'Nor do I,' he confessed, kissing the small of my back.

'But I think you'll enjoy the tight fit from this angle, once you lie flat again and squeeze me.'

From the moment he slid in and began to pump, my whole body quivered. I could feel every ridge, every slow, lovely inch he moved in and out of me, including testicles that pressed my inflamed lips when he was all the way inside. I'd never heard him moan with every motion, and the guttural sound of his pleasure ignited my passion again.

'Open your eyes, Mary Grace. See how beautifully right we look making love.'

Our reflection stunned me. Hyde's light brown hair rippled with his every move, alongside eyes that burned into mine as we gazed into the mirror. He rode me slowly, and I raised on to my elbows to watch his muscled body move in the morning sunshine, catching its light like an aura. My breasts bobbed above the mattress, and I gripped a handful of blanket to keep myself from coming too fast.

With a triumphant grunt, the man inside me succumbed. He drove into me again and again, his head thrown back, his Adam's apple quivering with his hoarse cries. The sight of his extreme pleasure prompted mine, and I found a sharper, sweeter release than I did the first time.

He fell forward, bracing himself on one muscled arm while wrapping the other around my shoulders. 'From the moment I first saw you, I had to have you,' he breathed, 'and you're mine at last. Be my wife, Mary Grace, so we can share this pleasure forever.'

His words should have filled me with joy, but I froze. When he pronounced me his at last, I realised why our sex sounded as much like recollection as present reality: Hyde Fortune spoke the words Father Luc had used, when he laid me on that table. Memories of the abbot's behaviour filled me with such disgust I couldn't stand the feel of Hyde's flesh against mine.

I struggled out from under him, wrapping myself in the blanket to ward off a chill.

He scowled. 'What have I said, to make you –'

'If this is your idea of a joke, it's unforgivable.'

He sat back heavily. 'You're not making any sense, love. One moment we're climaxing together, and now you're accusing –'

'You were there. You heard every word Father Luc said, and you're repeating him.' My head reeled with thoughts I didn't want to have, and my headache returned. 'All he wanted was to claim me. It was just a game to him, and now you're playing the same damn thing!'

'Mary Grace, how can you say that? We talked of love and marriage before you went to Heaven's Gate.'

'And how do we know it's not true? How do we know Father Luc isn't some demon puppeteer, pulling our strings for his own purpose – just like your poor mother said he was.' I clutched the covers around me, deafened by my pounding pulse and the fear that had again reared its ugly head.

'Then how is it I convinced the abbot to let you go?' he asked, wincing when I shrank from his touch. 'If he was in supreme command, and he intended to keep you for his own devious purposes, nothing I could've said would've set you free.'

'You told me yourself! He got what he wanted, so he cast me aside – like he did your mother. Do you know how horrible that makes me feel? And now you're sounding just like him.'

Unshed tears burned my eyes. It tore me apart to have such awful thoughts, but I couldn't go along with his idea of forever, if he was following the abbot's example as part of some fiendish plan. 'I don't think I should marry you, Hyde. And I'll only stay in this house if you allow me to repay you, as I sell my quilts. Thank you for the way you've helped, but –'

'Don't you dare insult me that way.'

Hyde Fortune made a formidable sight as he got off the bed to gather his clothes. 'If you think I'd take your money – or consciously imitate Father Luc – then you're more pitiful than my mother. I never dreamed you'd throw your life away, like she has, over such an outlandish obsession.'

He tersely pulled on his clothes. I cowered on the bed, knowing I'd spoken foolishly yet unable to shake the shadow of fate Father Luc had wrapped around me like a shroud. My heart thudded heavily, aware that if Hyde walked out under these circumstances, he would never return. Tears rolled down my cheeks, but I was too upset to wipe them.

He tied his shoes and stood up, jamming his hands into his pockets – to keep from choking me, I sensed. 'I've always believed you were heaven-sent, Mary Grace, by the same God who created you with such a lovely, responsive body. I'm appalled that a woman of faith can accept Luc as the devil – or feel he's woven us into a web of inescapable fate. But if that's what you believe, that's what will be true for you.'

He pulled something from his jacket pocket, and then flung them on to the mattress. 'I was going to ask you to wear these today, but it's pointless now. I'll send Sebastian with your things.'

As his footsteps faded down the stairway, I saw two circlets of gold on the sheets . . . the gypsy hoops Sybil had provided as part of my ceremonial disguise. Once again Hyde was reminding me of an ordeal I was trying very hard to forget, adding insult to the injury of his words as we'd made love.

Yet how could I see these earrings without smiling? Without recalling the bond I'd shared with an incredibly beautiful and brazen . . . and loyal friend. Sybil would be shaking her finger as she scolded me in that smoky voice, about how I'd just forsaken the love of a lifetime – a man who'd had her in his bed but never in his heart. A man she herself could only wish for. She would consider it an inexcusable waste of her time and teachings if I wallowed in my self-loathing instead of living my life boldly and fearlessly, as she did.

On impulse, I donned the gypsy jewellery. When I looked in the mirror, I watched the gold hoops sway, reflecting tiny rays of light to capture the imagination of the beholder. I couldn't miss my resemblance to Sybil, and couldn't help grinning because we'd played our own little game, and we'd won.

Yet also floating in that glass was a mystical reflection, images of lovers pleasuring each other until they cried out with joy. I could've sworn I saw Hyde gazing into my eyes, urging me towards my climax, and then throwing his head back to reach his own. Did these alluring hoops contain the erotic spirit of the woman who gave them to me? Or was I awash with wishful thinking?

I stepped towards the mirror to touch those elusive images. They vanished, leaving me with a sadness I dared not deny.

Had I been the pawn of a deceitful abbot, marked as his prey since before Papa died? Had Father Luc truly controlled the climate and lives on his timeless mountaintop domain?

It didn't really matter. I'd left that world behind, bringing home the astounding knowledge I'd acquired about myself, and about loving. A beautiful woman gazed at me from the glass, and I saw her because my friends at Heaven's Gate had opened my eyes to a wide array of pleasures. It occurred to me that I'd welcomed the attentions of those residents, and that even the abbot had made my body sing with his skill as a lover. It was his attitude I detested, his humiliating tactics and manipulation ... his lies about Hyde Fortune – the son he wouldn't acknowledge, and who'd kept all his promises to me from the start.

Hyde was right: if I didn't set my resentment behind me, it would eat me alive.

And Father Luc would win.

I yanked the top sheet from the bed and wound it around me. I hurried down the stairs and out the door, knowing this lovely house would never be my home if Hyde weren't sharing it. Waving to a neighbour lady whose eyes nearly popped, I trotted barefoot down the brick street. No sense in acting demure: the longer I waited, the less my chance for happiness.

Mount Calvary loomed at the end of the block, rows of sombre gravestones reaching out behind it. With a sense of destiny and completion, I rushed across the front lawn, my sheet flapping wildly around me. To the side door I went, where that engraved brass plaque proclaimed HYDE A. FORTUNE, MORTICIAN; where, weeks ago, I'd stood trembling with questions concerning my future.

I had the answers now.

I hesitated and then knocked, grinning when the door again opened of its own accord. This time, however, I didn't feel like a Gothic heroine entering at her own peril, and Hyde wasn't humping Delores Poppington in her casket. He slouched at his desk, raking his fingers through his thick, dishevelled hair. A snifter half-full of brandy sat before him, and he watched me warily as I approached.

I downed the rest of the amber liquor in one gulp. A delicious sense of decadence filled me as the fire sang through my insides, and I laughed low in my throat.

'Yes?' he asked.

'Yes,' I replied, gazing purposefully into his handsome face. 'It seems you've cast your spell upon me, Mr Fortune. It seems there's no escape, for I'm helplessly, hopelessly yours.'

I let the sheet slither down my limbs, to stand before him wearing nothing but a smile and those wicked little gypsy hoops. With a grin that was positively predatory, Hyde came around the desk, grabbing me up in a breathtaking kiss that declared him master of my fate –

at least when I wanted him to be. I returned the kiss with equal fervour, mistress of my own destiny at last.

'How do you do this to me?' I murmured against him, and then I laughed when he grabbed my bare arse in his hands.

Hyde fixed those hypnotic cinnamon eyes on mine. 'Am I not my father's son, after all?'

BLACK
lace

BLACK LACE NEW BOOKS

Published in August

WICKED WORDS 3
A Black Lace Short Story Collection
£5.99

This is the third book in the *Wicked Words* series – hugely popular collections of writings by women at the cutting edge of erotica. With contributions from the UK and USA, these fresh, cheeky, dazzling and upbeat stories are a showcase of talent. Only the most arousing fiction makes it into a *Wicked Words* compilation.

ISBN 0 352 33522 X

A SCANDALOUS AFFAIR
Holly Graham
£5.99

Olivia Standish is the epitome of a trophy wife to her MP husband. She's well-groomed and spoilt, and is looking forward to a life of luxury and prestige. But her husband is mixed up in sleazy goings-on. When Olivia finds a video of him indulging in bizarre sex with prostitutes, her future looks uncertain. Realising her marriage is one of convenience and not love, she's eager for revenge!

ISBN 0 352 33523 8

Published in September

DEVIL'S FIRE
Melissa MacNeal
£5.99

Destitute but beautiful Mary visits handsome but lecherous mortician Hyde Fortune, in the hope he can help her out of her impoverished predicament. It isn't long before they're consummating their lust for each other and involving Fortune's exotic housekeeper and his young assistant Sebastian. When Mary gets a live-in position at the local Abbey, she becomes an active participant in the curious erotic rites practised by the not-so-very pious monks. This marvellously entertaining story is set in 19th century America.

ISBN 0 352 33527 0

THE NAKED FLAME
Crystalle Valentino
£5.99

Venetia Halliday's a go-getting girl who is determined her Camden Town restaurant is going to win the prestigious Blue Ribbon award. Her new chef is the cheeky over-confident East End wide boy Mickey Quinn, who knows just what it takes to break down her cool exterior. He's hot, he's horny, and he's got his eyes on the prize – in her bed and her restaurant. Will Venetia pull herself together, or will her 'bit of rough' ride roughshod over everything?

ISBN 0 352 33528 9

CRASH COURSE
Juliet Hastings
£5.99

Kate is a successful management consultant. When she's asked to run a training course at an exclusive hotel at short notice, she thinks the stress will be too much. But three of the participants are young, attractive, powerful men, and Kate cannot resist the temptation to get to know them sexually as well as professionally. Her problem is that one of the women on the course is feeling left out. Jealousy and passion simmer beneath the surface as Kate tries to get the best performance out of all her clients. *Crash Course* is a Black Lace special reprint.

ISBN 0 352 33018 X

Published in October

LURED BY LUST
Tania Picarda
£5.99

Clara Fox works at an exclusive art gallery. One day she gets an email from someone calling himself Mr X, and very soon she's exploring the dark side of her sexuality with this enigmatic stranger. The attraction of bondage, fetish clothes and SM is becoming stronger with each communication, and Clara is encouraged to act out adventurous sex games. But can she juggle her secret involvement with Mr X along with her other, increasingly intense, relationships?

ISBN 0 352 33533 5

ON THE EDGE
Laura Hamilton
£5.99

Julie Gibson lands a job as a crime reporter for a newspaper. The English seaside town to which she's been assigned has seen better days, but she finds plenty of action hanging out with the macho cops at the local police station. She starts dating a detective inspector, but cannot resist the rough charms of biker Johnny Drew when she's asked to investigate the murder of his friend. Trying to juggle hot sex action with two very different but dominant men means things get wild and dangerous.

ISBN 0 352 33534 3

If you would like a complete list of plot summaries of Black Lace titles, or would like to receive information on other publications available, please send a stamped addressed envelope to:

Black Lace, Thames Wharf Studios,
Rainville Road, London W6 9HA

BLACK LACE BOOKLIST

Information is correct at time of printing. To check availability go to www.blacklace-books.co.uk

All books are priced £5.99 unless another price is given.

Black Lace books with a contemporary setting

THE NAME OF AN ANGEL
£6.99 — Laura Thornton
ISBN 0 352 33205 0 ☐

FEMININE WILES
£7.99 — Karina Moore
ISBN 0 352 33235 2 ☐

DARK OBSESSION
£7.99 — Fredrica Alleyn
ISBN 0 352 33281 6 ☐

THE TOP OF HER GAME — Emma Holly
ISBN 0 352 33337 5 ☐

LIKE MOTHER, LIKE DAUGHTER — Georgina Brown
ISBN 0 352 33422 3 ☐

THE TIES THAT BIND — Tesni Morgan
ISBN 0 352 33438 X ☐

VELVET GLOVE — Emma Holly
ISBN 0 352 33448 7 ☐

STRIPPED TO THE BONE — Jasmine Stone
ISBN 0 352 33463 0 ☐

DOCTOR'S ORDERS — Deanna Ashford
ISBN 0 352 33453 3 ☐

SHAMELESS — Stella Black
ISBN 0 352 33485 1 ☐

TONGUE IN CHEEK — Tabitha Flyte
ISBN 0 352 33484 3 ☐

FIRE AND ICE — Laura Hamilton
ISBN 0 352 33486 X ☐

SAUCE FOR THE GOOSE — Mary Rose Maxwell
ISBN 0 352 33492 4 ☐

HARD CORPS — Claire Thompson
ISBN 0 352 33491 6 ☐

INTENSE BLUE — Lyn Wood
ISBN 0 352 33496 7 ☐

THE NAKED TRUTH — Natasha Rostova
ISBN 0 352 33497 5 ☐

A SPORTING CHANCE	Susie Raymond	☐
	ISBN 0 352 33501 7	
A SCANDALOUS AFFAIR	Holly Graham	☐
	ISBN 0 352 33523 8	
THE NAKED FLAME	Crystalle Valentino	☐
	ISBN 0 352 33528 9	

Black Lace books with an historical setting

A VOLCANIC AFFAIR	Xanthia Rhodes	☐
£4.99	ISBN 0 352 33184 4	
INVITATION TO SIN	Charlotte Royal	☐
£6.99	ISBN 0 352 33217 4	
PRIMAL SKIN	Leona Benkt Rhys	☐
	ISBN 0 352 33500 9	

Black Lace anthologies

WICKED WORDS	Various	☐
	ISBN 0 352 33363 4	
SUGAR AND SPICE	Various	☐
£7.99	ISBN 0 352 33227 1	
THE BEST OF BLACK LACE	Various	☐
	ISBN 0 352 33452 5	
CRUEL ENCHANTMENT	Janine Ashbless	☐
Erotic Fairy Stories	ISBN 0 352 33483 5	
MORE WICKED WORDS	Various	☐
	ISBN 0 352 33487 8	
WICKED WORDS 3	Various	☐
	ISBN 0 352 33522 X	

Black Lace non-fiction

| THE BLACK LACE BOOK OF WOMEN'S SEXUAL FANTASIES | Ed. Kerri Sharp | ☐ |
| | ISBN 0 352 33346 4 | |

─ ─ ─ ─ ─ ✂ ─ ─ ─ ─ ─ ─ ─ ─ ─ ─ ─ ─ ─ ─

Please send me the books I have ticked above.

Name   ....

Address ....

....

....

.... Post Code ....

Send to: **Cash Sales, Black Lace Books, Thames Wharf Studios, Rainville Road, London W6 9HA.**

US customers: for prices and details of how to order books for delivery by mail, call 1-800-805-1083.

Please enclose a cheque or postal order, made payable to **Virgin Publishing Ltd**, to the value of the books you have ordered plus postage and packing costs as follows:

UK and BFPO – £1.00 for the first book, 50p for each subsequent book.

Overseas (including Republic of Ireland) – £2.00 for the first book, £1.00 for each subsequent book.

If you would prefer to pay by VISA, ACCESS/MASTER-CARD, DINERS CLUB, AMEX or SWITCH, please write your card number and expiry date here:

....

Please allow up to 28 days for delivery.

Signature ....

─ ─ ─ ─ ─ ✂ ─ ─ ─ ─ ─ ─ ─ ─ ─ ─ ─ ─ ─ ─